HIDDEN GATES

The P.J. STONE GATES TRILOGY

BOOK 1

AVA WIXX

First Edition: October 2025
Published in the United States of America by
Wicked Wixx Press.
The Wicked Wixx Press Logo is a trademark of
Wicked Wixx Press.
Originally published under the title
Enemy Through The Gates: 2012

Cover Art, Ava Wixx Logo, Wicked Wixx Logo, & Interior Book Graphics by Lindsay Tiry of LT Arts
Trilogy Logo by Jordan P. Fremgen

Print ISBN: 978-1-955950-42-8
Kindle ISBN: 978-1-955950-43-5
EPUB ISBN: 978-1-955950-44-2

For more information visit: avawixx.com

Acknowledgments

I have a whole list of people that deserve to be thanked here, and with that in mind, I was going to simply use my original acknowledgments from the first version of Hidden Gates buuuut …I'm currently in the process of moving and all of my books are in boxes. I would rip all those bad boys all open to find my copy of the old Hidden Gates but let's face it, that seems like entirely too much work and I'm already stressed from all the packing as it is.

I would rather list no one here than risk accidentally leaving someone out. So to avoid such a catastrophe, I'm simply going to thank all of the readers out there that have given my books a chance. You mean the world to me. Thank you.

This book has been on quite a journey. It was the first novel I wrote, or even attempted to write, and I began my feverous ramblings in 2011 and finished up several months later. The entirety of it was written by hand in purple pen in a three-ring binder. It was quite a mess, to say the least. But after a lifetime of consuming books on a ravenous level, I felt like I'd finally found my passion. (Full disclosure: I am neuro-spicy, so I have attempted and discarded quite a few 'career passions' over the years. But books—books have stuck with me through thick and thin so I hoped this time would be different. Spoiler: It was and still is.)

Because I lack patience, I self-published this novel under the title of "Enemy through the Gates" in 2012. Shortly, after that, it was picked up by Dragonfairy Press and republished under the title "Hidden Gates" in 2013. The next book 'Broken Gates' was published the following year. Then I left Dragonfairy Press and was once again on my own. Without bothering to query (again with the lack of patience) I republished the first two books in the trilogy, along with the conclusion "Open Gates" under my own imprint "Tik Tok Press". (Yeah, I picked that imprint name before TikTok existed sooo... it was kind of like being named Karen after that became a thing. Bad timing, for sure.) I re-released them with new covers a few years later and there they sat, largely unnoticed by the world as I continued my writing journey.

Fast forward to after the pandemic, which is when I made the decision to take up a pen name instead of continuing to use my legal name. I had to temporarily leave behind my backlist as I began publishing my new material under Ava Wixx and the imprint 'Wicked Wixx Press'. (Why? Because publishing is expensive and I couldn't re-publish everything under Ava Wixx all at once.)

This brings me back to Hidden Gates— This book holds an extra special place in my heart, plus, you, know, it has dragons ... and I felt it was time to put it back into the world. (Also, I sold a whole bunch of my jewelry and purses on Poshmark to raise the extra money. Heh.) Even if Hidden Gates and the rest of the trilogy once again sits largely unnoticed, I will at least have the joy of knowing that they're out there, and that's enough for me when it comes to my first book babies. Because, yes, my storytelling and prose wasn't quite what it is today, (I like to think I've improved over the years. Please lie to me if it hasn't.) but none of that matters in the end to me. This series is perfectly imperfect and I wanted to leave it largely untouched in this edition. I did go over it for any glaring errors but I wanted to leave these books as is for, I guess, a sense of personal nostalgia. As for the rest of my books, well, I'm a bit more practical when it comes to them. Make of that what you want. *winky face*

Also, added sidenote: I wrote this book in 2011 and it's set in that time frame. That means no widespread use of smartphones with accompanying cameras, social media was in its infancy etc. So please keep that in mind when reading. I hope you enjoy P.J.'s story as much as I enjoyed writing it. She is such a flawed character, and I will always love her for all her imperfections ... for they are many. (Even if I wanted to throttle her quite a few times when I was creating her because she really did like to do her own thing and ruin my plans. *facepalm*)

Anywho ... Happy reading! I'll let you get to it without any more of my neuro-spicy babbling. ;)

~Ava

Content Warning

Attempted rape, coerced sex, attempted suicide, gun violence, attempted murder, murder, teenage dumbassery, and probably a few other things I forgot about because it's been over a decade since I wrote this book.

Always be yourself...
Unless you can be a dragon,
then
always be a dragon.

Chapter 1

"**H**ey P.J." Evan's raspy voice commanded my attention, and I glanced over to meet his deep brown eyes, mine widening with surprise. "I was wondering what you were doing this weekend?"

"Me?" I squeaked. Evan Thompson was actually speaking to me, *and* he knew my name.

"Yeah, you. I don't see anyone else around, do you?"

My eyes traveled the length of the empty hallway and back. *When did that happen?* "No, I just—" I was silenced when Evan caressed the side of my face, his fingers slipping into my hair. The contact of his skin on mine made me tingle with awareness, his powers invading my system.

"How have I never noticed you before?" His voice had dropped down into a more intimate tone, his eyes flashing with lust just before he pushed me back against the wall, capturing my lips with his. I groaned with pleasure as his tongue slid into my mouth to intertwine with mine, his muscled body pushing firmly against me. The hand that wasn't holding me captive by my hair moved down to—

"What?" I was startled back to reality when someone pinched the fleshy part of my arm.

Bryn's azure eyes glittered with amusement. "Daydreaming again? Who was it this time? Let me guess." He leaned back in his seat, scanning the room around us. His head tilted in Evan Thompson's direction, who happened to be sitting in the exact spot my vacant gaze had been fixated on for the past half hour. Bryn snorted, his eyes rolling. "Really? Evan Thompson? Like you have any chance at all with him."

I shot Bryn a death glare. "Hey! I might not have had a shot with him in high school, but we're in college now so it's different."

Bryn interrupted me with another eye roll. "Here we go again. Nobody changes on an intrinsic level just because they're older. Ageing up doesn't make a someone like Evan any wiser. And as for the rest—" Bryn swiped his hand in my general direction. "Well, to put it bluntly, your tits growing about half a cup size isn't gonna change anything either. Trust me when I say you're probably the only one who can tell the difference."

I brought my arms up over my—*fine*—less than ample bosom, to protect them from his hurtful words. "You noticed," I grumbled.

He snorted. "I'll tell you what I noticed, you prancing around like they're suddenly D cups."

"Okay, this is just weird. Can we *please* not talk about my cup size, or lack thereof anymore? You may be my best friend, but you're still a guy. Besides, I have plenty of other qualities that might interest someone like Evan Thompson." Bryn gave me a pitying look before going back to doodling in his notebook. He obviously thought our conversation wasn't worth his time anymore.

"Fine. Whatever, Bryn *Aries* O'Bannon," I hissed. "Nobody asked you anyways."

Bryn clutched the sides of his desk, turning to deliver me a death glare of his own. "Quiet, Paige *Joplin* Stone. You wanna use my middle name for everyone to hear, then two can play at that game."

"Shut up!" I cringed at hearing my middle name said out loud. "My name is *P.J.*"

His lips curved up slightly at the corners. "What was that, *Paige Joplin Stone?* I couldn't quite hear you."

A few people turned around in their seats, their interest piqued by my and Bryn's exchange. Not that I could blame them, there usually wasn't much excitement in Creative Writing 1. More than half the time our professor, if you wanted to call him that, gave us a topic to write about and left us to our own devices. The only reason why everyone didn't immediately clear out was because he checked attendance at the end of class. *So why does my conversation have to suddenly catch everyone's attention?* Realizing I could be blown out of the water and my entire chance of having a new cooler reputation ruined, I shot Bryn a pleading look. "Okay. Fine. I'll shut up if you do. Just please don't say that name out loud *ever* again."

Running his hand through his thick black hair, Bryn gave me his patented lopsided grin, complete with dimples. "Well, I don't know. What are you willing to give me for my silence?"

Anger bubbled up within me. Most of the time, Bryn was great, my partner in crime since we were five, but lately he was becoming relentless in his harassment of yours truly. Truth be told, he knew way too much about me for it to be even the tiniest bit amusing, case in point with my middle name. Bryn was the only person, outside of family, staff at our school, and my doctor, who was privy to such top-secret information. It was hard enough making it through community college relatively unscathed, without such handicaps as everyone knowing my middle name is Joplin because my quirky mother's favorite singer is Janis Joplin. Because even after such a short time I'd discovered community college, unlike university, was basically high school 2.0. People liked to latch on to the stupidest shit to tease someone about and I refused to be another casualty. Honestly, I should have matured past the point of caring, but unfortunately when you wade into the marsh, you eventually become one with the creatures there.

"I swear to God, Bryn, if you don't shut up right now, I'm never gonna talk to you again."

Bryn barked a sharp laugh. "Please. You'd never be able to find someone who puts up with you the way I do, and you'd come crawling back to me in less than a day."

"I hate you," I grated through clenched teeth.

"You love me." His eyes twinkled brighter, which only made me want to scratch them out.

"No, I hate you," I repeated with more vehemence.

"Whatever you say." He focused back on his stupid drawing.

I sat and stewed for the rest of the class until our professor returned to release us from our torment. *Thank the heavens.* I gathered my stuff, jamming it all into my bag, and bolted for the door. I usually waited for Bryn since we always grabbed lunch together in between our shared class schedule, but since I was still mad at him, I didn't bother.

I made it about halfway down the hall before he caught up with me. "Awe, come on, I was only kidding. Don't be so touchy."

I turned my head to avoid eye contact with him, speeding up my pace. He matched my gait with ease on his longer legs. *Damn Guardian genetics. It seems like only yesterday I was almost as tall as him. Now he towers over my 5'9", which isn't exactly short for a girl.*

"Okay, I'm sorry. Is that what you want? An official apology?" When I didn't respond, he continued, "Someone like Evan Thompson would never notice you because you would never even blip on his radar. You've seen the trashy girls he's with all the time. You're too good for him. It was kind of a compliment, what I said before—in a backhanded sort of way."

"Very backhanded," I grumbled. "And I'm not going to comment on the use of trashy to insinuate something that sounds suspiciously close to slut-shaming, even if you are trying to make me feel better." I sighed heavily. "Whatever way you describe them though—it's not like he can *really* be with any of those girls—not in the long run anyways—he's a Gatekeeper."

No, Evan couldn't be with a *regular* human, or Regs as we referred to them, at least not settle down with one, because our world had rules. Our world—*my* world—was very different from the one most people knew. In my world, there were portals, gates if you will, that linked our dimension to thousands of other dimensions. Living close to these gates were small groups of people with special gifts. These people have existed as far back as recorded time.

These people—*my* people—existed to protect our dimension from any outside threats. We passed down our genetic gifts from generation to generation, which ensured the future safety of the earth. So it was kind of important to keep our bloodlines strong.

Evan, as a Gatekeeper, would be expected to choose a Seer as a future mate. Technically, we could go out and date whoever we wanted, we could also have kids with whoever we desired, but it'd been ingrained since childhood that it was our duty to pass on our DNA for the protection of the planet. *Talk about pressure.*

I, being a Seer, can only reproduce another Seer if I have a child with a Gatekeeper, or a male descendent from a Seer line. An anomaly of Guardians is that they only produce male children, so if I were to have a kid with one, I would put a halt to the possibility of another Seer being born, as only girls possess active Seer powers. Seers are the most important group among our people. No one else can really do their job if there aren't any Seers around. Therefore, a lot of work goes into perpetuating our lines. Thankfully, my kind existed all over the world, so we hadn't run into any dicey line crossing like blue bloods of days gone by. Although our intermingling was carefully planned since it was expected of us to remain close to our chosen clan and specific areas of power throughout our lives. *Yeah, being a member of my world, specifically a Seer, kind of puts a kink in my love life.*

"Evan being a Gatekeeper doesn't matter. You deserve someone better. Someone who can appreciate you for who you really are."

"I don't think that guy exists, Bryn. My choices are kind of limited." I expelled a long breath. "You're right when you said no one else would put up with me. At least when I'm forced into a marriage one day with someone that repulses me, I'll still have you to comfort me as I cry myself to sleep every night."

"Awe, come on, I was just giving you a hard time, and you know it." He ducked to bump my shoulder with his.

"We both know it's the other way around. Who would put up with me and my—"

"Dark and broody moods?" I interjected. "You're quite right. Me and only me. You shouldn't antagonize me, Bryn. What you really should be doing is kissing my feet." I bit my lower lip, trying not to laugh. "Kissing my toes and massaging my feet for putting up with you all these years. How Tammie did for an entire year is beyond me."

He scowled. "I broke up with her, remember? Not the other way around."

"And I don't understand why." I studied his face for some kind of clue. Tammie Masterson had been Bryn's girlfriend for well over a year. I'd never really liked her because he was way too good for her, but that aside, they had seemed pretty happy together. Although she was constantly jealous of all the inside jokes Bryn and me shared. But whoever dated Bryn was going to have to deal with that because I was there to stay. One day Bryn would be my personal Guardian, and there was no interfering with that relationship. Everyone knows a Guardian's most important job is protecting his Seer. *As it should be.*

"I really don't wanna talk about this right now."

"But I do. Why won't you tell me why you guys broke up? You used to tell me everything. It's been almost a whole month, and I still have no clue what happened between you guys. Aren't I your best friend anymore?"

Bryn's eyes darkened. "You know you'll always be my best friend. There are just some things I can't talk to you about." When my lower lip stuck out at him, his face softened. "At least not right now."

I took his hand in mine, giving him my best puppy dog eyes. "Please, Bryn. Please tell me. I'll do anything you want. Pah-leeeeeezzze."

He stared at me, his brows drawing together. "Be careful what you say," –he turned and started walking again– "what I want might be more than you're willing to give me," he muttered under his breath.

What could he possibly want from me that he would think I wouldn't give him? He was my best friend in the world, and there was nothing I wouldn't do for him—nothing.

I scurried to catch up to him. "Bryn, what are you talking about? I hope you know I would do anything for you. You know that, right?"

"Just drop it. I told you I don't wanna talk about it." We walked a few moments in silence before he spoke again, "So what time did your mom say for us to come over tomorrow night again?"

Bryn and my birthdays were a day apart. Mine was today, and his was tomorrow. Somehow we ended up having a joint sixth birthday party, and it just kind of stuck. It had become a tradition with our families to combine our celebrations, and since our families were so close, no one objected—in fact, quite the contrary. "I don't know, seven-ish I guess. You know"—I interlaced my fingers with his– "I'm still older than you for a few more hours. Older and wiser."

You know that saying...*speak of the devil and he shall*

appear? Well, in this case, the devil was a *she* because Tammie chose that exact moment to walk out of a classroom just as we were passing it. She stopped abruptly, looking up at Bryn like a deer caught in headlights, the two of us dwarfing her small five-foot-something frame. She self-consciously ran her fingers through her long blonde curls. "Hey, Bryn. I was hoping I'd see you today. I wanted to wish you Happy Birthday, and I was hoping that maybe..." Her voice trailed off as she took in the sight of Bryn holding my hand. "Oh, I see," she said. "I can't say that I'm surprised." She whirled on her heel, heading off at a dead sprint.

Realization dawned on me. I dropped Bryn's hand. "Really? Is that what you don't wanna tell me? Does she really think something is going on between us? Is that why she was always so jealous of me?" I laughed. "That's ridiculous, absolutely ridiculous."

Bryn's eyes clouded over, darkening his entire countenance. "Yeah, absolutely ridiculous," he said through clenched teeth. "Look, I forgot I have some math work to finish up before class. You go ahead and have lunch without me, and I'll see you later." Bryn jogged off in the opposite direction of where Tammie had gone, before I could argue with him.

"Weird," I muttered to myself. *I'm in the same class and I don't remember an assignment. What the hell just happened.* I had a sinking feeling that I really didn't want to know.

Ugh. See. Community college really was like high school 2.0. All the same stupid people I'd been forced to be around almost my entire life. And I had such high hopes. Why? A deep-seated denial of my reality, I supposed. If only I didn't have to stay close to home because I was a Seer I could have jettisoned off to a university in Paris, Milan, or I don't know, somewhere—anywhere as long as it was far away from our podunk Pittsburgh suburb where my entire life was basically already planned out for me.

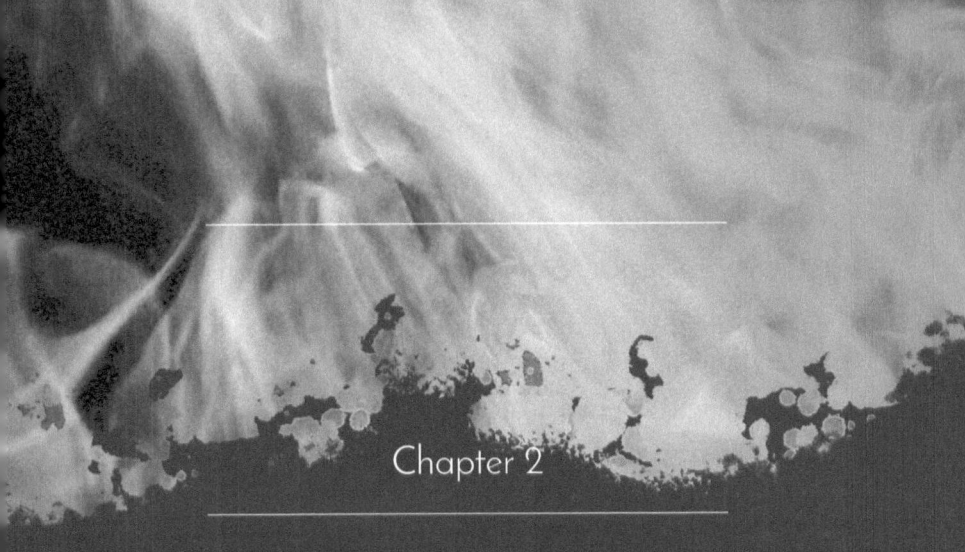

Chapter 2

"**D**o you think Bryn's been acting weird lately?" I asked Jenna between bites of pizza. Another thing our local community college had in common with high school was crappy cafeteria food. Although, bad pizza was still better than no pizza no matter the situation, in my opinion.

Jenna gazed over my shoulder, twirling a purple piece of hair around her finger, her eyes shining with adoration. "How am I supposed to know? You guys have your own language, one that even I've never been able to understand."

I frowned. "I don't have time for your stupid Speaker jokes. I'm being serious here."

Jenna turned her dark brown eyes on me, a smile stretching her olive-toned cheeks wide. "So am I—being serious, that is. You guys are a mystery even to me."

"What's that supposed to mean?" I so wasn't in the

mood for one of Jenna's cryptic conversations. Speakers had their own unique brand of humor, one that I had a hard time getting on board with, mostly because I didn't get it. As a Speaker, everything in Jenna's world revolved around language because she had the ability to understand any language of any species. For her to say that Bryn and me had a language of our own, one that she didn't even understand, was only something she would find amusing.

Jenna's gaze slid back over my shoulder, her eyes glazing over again as her skin flushed. "Evan Thompson really is hot. All that lean golden muscle, topped with his golden-brown hair, and chocolate eyes that I could melt into—Mmm Mmm Mmm—tasty. I would love to feel more than just his Gatekeeper magic sliding into me, if you know what I mean."

"Hey," I snapped. "You can pretty much date whoever you want. Don't dip into my shallow pool." I sighed, letting go of my hostility. "Not that it matters anyways. I have about as much of a chance with him as you do."

Jenna raised one dark eyebrow at me. "Actually I do have a chance with him. At least if I'm only interested in getting into his pants." She paused to flip her purple hair over her shoulder. "And darling, I most certainly am."

I groaned. "Jenna, come on. You're not gonna sleep with him."

"Who said anything about *sleeping* with him?" She giggled. "If I have my way with him, there definitely won't be any *sleeping* involved."

"Whatever," I mumbled. And she would, Jenna was the type of person who could just go up to a guy like Evan and offer him sex. Me...not so much. I was beginning to think I was the last card-carrying member of The V Club locally in my age bracket. Hell, I'd barely gotten to second base. I was definitely way behind my peers in the sexual experience department, even though it was by choice. I still had the same hormones pressuring me on a daily basis that my friends did, but I wanted something more than just the physical. *Call me crazy.* And even though I daydreamed about a lot of guys, when it got down to it, I wasn't really interested.

Some days I envied Jenna, with her constantly changing hair color and brazen attitude towards life. She did whatever she felt like whenever the whim hit—again, me...not so much. I seemed to always fall victim to over-analyzing everything. I couldn't do anything without dissecting it twenty different ways, and by that time, the opportunity to be spontaneous had passed me by.

"Oh, why don't you just do it with Bryn and get it over with?" Jenna asked, breaking into my mental pity party.

"What? You can't be serious!"

"I never kid about sex and...well, sex. Sure, he's not long-term material with him being a Guardian and all—yours to be specific—but why not at least do it for the first time with someone you trust? And you do trust him, don't you?" She eyed me speculatively, as if trying to decode something in my expression.

I flushed under her scrutiny. Yes, Bryn was hot, but he

was my best friend, and one simply didn't do those kinds of things with their best friend. Besides, there could be no future between us, so what would be the point really? "Umm...I can't sleep with him, *especially* because he's gonna be my Guardian. I won't even bother ticking off the rest of the reasons because there's only one that's really important. He's my best friend, and even if I wanted to, which I don't, he's not interested in me like that."

"Sure he's not. Because him being a guy, if you offered him sex, he'd turn it down," Jenna deadpanned.

"I'm not doing that, and he wouldn't be interested anyways. Don't be ridiculous," I snapped. First Tammie and now Jenna, when were people going to get it through their thick heads that nothing had or would happen between me and Bryn?

"Speaking of Bryn," Jenna murmured.

I turned just in time to see Bryn enter the cafeteria. His blue eyes scanned the room, lighting up when they landed on me. As he headed our way, I couldn't help but notice again how much he'd grown recently. Since coming into his powers, he'd sprung up to almost 6'4". Instead of being long and lanky like most boys our age, he had already filled out quite nicely. I smiled at him as he pulled out a chair beside me, curling gracefully into it. He ran his hand through his thick black hair, giving me his lopsided grin, complete with dimples.

My smile widened in response. "Hey. I thought you had some work to do or something?"

"Yeah. I guess I got stuff mixed up, because as it turns

out, we didn't have an assignment." *Huh.* Maybe I was reading too much into things, as usual, and Bryn had simply gotten confused. It happened to the best of us sometimes. "So what were you guys talking about?"

"You," Jenna said.

"Nothing," I said at the same time. I shot her a dirty look before turning back to Bryn. "Well—"

"What about me?" Bryn's eyes sparked with curiosity, and I knew I had to work fast. If I didn't change the subject immediately, Jenna would tell him exactly what our topic of discussion had been about.

"Our dear friend Jenna actually thinks she has a chance with Evan Thompson," I blurted out in a Hail Mary effort.

Bryn tilted his head at me, signaling that he knew I was changing the subject, but then he turned to Jenna and grinned. "What, you just gonna walk over and offer to do him?"

"How'd you guess?" Jenna laughed.

"Gee, I don't know." Bryn chuckled into his sandwich. "Because maybe that's what you always do."

Jenna pretended to turn pensive, twirling a purple piece of hair around her finger again. "Huh. Well, I guess you're right, I *do* always do that."

Whew. Crisis averted. No need to put any ideas about sex with me into Bryn's head. I was fully confident that he didn't think about me in that way, but he was still a guy; Jenna was right about that part. Then again, better safe than sorry. *Time to bring up a new topic completely off sex.*

"Sooo ... how's your badass in training stuff coming along?" I directed my question at Bryn.

"Fine, I guess."

"What about you?" Jenna interjected. "Any premonitions" —From the corner of my eye I could see Bryn furiously waving his hand at her in a slashing motion—"...yet?" Jenna finished up hesitantly.

I scowled. *Damnit.* Just when I'd gotten my mind off of one problem, I had to be reminded of another. "Nothing. I've got nothing. So maybe I won't have to worry about you dipping into my shallow pool after all because maybe I can date whoever, too." Most Seers my age had at least gotten some small premonitions. Me—not even a blip on my premonition radar. Maybe I was some weird Seer anomaly that was born without powers. If that was the case...well, at least my dating worries would be over. *Hooray?*

Bryn sighed loudly. "Some Speaker you are. Do you not know what this means?" He waved his hand in front of his neck in a slashing motion again.

Jenna scrunched up her face. "Obviously not."

I placed my hand on top of Bryn's. "It's okay. I might as well face the truth. Something went wrong with me, and I'm never gonna actually *see* anything."

Bryn interlaced his fingers with mine, giving my hand a squeeze in an effort to comfort me. "Maybe the problem is you're putting too much pressure on yourself. Just relax."

"And you know what's a great thing for relaxation? Sex," Jenna added.

I groaned. "Come on, Jenna—seriously—enough already."

"Fine. Oh, hey, you gonna go to Ryan's party tonight? It's gonna be aaawe-some," Jenna said, finally changing the subject on her own. *Thank God.*

"I don't know. Maybe. Our birthday celebration isn't until tomorrow night, but I'm just not sure if I feel like dealing with another of Ryan's parties." I slumped back into my seat, withdrawing my hand from Bryn's, causing him to frown slightly.

Normally I'd be all gung-ho about going to one of Ryan's parties to scope out the place for any eligible guys I could actually date, but at the moment, the thought was just depressing. I mean, Ryan graduated with us and here we all were still going through the motions a year later. *Ugh. Who am I kidding anyways?* I wouldn't find anyone but the usual drunk fools interested only in sex and nothing more, just like in high school. "You going, Bryn?"

He shrugged. "I am if you are. Could be fun."

"Pleeeaase." Jenna clasped her hands in front of her. "You can get ready at my place, and we can go together."

I sighed. "I don't know why you always beg me to come to these things since you ditch me for some rando practically before we're even in the door."

"Don't worry, I'll be there," Bryn chimed in.

"Fine," I agreed, even though I was sure to regret my

decision. At least I'd get to hang out with Bryn and have a few beers.

Jenna gathered up her things, beaming. "Good. Just come over to my house after dinner, and we can get ready." And with that, she headed off in Evan's direction, but not before pausing to adjust her v-neck T-shirt to better show her cleavage—which I admitted with envy, was much more impressive than mine probably ever would be.

"Should I just meet you guys there?" Bryn asked, causing me to drag my eyes away from Jenna and her soon to be spectacle with Evan.

"Yeah, I guess. By the way, you ever gonna tell me what happened with you and Tammie?"

Bryn's jaw ticked with sudden tension. "Why won't you just let it go, Peej?"

My insides warmed. Despite Bryn changing so much on the outside, most of the time he still said my name so it sounded like one syllable, something he'd been doing since we were kids.

"You know I can't do that. It's just not possible. You might as well just get it over with and tell me now so you can save us both all the trouble."

Bryn stood abruptly, pushing his chair back with enough force for it to hit the wall behind us. "Let. It. Go. There are just some things that I can't talk to you about. You better get used to it now." He stalked out of the cafeteria without finishing his lunch.

Huh. Then again, maybe I wasn't reading too much into things. *Bryn is definitely acting weird.*

Chapter 3

"I can't believe I let you talk me into this," I hissed.

Yanking at the hem of my dress, I attempted to stretch the fabric which was lacking in length. Of course, when I managed to make any headway at all, my lackluster cleavage was exposed to the point of scandal, and I was right back at the drawing board with too much skin being showcased. *Little black dress, my ass! How about* too *little black dress.*

"Oh hush. I would kill for your stems. Instead, I have to make do with these stubby little things." Jenna motioned briefly to her legs. "And it's too late now. We're almost there."

I gulped as Ryan's house came into view, framed in the window of Jenna's bright yellow Volkswagen bug. She parked at the curb, turning to me with a serious expression. "So...what do you think of the new hair color? Too much?"

She had gone from a dark purple color to a shade of red that matched most fire trucks. It would definitely turn heads. I just wasn't sure it would be in the way she wanted. I tried to remain tactful though. "If attention is what you crave, then you definitely chose the right color."

She frowned, her eyes narrowing. "You don't like it, do you?"

"It's not that I don't like it—it's just—well, I liked the purple better." And that was very true. I liked the purple a whole lot better.

"But now we both get to be redheads." Her peach glossed lips curled upwards. She really didn't care much that I didn't like her new hair color. Besides, it would probably change by next week. *It's a wonder all of her hair hasn't fallen out yet, seriously.*

"Yeah, but only my shade of red can be found in nature." I smirked.

Why anyone would purposely dye their hair red was beyond me. My natural color was a bright strawberry blonde, which I had managed to darken to a nice auburn shade through the use of frequent Henna applications. I was still stuck as a redhead, but at least the current darker hue was less traumatizing to my retinas whenever I caught a glimpse of myself in any shiny surface.

We exited Jenna's car, heading up Ryan's walkway. All the while I fidgeted with my borrowed dress. I felt like an adult trying to squeeze into little kids' clothes, and I suddenly wanted to go home very badly. "I don't think I should be wearing this in public," I grumbled under my breath.

Jenna whipped her head in my direction. "Okay. I'm done. You look super hot, so stop complaining. I don't wanna hear another word about it." She turned the knob on Ryan's front door, and boisterous voices accompanied by loud music slammed into my chest. When I balked, Jenna took my arm, yanking me over the threshold.

We barely made it a half dozen steps inside before she spotted Evan. "It looks like I have a date with destiny." She dropped my arm, heading towards Evan with a huge grin on her face. When he saw her approach, he let his gaze travel over her from head to toe, a grin of his own spreading across his face. I guess he liked what he saw and was going to take her up on her offer from earlier. I turned away abruptly, not wanting to witness any more.

"Hey." Bryn was standing nearby, his gaze sliding over my teeny tiny dress. "Did you let Jenna dress you?"

A sharp laugh escaped my chest. "Is it that obvious?"

He grunted, a slight smile tipping up the corners of his full lips. "To me it is." He snagged my hand in his. "Let's get you a beer. It'll help."

"What would really help is pants because this dress is so small it could be a shirt. I really don't know how she talks me into these things sometimes." I grimaced self-consciously as we passed by a group of guys who I didn't know, all of them eyeing my bare flesh. *Thanks, Jenna.*

I attempted to adjust my dress again while Bryn filled up two plastic cups with beer from the keg. He handed me one and I took a sip, crinkling my nose in disdain. "What is this? Some crap light beer? Ugh. At least get a decent light beer, if there is such a thing."

Bryn took a swig of his beer, chuckling at my still scrunched up face. "Underage beggars can't be choosers."

"Yeah, yeah," I grumbled. I tipped the cup up, chugging down the rest of the subpar beverage. I decided I would make up for in volume what was lacking in quality.

Bryn quirked one dark eyebrow, raising his own cup to his lips again. I glared in response. "Don't you give me that eyebrow, Mr. O'Bannon." I began pumping the keg for a refill.

Bryn's eyes met mine over the rim of his cup. "What? I didn't say a word." His lips curled up, showing his dimples.

"You didn't have to, your eyebrow said it all." It was then I remembered what Jenna said earlier about Bryn and me having our own language. Maybe I could see her point. "It's a party. I'm just trying to have fun." Bryn still didn't say anything. He simply looked at me with his way too expressive eyes. They currently were asking me if I thought getting completely smashed was the answer to my problems. I narrowed my eyes and scrunched up my nose. *Yes, yes, it is.*

As I polished off beer number two within five minutes, Bryn decided I was temporarily cut off. I knew he was worried that I would get too chatty, like I sometimes did when I was drunk, and start complaining to the wrong person about my lack of premonitions or something. I had one little incident in the girls' room at one little mixed party like this one, and Bryn had been paranoid ever since. It wasn't like any of the Regs believed me anyways. They just thought I was completely smashed and probably on drugs to boot.

Bryn snagged my empty cup, setting it down near the keg. He took my hand again, tugging me back into the other room. I giggled. *Lookout! Lightweight coming through!* I scanned the room for any signs of Jenna and Evan. Just as I suspected—they were both conspicuously absent. "It looks like Evan took Jenna up on her offer," I called to Bryn over the music.

Ignoring me, Bryn practically pushed me down on the couch. "Sit," he ordered. "I'm gonna get you some water. Don't go anywhere." He narrowed his eyes at me. "And it's probably best if you don't talk to anyone until I get back either."

Bossy much?

I giggled again as he walked away, really starting to feel the effects of those two beers. But hey, at least I hadn't thought about my dress or boyfriendless situation for a couple of minutes. Sometimes it was nice having the super low tolerance to alcohol that all Seers shared. I couldn't imagine being like Bryn or Jenna, or anyone else of my kind, who didn't seem to get drunk. The best they were able to do was get buzzed. That was the reason my kind watched Seers like me so closely at public functions where drinking was involved.

"Hey, pretty girl. How are you doing tonight?" A guy

with longish sandy blond hair, tanned skin, and bright crystal blue eyes sat down next to me. He was one of the guys who had been eyeing me when Bryn and I had gone in to get our beers just a few minutes ago.

He was kind of cute, and I could sense some power coming off of him. It was very faint though. When I reached for it mentally, it brushed against mine, feeling like thousands of tiny fingers running up and down my exposed skin, causing goose bumps to erupt along my flesh. I tilted my head to study him for a moment. Like called to like, and I just knew. *Seer.* I mean, he wasn't—obviously—but I was picking up on the dormant power in his blood. *Maybe he's exactly what I've been searching for.*

"Hey, yourself." I grinned, all tension leaving my body. "What does it look like I'm doing?"

"Well," His eyes slid over me blatantly. "It looks like you're wasting that dress sitting all alone on this couch."

Pushing my self-consciousness aside from before, I decided to let his attention empower me. Sitting up straighter, I flipped my hair over my shoulder. "Mmm ... what do you suggest I do instead then?"

"Come with me." He pulled me up from the couch and I stumbled into him.

A wave of uncertainty washed over me. Normally going off at a party with some strange guy would one-hundred-percent be a bad idea. But—but this one was from a Seer family, and he would have had it drummed into his head since practically birth how important someone like me was. In fact, because of his status as Seer descendant he could even be future boyfriend material. *So why not go with him? What will it hurt? Maybe he wants to talk away from the Regs about our world without worrying about sounding completely insane.*

Deciding to ignore my initial worries, I allowed him to lead me out the back door, and into a small patch of woods at the edge of Ryan's property. He pulled a slim flask out of his pocket, taking a swig, before offering it to me. "It's Southern Comfort mixed with some lime."

I took it from his hand, the metal warming in my palm. I eyed the thing suspiciously like it would jump up and bite me. "Yeah, I don't know, I'm already kinda buzzed."

He responded with an easy grin. "It's just Southern Comfort, it's not that strong. Give it a go."

Well, I don't want the happy buzz I have going to wear off. What will one little taste do to me? I brought the flask up to my nose for a quick sniff. I tried to ignore the almost sickly sweet aroma that tickled my nostrils. Taking a shot's worth into my mouth, I forced myself to swallow. "Blak. That stuff is horrible." I winced at the slight burn it left in its wake.

He grabbed the flask from my hand, taking another swig. He then screwed the top on, stuffing it back into his pocket. I was still processing the horrible taste of Southern Comfort, when I found myself abruptly pushed against a tree, a slug-like tongue shoved down my throat.

My world spun at its axis. "Hey," my protest came out in a slur. Slobber from his sloppy kisses ran down my neck. "Hey, wait a second. Stop." I pushed at his chest, but my strength was no match for his. Rough hands roamed over my body as I continued to fight. When he reached down to hike up my dress, stark panic took hold. "Stop," I squeaked, my heart thrumming loudly in my ears.

"Awe, come on, baby, it'll be good. Just relax."

Like a brick to the face, his words hit home my galactic mistake. I didn't even know this guy's name, and I had wandered off into the woods with him when I was already halfway toasted. It didn't matter what kind of family he was from. Blood doesn't automatically make someone a good person. I'd rationalized my decision because I wanted it to be true. How stupid could I get? Seriously ... I had entered willingly into after school special territory because I—what? Wanted a boyfriend? What a fucking idiot.

"Please. Stop," I pleaded, my words sounding more slurred than I would have liked. "I'm a virgin."

He laughed, the sound echoing inside my head. "Yeah, I don't believe that for a second."

A loud rip rent the air as he fumbled with the zipper on the side of my dress. I kicked, scratched, and attempted everything in my power to escape, but I was no match for the guy in my current state. A scream gurgled up my throat even though I knew no one would hear me over the deafening music. I let it loose anyways, the sound swallowed up almost as soon as it left my mouth. *I'm such a fucking cliché—a drunk idiot who's about to pay the ultimate price for not thinking it would happen to me.*

Completely unbidden, Bryn's face rose up in my

mind's eye. It wasn't merely because I was wishing that he would come to my rescue, even though I was. I just couldn't help but think of him in that moment, I wasn't sure why.

"Please, I don't want this. I'm not lying—I'm a virgin. Pleeeaaase ..." I whimpered, his hands skimming up and over my underwear. Bile rose in my throat. *I don't wanna lose my virginity this way! Why did I leave the house? How could I be so stupid? Fight him! Fight him harder! You have to fight him! Don't stop fighting! It's not over until it's over!*

"Get the hell off her! Now!" Suddenly the guy was pulled from me and tossed to the ground. My eyes locked onto Bryn, and my throat constricted, tears burning my eyes. "I should break your face. I should break every bone in your body," Bryn snarled.

I'd never seen Bryn look so—so dangerous. His long black hair had fallen forward into his flushed face, his eyes raging with violence. As he picked up the wanna-be rapist by the neck, holding him a good few inches off of the ground, a low growl emanated from the back of his throat. For the briefest of moments, I could have sworn, his eyes sparked an even brighter blue, as if they glowed.

"I'll-I'll leave," wanna-be rapist sputtered, while gasping for air. Bryn released his grip, letting him drop to the ground with an audible thud. "I'm leaving," wanna-be rapist wheezed, an edge of panic lacing his words. He scrambled up, moving faster than I'd ever seen anyone run while intoxicated.

Bryn watched him go, anger rolling off of him in

palpable waves. When wanna-be rapist was out of sight, he turned back to me, his expression softening. "You okay, Peej?"

I blinked up at my savior—*Bryn*. Bryn, who I'd known practically all my life—suddenly he seemed like a stranger. He really was becoming a Guardian—*my Guardian*—and for some reason that caused my chest to constrict, stealing my breath. I didn't want things to change. I didn't want to lose him. I could no longer hold back the deluge of emotions that had been threatening to overwhelm me. I slid down the tree, sobbing hysterically.

Bryn dropped down on one knee, tipping my face up with his long fingers. His features contorted with anguish, his skin suddenly taking on a ghostly pallor. "He didn't—he didn't—I thought I got here in time."

"No. He didn't," I croaked. "But he would have...he was going to."

Bryn exhaled one long breath. He hesitantly wrapped his arms around me, but when I sank into him, his hold grew fiercer. "What were you thinking? Going off with him? I told you to stay put," his voice was harsh, making me cry harder.

"I don't know. I wasn't—thinking, that is. I'm sorry, Bryn, so sorry." My apology, like my thoughts, was slow and muddled.

He let go of me, tipping my face up towards him again so he could meet my gaze. "Hey, why are you apologizing to me? I was just worried is all—scared that—" He stopped talking when I caressed the side of his jaw, trailing my fingertips over his warm skin. I'd never realized how truly beautiful Bryn was. I mean, I noted on some level he was hot, but I never actually took notice.

I studied the face that had been one of the most important ones in my life since I was the age of five. I let my gaze roam from his startling blue eyes that were currently churning like a storm at sea, to his high sharp cheekbones, to his full, perfectly shaped lips. The contrast between his strikingly blue eyes and his black hair and pale skin was nothing short of perfection. *Bryn has the most beautiful face I've ever seen.*

"Do you think I'm pretty, Bryn?" I whispered. His brows furrowed as he gazed down at me. "Because I think you have the most beautiful face I've ever seen." *Did I actually just say that out loud?*

"Peej—"

I brought my index finger up to his lips slowly, as if my hand weighed more than it normally did. "Shhh… No, really. Do you think I'm pretty?"

He swallowed, causing his Adam's apple to dance up and down in his throat. "No—I think you're beautiful."

I frowned. "You're just saying that so I don't feel bad, you know, because I said you're beautiful."

"No. I mean it." He tucked a stray piece of hair behind my ear, his hand lingering a moment too long. "So beautiful."

His lips met mine with an undercurrent of electricity. The kiss started out soft and sweet but began to gain momentum quickly. I gasped as his tongue slid in to deftly take control of my mouth. An unfamiliar feeling of liquid heat pooled in my middle, causing a moan to escape from me. I wrapped my arms around his shoulders in an attempt to pull him closer. It was like my body was on fire, and Bryn was the only one who could bring me relief.

And just as suddenly as it had begun, the kiss ended.

Bryn stood quickly, leaving me on the ground to stare up at him in a daze. He swore under his breath, turning away from me to run his hands through his hair. "That shouldn't have happened," his voice broke an octave lower than normal, causing my stomach to do a little flip-flop.

"Bryn." His name, carrying an unsaid plea, felt new and unfamiliar on my tongue. I wanted his lips on mine again, so much so that almost being raped didn't even seem relevant anymore. Following my duty didn't seem relevant anymore either. Nothing but tasting Bryn's mouth again mattered in that moment.

"Bryn," I repeated, bringing my fingertips up to touch my lips, imagining his were still locked with mine. It didn't matter that he was a Guardian and I was a Seer. He was Bryn—*my* Bryn.

Bryn turned back towards me, acknowledging my silent plea with wide eyes. Tension was etched into every line on his face. "You're drunk, and that shouldn't have happened."

Maybe I was buzzed, but I wasn't drunk. And for the life of me, I couldn't remember why kissing Bryn was such a bad idea. I might have had the memory a moment ago, but it was now buried beneath the fog in my brain. I'd never imagined kissing someone could feel so—*right*. So there was no reason why it shouldn't have happened or why it shouldn't happen again.

"Why?" I whispered. "Why shouldn't it have happened? I want—I want you to kiss me again." When Bryn didn't move, my cheeks heated with embarrassment. I was having a banner night filled with stupidity. Of course Bryn didn't want to kiss me again, we were friends—best friends. He obviously didn't think of me in a sexual manner—like I'd told Jenna earlier in the day. More than likely I'd initiated our kiss without realizing it, and then somehow misread his response.

Bryn's eyes filled with to the brim with despair. "I'm a Guardian, Peej. That's why it shouldn't have happened."

"Oh," was all I managed. How could I have forgotten? *Maybe I am drunk.* Of course—there was no possibility of a future for us. I would marry a Seer descendant or a Gatekeeper one day, not a Guardian. I brought my fingertips back up to touch my lips—they yearned to be pressed up against Bryn's again—and suddenly none of it mattered anymore. *Maybe I didn't imagine the spark between us, after all.*

"I don't care," I whispered, gathering my feet under me and pushing off them to stand. I swayed for a second, dizziness temporarily tilting my world, before Bryn caught me in his strong arms. "I don't care," I repeated as I studied Bryn's beautiful face from only mere inches away.

"You should care."

"I want you"—even as I was saying it, I could hardly

believe the words that were coming out of my mouth—"to be my first time." Not stopping to get a reaction from Bryn, I took a step back, tugging my tattered dress from my body. I stood in front of him in only a little black thong and matching lace bra. Goose bumps erupted along my flesh in response to the cool night air.

"Peej—" Bryn's voice cracked, and I averted my gaze, not wanting to see any kind of rejection there. I was hoping I hadn't misread the situation again. He hadn't said he didn't want me, just that we couldn't be together because I was a Seer and he was a Guardian.

"Don't you want to? Be my first? I thought you said you think I'm beautiful." Still not wanting to meet his eyes, I watched his fists clench and unclench, the muscles in his forearms rippling.

He strode forward, taking my face in his hands. "I want it so much it hurts." There was a fierceness in his gaze that I'd never seen before, and I realized I liked him looking at me that way.

We somehow found our way back to the same tree that the wanna-be rapist had been trying to take advantage of me against. None of that mattered once Bryn claimed my mouth again. I eagerly welcomed the taste of him on my tongue, the feel of his callused hands on my skin, and the press of his body against mine. I gasped into his mouth as he pivoted his hips into me, spreading my legs. Feeling that part of him pressed so intimately between my thighs was a shock—even if it was a good one. When I instinctively locked my ankles behind his back, Bryn froze. "We can't," he protested against my lips, before pulling away. "We just can't."

"Bryn, no—" I started to protest, but he didn't let me finish.

"No, we can't," he growled. "God knows how much I want to, how often I've thought about it. That's why Tammie and me broke up—because it wasn't right. I couldn't get you out of my head. It wouldn't have been right to be with her when I was thinking about you the whole time. But it doesn't change the fact that you're a Seer and I'm a Guardian. You're too good for me, out of my league."

I blinked at him in surprise, letting his words fully sink in. I was the reason he broke up with Tammie? He wanted me? Like *really* wanted me? "You can have me." I realized as I said the words, that I always had—and always would be—his for the taking. I'd simply been in denial before. Something I excelled at, apparently.

"Be careful, Peej," his voice was low and husky. "If you keep offering, I might actually take it."

I stepped into him, resting my hand on his arm. "I wouldn't offer it if I wasn't willing to let you have it." His sea storm eyes threatened to pull me under, to wash away any thoughts of anything but him. "Don't you see? I'm not too good for you. If anything, it's the other way around. You're always watching out for me, taking care of me— what have I ever done for you except be a major pain in your ass?"

The corners of his lips curled up slightly. "You don't

even know how great you really are, which is part of why *I love you."* As soon as those three little words trickled out, his mouth clamped shut, his face going taut with tension again.

My mouth dropped open, ready to catch any nearby flies. "You love me?"

"Yeah, you know that. Of course I love you," he said gruffly, not meeting my eyes.

"No—you *love* me?"

Bryn stood still and silent, hardly breathing.

"How long? Just—how long?"

"I don't know," his voice was so low and soft that if I hadn't been standing so close, I never would have heard it. "Maybe always. It just took me awhile to figure out what my feelings really meant."

As his words sank in, it made me question my own feelings. Could I be in love with Bryn and not even know it? I considered all the times I'd gone a bit crazy when he'd been with Tammie, even though I thought it was simply because he was my best friend, and I was merely jealous of his time. But maybe not, maybe it had been more.

Next, my mind flipped through all the times when I'd gotten petty with girls when I felt like they were trying to flirt or make a move on him. Again, I'd thought it was just because I was jealous of his attention ...

Holly Hell, I'm a certifiable idiot. It was more than friendship level jealously—much more. I'd always thought of Bryn as mine. *He belongs to me.* His lopsided grin, his black hair, his cobalt eyes... Even the mix of deodorant, soap, and his individual spicy scent that made him—*home.* I'd come to think of him as home. Everything about Bryn was home for me.

"Every time I'm with you, it's like coming home," I murmured.

"What does that even mean?"

I stepped closer to Bryn, pressing my body tightly against his. "It means I love you, too." Why did it take almost being raped for me to figure it out? Now I understood why I'd thought of Bryn when the wanna-be rapist had his hands all over me. It was because his was the face I loved, the one I truly longed for, the one I would have had trouble looking at again if he hadn't arrived in time to stop the rape from happening.

Bryn opened and shut his mouth as though he didn't know what to say, before his face hardened with determination. "You'll get over it when your mom starts setting you up on dates with guys you can actually be with, guys that a real future is possible with."

My thoughts began to sharpen, the effects of the alcohol finally starting to wear off. I let out a strangled cry of frustration. "But I don't want other guys—I want you." *If only I'd figured it out sooner. Everyone else saw it but me. I'm the official Queen of Denial.*

"I won't be strong enough to watch another guy walk away with you once I've had you. It's just better for me not to know." His voice turned pleading, "Let it go, Peej. I'm gonna be your personal Guardian one day—and that day isn't that far off anymore. I won't be able to handle it if we have some kind of thing like you're suggesting. I know I'm a guy, but I want more than just sex from you."

"I'm not trying to suggest that we have some little thing that's just about sex. Didn't you hear me? I love you, too."

"Put your dress back on. *Now,*" Bryn said between clenched teeth. Instead, I unhooked my bra, letting it slip from my arms. I loved him, too. I wanted him. Why couldn't he see that wasn't something someone like me could just throw away? He knew me better than anyone, after all.

Bryn groaned, his eyes locking onto my nearly naked body. "You'd put it all on the line for me, give it all to me, wouldn't you? Because you think you have a choice." His voice came out sounding strained to the point that it almost hurt me to hear it, "But you don't have a choice. *We* don't have a choice. *Put. Your. Clothes. Back. On. Now.*"

"No." I raised my chin at him defiantly. "There's always a choice. We'll find a way. You're not gonna run away from this—from me."

"Put. Them. Back. On. *Now,*" Bryn snarled.

He'd never talked to me so harshly before. Even though I wasn't afraid of him, I still scuttled backwards, startled. My thoughts may have been clearer, but I was still buzzed, my balance off-kilter. The ground quickly came up to meet me, my head banging on the hard dirt.

"Ow," I grumbled, suddenly nauseated. "I don't feel so good anymore." I rolled onto my side, my gut twisting. Everything in my stomach ejected forcefully. *Fabulous.* I closed my eyes, wishing the ground would open up and swallow me whole. "Go away, Bryn. Just leave me." *My humiliation is complete.*

"Haven't you reached your maximum of stupidity for the night yet? Apparently not if you think I'm leaving you here. I'm gonna give you my shirt. It should cover you better than Jenna's dress did."

"Why can't I just put the dress back on?" I mumbled.

"Because it's ripped, and you just threw up on it." If I didn't know better, I'd swear Bryn was laughing at me. *No. He wouldn't dare.*

"Okay. But you can't tell Jenna what happened." My world was spinning. All I wanted was to go to sleep, until a thought occurred to me. Bryn would be walking around with his shirt off in front of everyone—everyone as in all the other girls at the party. Jealousy spiked through my fuzzy, probably concussed brain.

"No. I'll wear the puke dress," I mumbled, my eyes still shut. I had no desire to see whatever was swimming in his beautiful sea storm eyes. I felt Bryn lift me up in his arms, already bare-chested. *When did that happen?* "You can't walk around without a shirt on," I stated. *Why does he not understand this?*

He chuckled. "I think me walking around without my shirt on is gonna cause less of a stir than you doing it."

"I said I'd wear the puke dress." *What do I have to do to make him understand? Geez.*

"What's your problem with me being shirtless?" I could hear the amusement in his voice.

"Because you're mine." I snuggled in tighter to his muscular chest. "And I don't want the Jennas of the world to get a good look at what they've been missing and steal you away." I inhaled deeply, letting Bryn's spicy scent surround me in comfort—*home*. As I drifted off to sleep, I heard Bryn whisper something that I'd never forget.

"There's never any danger of that. I'm yours. Always."

Chapter 4

A t first, I thought it was a dream.

Something pulled me up and out of my body—an invisible force or power—not a completely unpleasant sensation, just different than anything I'd ever experienced before. Off in the distance, an unusual purple light pulsated, the lure of it drawing me in like a moth to flame.

I focused my mind completely, the light drawing closer to me—or I drew closer to it; I wasn't really sure which. Arriving at the origins of the purple light, I found myself completely mesmerized.

The air was cool, and yet it was charged with an unseen current, almost like static electricity causing all the hairs on my body stand on end. Directly in front of me, it was as if a piece of sky had been ripped into the side of the forest, the jagged edges swaying with pulsating shades of purple and blue. The shape of it was irregular, moving as I imagine pure energy does, with a kind of pattern that no naked eye could pick up on—even a Seer's naked eye. It was absolutely stunning—beyond anything I could actually put into words beyond my clumsy attempt. A sort of pity washed over me for all the Regs that would never get to see such a magnificent sight.

As I stood, or hovered, or whatever; shapes began to emerge from— *The gate. Yes.* I belatedly realized I was seeing one of the gates for the first time even though it was so painfully obvious now that I thought about it. Truly *seeing* it. But my elation was short-lived as the shapes that emerged from it took form. They looked humanoid, and yet were *other*. There were so many of them—too many to count—and I couldn't distinguish between them since they appeared uniform in shape and size to me.

Huge eyes bulged out of their too tiny, pinched faces. Luminescent, dewy skin glowed with a soft light that reflected the gate's hues, making them all seem to pulsate with the same blues and purples. They glided out of the gate slowly, their thin bodies levitating inches off the ground, ghostly in nature. As I stared at them, a chill ran up my spine.

Dangerous. These creatures are dangerous and they're creeping into my world completely unnoticed. Where are the other Seers? Why aren't they here watching this with me? Where are the Gatekeepers to shut the gate on these pesky humanlike creatures? And where are the Speakers and Guardians to demand that they return to whence they came or they'd get some major smackdown laid on them? I seemed to be the only silent witness to the breach of our world.

Abruptly, they blurred off into the distance, too fast for my eyes to track, disappearing completely. My heart exploded in my chest. *I have no idea where they went! Holy shit! They could be anywhere—I have to tell everyone before it's too late! I have to—*

"P.J. Hey, P.J. Wake up," Jenna groaned. "You're having a nightmare, and I'm trying to sleep."

My eyes popped open as I attempted to sit up, my heart pounding a rapid rhythm against my eardrums. Clutching at my temples, I wondered if brain matter was actually oozing out from the internal pressure. "What happened?" I squinted in an attempt to bring my surroundings into focus but my eyes refused to cooperate.

"I'll tell you what happened. You got too drunk, you puked on my dress—but not before managing to rip it—and then you passed out. Me and Bryn brought you back to my place where I've been trying to sleep."

The events from earlier in the evening came flooding back with crystal clarity. I groaned as my sluggish brain tried to process everything. Despite my best efforts all I managed was a squeaked, "Where's Bryn?"

"I made him go home. He wanted to stay, but I was afraid if my parents came home early and found him here, they'd blow a gasket," Jenna said around a yawn. "Now go back to sleep."

"But he's my Guardian," I groused.

"As my mom would say, he's not your Guardian yet, so go to sleep." Jenna flopped over on her bed.

"Wait. I had a premonition. We have to warn people." Finally that got a real reaction out of her, but not the one I expected.

"You got drunk, hit your head, and passed out. You didn't have a premonition, you just think you did." Jenna flung a pillow, hitting me in the face. "Now go to sleep."

"Fine," I muttered to myself as I stumbled out of Jenna's guest twin bed. If Jenna wouldn't listen to me, I would find someone who would.

I crept out into the hallway, tripping over a pile of something in the middle of the floor. "What the hell?" I screeched as I lurched forward in the dark. Strong, familiar arms caught me before I face-planted.

"What are you doing?" Bryn stage whispered. "Go back to bed."

"Wha-what are you doing in the middle of the floor? It's a good way to get kicked in the head, and send someone hurtling to their death, I might add."

"I wasn't in the middle of the floor, I was tucked against the wall. You just don't have any depth perception."

"Hey. It's dark. I—"

The hallway light flicked on, and a very annoyed Jenna glared out from under a tangled mess of red hair. "Seriously? I told you to go home."

Bryn glared back at Jenna. "I couldn't just leave her. I was worried. Besides, if someone hadn't let her go stumbling around in the dark, you would've never known I was here."

"I'm not her babysitter," Jenna snapped.

"How about trying to be a concerned friend?" Bryn growled.

They're both completely exasperating. "I have no time for this. I have to warn everyone about the premonition I just had."

Bryn's head snapped back towards me. "What? What'd you see?"

"Nothing. She was drunk and hit her head, remember?" Jenna said, sighing demonstratively. "So can we all just go back to bed, please?"

Bryn studied my face for a second before responding. "Do you really think you had a premonition, or do you think Jenna could be right?"

I met Bryn's gaze, thinking of the kisses we shared earlier, shivering. Recognition of my reaction to him played briefly across his face before he glanced away. I swallowed, trying to fight the sudden dryness in my throat. It finally dawned on me that I still had Bryn's shirt on and almost nothing else underneath. He hadn't bothered to find another shirt, so he stood in Jenna's hallway in nothing but his jeans and socks. I found myself wondering if Bryn was a boxer or brief kind of guy, or maybe he went commando? I wanted nothing more than to close the distance between us. I would run my hands over his finely honed muscles and smooth skin, dipping my hands underneath the waistband of his jeans to find the answer to my question.

"What's wrong with you guys? I'm getting some really weird vibes from you two right now." Jenna swung her gaze back and forth between the two of us. "Well?"

I couldn't let Jenna know. What happened between Bryn and me, and the potential of what could happen between us in the future—that was staying between just the two of us. I had to say something to distract her fast. "It felt like a premonition, but I don't know. Bryn—what do you think?"

He was careful not to meet my gaze again as he spoke, "If it was something that major, then someone else had to have seen it—another Seer, I mean. You should just go back to sleep, and we can figure it all out tomorrow."

"Yeah, I guess." Standing out in Jenna's hallway made the premonition, or whatever it was, seem too surreal to be plausible. Besides, Bryn was right, how could it be possible for me to have been the only one to see such an important vision, especially when I'd never had any before? Chances were, with having hit my head combined with having been buzzed, I'd just had a very realistic dream. And of course, in my dream I'd be the only one who could save the day. It was an excellent way for my psyche to make up for the fact that I hadn't had any real premonitions yet—just give me the Mac Daddy of all premonitions to make myself feel extra special.

On to more important issues, I suppose. "Are you gonna keep sleeping in the hallway?"

"Probably." Bryn ran a hand through his hair. "It would make me feel better to kind of stand guard for you, since I will be your Guardian one day." He stared me down, raising his eyebrows. *Yeah, yeah.* I knew what he was trying to get at, and I didn't care. I let my gaze briefly pass over his smooth, muscular upper body before returning to his perfectly chiseled face.

"You could keep a closer watch if you stayed in Jenna's room with us." I bit my lower lip and smiled at him. "I mean, you could always stay in my bed, with me, so you could keep a *very* close eye on me."

"Oh, hellz, no," Jenna interjected. I'd almost forgotten she was standing there. "If he wants to be all creepy and stay in the hallway, fine. At least he has a leg to stand on with the whole future Guardian thing with that situation. But if my parents caught him in bed with you, no matter how platonic we all know it would be, there'd be no escape from punishment for any of us."

I quirked an eyebrow at Bryn, asking him a silent question. How platonic would it be now that we'd crossed that line? Would he be able to just hold me, like he used to, under the guise of friendship? Or would things be different now that he knew I loved him and wanted him, too? Judging from his tormented expression, I was guessing the answer was no. *Is he imagining what it would be like to be naked in bed with me right now?* I heaved a sigh, considering the tantalizing possibility myself.

Jenna looked at me sharply. "Seriously—what is going on with you guys?"

I forced a yawn. "Going back to bed now." Luckily it was always easy to distract her.

"Finally," she muttered, flicking the hallway light off.

I stumbled back into bed and crawled under the sheets, shutting my eyes against my pounding head. I thought with how crappy I felt, the minute my head touched the pillow I would have had an instant ticket to dreamland. Instead, my very awake mind swirled around Bryn. Bryn, and his currently half-undressed state, residing right outside Jenna's door. It was like the kiss we shared earlier had unlocked all these feelings that had been pent up for years.

I sure would like to unwrap him for my birthday present. Ugh. I'm starting to sound like Jenna. I just wanted to be near him—something that I'd always craved. I just happened to actually know my motivations now.

I stumbled out of bed and crept back into the hallway. This time I had a pretty good idea where Bryn had situated himself so I wouldn't trip over him again. When I dropped to all fours, reaching my hand out to search for him, his sigh surrounded me in the dark.

"What are you doing?" he whispered, tension evident in his voice.

"Where are you?" I asked, ignoring his question. His hand encircled mine in response, tugging me forward. "You'd think Seers would have better night vision," I grumbled.

When I finally made contact with his bare skin in the dark, I pushed my way under his arm to snuggle up close to him. "I still don't feel good." I ran my hand slowly over his chest and inhaled his scent deeply. *Mmmm...there is nothing like the spicy aroma of Bryn mixed with soap.* I was sure I could make a lot of money if I bottled and sold the purely masculine—and suddenly very sexy—scent that was all Bryn.

His muscles tensed beneath me. "So go back into your nice, comfortable bed."

"But you always make things better when I don't feel good," I pouted. There had always been something comforting about Bryn's presence. I couldn't even begin to count how many times we'd spent the night together with me in his arms. Of course, things were a little different now that we'd crossed a line earlier.

"Things are different now," Bryn said warily, as if he'd just read my mind.

"So what? Now I can't be close to you anymore?"

"You know what I mean, Peej."

"Just hold me," I commanded. I wasn't going to let him push me away—literally or metaphorically.

A whoosh of air tickled the side of my face as he sighed heavily even as he brought his arms up to encircle me. I snuggled into him, my head on his chest, and one leg over his. I was happier than a clichéd bug in a rug. The tension in his body only lasted a few awkward moments before his breathing slowed and he drifted off to sleep. Feeling safe and content in his arms, I wasn't far behind.

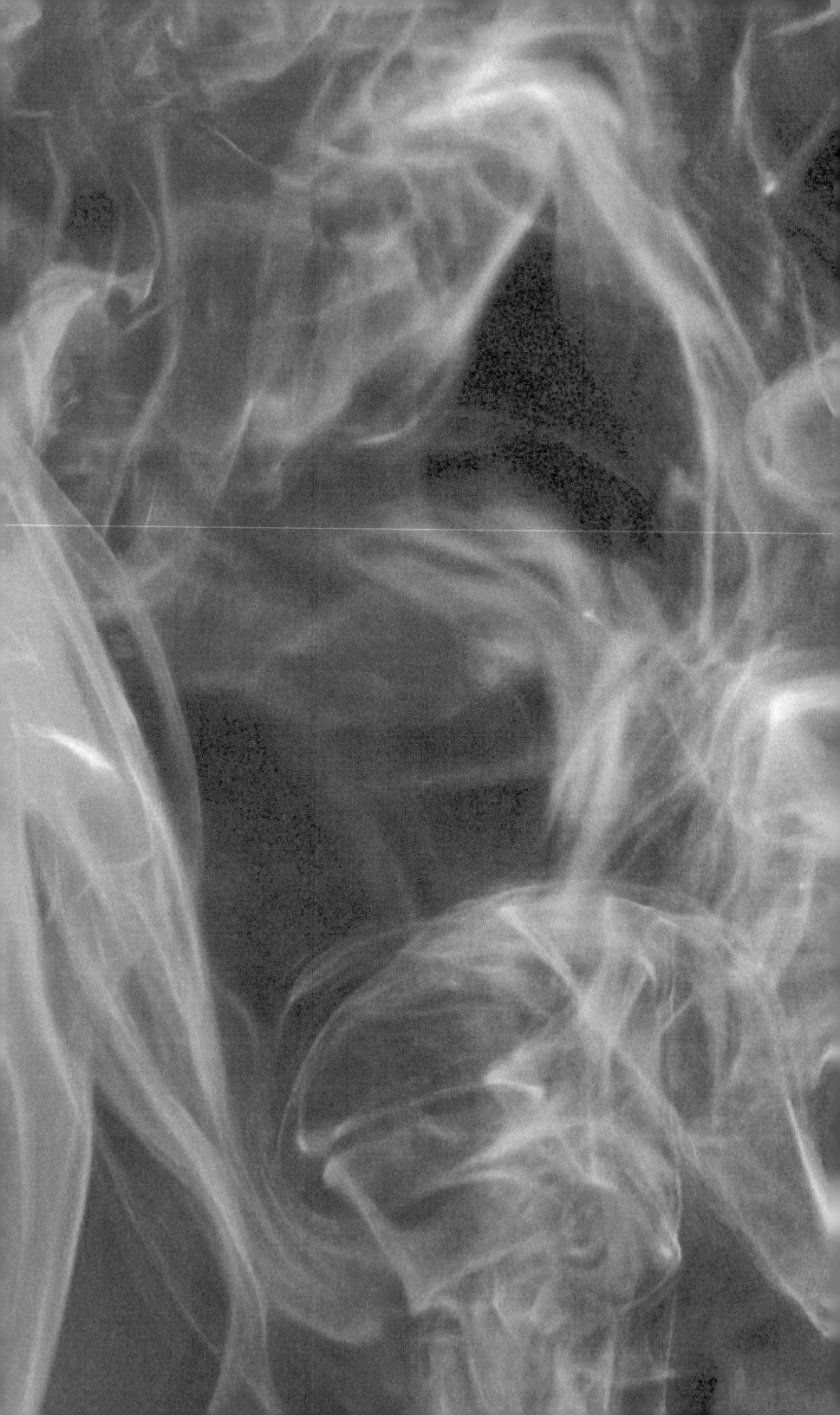

Chapter 5

When we woke the next morning, things returned to an awkward state between me and Bryn. He still insisted on keeping his hands to himself, despite my protests. And as soon as he disentangled himself from me, he was gone so fast I was surprised there wasn't a Bryn shaped hole in the door.

Why is he being so stubborn? It's not that complicated. I'm into him and he's into me. I mean, sure, a romantic relationship between a Seer and her future Guardian is in taboo territory, but aside from that ... no big deal. He needs to just accept that I'm not going to give up now that I'm no longer lying to myself.

I glanced at the clock, noting that I didn't have long before Bryn and my joint birthday celebration, so I needed to get a move on getting ready. It was generally low key—just our families, a nice dinner, some cake and ice cream to follow, and then, of course, presents. I usually had a good time sharing the birthday spotlight with Bryn, but I had to wonder how high the tension meter would be between us tonight. If the nervous flutter in my stomach was any indication, fairly high. *Okay, get out of your head and concentrate on the task at hand.* I popped open a tube of my favorite lip gloss.

"What's wrong, peanut?" I met my mom's gaze in the vanity mirror. She was hovering near the doorway to my room, her finely featured face and green eyes filled with concern. I noticed that she had styled her shoulder length reddish hair into a neat updo. *A chignon, maybe?* She never wore much makeup because she had a simple, natural beauty. Today was no different.

"Nothing. Why?" I responded, setting down the lip gloss I'd just applied.

"Oh, I don't know, maybe because I've been standing here saying your name for the last few minutes."

I forced a smile onto my face. "I just have some things on my mind. Nothing's wrong exactly."

She nodded and gave me a knowing grin. "A boy wouldn't have anything to do with what you're thinking about, hmmm?"

My mom was pretty cool as far as moms were concerned, but I also knew I couldn't talk to her about Bryn. She wouldn't approve of me wanting to be with him unless he suddenly became a Seer descendent or a Gatekeeper. Still, nothing wrong with testing the waters a little. I'd been known to misjudge situations a time or two in my life and maybe this was one of them. *Fingers crossed.* "Well…I don't know. It's just—have you ever wanted to be with someone that wasn't who everyone expected you to be with? You know, when you were younger, before Dad?"

My mom came farther into my room and peered at me with understanding. "Oh, I see. You have a crush on someone you know you shouldn't."

"Well, not exactly." I knew no such thing. My feelings for Bryn were too right to be wrong—as cliché as it sounded.

My mom sat down on the edge of my bed. "Let me guess, an ungifted human or a Guardian?"

"How did you know?"

She laughed. "Oh, honey, the forbidden fruit is always the sweetest when you're young. But those kinds of things pass—puppy love always does."

"But what if it doesn't? What if it's more than puppy love?" Too late for the *what if* it's more than puppy love part.

"Don't be silly, of course it'll pass." She studied me for a moment before her smile seemed to up in wattage. "It's about time I start setting you up with some eligible young men, men who you could have a future with."

My heart dropped into my stomach. *No, no, no, no, no.* Eligible young men meant only Seer descendants and Gatekeepers who were actually future husband candidates. It was very common with parents amongst our people to make introductions of the kind my mom was referring to. There was even a term for it—*Suiridhe*; it meant wooing—or rather, forced wooing. Somewhere along the line, the younger generations had begun calling the whole process Sudding—maybe because we felt like we were getting hung out to dry after the wash, not really getting much of a say about who we eventually settled down with.

Parents paid attention when couples in my community had children, and they took notes as those children grew up. My mom probably had a list of guys that she thought I should give a chance—literally. Some parents, like mine, would give their children a little bit more say in the process, but when it came down to it, the final choice was out of my hands. Hell, we were all kept close to home for that reason, too. It was common practice to live with your parents until a match was made and then the cycle would begin anew. Everything was done to perpetuate our lines and gifts, which ultimately was for the good of our world safety.

Families with the most coveted, gifted children, like Seers, always held the advantage. *Bonus for me.* So all my mom had to do was start making phone calls to the eligible guys' parents, and soon enough, I'd have guys lined up around the block to date me, whether they wanted to or not. Some of them would be local and others would travel or actually move here for the opportunity to be matched with a Seer. The entire scenario was ludicrous.

My mind flashed to Bryn telling me just last night that my feelings would all pass when my mom started setting me up, that I would move on and leave him behind. Bryn had known it was only a matter of time before my mom started my Sudding. After all, I wasn't officially dating anyone, and I'd just had my nineteenth birthday. "Aren't you worried about my feelings for this other guy?"

My mom got up and headed for the door, pausing to fix me with her gaze. "No. I don't worry about you, honey, because when it comes down to it, I know you'll do the right thing. I'll see you downstairs when you're ready." She pulled my door shut behind her, leaving me alone with my thoughts.

Shit, shit, shit. My worst fears were coming to fruition. I was going to be set up with guys who weren't Bryn, and I would eventually be expected to pick one of them. An arranged marriage it was not, but it suddenly felt eerily close. The thought of letting anyone else but Bryn touch me intimately made my stomach suddenly queasy. Something that never seemed to bother me before with all my daydreams about other guys. But now—now ...

What the hell am I gonna do? I drummed my nails along the top of my vanity. It wasn't even an *us* against the world situation. Currently it was just *me* against the world. I couldn't even get Bryn to fight for me.

But wait ... What if I could do exactly that? Get Bryn to fight for me. Then at least we'd stand a chance. I grinned at myself in the mirror. *Finally, I have a plan. Sort of. Well, I know what direction I'm going in now at least.*

Determination shot through my veins, and I stood, briefly scanning my purple accented room, already mentally picking through my closet. I yanked my current shirt over my head, letting it drop to the floor. Normally, I was a bit of a neat freak, but at the moment, even I didn't have time to worry about a few misplaced articles of clothing. As I considered my options, I reached into the top drawer of my dresser, snagging a candy bar from my secret stash. I was going to need some chocolate fortification before I set to work on myself.

As I munched, I glanced at the calendar hanging on my wall with September 23rd and 24th circled in thick, black Sharpie. Not only were yesterday and today important because they were mine and Bryn's birthdays, but the dates also symbolized a rebirth of sorts for both of us. Last night at Ryan's party had changed everything, and it would for the better ... somehow.

I MADE MY WAY DOWNSTAIRS, dressed like I was ready for a red carpet somewhere. Instead of my normal casual wear, I donned a party dress. *It is a party after all.* The dress wasn't as tiny as the one I had on last night, but it showed off what assets I had very nicely. Plus, the green glossy material really made my green eyes pop. I also actually took the time to curl my hair and applied a full face of makeup. *I look pretty damn good, if I do say so myself.*

All eyes turned towards me as I entered the living room, but I currently only cared about one person. *Bryn.* He was lounging in his usual spot at the corner of the couch, a glass of soda in his hand. When he spotted me, the smile on his face instantly dropped. His intense gaze roved over my body from bottom to top before it flicked away. And yet what I saw there in his deep blue eyes before he turned was exactly what I had been going for—*possession*. A part of him acknowledged that I belonged to him, just like I knew he belonged to me. After what happened last night combined with my birthday glow-up had made him consider the real possibility of actually possessing. *Boom! My plan has launched successfully.*

A chorus of *Happy Birthdays* greeted me before my mom ushered everyone into the dining room for dinner. Bryn and I took our traditional seats next to each other in the center of the table.

"What are you doing?" Bryn hissed.

I widened my eyes and blinked at him in feigned confusion. "I'm sure I don't know what you mean."

He quirked one dark eyebrow at me. "Yeah, I don't believe that for a second."

"What you choose to believe or not believe has nothing to do with me." I bit back a smile. "Now let's just have a nice dinner and enjoy ourselves."

Dinner went smoothly, and Bryn started to relax a bit. He even let me hold his hand like I normally did. It was only when we were opening presents that things took a turn towards the more interesting.

"Kevin," my mom addressed my dad. "I was just telling P. J. earlier that I think it's time for us to start setting her up on dates with some proper young men…you know?"

My dad nodded in agreement, his glasses catching the light in an ominous way. "Sure."

Bryn's mom, of all people, piped up. "It's about time you started *Suiridhe*. Some of the other single Seers about your age started already. You better get going before you miss out on someone good." It was like they were talking about going shoe shopping or something. *You better hit the sale before all the best shoes are gone.*

I lifted my gaze to ensnare Bryn's as I responded, "Sure. I'd love to, Mom. It's not like I have any other prospects of my own to worry about. Not really." Bryn sucked in a startled breath and dropped my hand. I dipped my head and raised my voice for effect. "The sooner the better."

"Oh, good, honey, I'll get started right away." My mom called over her shoulder as she headed back into the kitchen, "Anyone need anything while I'm in here?"

Bryn vaulted to his feet. "I'm going for a walk."

"I'll go with you." I wasn't going to let him get away that easily.

"No," he snapped.

"Well, why not?" I quirked an eyebrow at him in silent challenge. He knew he couldn't make a big a deal about wanting to get away from me without raising questions he wouldn't want to answer. His jaw ticked with tension. He then abruptly spun on his heel and headed for the door without another word. Of course, he knew I would follow him.

"We'll be back in a couple minutes," I called to no one in particular. Bryn and me going off by ourselves was a common occurrence, and no one in either of our families would give it a second thought.

I stumbled several times, my high heels making it difficult to keep up with Bryn. He was practically sprinting down the street. "Hey, wait up," I wheezed.

"And why would I do that when I'm trying to get away from you?" Bryn snarled, ducking into the woods that sat across from my house.

"Bryn, please."

He whirled around, his face contorting in agony. "What the hell are you trying to do to me, Peej? Seriously, are you trying to punish me or something?"

"No, I—"

My words were swallowed up when his mouth found mine, his tongue forcefully pushing past my lips. His heady taste and raw masculine scent invaded my senses, overpowering me. His hands tangled in my hair, and just like the night before, I found myself pushed up against a tree by Bryn.

The way he was kissing me was different than before though. There was an undercurrent of desperation, making him more forceful. All my nerve endings crackled with his energy, causing a wave of pure lust to slam into me. "I can't lose you. I just can't," he rumbled into my mouth.

My insides danced with glee. Had my plan worked that quickly? Had the mere threat of me being with someone else driven Bryn into my arms? *Time to find out.* "I wanna be with you, Bryn. I don't wanna be with anyone else. Ever."

He froze, breaking our kiss, his chest heaving. "Yeah, okay. Yeah. We'll find a way. Somehow, we'll find a way." His lips crashed into mine again.

Yes. Bryn is going to fight for me—for us. Somehow, we'll make it work.

We kissed and groped each other for minutes, hours— I wasn't sure how long, but before things progressed into X-rated territory, Bryn pulled away, breaking all contact between us. "Not like this. Your first time can't be like this."

My insides churned as I gasped for breath. *How did I manage to lie to myself so thoroughly about my feeling for Bryn until now?* I wanted him more than I imagined I could ever want anyone or anything. "You can't take it back. You can't say we'll find a way and then take it back. That would be even worse than if you'd never said anything at all." *It would kill me.*

Bracketing my face in both of his large hands, he leaned in, our breath intermingling. "No. There's no going back. I want this." He shook his head slightly. "No. I *need* this. I need you. I can't imagine my life without you. Just being your Guardian isn't enough—it'd never be enough."

"What do we do then? How do we—?" I swallowed around the lump in my throat. I hadn't put much thought into my plan beyond the getting Bryn to fight for me part, and honestly, I hadn't expected it to work so fast.

"I don't know … yet. So we have to keep it a secret. We

can't tell anyone. At least until we figure out what we're going to do."

I nodded in agreement. "Of course."

"But once we graduate from college we can go somewhere else if they won't agree. In the end, they can't stop us—no one can stop us."

That wasn't exactly true. I was only going to college at all to learn how to help run my family's construction company, the business side of it. I didn't have aspirations beyond that—because I wasn't allowed to. If we set out into the world on our own, I wasn't sure we'd thrive the way we hoped. We simply weren't prepared like other humans. Plus, there was the immediate problem of my dating status.

"Yeah, but what about now? What about my mom and the Sudding…" My voice trailed off as I zeroed in on the torment in Bryn's eyes.

The muscles in his jaw feathered as he clenched his teeth. "You go. You pretend. We bide our time. And we do this" —he slammed his lips against mine, delivering me a feverous kiss that left me slightly dizzy— "in secret."

"O-okay."

His thumbs circled my cheeks gently. "I love you, Peej —so much, it hurts."

I gnawed on my lower lip. His eyes spoke of promises, promises of hope and love. I wanted nothing more than to drown in those promises. "I love you, too."

"Come on." He slid away from me and interlaced his fingers with mine, tugging me away from my now favorite tree in the whole world. "We better get back before they start to wonder what's taking us so long."

"But wait—" I teetered on my heels, trying not to let Bryn pull me forward. "I didn't give you your birthday present yet." Reaching into my dress, just above my left bra cup, I produced a slim leather wallet.

Bryn's eyes widened slightly. "How did I miss that?"

I snorted. "Well, to be fair, I had it more under the strap, and you kind of skipped over that area of my body and got right down to business with your groping. Not to mention that you were completely over my clothes and—"

Bryn waved his hands in defeat. "Okay, okay, I get the point. Can I have my present now?"

I set the wallet on his upturned, waiting palm, my stomach twisting with nerves. The wallet was something I would give my friend Bryn, but he was more now...so much more. Maybe he wouldn't like it. Maybe he would think it was stupid. Bryn was always such a hard person to shop for. I'd simply noticed that he needed a new wallet. His old one was on its last leg, not to mention it had a Velcro closure. *I mean, Velcro? Seriously?* So I got him a nice little leather wallet with his initials on the front. I'd also added another personal touch on the inside...

"Is this a picture from our first birthday celebration together? What were we, like, five?"

"No, six. We didn't officially start celebrating our birthdays together until we were six." I was momentarily swept away to another time. I saw Bryn as the tiny mischievous boy that I'd come to call my best friend. His black hair had fallen forward into his sparkling blue eyes. He had given me his patented lopsided grin complete with dimples, just as he smashed a piece of cake into my face. Of course, I reciprocated, and a full out cake war had ensued. That's when my mom had snapped the picture of us that I put into Bryn's wallet. We were both completely covered in chocolate cake and grinning like loons at each other.

"Peej—"

"I know it's stupid. I guess I'm just being overly sentimental. I don't know what—"

"I love it," Bryn cut me off. "The fact that you noticed my old wallet is falling apart—I don't know, maybe I'm being overly sentimental too, but I think it's cool that you pay so much attention to me, that you notice the little things no one else does. And the picture…I love it, too."

Warmth bloomed in my chest, and I smiled at him. "I'm really glad you like it—all of it."

"My turn," Bryn muttered, reaching into his back pocket.

When he offered me a small black velvet box, I gasped. No male besides my dad had ever given me jewelry before. With trembling hands, I took my gift from him and popped the lid off. I gasped again. "Bryn, I love them! They're just the ones I wanted—the ones I told you I saw at the mall with Jenna last month."

Winking at me in the dim light was a small pair of blue sapphire stud earrings. The dark blue color reminded me of Bryn's eyes when they were churning with deep emotion, their shade often seeming to change with his moods. Plus, sapphire happened to be both of our birthstones. *They're absolutely perfect!*

"Yeah, I know. I had Jenna show me which ones."

"But how did you afford them? I mean, they weren't exactly cheap—"

Bryn stepped forward and cupped my cheek, snagging my gaze with his. The charge of electricity that passed between the two of us stole my voice. "I just wanted to make you happy."

I completely in Bryn's thrall, unable to look away. "We'd better get back for real this time—" He cleared his throat, dropping his gaze from mine. He took my hand within his, tugging gently. "—before I do something we'll both regret."

As I trailed along mutely behind Bryn, heading back to our party, I thought if I could find my voice, I would tell him that *whatever* he wanted to do—*I* most certainly wouldn't regret it.

Chapter 6

Keeping a romantic relationship secret isn't as fun as movies and TV would have us believe, nor is it as easy. Spending time with Bryn had become a newly discovered form of torture. Being close to him, holding his hand—those simple things alone caused the almost undeniable impulse to explore every inch of his skin with my fingertips, followed by my tongue. I yearned to map every nook and cranny of his body, to feel and taste the finely honed muscles that that lay under his smooth, pale flesh, to kiss not only his lips but his sweet, salty skin. I craved closeness to him—a closeness I wasn't even sure I fully understood, being that I was still a virgin. When I was near him, it was if my body thrummed in anticipation of even the slightest brush of his flesh against mine. We were in love. The kind of deep, soul-changing love that happens only once in a lifetime.

And despite my feelings for Bryn, I found myself in the

nightmare scenario of going on a date with someone my mom set me up with. *Someone who is not Bryn.* I'd reluctantly chosen to wear black skinny dress pants and a black and white striped one-shoulder top, paired with black gladiator sandals. What I really wanted to be in was jeans and a T-shirt, but I had to at least look like I was trying. Bryn was aware of my pending date, knew it wasn't real, at least on my end, and yet I couldn't shake the feeling that I was betraying him—us. If only I could go back in time and sew my lips shut so I didn't bring up the subject of Sudding to my mom at all. I could have used some other means to make Bryn jealous ... *It doesn't matter. You're here now and you have to deal with the mess you made.*

I knew what I had to do, what I was going to do, but I wanted more than anything to be alone with Bryn somewhere—anywhere, his heated lips pressed against my skin. Goosebumps erupted along my flesh at just the thought. I didn't know how much longer I'd be able to keep our relationship under wraps, not with the way he made my insides burn. Every fiber in my being cried out in yearning when I wasn't with him. And my blood boiled, shoving desire through my veins every time Bryn was in a five foot radius of me. *How has no one picked up on that yet?*

When the familiar sound of the doorbell chimed, dread snaked through my chest, squeezing the breath from my lungs. *Run! It's not too late! Run out the back door before anyone sees you! No. Stop. You can't.* I had to keep up appearances, to pretend that nothing had changed between me and Bryn, even if—even if I kind of wished he'd appear in a jealous rage and demand for me to not go on the date.

"Honey, Jeremy is here," my mom called to me, her voice much too cheery for my taste. I somehow managed to peel myself off the couch, trudging towards the front foyer. "Here she is," my mom nearly sang. "P.J., this is Jeremy. Jeremy, this is my lovely daughter, P.J. Don't mind her, I think she's a little nervous."

Glaring at my mom, I hissed, "I'm not nervous."

"Hey," Jeremy said.

I forced my gaze up, curiosity taking over, the need to assess my adversary strong. Jeremy had a pleasant enough face. I took note of his sandy brown tousled hair, bronzed skin, dark brown eyes set over a long straight nose, high cheekbones, full firm lips, and a square masculine jaw— quite handsome if I was being honest with myself. I wouldn't have been surprised to find his picture adorning the walls in one of those preppy clothing stores like Abercrombie & Fitch. Jenna would already be wiping drool off her chin if she were in my shoes. She'd probably have him half undressed by the time they reached his car. *But of it matters to me because he's not Bryn.*

"Hey," I replied coolly.

My mom grinned at me, obviously very pleased with herself. "Now you two have a good time." She proceeded to usher us out the front door, closing it behind us with an ominous finality. I sucked in a shaky breath, again fighting the urge to bolt.

"So..." Jeremy trailed off before clearing his throat. "I

know this is kind of awkward, but I thought we could go get something to eat and talk, try to make this as painless as possible."

I'd forgotten to consider the very real possibility that whoever I went out with wouldn't be thrilled to go on our date either. "Yeah, okay," I agreed with a tentative smile. I trudged along behind him, halting when we arrived at a brand new, dark green RAV4. *Probably his parents.* After all, there was very little autonomy from parents in my world, not like Reg children. I let him open and shut the door for me as I climbed into the passenger side. I waited in silence as he rounded the car, letting my gaze settle on a patch of trees by my house.

My lungs seized. Bryn was there, standing right by the trees. Our gazes collided for one intense moment before he seemed to melt into the shadows. My pulse pounded against my eardrums. *Why did he come to watch me leave on my date? Why would he do that to himself?* I raised my palm to the window, touching my fingertips to it. *I wish I could touch you, kiss you, tell you everything is going to be okay.* A lump formed in my throat, and I attempted to steady my heartbeat.

The engine in the RAV4 revving to life pulled my mind back to the interior of the car and the date I was supposed to be on. I forced my gaze away from the dark night, and from where Bryn still lurked somewhere. I glanced over at Jeremy, giving him another tentative smile, to which he returned one of his own.

"Music?" he asked.

I bit the inside of my cheek. "Yeah, sure."

"My iPod is down there in the console, already hooked up. I'll let you pick our soundtrack for the evening."

With trembling hands, I scrolled through his music selection without another word. I decided on Seether's *Fake It* for the first song, feeling it was definitely appropriate for the situation, and Genius-ed it. Once the selection was made, I turned it up loud enough to where it would make conversation relatively difficult. Jeremy obviously took the hint, and we rode in silence—except for the music. I stared out the window, watching the world blur by without really paying attention to where we were going. When the car finally rolled to a stop, my gaze snagged on the warm glow of *Tony's* restaurant sign shining through the windshield. Pittsburgh and the surrounding suburbs are jam packed with local mom and pop Italian places, so Jeremy bringing me to one wasn't that odd, but it definitely wasn't a coincidence that he had chosen my favorite.

Frowning, I asked, "My mom told you, didn't she?"

Jeremy blinked several times, a puzzled expression settling on his face. "It's okay, isn't it? I mean, was your mom wrong?"

"No," I sighed, fingering the buckle on my seatbelt. "She was right. This place is my favorite."

"Okaaay," Jeremy drawled, obviously considering what to say next. "Look, I know this is awkward, like I said before, but there's no need for it to be painful. It's not like I was exactly thrilled when my parents informed me that I had a date with someone that I'd never met before. But then again, it's not as if I'm seriously seeing anyone right now anyways, hence the Sudding." He smiled at me. "And now, after meeting you, even though I can tell you're also less than thrilled to be here, I'm thinking this might not be such bad a thing after all."

So much for him not being interested in me. He seemed nice enough, and I didn't relish the idea of being mean to him, but what was the point, really? "Look." I tugged on my seatbelt nervously. "I'm here because my mom has it in her head that it's time for me to start dating *proper young men,* and obviously I don't have to clue you into what she means when she says that, but—" *But what?* I couldn't exactly tell him that I was in love with someone else. It no doubt would get around, and my mom would demand to know more details about the supposed puppy love I'd already illuded to. And I couldn't afford for her, or anyone for that matter, to find out about me and Bryn.

"But what?" Jeremy asked. "Are you, well, are you— there's no proper way to ask this, so I'm just going to—are you into girls or something?"

"What?" I *so* hadn't seen that question coming.

"Well, you're not married, and you're not in a serious relationship, so if you're not into girls, then I don't see why you can't at least have dinner with me, give me a chance. Unless you think I'm completely repulsive?" He met my gaze, grinning, knowing full well he wasn't repulsive.

An image of Bryn flashed in my mind's eye. Heat rolled

over my skin, an unavoidable reaction to the thought of his body pressed up flush to mine, his lips trailing down my—

I shoved the image out of my brain, since continuing that train of thought would lead to no good, possibly causing me to combust right where I sat. I internally snickered. *Yeah, the concept of me not being into guys is absolutely ridiculous.* "Fine. Dinner. But that's all I'm promising." I'd at least pretend to give him a chance, and then tell my mom there was no chemistry or something of that ilk. *Next contestant, please.*

Jeremy reached for his door, giving me a hundred-watt smile. "A chance, that's all I'm asking for."

Mmm hmm ... don't get your hopes up, buddy.

I unhooked my seatbelt and slid out of the door to meet him beside the car. He offered me his arm, which I eyed warily before stalking off towards *Tony's*. I'd have dinner with him, but I never said I would touch him. So far, I'd managed to avoid the connection with his Gatekeeper powers by not opening myself up to them, and by not having skin-to-skin contact. I was planning on keeping it that way. For some reason, that fact was important to me, no matter if it didn't really make any sense.

About forty-five minutes later, numerous glasses of soda consumed, and our meals completely devoured, I had discovered that Jeremy wasn't that bad. All things considered.

"Then what'd you do?" I laughed, trying not to squirt soda out of my nose.

"So there I was, out in the woods, by myself, completely naked, no phone, no keys, nothing. My only choice was to hoof it home. Luckily, a few blocks from where I was, I found a trash bag that didn't reek too bad that covered me up until I got home." He paused to laugh himself. "You shoulda seen the look on my dad's face when I tried sneaking in the back door. Of course, he was so proud when he found out the whole thing was because I was beginning to come into my powers."

I took another sip of soda. "I never knew that could happen to Gatekeepers. I wonder if it happens to a lot of you guys?"

Jeremy averted his gaze, his face flushing. "As far as I know, I'm the only one, although I'm not gonna be making my incident public, so maybe that's why I haven't heard of it happening to anyone else."

"Well, I'm just glad being a Seer doesn't run that risk. I have enough potential for embarrassing situations as it is. I don't need to worry about zapping all of my clothes out of existence when I go to manipulate energy around a gate."

"I'm guessing there'd be a lot fewer complaints if you were seen around town naked."

Our gazes locked for a moment before I turn away, clearing my throat. "Are you better now? With your powers? That doesn't happen on a regular basis, I mean?"

"No, it hasn't happened since then." His attention was

temporarily distracted when our waitress brought back his change from our check. He took out a couple of bills, leaving them in the book for her.

I spotted my opportunity and seized it. "I guess you're ready to go then?"

"Yeah, I guess. I don't suppose—"

"No," I interrupted. "I need to be getting home. I have to get up in the morning pretty early for...church." Yeah, I hadn't been to an early Sunday service in—ever. But he didn't need to know that.

"Oh." Disappointment shimmered in his eyes. "Then I guess I'd better get you home."

A wave of guilt crashed over me. I mean, Jeremy was a nice and charming guy, and if it weren't for Bryn, I might have been interested. "Thanks for dinner and everything," I said, ducking my head and tucking my hair behind my ears before making a break for freedom.

He caught up easily, walking me to his car in silence. Once inside, I turned up the music for the ride home, which effectively kept Jeremy from talking to me anymore. I heaved a sigh of relief when we pulled into my driveway.

Jeremy turned the car off and opened his door. "I'll walk you up."

"Oh, you don't have to..." But he was already making his way around the car. *Why can't he just take the hint already? Ugh. Don't make me be mean, Jeremy. Please.*

I managed to avoid his touch as I awkwardly hopped out of the car to keep his grubby hands off of me. But that didn't deter him from escorting me all the way to my front door where he turned to face me. "Well, I'm really glad I met you, P.J., even though I know you're still feeling weird about this whole thing. I'll call or text and maybe we can go out again. I hope you'll be more open to it since you can see that I'm not that bad of a guy."

I held back a snort. *Yeah, not that bad of a guy but horrible at reading people, apparently.* I didn't want to be mean, but I didn't want to lead him on either, but I also needed to consider self-preservation. Ultimately, would it be better to hang out with him again for appearance's sake, or move on to the next guy my mom probably already had lined up? It would most likely be more believable to go out with Jeremy a few more times before I dropped the no chemistry line on everyone. I had to at least pretend I was giving him a real chance.

I sighed. "Yeah, okay. We can hang out again, I suppose."

His lips stretched wide into a grin, lighting up his handsome features. "All right, talk to you soon then."

He leaned in, giving me a quick peck on the cheek before I had a chance to react. Just the briefest sense of his powers zapped along my skin, snapping into sync with my pulse. My breath caught in my throat at the intoxicating rush. He paused to lock eyes with me, giving me a smug smirk before heading down my walk.

Shit. Our powers had connected, and that wasn't a good thing in this instance. With my people, power was an extremely enticing lure. If Jeremy thought we had a power connection, it would only heighten anything he might already be feeling for me. I stood there, frozen with trepidation as he drove away. Another few heartbeats passed before I turned to go into my house.

No. Wait. I have to see Bryn. Now.

Spinning on my heel, I took off at a dead sprint for Bryn's house. *Please be there. Please be there. Please ...* I crept into his backyard, and zeroed in on his window, breathing a sigh of relief when I spotted the light on in his first-floor bedroom. *Thank God he's not off brooding somewhere.*

Sucking in a few calming breaths, I hovered outside his window, listening for any signs that he had company. It would be an utter disaster if his parents found out I was sneaking into his bedroom when I was supposed to still be on my date. And not just any date, but the first of my Sudding.

Satisfied when complete silence met my ears, I tapped on the window softly. Almost immediately, Bryn's face appeared on the other side of the glass. Gaze locking with mine, he yanked up the blinds and shoved up his window so I could crawl through.

Nervous energy and excitement sizzled through my veins at the mere sight of him, and I eagerly wrapped my arms around him, fully expecting him to welcome me into his embrace. But instead, his arms remained limp at his sides, his body rigid.

Drawing away from him, I stared up at his face in confusion. "What's wrong?"

His jaw muscles feathered with tension as he stared

back at me, his gaze churning with emotions I couldn't quite read. I swallowed around the sudden lump in my throat. "Bryn?"

He abruptly backed me against the wall, caging me in when his hands came to rest against the wall on either side of my head. My pulse set off at a gallop, my breath catching in my throat. "Bryn?" Uncertainty caused my voice to waver. He seemed so—so angry, and yet—yet instead of being worried or afraid a warmth simmered low in my belly.

"I couldn't stand watching you leave with him," Bryn growled. "I had to fight everything in me to not come after you." His chest heaved as he sucked in ragged breaths. "You're mine. I won't share you."

"It's not real, Bryn. You know that. I'm yours—all yours."

He stared at me a few more seconds, his nostrils flaring. "It seemed so real, Peej—like I was losing you. It was like a nightmare I couldn't wake up from."

I slid my fingers along his arms. "I'm here now. And I'm yours. Always."

Bryn captured my lips with his, taking my mouth forcefully, dominating me like never before. I welcomed the heat of his jealousy as it morphed into fiery passion that spurred him to roughly explore me with his tongue and mouth. Our clothes fell away, and soon we were both left in nothing but our underwear.

We suddenly found ourselves suddenly in undiscovered territory, our make-out sessions previously not going beyond heavy petting, and we'd definitely never been fully naked in front of each other either. Our physical relationship was so new that we were both still in awe of the simplest things, like kissing and touching. But tonight—tonight Bryn didn't show any signs of stopping. And I sure as hell wasn't going to protest. I'd wanted to give my virginity to him since that first night in the woods. He was the one who thought it wasn't the right time or place. He kept insisting that I should have more for my first time, some deluded idea that I should expect it since I was a girl. The sentiment wasn't misplaced, even if it had left me beyond frustrated on more than one occasion.

"I need you, Peej," Bryn rumbled as his fingers deftly dipped into my underwear. I moaned, his long fingers exploring areas where no boy had ever gone before.

"Yes," I gasped into his mouth. Setting me on his bed, Bryn made quick work of removing my last scraps of clothing. He sucked in a ragged breath as his rapt gaze roamed over my exposed flesh.

"Bryn," I pleaded, reaching for him.

"You're so beautiful," Bryn whispered in reverence. He then came to rest over me, his pelvis cradled in between my thighs.

When did he manage to get his boxers off?

My heart thrashed against my ribcage. *This is happening. I'm going to have sex with Bryn. Me and Bryn are going to have sex.* Then my gaze locked with his, and I was pulled into the fathomless depths of his sea storm eyes, where all my trepidations seemed to drown in the abyss.

"You still taking the pill?" Bryn rasped.

Reality check. "Yeah." My mom would be absolutely furious if she knew I was using the pill for its intended purpose and not just to regulate my period. Especially if she found out I was using it with Bryn on the heels of a date with someone she had set me up with. "What about your parents—"

"Not here." He dipped his head, showering me with more kisses before pulling away again. "You ready? I don't wanna hurt you."

The way he was looking at me, the love that emanated from him—I felt like the most beautiful and special girl in the entire world. Someone who could do that for me, make me feel so cherished, deserved to have everything that I was—mind, body, and soul. So far, Bryn had only received two of those three. *Tonight, he is going to have everything.* "Yeah, I'm ready."

As he pushed into me, filling me in a way I'd never been able to fully imagine, I gritted my teeth and dug my nails into Bryn's shoulders. I thought I'd been prepared, since I'd heard from friends that the first time for a girl is almost always painful. But no amount of mental preparation could have readied me for what I was currently experiencing. The sharp jab deep inside my body and the burning. Thankfully, as Bryn rocked back and forth inside of me, slowly the pain ebbed into pleasure.

I finally understand why people like Jenna are so sex-crazed. This is—this is—

My entire world narrowed down to Bryn. I could no longer tell where I ended and he began.

Bliss. This is bliss.

A warmth like I'd never experienced before bloomed in my center as our powers converged. Soon it roared into a fire of need, rampaging through my system, spreading outward and erupting into spasms of ecstasy.

Holy shit, it definitely was never like that when I took care of myself.

Bryn slid his hands into my hair, forcing me to look at him. Shuddering, he pulsated within me, his muscles straining. "Fuck," he growled.

Melting into the bed, I smiled when he collapsed above me, careful not to crush me with his massive form. I ran my hands through his silky, tousled hair, then down over his sweaty back. He curled into my touch, leaning forward to kiss me with a slow languidness that spoke of shared intimacies, and unspoken promises. "I love you, Peej. More than I can even begin to explain." His voice was so low and husky it seemed to brush things on my insides, making me shudder in turn.

I sighed contentedly. "I love you, too."

If only we could stay like this forever. But our love wouldn't be enough to protect us from our parents' wrath if they found us like this.

I must have frowned because Bryn's brow furrowed. "What's wrong? Did I hurt you?"

"No, Bryn." I bit my lower lip, briefly replaying the highlights of what we'd just done. "You made my first time more amazing than I ever could have imagined." A smug grin exploded across his face. "I just wish I could stay here with you and not worry about anything else."

He rolled onto his back, tucking me into his side so my head rested on his chest. "I hate this, Peej. I just wanna be with you. I wanna be able to touch you when I want, kiss you when I want. I wanna yell from the rooftops that you belong to me." He pulled his fingers through my hair. "I don't wanna have to watch you go out on dates with other guys." His fist balled at the base of my neck.

"It wasn't so bad tonight, was it? I mean, yeah, it sucked that I had to go on that date, but" —I lifted my head so I could meet his gaze—"look at where we ended up."

He scowled. "I'm sorry, Peej. I really wanted your first time to be special, not in my bedroom because I was crazy with jealously over some guy that you're not even really dating. I just—"

"Shhh…" I brought my finger up to his lips. "I'm glad it happened. I wanna give everything that I am to you, Bryn. The rest doesn't matter. Tonight was the best night of my life so far, because I just shared something with you that I've never shared with anyone else. You own me now—heart, soul…and body."

"You own me, too, Peej. Everything that I have—that I am—belongs to you and only you. Always." His lips sought mine, our kisses becoming feverous again. I wanted so badly to stay in his arms, kissing, exploring, learning all there was to know about pleasing him, and discovering what I liked best, too. But we couldn't stop the outside world from happening. Eventually it would seek us out.

"Hey. I should probably go." I started to get up, but Bryn pulled me back down to ensnare my lips with his again. "Bryn." I tried to chastise him, very unsuccessfully, especially since my body seemed to have a mind of its own. I groaned as he rolled me under him, obviously not liking the idea of me leaving quite yet.

"Five more minutes…" I murmured, giving myself over to him.

BLINKING MY EYES OPEN SLOWLY, I drowsily noted the rays of sunlight streaming in through Bryn's bedroom window. Sudden adrenaline spiked through my system as I jolted upright. "Oh, shit!" Bryn grumbled something incoherent as he reached for me, trying to pull me back down into bed.

I slapped at his hand. "Bryn—no! Wake up! We fell asleep."

He slitted his eyes open, and propped himself up on his elbows, his gaze lazily darting over my rumpled appearance. I saw the moment realization sparked in his brain, wiping the contented look of his face. "Fuck!" He leapt from bed, pulling on a pair of athletic shorts.

I, meanwhile, was frantically searching for my clothes.

"Oh God—Bryn—we're gonna be in so much trouble. They're gonna know. They're—"

"Calm down, Peej. Don't panic. My parents obviously didn't check in on me when they got home, so our cover isn't blown yet."

I grabbed my cell phone out of my purse and swore under my breath—*25 missed calls.* Just then my phone began to vibrate in my hand. It was Jenna. "Hello?" I squeaked.

"Oh my God! Where are you? Your parents were freaking out. I told them you came over to my house after your date to tell me about it and fell asleep, but they're gonna be expecting you home soon."

Relief washed over me, and I exhaled the tension from my body. Bryn was right. Our cover wasn't blown yet. "I'm on my way home now. Thanks, Jenna."

"Wait!" Jenna yelled. "I better get all the details later. It's the least I deserve."

"Yeah, okay. But I have to go now. I so don't wanna get busted."

"Yeah, yeah, yeah. Bye." She hung up in a huff. What exactly was I going to tell her? Guess I could worry about that part later. For now, the important thing was that I had to get home before anyone discovered what really happened to me.

"Jenna covered for you?"

"Yeah, thank God," I said as I pulled my shoes on and headed for the window.

Bryn caught my wrist just as I managed to scramble

over the sill, tugging me up so I had to stand on my tippy toes to reach him. "I need to see you later."

I smiled up at him. "I hope you don't think we're gonna be getting naked again for the next couple of days. I can barely walk."

He delivered me one of his patented lopsided grins, complete with dimples. "We can do other...*things.*"

I'm not really sure why I had the urge to ask—no, the *need*—but I just couldn't help myself. "What was it like—with Tammie? I mean, was I as good?"

His brows furrowed. "I didn't go all the way with her. Last night was my first time too, Peej."

My jaw dropped. "But you were with her for over a year, and you've been making such a big deal about my first time and—" *And he was so good.* How was he so good at those things if he'd never done them before?

"Girls look at their first time a lot differently than guys do. I just wanted to make sure it was special for you." He locked gazes with me. "I told you I couldn't get you out of my head. It would've been wrong to do it with her while I was imagining it was you the entire time. I knew as long as my first time was with you, it would be special for me."

My cheeks heated. "Oh, but—"

"We did other stuff. Mostly she did—um—things to me," Bryn answered before I could ask. "And yeah," He grimaced. "They were good, I mean, of course I enjoyed them—I liked Tammie, but ... she wasn't you."

I knew it was absolutely ridiculous, but just the idea of Tammie doing anything even remotely sexual to Bryn, and him enjoying it to boot—despite the night Bryn and me had just shared, caused jealousy to burn through my veins. "Teach me," I growled. "Teach me so I can do all of those things to you. I wanna learn how to make you happy, Bryn."

He gently tucked a piece of hair behind my ear, trailing his fingers down the side of my neck. "You've already made me happy, Peej. You're so amazing—beyond amazing—I can't even describe…"

I jerked out from under his touch. "You know what I mean, Bryn. I need to learn."

"I mean, yeah, I'll be happy to teach you." He grinned at me, mirth and heat intermingling in his eyes. "There are a few things I wanna learn to do to you, now that you've broached the subject."

He fisted the back of my hair and brought my face to his, slipping his tongue into my mouth to briefly intertwine with mine, before he playfully pushed me away from the window. "Now go before I don't have the strength to let you."

"Okay." I bit my lip, fighting a smile.

My steps were slow and labored as if my legs were protesting the thought of leaving him. I willed myself not to glance back at him for fear that I would throw into his arms again. I hurriedly made my way home with what I was sure was a big goofy grin on my face.

Chapter 7

My mom spun around and crossed her arms over her chest, silently watching me as I sheepishly shuffled into the kitchen through the back door. "Morning." I gave her a a little wave and grimaced.

"Nice of you to call to let us know you were safe. I was frantic with worry." She fidgeted with her reddish hair that was currently pulled into a low ponytail at the nape of her neck, a sure sign of her motherly anxieties, since it was clear she hadn't bothered to wash or style it. I also noted the dark smudges under her eyes, probably caused from staying up late worrying about me. I internally sighed. *Great. Like I don't feel guilty enough for lying to her about Bryn.*

"I didn't mean to fall asleep. Plus, you know, you're always frantic with worry so even if I did call, which I meant to, I swear, you would have found something else to worry about. It's what you do," I mumbled, averting my gaze. I was almost positive she'd be able to tell I wasn't a virgin any more just by looking at me.

"True," she stated. "But that's beside the point. Next time, at least call." She turned back to the stove to continue cooking breakfast. "And no allowance this week. I'll probably need to use the money to buy hair dye to cover all the gray you're giving me."

My arms fell limp at my sides, and I stared at the back of her head. *That's it? A week without allowance? No yelling? No crying? No accusing me of betraying my duty and for messing my life up or some shit? Nothing but the loss of my allowance?* I wasn't going to stick around to press my luck.

"I'm gonna go shower," I mumbled as I scurried out of the kitchen.

Only when I was safely behind my closed door did I dare release a sigh of relief. I pulled out my phone and texted Bryn.

> In the clear.

A few seconds later, my phone beeped in response.

> Wasn't worried. Need 2 c u later.

> I'll text u when I can get away.

> I'll be waiting.

My body suddenly felt lighter, my mood buoyed at the

possibility of seeing him again soon. *Bryn is mine.* And I was beyond lucky to have him. But being separated from him—it was bad enough when I'd lied myself into believing he was only my best friend. Now that we were so much more, it was almost as if I could barely breathe being away from him.

Heaving a loud sigh, I shuffled into the bathroom for a quick shower. As the water warmed, I stripped off my clothes to study myself in the mirror. On the surface, maybe I didn't look any different, but the eyes that were reflected at me were those of a stranger. She seemed to hold some dark, delicious secret of what it meant to be touched so intimately by the man she loved. Her gaze danced merrily with the knowledge of what it felt like to be made love to by her heart's desire. She smiled at me. I smiled back. I paused another moment to study the rest of me for changes. Unfortunately, I hadn't sprouted a more curve-atious body overnight. I was still a tad too skinny and a tad too tall. "But Bryn thinks I'm beautiful," I murmured to myself. And that was all that mattered, especially since I would never fully live up to my own standards set by years of devouring fashion magazines.

When steam began to fog the mirror, I hopped into the shower with a smile that just wouldn't die on my face. Humming to myself, unable to pull my thoughts away from Bryn, snatches of last night kept flashing across my mind, causing my shower take longer than planned. By the time I finally turned the water off, the bathroom had transformed into a sauna. After wrapping a fresh towel around my middle, I pranced back to my room.

"Someone's in an awfully cheerful mood today." I stopped short when I spotted my mom in my room setting some folded laundry on my bed. She smiled at me, obviously thinking my good mood had something to do with my date last night, and not Bryn. "Want to tell me about it?" Her green eyes danced with eagerness.

My face heated as an unbidden memory of Bryn and me locked together in bed flashed across my mind. "There's nothing to tell. Can't a person just be in a good mood for no particular reason?"

"No, *you* can't be in a good mood for no particular reason. I know you too well, peanut." Her expression was expectant, as if her words would loosen whatever secret I didn't want to tell her.

"There's nothing to tell," I repeated, fidgeting from foot to foot.

She frowned, disappointment dancing across her features. "Fine. If you don't want to share with your mom, I guess I can live with that. But can I assume you're going to have a second date with Jeremy?"

"Yeah," I grumbled, leaving it at that. Let her draw her own conclusions.

"Good," she said, sounding very pleased with herself. "Come downstairs when you're dressed, and I'll heat up some breakfast for you."

"Okay." I waited for her to leave before getting dressed, pausing to text Jenna before I headed downstairs.

> U need 2 get here ASAP—can't deal with mom interrogating me about last night.

> K. But we need 2 go somewhere so u can fill me in. Leaving now, c u in 10.

> K. Pretend we already had plans.

She didn't text me back, but I knew she'd be on it.

I stalled a little bit longer before heading downstairs, giving Jenna time to get to my house. Just as I was coming down the stairs, the doorbell rang, and I dashed for it. "Jenna's here, Mom. Last night we made plans to hang out today," I called.

"You still need to eat breakfast," my mom called back. "Maybe Jenna will want something, too."

I flung the door open, never more relieved to see Jenna…and her now *blue* hair? "That red lasted even shorter than usual," I observed.

"Yeah, well, I had to do something last night since a certain someone was M.I.A. after her date, and I had no prospects of my own," she retorted.

"Shhh," I hushed her. "My mom has bat ears. We have to eat before we go anywhere," I added. Well, at least Jenna's new hair color might distract my mom for a few minutes while I scarfed down some food. I trailed into the kitchen behind her, my nerves at an all time high, when suddenly my entire world tilted.

It was like the dream/premonition I thought I'd had the other night at Jenna's after Ryan's party. I was pulled up and away from my body, drawn to the pulsating soft purple glow of the same gate. I saw in fast-forward the same imagery I had before: *There were so many of them—too many to count—and I couldn't distinguish between them since they appeared uniform in shape and size to me. Huge eyes bulged out of their too tiny, pinched faces. Luminescent, dewy skin glowed with a soft light that reflected the gate's hues, making them all seem to pulsate with the same blues and purples. They glided out of the gate slowly, their thin bodies levitating inches off the ground, ghostly in nature. Abruptly, they blurred off into the distance, too fast for my eyes to track, disappearing completely.*

But this time, instead of panicking, I conjured a mental image of what the 'aliens' felt like to me, let their energy signal vibrate within me, and almost instantly without any further effort, I found myself zooming along behind one of them as it made its way to ... *Tennessee, yes.* Somehow, I just ... knew, despite having never been there before.

I watched as it glided into the bedroom of an older man—his dark hair was a similar shade to Bryn's, I noted —and well, the 'alien' proceeded to ooze into the man. It was if the 'alien' went liquid, flowing into the man, only to reform inside of him. He still looked like the man he had been, and yet...I could *see* the 'alien' shining through his visage. The disturbing and wholly unnatural dual imagery caused panic to shoot through my system, and despite myself, I opened my mouth to scream, but instead was hurtled back towards my body.

Everything went dark.

onsciousness found me slowly, my pulse pounding dully as if someone had done a tap dance on my skull. Nearby, my mom was hunched over, whispering in an agitated tone. "No, doctor, I said she passed out cold. Yes, that's what I said. Out cold. Mmm hmm. Mmm hmm. Well, get here as soon as you can then. I'm all but certain it was a premonition, but because she's never had one before, I can't be one-hundred percent, and I don't want to risk it. Mmm hmm. Okay. Thank you." The telltale beep of the cordless phone let me know my mom had hung up.

I sat up slowly, waving absently in her direction. "I'm fine, Mom. I don't need a doctor."

"Oh, honey, you're awake. Good." My mom perched on the edge of my bed, putting the back of her hand to my forehead in the way that all mothers seem to do.

I shoved it away with annoyance. "I said I was fine. I just had a premonition is all."

My mom's gaze darted over my face, accessing, before a smile slowly curled her lips up. "That's great news! What did you see?"

"It was horrible—I saw a gate and it was beautiful but then these aliens came through and then I followed this one alien, well not me exactly but my consciousness or whatever and then the alien slid into this old guy and I could see him hiding underneath him—inside him—like he took over almost like a possession." I inhaled deeply, not having bothered to take a breath during my entire long, run-on sentence of babble, but at least I'd gotten it out—sort of.

My mom's expression sobered, and she clicked her tongue. "I'm sorry, honey, but that's just not possible. There's never been a time when a lone Seer witnessed such an event. On top of that, anytime any of the gates have ever been breached, the offending aliens have never made it more than a few steps into our world. That's why all of us exist, to prevent such things from happening. Usually, a Seer's first vision is something pretty benign... you know that. Your first vision wouldn't be of an impending breach. You aren't ready for that yet. A Seer's mind won't show her something she's not ready to handle." She clicked her tongue again. "Maybe you passed from low blood sugar or something. Good thing the doctor is on his way. I don't think your little episode had anything to do with your powers. What I do think is—"

"No, Mom, it was real!" I exclaimed, throwing my hands in the air.

She patted the top of my head gently. "All right, honey. Just calm down and we can talk about this later." Which meant she didn't believe me and was just patronizing me until she had something better to dissuade me with.

Fine, I can bide my time, too.

I crossed my arms over my chest and waited.

ABOUT AN HOUR later I had a clean bill of health but wasn't any closer to convincing anyone that my premonition was real. I was at the point where I was beginning to have doubts myself. *Maybe it's pointless to persist with the fight?* After all, the arguments for me having dreamt or hallucinated the whole scenario were making a whole lot of sense.

Besides, I had more important things to worry about at the moment. I was almost to Jenna's house, and I didn't have a single believable excuse for where I'd been last night. At least not anything Jenna would buy. I couldn't exactly say I was with Jeremy because then if I slipped up about some detail from our date, she would know I was lying. I wished I could just tell her about me and Bryn, but the fewer people who knew, the safer our secret would stay. *Yep, having a secret love just isn't all it's cracked up to be.*

I'd barely raised my hand to ring Jenna's doorbell when she was pulling me into her house, only to then drag me up to her bedroom. She flopped onto her bed and turned to stare at me expectantly. "Spill," she demanded.

I sighed, my gaze darting around her room. "Well, there's really not much to spill—we fell asleep is all."

"Liar," Jenna hissed. "I'm a Speaker, remember? I can understand all kinds of language, including body language, and you"—she waved her hand in my general direction— "are hiding all kinds of secrets."

I pressed my lips together and narrowed my eyes. "You're a Speaker, not a mind reader. You've been known to make mistakes before."

Her eyebrows crept up her face in disbelief. "Please. You can't possibly think that's going to work. So spill—now."

I grunted in annoyance. "I don't have to put up with you accusing me of stuff that I'm not guilty of—I fell asleep, and that's all."

She stared at me for what seemed like an eternity before she slumped back on her bed. "Mmm ... Okay."

What? Some Speaker she is if she actually bought that. "Okay?"

She shrugged. "Yeah, okay."

My phone beeped, letting me know I had a new text message. I popped it open to see it was from Bryn.

Getting impatient—need to see you. Meet me in 15 @ our tree.

Okay.

My cheeks heated at him mentioning *our tree*. I'd come to think of it as that, but I was pleasantly surprised to know he had, too. My stomach did a backflip as an image of Bryn kissing me while I was pressed up against my favorite tree in the whole world—where he'd finally decided to be with me.

"Aaand who was that?" Jenna drawled as if she wasn't interested.

I shut my phone and avoided her gaze. "Bryn. It was Bryn. But umm...I've gotta go. We'll talk more later." I stuffed my phone in my pocket and hurried from her room. "Thanks for covering for me—love ya!" I called over my shoulder as I rushed through her front door, slamming it behind me.

I didn't want to upset Jenna, but I needed to see Bryn more than anything else in the world right now. The walk over was a blur. I was floating on a cloud of joyous anticipation, and I would have run, but I didn't want to show up a sweaty mess to see Bryn.

I hardly made it a few feet into the spattering of woods across from my house when warm, strong arms encircled me from behind. "I missed you." Bryn spun me around, capturing my lips with his. I allowed myself to sink into him, his spicy scent and heady taste welcoming me home.

"I missed you, too," I murmured, running my hands eagerly over his muscled shoulders and torso. It felt like I hadn't seen him in months, not hours. His hands explored my flesh, emboldened by the nature of the time we'd shared last night. It wasn't long before we could have been arrested for indecent exposure.

"I'll never get enough of you, Peej. It's like a dream—us being together," Bryn rumbled. "I love you so much."

"I love you, too."

"Oh. My. God." Jenna's voice shattered our happy little love bubble. Panic swept through my system, ratcheting up my pulse. Bryn and me fumbled to put back on and straighten our clothes, all the while Jenna stood in the clearing gaping at us. "I can't believe you didn't tell me!" she exclaimed.

"Why would I tell you?" Bryn grated.

"Not you—her." She pointed an angry finger my way. "I mean, I know he's your best friend and all—and now I can see why—but I'm at least your best *female* friend." She crossed her arms, glaring at me with indignation.

"You followed me?" I couldn't believe she actually followed me—well, then again, maybe I could. I would do it if I were in her shoes. "You didn't believe me at all. You just said you did so I wouldn't think about it and I'd be sloppy." *How the hell did I fall for that? Seriously? My eagerness to see Bryn turned me into an idiot.*

"Ding, ding, ding. We have a winner." Jenna smirked. "I knew you were hiding something really big and juicy. I just never in a million years imagined it was this." She motioned to both Bryn and me. "And you guys are in love? I mean, having sex is one thing, you know, being friends with benefits or something, but this is some really serious shit."

"You heard us?" I asked incredulously. "But if you followed me—" I stopped to stare at her for a stunned moment. "You were watching us? Oh my God, Jenna—ewww!"

"No! I wasn't watching you like a voyeur or something! I just wanted to see what I could find out, and then I got distracted by a chatty squirrel who, by the way, said he would normally be annoyed by you guys, but after the other night when he heard you professing your love for each other, he is now okay with you guys being here. I kind of thought he was exaggerating the whole love thing, but apparently not."

Damn Speakers. And damn chatty squirrels. "You can't tell anyone—please," I begged.

"Well, duh. Like I said, this is some really serious shit. I can't believe you guys are in—did you guys have sex? Did you lose your virginity to him and not even tell me? Please tell me it isn't so." Her face scrunched up in horror.

I choked back a laugh. She was more upset at the prospect of me losing my virginity and not telling her than anything else. "Last night."

She sniffed. "I suppose I can forgive you since you've only been keeping that vital information from me for less than twenty-four hours." A huge grin broke out across her face, and she jumped up and down, clapping. "Oh—oh—I'm so excited! I need to hear every last detail!"

Bryn shook his head as his eyes widened. "Please don't. Our sex life is not up for public discussion."

Bryn and me have a sex life. We've had sex. I inwardly sighed. *Life is good.*

Jenna waved him off. "Puh-lease, it's not public, it's just me. And I bet you're super pumped to finally have P.J. after all this time. I kept trying to get her to have sex with you, but I just couldn't tell if she was into you or not."

"What?" Bryn and me exclaimed at the same time.

"Yeah, Speaker here." She pointed demonstratively at herself. "I've known Bryn had a thing for you for awhile, P.J., but you were the tough one to figure out. Sometimes I felt the vibe, and other times, well...I guess it was just because you hadn't figured out your own feelings yet." She nodded to herself.

So that was why Jenna was always telling me to just get it over with and have sex with Bryn. I couldn't count how many times I'd heard her say that. In fact, I distinctly remember her saying it the day of Ryan's party. "Well, you could have told me he had a thing for me."

"No, I couldn't have. You would have freaked out and run for the hills so fast none of us probably ever would have seen you again."

"She's right," Bryn agreed.

"Hey!" I shouted indignantly. I glanced from Bryn to Jenna and back again. "Fine, maybe that's true." I cracked a smile. "I guess I had to figure it out myself."

"So, what are we gonna do now?" Jenna asked.

Bryn scowled at her. "We? I don't think so. This is between me and Peej—"

"And me now," Jenna interjected. "Because I know the secret and all. I can help you, you know, to keep it that way—a secret."

Bryn sighed as he glanced at me, exasperation splashed across his features. "Why do I have such a bad feeling about this?"

I grimaced. "Because you're not stupid, that's why."

"MAYBE IT'LL BE okay that she knows," I said to Bryn, though even to myself I didn't sound convinced. "I mean, it did help to have her cover for me the other night when I fell asleep at your place."

My mind danced away to that glorious night, a brief reprieve before I was forced to consider the reality of the present. A sense of grief washed over me as I considered how few of those intimate moments we might get in the near future. And if we got caught? Dread replaced grief as my stomach twisted with the mere possibility.

"Hey." Bryn tipped my face up so he could capture my gaze. "Don't panic. We'll figure it out."

Determination was etched into his pupils, his irises... his very soul. The storm of emotions raging within him reminded me that he would fight for us. That's all that really mattered. "And if we do get caught before we're ready? Then what?"

He ran his fingers down along my jaw, tracing the same path with his lips a moment later. I shivered. "Then no matter what happens, I'll find you. I'll come for you. No one can keep us apart. We'll be together in the end..." His voice trailed off with words left unsaid. He was saying if we got caught, if we were separated, he would come for me no matter what no matter how long it took. "But we're not caught yet, so let's enjoy the time we have together."

I buried my hands in his hair, tugging, as he kissed a trail of fire down my neck. "I just wish I could have figured this all out sooner," I mumbled, trying to temporarily fight the effect Bryn's lips on me.

"What?" he rumbled, his voice was low and husky. *He's so hot. There's no way I can concentrate with him being all ... him.*

"U-us—how I feel about you. I wish I figured it out sooner. I mean, I've been in love with you, and too blind to see it." I gripped his hair, pulling his head up so I could meet his gaze. "I somehow managed to miss when my love changed and grew to be more...adult. And now look at us."

Bryn's eyes glinted with amusement. "Yeah, look at us now. Although I suppose I should have guessed that one day you'd have me wrapped around your little finger. After all, you were the only girl who never had cooties as far as I was concerned." I laughed, playfully swatting at him. I'd forgotten about that. Like a lot of little boys, Bryn had gone through the "all girls have cooties" phase, but with one exception: in his case, it was more "all girls have cooties, except P.J.".

"Yeah, our version of doctor has changed a little over

the years." He smiled devilishly, turning my insides to goo. "Now take off your clothes so I can give you a full exam."

"Bryn." I giggled as he playfully tugged at my clothes. It was just so right being with him—someone I'd shared almost my whole life with, someone who knew me better than any other person on the planet.

My phone beeped. "Hold on," I chastised him. "It could be my mom. She's figured out how to text now, you know."

I sobered the second I realized who it actually was— Jeremy.

> Was really hoping we could go out again soon.

Gnawing on my bottom lip I stared at my phone, considering. I wanted to say no and be done with it, but was that the best choice for me and Bryn in the long run? If I raised too many suspicions, people would start to ask questions, and in our case, questions were bad. It would be best if I took my time so I could appear to seriously be weighing my options with the Sudding guys. It had to look like I was actually giving them chances. I had to appear unattached and completely available to the outside world.

I was still staring at the message when Bryn slipped my phone out of my grasp. "That's a resounding no," he growled.

"Hey, wait. I have to, remember?" I made a grab for my

phone, but he kept it just out of my reach with his long arms.

"You don't have to anything. You went on a date with him, now it's over, time for Mr. Gatekeeper to move on along from you."

"Bryn," I snapped. "Just give me my damn phone."

"Why? Do you *want* to go out with him again or something?"

He can't be fucking serious right now, can he? "You know I need it to look like I'm giving these guys the proper consideration everyone expects me to. Besides, he was a nice guy. I should be able to get another date out of him, therefore buying us more time, without him trying something with me."

"You are not going out with him again," he gritted out through clenched teeth, his entire body trembling.

I threw my hands up in the air. "What the hell is wrong with you? Why are you acting so jealous all of a sudden?" Notching my chin up, I glared at him. "No matter how much I love you, there's absolutely no future for us if this is how you're gonna act. It'll poison our relationship."

He stared at me for another couple seconds, his jaw ticking with tension, before he hunched into himself, and his gaze slid to the ground. "I'm sorry, Peej, this is—this is hard. Us—our relationship is new, and watching you drive off with him before..."

Wrapping his arms around me, I found myself completely engulfed with his scent and warmth. He sighed heavily and rested his chin on the top of my head. "It was as if you reached into my chest and ripped out my heart with your bare hands, taking it with you." He ran his fingers through my hair. "I don't mean to order you around. I know you hate that kind of stuff. I'll try harder, I swear."

His words effectively washed away my anger. After all, I'd probably be acting a little jealous, too, if the shoe were on the other foot. "I'm sorry, too. I could never walk away from you no matter what you did. I probably shouldn't be telling you that. It just encourages bad behavior, but maybe it'll make you feel better."

"No. I don't wanna be one of those controlling assholes. I'll try harder—really." He kissed the top of my head. "We'd better get back though. You leave first. I'll wait a couple minutes to make sure no one sees us leaving the woods together."

"Why? It's not like we're not allowed to be seen together—we're best friends. Everyone knows that." I jutted my lower lip out at him in a faux pout.

"Just humor me, okay?" He dipped his head to give me one last thorough kiss, leaving me breathless. He pushed me in the direction of my house, taking the time to swat me on the behind in the process.

"Hey!" I giggled as I walked away from him.

"Sneak over to my house later, if you can." He delivered me one of his patented lopsided grins, complete with dimples, causing my heart to take off at a gallop. Bryn was too adorable for his own good.

"Yeah, okay." I shook my head trying to dislodge my naughty thoughts, to no avail. Bryn was a drug, one that I was quickly becoming addicted to in ways I was sure I didn't understand the full scope of yet. Stumbling towards home, I lost myself to a Bryn induced haze of lust.

"Paige," a voice whispered, seemingly coming from the very woods themselves.

I froze. *No one calls me Paige.* Which meant whoever it was probably didn't know me. And if that was the case, why were they lurking around in the woods waiting for me to be alone? Goosebumps erupted along my flesh as a chill raced up my spine.

"Paa-aige," the voice whispered again, closer and now distinctly male.

Spurred into action by panic, I spun around and dashed back in the direction of Bryn.

"Paige." The voice sounded like it was right behind me and having watched one too many horror movies growing up, I wasn't about to make the mistake of looking behind me to check. I let out a scream of panic, regardless, as I tried to run faster. Suddenly my vision blurred, and I was falling.

"WHAT HAPPENED?" I opened my eyes to find someone's black boots directly in my line of sight. *What the hell? Why is someone putting their boots in my face? No, that's not right.* The moments prior to me losing consciousness slammed into me. *Okay, I'm on the ground and my face is in somebody's boots, not the other way around. That makes much more sense, all things considered.*

Shooting to my feet, I pinwheeled my arms before pitching over to end up sprawled right back where I started on the ground. *Well at least my face isn't in the dirt anymore.*

My eyes widened and my heart thrashed against my ribcage as my gaze went up and up ... and up from the boots that were attached to a massive man. He had to be somewhere around 7 feet, since it was obvious he would tower over even Bryn. And he was broad with clearly defined muscles, not bulky though. Dark auburn hair that I would have mistaken for brown glinted in the sun streaming through the spaces in the canopy of trees above us. It was pulled back in a low ponytail at the nape of his neck. *Holy crap, he's huge.*

Frozen in terror, I continued my perusal of my potential assailant, sweat trickling down my spine. The man's skin was pale and smooth, his features rugged and yet angular somehow. But it was his eyes that stole my breath and sent my pulse to dangerous levels. They were such a bright green they seemed to glow in the low lighting.

What does he want? If he was going to attack, he would have already, right? *Which means he might just be an asshole trying to intimidate me. And if that's the case ... rude much?* Swallowing around the lump in my throat, I lifted my chin and met his startling gaze. "Who the hell are you?"

He took a hesitant step forward, his spooky green eyes fixated on me. Despite my desire to seem unaffected, I found myself scrambling backwards to put more distance between us. *Don't be an idiot and stop poking the bear.* After all, no amount of bravado would stop someone like him if they put their mind to doing something to me. I was at a clear disadvantage in more than one way. Bryn, where are you? But I knew if he was anywhere within ear shot he would already have come to my rescue, therefore it was clear I was on my own dealing with this guy.

Tensing, I waited for any find of tell that would alert me to his motives. I flinched slightly when his face twitched, a smile cracking his serious façade. "I like you," he rumbled, his voice low and scratchy.

"And I should care because?" I slapped my hand over my mouth. *What the hell is wrong with me? Don't poke the bear, damnit.*

His spooky green eyes lit with amusement. "Yes, I definitely like you." He tilted his head, the motion abrupt, causing me to flinch again. "You may call me Khol."

I bit my lip to keep from saying something else I didn't mean to.

He made a rumbling sound before speaking again. "I mean you no harm. I have come a very long way to see you."

A snort escaped me. "Then why did you scare the crap

out of me and then just stand there while I was lying on the ground passed out?"

"I did not mean to scare you. I am out of practice with this form of communication. It proved to be too much for you. In time, you will grow accustomed."

I blinked rapidly at him. "What are you talking about? What form of communication?" *Maybe he's foreign and English isn't his first language.*

"You are currently in a state similar to a dream. Right now, your consort is trying to resuscitate you. I did not mean to scare him, either. He is very worried."

Did he just say consort? *Seriously?* "Why are you here?" I could have asked a thousand other questions, but I figured it was best to skip to the most important one first.

His lips curled up at the corners slightly. "I had a desire to meet you. Your power has been a constant draw to me these past few weeks. I could no longer resist."

"My power?" *Umm...what power? Last time I checked, I was running on empty.*

"Yes. Your power. You are just beginning to come into your gifts. You will be a very powerful Seer, the likes of which haven't been seen for a millennia. That kind of power draws many kinds—some who will wish to steal or control it, some who will wish to destroy it, and some who will wish to protect it and you."

My mind reeded, and an impending headache bloomed across my temples. "Which are you?"

"I fall into the category of wishing to protect it...and you." His gaze swept over me with an unreadable emotion.

"Yes, I do not wish to see harm come to you." His eyes flared brighter, causing me to shrink back from him even more. *Yep, they're definitely glowing.*

"What are you?" I whispered.

"All you need to know right now is that I am a friend and I hold magic that is extremely old. Magic that I do not wish to reveal is still in existence. Because of this, I have placed a binding on you to prevent you from discussing me with anyone. One day I may lift it." He shrugged his shoulders. "Or perhaps not."

He leaned forward, gaze narrowing slightly. "I know of what you have seen in your visions, because I have chosen to link myself to you. Trouble looms in the future, the kind of which this world has yet to see. Although we have not been able to ascertain how to eliminate the problem yet, for now, take comfort in knowing that you are not alone." I opened and closed my mouth like a fish out of water.

He invaded my space farther, offering me his hand. Reluctantly, I accepted it. I wasn't naive enough to trust him just because he claimed to be a friend, but I would play along if it kept him docile and me safe.

A squeak rushed out of me as I was jerked against his chest, and he ran his nose up the side of my neck, inhaling deeply. "Mmm ... delicious. You smell of power and innocence, a rare combination." He leveled his face with mine, our breath intermingling, and his spooky green eyes illuminating his features. "I have been asleep for a long time, and I find your allure almost too great to resist. I

could easily take what I want from you—make you mine."
His gaze darted over my features. "And yet—"

His grip on me loosened, and my knees buckled, sending me to the ground. "Your heart belongs to another. I will respect that—for now."

He disappeared into thin air right before my eyes, and as I stared at where he'd just been standing everything slowly faded to black.

uriouser and curiouser? Well, I had that beat with complicateder and complicateder. Technically not a word, I know, but definitely a fit for my current life circumstances. Case in point, Mr. Creepy Eyes from the woods aka Khol. Who—or what was he? His sudden appearance coupled with his portent of doom had my anxiety levels spiking. According to my self-proclaimed friend, both my premonitions/visions were real, and they indicated bad things on the horizon. Add in the fact that nobody believed me and that I was currently involved in a secret relationship with my future Guardian while pretending to date other guys … yep … complicateder and complicateder.

"She'll be fine," my mom talked in a hushed whisper, "the doctor checked her over again and said it's just low blood sugar…or rather, he couldn't come up with a better explanation. But he's sure there's nothing seriously wrong with her. She just needs to take better care of herself. I'll make sure to tell her you were worried, but you can go on home now."

"Can't I stay just a little longer?" My ears perked up at Bryn's voice. "In case she wakes up. I just—"

"Awe, honey. You're going to make a wonderful Guardian one day, but today isn't that day. Now head on home, and I'll tell her to give you a call later."

But I don't want Bryn to leave. I wanted to be held in his comforting embrace. I wanted to surround myself in his essence. I just wanted...him. My eyes fluttered open with effort. "Bryn," I whispered, fatigue pulling at me. It probably wasn't the best idea to beg for him to stay. It might give something away, but at the moment none of that seemed to matter. *I need him with me.* "Please let him stay." She frowned at me. "Mom," I pleaded. "He's stayed with me like a million times before, why can't he now?"

"Because, peanut, the two of you are too old for some of the things you used to do. It just wouldn't be right." I almost wanted to laugh. She'd probably have a coronary if she knew some of the things we'd been doing together. The bright side was that she obviously still thought Bryn and me were completely platonic best friends. "Besides, I don't think whoever you end up in a serious relationship with is going to appreciate Bryn being so close to you all the time."

"He's gonna be my Guardian," I groused.

"Guardians don't stay in the same room or in the same bed with their charges, sweetie. It just isn't done. You don't see mine constantly hanging around. Your father wouldn't be very pleased if he did." She ruffled Bryn's hair. "Now head on home, and you two can hang out tomorrow."

"But, Mom—" I protested, watching Bryn shuffle towards the door, his eyes lingering on me with concern. "Fine. Whatever." I glared at my mom once Bryn had left. "You're being absolutely ridiculous. What do you think is gonna happen anyways?" Probably something along the lines of *exactly* what would happen. *Oh, the irony.*

"I just wouldn't be a very good mother if I let my daughter have her straight male friend stay over in her room." She had taken on the *"there's no point in arguing with me"* tone that all mothers seemed to have in their bag of tricks. Even I knew when the battle was lost, so I decided to change the subject away from Bryn completely.

"Jeremy texted me earlier. He wants to go out again."

"Really?" Hope danced in her eyes. *Yep, subject change is a success.* I had my mom hook, line, and sinker. "So what did you say?" She sat back down on the edge of the bed, expectancy radiating from her.

"Well, nothing yet. I kind of passed out and forgot about it until now." Not to mention Bryn's mini-meltdown in between those two things.

"You said he was nice, right? And he's cute, so you should definitely say yes. Where's your phone? You should text him right away." She swiveled her head around, scanning all the surfaces in my room for my phone.

I really didn't like how excited she was. I was determined to be with Bryn, but it was going to kill me to disappoint my parents so much. If only there were a way we could all be happy. I sighed. "It's probably still in my purse."

"Oh, of course." My mom scurried over to pull my phone out of my bag in a blur of excited movements. She handed it to me, sitting back down on my bed only to resume her expectant stare. When I didn't move to immediately open my phone, she sighed impatiently. "Well, go ahead, peanut."

Thinking about how Bryn had reacted in the woods, I scowled at my phone. Even though I didn't like being told what to do, I most definitely could be motivated by guilt. If I said yes to a second date with Jeremy, no matter how hard Bryn tried to hide it, I knew it would hurt him. And that was something I wasn't interested in doing. "I think I'm gonna say no," I mumbled.

"What? Why?"

"He was nice and all, like I said, but there didn't really seem to be a spark with him, you know?" I raised my gaze to meet my mom's, silently pleading that she would let the issue drop. But of course, I should have known better.

"Oh, is that all? You said he didn't even kiss you yet. How can you know for sure?"

"Because I don't *want* to kiss him, that's why. I also don't need to kiss Jenna to know that there's no spark between us. Should I just go around kissing everyone I see to find out who I have a spark with? Hell, why not go a step farther, why not—"

Her face scrunched up. "There's no need to be crass, missy. I just think you should try kissing him before you dismiss him so easily."

"I don't want to."

"You're going on a second date with Jeremy," my mom snapped, motherly determination etched into her face.

I narrowed my eyes at her. "No, I'm not. And you know you can't make me."

"No, but I can make you wish you did. You're grounded until you set up a date with Jeremy."

"You can't do that!" I screamed at her rapidly retreating form.

But the closed door staring back at me said she intended to. I shrieked in fury and hurled a pillow. *There's no way I'm putting up with this. No way.*

Anger fueled my next decision. I opened my phone and texted Bryn.

> Meet me—now.

Not waiting for his response, I had the screen popped out of my window and was scrambling down the drainpipe before I could rethink my course of action. Keeping to the shadows created by oncoming dusk, I skulked across my front yard before making a mad dash for the cover of the woods across the street. Nibbling my nails and tapping my foot I waited. What seemed like an eternity later, but what was probably only about five minutes, Bryn jogged into my line of sight.

His presence loosened something in my chest, and I rushed him, wrapping my arms around his waist. "My mom—she grounded me until I say yes to going out with Jeremy again." I sobbed into his shirt.

His fingers tightened against my back. "But I thought you were gonna go anyways."

"No. Not after"—I struggled to catch my breath—"not after how you reacted. I couldn't stand the thought of hurting you again."

He tensed before letting loose a long sigh. "I understand why you have to go. I overreacted before. You won't hurt me, I promise. I trust you." He pulled away from me, cupping my face in his rough hands. He dipped to slowly kiss away my tears, each caress gentle but firm against my skin and I swayed in his direction completely under his spell.

My eyelids fluttered shut under his tender ministrations. "I just don't understand what's supposedly wrong with being with you. So what if our kids are all Guardians. I can't bring myself to care as long as I'm with you."

People often ask what the meaning of life is. What's the point in all of this? As far as I could tell, life is pretty much pointless without love. If you have it, then you're truly rich, and if you don't, then nothing else really holds any value. What would my life mean if I married a

Gatekeeper or Seer descendent for the sake of duty? It would mean nothing to me, even if it did to others. Bryn gave my life meaning. He made everything else worthwhile. He always had, and hopefully, always would.

"Because you're special, Peej—so special. You deserve to be with royalty, not a Guardian like me." I opened my mouth to protest and was silenced when one of his long fingers pressed against my lips. "But I'm not a complete idiot, although I am plenty selfish. I want you all to myself. I'm not gonna walk away from you so you can be with someone else, someone born into the right family. Somehow I got lucky, and you love me back. I'll fight for you as long as you want me."

"I'll always want you," I whispered.

"Then I'll always be yours," he said gruffly, his lips meeting mine in a brutal kiss. The taste and feel of him helped to sooth my frayed nerves. Loosing myself in him, I slid my hands into his silky hair, moaning when he abruptly shoved me against a tree. It seemed to be fast becoming me and Bryn's thing. Or maybe it was because we didn't have any other place to go?

"Take your hands off of my daughter. Right now." My father's deep voice boomed across the clearing.

My muscles instantly locked up as I gasped into Bryn's mouth. *We're caught. Oh, my, God, we are caught.* We separated quickly, stumbling away to stand a few feet from each other. But it was obviously too late.

"Sir, I—" Bryn attempted, but my father cut him off.

"Sir nothing." My father's voice vibrated with fury,

causing me to shrink in on myself. He stood across the clearing from us with his reading glasses still perched on the edge of his nose as if he'd rushed after me in such a hurry, he'd forgotten to remove them first. His face slowly went from splotchy to a dark shade of red as he stared at Bryn, seething. "How dare you take advantage of my family's trust like this! And how dare you take advantage of the sacred trust being a future Guardian affords you!"

"Dad—Daddy, please!" I interjected, making my voice sound small and childlike. "It's not Bryn's fault. Don't—"

He turned his withering stare onto me. "You, young lady, have disappointed me. We raised you better than this." He shook his head slowly in disbelieve. "Never in a million years did I expect to find you in this kind of situation when I saw you sneaking over her. I don't even want to look at you right now."

"I love your daughter, sir," Bryn croaked. "Please, all I want is to love and protect her. I never meant to disrespect anyone."

Ignoring Bryn's words completely, my father continued to speak to me. "Get your ass over here right now, Paige Joplin Stone. You're not to be alone with him for one second more—ever."

No, no, no, no, no! My throat and lungs constricted as I struggled to find air. *No! This can't be happening! I can't lose Bryn even for a short time! I can't!* Flinging myself at Bryn, I wrapped my arms around his middle in a death grip. "Please! You can't to this to me! I love him! You have to understand! Please! I love him!"

"Understand?" He scoffed. "What I understand is that you just turned nineteen and you haven't the slightest clue what real love is yet."

My voice steadily went up in volume and octave, as if I could force my point of view into my father's head if only I was loud enough. "That's not true! I understand what real love is!" I sucked in a ragged breath. "I would die for him! I would lie down and die for him! Don't tell me that's not real love! And If you take him away from me—" My chest heaved. "I might die, too!"

Rolling his eyes, my father grumbled, "Teenager dramatics," as he stalked towards me. He then eyed Bryn, his nostrils flaring. "You better let her go, son." Instead, Bryn's grip on me tightened as clung to him. My father hefted out a sigh ladened with annoyance.

Indignance pierced my fear. My father was annoyed? He was annoyed and I was fighting to stay with the love of my life? He was fucking annoyed? My future happiness hung in the balance, and he was annoyed. I lifted my fury filled gaze to his. "I hate you," I hissed. "I fuc—"

"Don't you *dare* finish that sentence, young lady. I am your father."

"My father? Ha! That's why I hate you. You're my father, which means you should want me to be happy. You shouldn't be treating me like a child who doesn't know what real love is."

He ripped his glasses off and pinched the bridge of his nose. "Okay, fine. You want to be treated like an adult, then you come back to the house, and we can talk about this like adults. Stop cowering in the woods, refusing to let go of *him*."

Peering up at Bryn, he nodded his encouragement, although tension lined his shoulders and jaw. Forcing myself to let go of him, I turned towards my father and notched my chin up defiantly. "Fine, we can talk at home then." I stalked past my father without another word.

The truth was that if my parents wanted to keep me separated from Bryn until I was out of their house, there wasn't a whole lot I could do about it. I would be lying to myself if I thought I had any real power over the situation as it currently was.

My father followed behind me silently, although I could feel his agitation hanging in the air between us. I stomped into our house ready to give him an earful but before I could formulate another thought, he was yanking me up the stairs by my arm. Taken off guard since I wasn't used to being manhandled by my own father, I went easily even when he shoved me into my room and locked the door from the outside.

I blinked rapidly for several moments before my brain finally came back online. It became instantly clear that he never intended to have any kind of conversation with me, he simply told me what I wanted to hear to get me away from Bryn. "You lied to me!" I screamed, not really knowing why I bothered. It was now obvious that there would be no reasoning with my father, he'd already made up his mind.

"You lied to me first," my father's voice lanced me

through the door. "And don't bother trying to sneak out again. Your mother has Eric watching for you now." My heart dropped into my stomach. With Eric on the job, there definitely wouldn't be any escaping since he was her Guardian—and Bryn's father. It would be like trying to escape from Alcatraz. *Unless ... unless ... no.* I shook my head. I was kidding myself if I thought Bryn's parents would be any less against a Guardian/Seer relationship than mine were.

Softening my voice to sound childlike again, I made one last plea, hoping this time it would tug on my dad's heart strings. "Daddy, please. I love him. Don't destroy me like this."

The only response I got was my father's footsteps thundering down the stairs.

I hurled myself onto my bed face first, sobs overtaking my body. At some point exhaustion forced me into lose consciousness.

I JOLTED awake when my bedroom door slowly creaked open. I forced myself to remain silent and still, my heart thundering against my eardrums. My room had fallen into dark with the onset of night, but my bedside lamp clicked on to reveal my mom in its soft glow. She gingerly perched herself on the edge of my bed, staring down at me with a pained expression. She reached for me, but her fingers curled into her palm before making contact.

"How could you, peanut? You know you can't be with him."

Fresh tears sprung into my eyes, and I blinked them back furiously. "Why? Why can't I be with him? It doesn't make sense when you really think about it. I love him—so much—more than anything. How can I be with someone —someone like Jeremy—after I've discovered I can have that kind of connection with someone else? Shouldn't love matter more than the rest?"

She sighed heavily. "Sometimes I forget how young you still are—how naïve. You're growing up so fast, and yet...you know nothing of the world."

"I know enough. I know that I love him. Mom— mommy, please." The tears finally broke free and slid down my face.

"Bryn's going to be sent away—to train elsewhere. He'll be assigned someone to guard when he's ready."

"Someone that's not me?" I croaked, not wanting to say the words out loud but needing to verify.

She flicked her gaze away. "Yes."

"No!" Frantically I grabbed for my mom's hands. "No! Please! He's my best friend, too! He's not only my lover, but my best friend, too."

Horror dawned in her eyes and only then did I realize what I'd done. "Your lover?" she breathed.

"No—that's—um—that's not what I meant. I just meant that—" *God—what did I mean?* I'd never used the word lover before in my life in a serious manner, and I chose now to start? Why couldn't I have said boyfriend?

Because he's more, so much more.

My mom's complexion went ashen. "Have the two of you—did you more than kiss him—did you—did you have sex with him?"

I swallowed hard, not sure how I should answer. Maybe if I told the truth, she would take our relationship seriously? Or perhaps a lie was the way to go? I was too frazzled to think clearly. My unhelpful mind conjured up an image of Bryn and me wrapped in each other's arms, our sweaty bodies writhing against each other. I flushed.

Her hand flew to her mouth. "Dear Lord, your face just told me all I need to know." She stood abruptly, heading for the door. "I thought we'd raised you better than that. I thought you'd know better than to let a common Guardian defile you."

Ice raced along my spine as shock settled into my system. "Defile me? But I thought you said the forbidden fruit was the sweetest—I thought you'd maybe understand—"

"To daydream about, to look, but not touch, not to slum with. You gave your most valuable gift to a common Guardian. I would never have even considered you doing such a thing—even after what you'd said to me before. Especially because of what you said before—you *knew* it was wrong."

"I know no such thing! I gave him everything because I love him! That could never be wrong!" Sobs wracked my chest and I struggled to fill my lungs with air.

I couldn't believe the things she was saying. Who was

this woman standing before me? Certainly not the caring, loving mother I'd grown up with. *My mom* would never say such horrible, cruel things. Bryn and my family had always been like one since I was a child, at least that's what I'd thought. Maybe to my parents Bryn's family were simply beloved servants and nothing more. Perhaps I'd never truly understood the class lines that were drawn within my society. How could I when I was at the top of the tier? I'd always thought of Guardians and Speakers as different, no better or no worse...just different. Was that why Bryn put me on a pedestal? I'd been under the impression that my people would be upset and angry about me not having a Seer child if I chose Bryn—possibly I'd become sort of a social pariah—but now I was beginning to realize that I might truly be shunned. So much more was at stake than I'd ever understood... But in the end, it still didn't matter. I would give up anything and everything to be with Bryn.

"We'll be lucky to make you a good match after this. With Bryn being sent away, people will assume the worst, whether or not it's the truth. No decent Gatekeeper or Seer descendant will want you after you've been with a Guardian." She shook her head as tears of her own leaked from the corners of her eyes. "I wanted so much for you..." She slammed and locked the door behind her.

I sat in stunned silence, my ragged breathing echoing in my ears. The things that my mother had just said sounded like they were pulled right out of the 1800s, maybe a Jane Austen novel. *We'll be lucky to make you a good match after this.* There had to be some kind of nightmare. Yes, I must have fallen and hit my head, and this was all some kind of huge nightmare—a coma-induced nightmare.

My phone beeped, and I dashed for it, praying it was Bryn—and it was.

Remember, I'll come 4 u no matter what.

I hastily hit send to call him, and he answered on the first ring. "Peej," he whispered, his voice holding the same kind of desperation that was currently seeping out of all my pores. "They're sending me away—now—like right now. I won't have my phone—maybe no phone at all, and I don't know if I'll be able to contact you anytime soon. But I'll come for you, I promise. Don't lose hope and never forget that I love you. Always." He paused as if listening to something. "I gotta go," he said hurriedly. "I don't want them to know we talked—to know about our plan. They need to think they've separated us permanately."

"No wait—Bryn—I love you, too." But the phone had already gone dead. I stared at it as my stomach churned. It was really happening. I wouldn't see Bryn for an indefinite amount of time. He was gone.

A scream of raw agony erupted from my chest and tore from my throat. Without thinking, I blindly reached for the nearest object, my lamp, and hurled it against the wall. Screaming again, I grabbed at anything that wasn't nailed down, smashing and destroying everything in my path as I rampaged through my room.

Things I'd had since childhood, things that I cherished, were ripped apart and smashed to smithereens because none of it mattered anymore without Bryn. At some point when my eyes were blurry, my throat hoarse, and my legs could no longer support my weight, I sank to the floor and curled into a ball.

Eventually, the sweet oblivion of sleep overtook me once more.

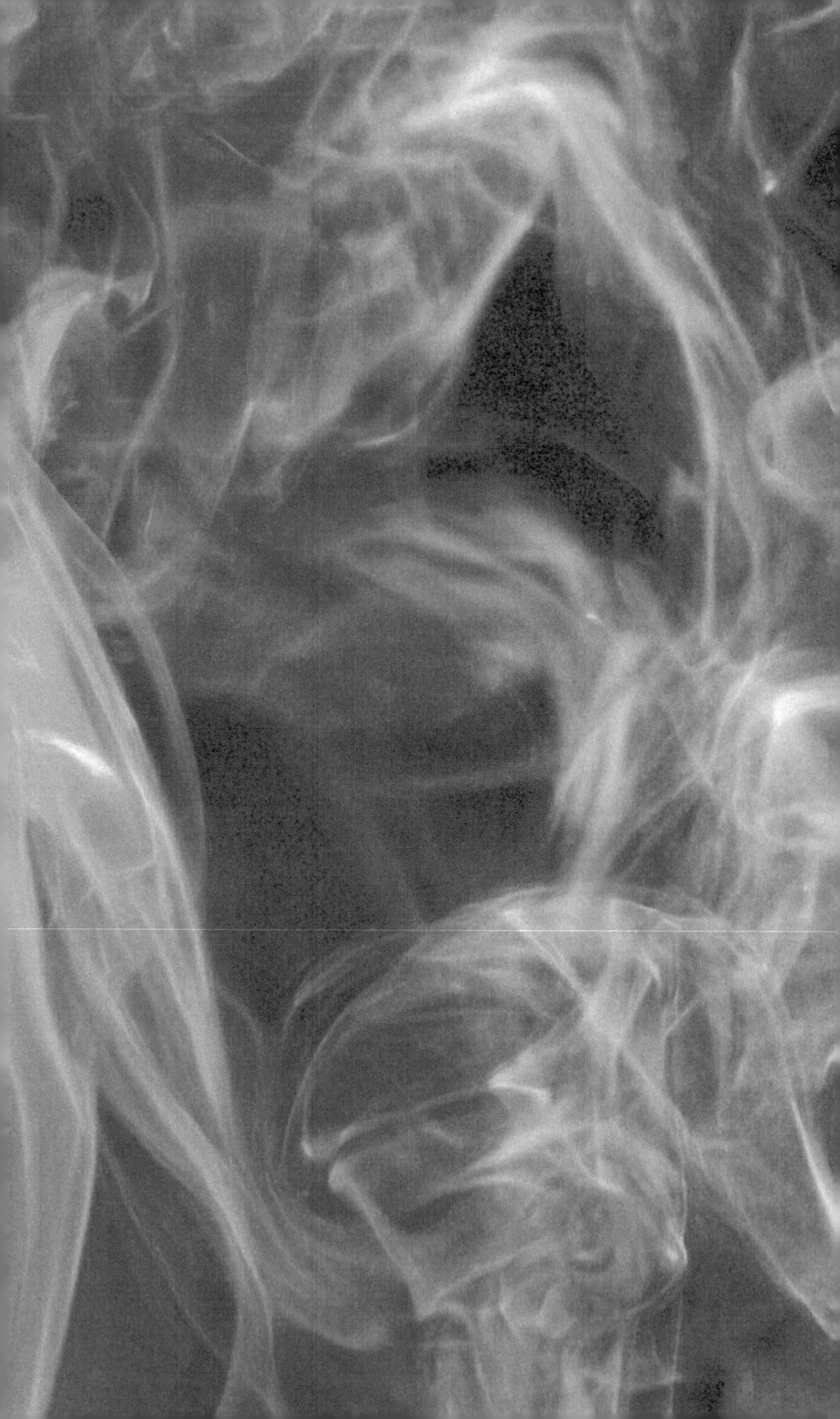

Chapter 10

"**W**ell, what do you suggest we do with her then?" My mother's strained whisper wafted through my door.

"It's just more teenager dramatics. She'll get over it eventually," my father stated blandly.

"She doesn't talk to anyone, she's barely eaten, and she just sleeps all the time."

Of course I sleep all the time! I wanted to shout. When my dreams all seemed to contain Bryn, and my reality was lacking it didn't seem like much of a choice.

"She'll snap out of it. You'll see." *Yep, my father is seriously deluding himself.*

"And if she doesn't?"

"Then we'll come up with something."

Please, like what? Are you going to send away my best friend and who is also the love of my life to prevent me from ever seeing him again? Oh wait ...

My parents' footsteps retreated down the hall, and I heaved a sigh of relief into the dark. I wished they would just leave me alone already.

"Hello, little Seer." A vaguely familiar voice drifted through my mind, attached to an image of Khol, the guy from the woods with creepy green luminescent eyes.

"What do you want?" I grumbled, not sure if I was imagining his voice or not. *Maybe delirium has set in.*

"I am not a figment of your imagination."

"Then how did you know what I was thinking if you're not all in my mind? Besides, that's just what a figment would say." I scrunched up my face in a display of my skepticism.

"As I said before, I linked myself to you. It comes with certain advantages, such as me being able to communicate this way with you, the way I did in the woods, along with being able to sense your emotions."

Advantages maybe for him, but distinct disadvantages for me. "You know, one would think that I would have gotten some kind of say in this whole linking process. I mean, I don't like you just being able to pop into my head, and I most certainly don't like you being able to sense my emotions."

His laugh rumbled through my brain. "All the most powerful Seers of old were linked to...*creatures*...such as myself. It should be a great honor to find yourself linked to one of us, and you want to throw me away? You are fortunate indeed that I chose you. There are very few of us left, and most of us still sleep."

"Yeah, well... You won't tell me what you are so ..." I flopped onto my stomach as if he was really in the room and I could turn away from him.

"All in due time."

He paused long enough that I thought he wasn't there anymore. "Hello?" I mentally called.

"Watch the second showing of the evening news tonight."

"What? The rerun of the news?"

"Yes, watch the—rerun of the evening news, and then we'll have something to discuss." And with that, I felt a mental pop that let me know he was actually gone.

Weird. Or was the weird part how casually I was accepting this creepy guy into my life? Or maybe I'd grown up with so much weird that one more thing didn't really seem like a big deal. Especially now.

Not that any of it matters. I had no idea what time it was, and I didn't care about the stupid evening news or Khol's demand that I watch it. I slid my eyes closed, wanting nothing more than to doze off again so I could dream of Bryn.

Just as I was on the precipice of dreamland, my new T.V. clicked on. With a start, I sat up in bed to snap at whoever had turned it on. Swinging my head around, I realized I was still the only one in my room.

I growled under my breath. Realization dawned when I saw the evening news on display. *How the hell did Khol manage that and why is he insisting that I watch this?* I swiped at my eyes, my focus still a bit blurred.

A blonde anchorwoman was speaking. "And tonight we have a special treat... We have Senator Bill Wexington in our studio. As many of you know, he's been touring our illustrious state of Pennsylvania the last couple of days, trying to garner as many votes for the upcoming election as possible. When he asked to stop by and chat with us, we couldn't have been happier."

The screen split. The female anchorwoman remained on the left side, and on the right appeared an older man with silver hair. The title *Senator Bill Wexington* scrolled across the bottom of the screen. Stifling a startled gasp, I slapped my hand over my mouth.

I know him. It's that man. Only when I had seen him, he had been at least twenty years younger, but there was no mistaking who he was.

As he began to talk, I saw a quick flash of the alien *under* his skin. It was like seeing two men, one a human and one an alien, taking up the same space. Their features were mingled together somehow, and yet they were separate. "Oh my God," I whispered, horrified. "How is this possible?"

"Apparently your vision was one from the past. It has been many years since the creature has merged with the man," Khol said in my mind. "They are one now."

"But how? Why?" I stared at the screen, unable to tear my gaze away.

"Your vision showed the how. Obviously, it was important for you to see what you were shown. As you already know, Seers bear witness to all that pertains to the gates."

"But if that happened so long ago, why didn't any other Seer have a vision pertaining to it when it actually happened?"

"I can only offer you an educated guess as to why no one else saw it in real time. You are the strongest Seer to be born in a long time, as I've previously stated. Perhaps, no one else had the power to see it until you came along. Your powers are only just beginning to awake, so you were shown as soon as you were able to receive the vision."

"Oh. I mean—" I would stick a pin in the subject of me being a super powerful Seer who got a vision of the past because I wanted it to be true although I didn't necessary believe it. "Fine, but why can't anyone else *see* what he really is now then? I'm sure I'm not the only Seer who's laid eyes on him in all this time. Hell, I bet a bunch watched this news broadcast."

"Yes, there is that as well." Khol paused for a few heartbeats as I stared, mind reeling, at the T.V. What did this 'alien' want? Why did he lay low for all these years only to emerge now? Or had he? "There are many questions for which I do not have the answers as of yet, my little Seer."

My little Seer? "So what do we do then?" I asked, choosing to ignore his little term of endearment, at least for the moment. I was certainly not *his* by any definition I was aware of.

"We watch. We wait. We gather power. When things become clearer, we make a move."

"Great. So basically, we do nothing." I fumbled for the T.V. remote, turning it off.

Khol sighed, the sound echoing in my mind. "Watching, waiting, and gathering power is not nothing."

"Whatever. I don't care anyways." I slid back down in my bed, shutting my eyes. None of it meant anything without Bryn.

A low growl ricocheted within my brain. "Your childish woes are nothing compared to what we could face. More than just you will be affected—this is my world, too." I didn't respond and crossed my arms over my chest, hoping that by being linked to me, he would pick up on what my body language was saying.

Another growl pummeled my senses. *Huh. So it worked.* "Stop being so childish," Khol grated, anger evident in his voice.

"Leave me alone," I snapped. Abruptly I felt the mental pop signaling that he was gone from my mind. I heaved a sigh of relief. I didn't want to deal with anything right now, let alone crazy aliens who were up for Congress or whatever.

I blinked into the dark, waiting for sleep to claim me once again so I could be whisked off into Bryn's imaginary arms.

Unfortunately for me, Khol had other ideas.

A low growl rumbled through my room—one that was definitely outside of my head this time. Jolting up, I almost choked on my own tongue as I took in Khol, live and in the flesh, taking up way too much space in my suddenly small room. He stalked towards my bed in the dark, his luminescent gaze throwing shadows across his angry expression. The air buzzed and crackled with the foreign energy of his powers which had every molecule in my body quivering with excitement. Whatever Khol was, my powers liked the feel of him.

"What are you doing here?" I demanded.

"Making you understand," he spoke through clenched teeth. He halted at the edge of my bed, glaring down at me.

I lifted my chin and met his gaze steadily. "Make me understand what? That you're good at intimidating me? You've already made that point clear before." Then I had a thought that made me relax slightly. "Wait, are you really here? Or just here like in the woods before?" *Because he got here awfully quick. Maybe the connection is just better this time around.*

"I am here, in the flesh this time. I would not be able to make the point that I am going to otherwise." His eyes glinted with something I couldn't decipher, setting me on edge again. *It's extremely difficult to get a read on someone with green glowing eyes.*

"Okay." I gulped, nothing left to say. What kind of point needed him to be in the flesh to make it? Was he going to smack me around? Torture me into complying with him? My mind was reeling with possibilities, compiling a list of all the horrible things he could do to me. Sweat trickled gathered around my hairline.

Faster than I'd ever seen anyone move, even fully matured Guardians, he leaned down and crushed his lips to mine. When I gasped, he took the opportunity to plunge his tongue into my mouth. White-hot heat surged through my body, igniting all of my nerve endings. My lips moved against his with enthusiasm, and I shuddered with pleasure as his hands skimmed down my body.

I want—

I want—

Bryn. An image of him skittered across my mind and instantly cooled my heated skin. *I love Bryn, and only him. How can you be letting some—creature kiss you?*

"Stop!" I shoved Khol away from me. Although with how easily I managed it, I knew he had let me. "What the hell was that?" I swiped at my mouth with the back of my hand demonstratively.

A satisfied smirk spread across his face, and his eyes glowed even brighter than before. "I was making a point. Teaching you a lesson, if you will."

"Teaching me a lesson? Really? And what would that be? That you're an asshole that forces unwanted attention on females that are smaller and weaker than them?" I ground my teeth together so hard my jaw started to ache.

"No—that Bryn is not the only one who can stoke your fires. That you need to get out of this bed and start focusing on the bigger problems at hand. Your life hasn't ended because he is gone."

Stoke my fires? Who the hell talks that way? "Yeah, I have hormones, so what? And you're a really good kisser—congratulations. I'm sure practically any hot guy could waltz in here and get some kind of reaction out of my body. That doesn't change the fact that I love Bryn and will never want to be with anyone but him. Love means something to me, and Bryn does it for me physically—*and beyond.*"

Khol's smirk remained firmly in place. "Bryn is not the one for you. You will figure that out eventually, in your own time. As you grow into your powers, you will find that you will crave...more."

More? "Whatever. Now that you tried to teach me a lesson—and failed—will you please leave so that I can go to sleep? Dream Bryn is waiting."

"I will leave and let you go to sleep—after you promise to get out of bed and resume your life starting tomorrow. Only then will I leave." Khol crossed his thick, muscular arms over his chest, narrowing his eyes at me. I didn't know him very well, but I could tell he meant business.

"Fine. Whatever. I agree. So leave. *Now.*" What was he going to do, come in the morning, drag me out of bed, and force me to go to school? *Yeah, right.*

He produced a newspaper seemingly out of thin air, tossing it to me. "There is an article about Senator Bill Wexington in there. I thought you might want to read it."

I glanced down at the paper for a second, and when I looked back up, Khol was gone. *What the hell?* I turned back to the paper and searched for the article he had mentioned, my curiosity too great to ignore it.

When I was done reading the article, I was even more confused. "So aliens are fans of gun control," I muttered to myself. "So what? Some level of gun control is necessary to keep people safe. Was there a point to him wanting me to read this? Seriously." *Ugh.* All the article told me was that Senator Bill Wexington didn't fully stand behind the Second Amendment of the Constitution. It wasn't like he was making any highly suspicious suggestions for his campaign to get elected to Congress though. I wasn't a political person, but even I knew Senator Bill Wexington wasn't the first, nor would he be the last, politician to suggest gun control in some form. Besides, most of the time people campaigned with extreme platforms and usually dialed it back if they made it into office.

My phone beeped, signaling a new text message. My heart sped up in anticipation. Even though I knew that Bryn didn't have his phone, I kept hoping he'd find a way to contact me. So far I'd heard absolutely nothing from him, and even a text message at this point would make me jump for joy.

The text was from Jenna. I heaved a sigh of disappointment. I hadn't talked to her since Bryn had been shipped away and I'd sunk into the depths of despair, but I did grace her with responses to her text messages once in a while. I think she understood, mostly, that I wasn't up to talking about everything that happened.

I opened my phone and read.

So who was the guy who wasn't Bryn u were just making out w/ ???

My jaw dropped open. How the hell did she know?

IDK what ur talking about.

LIAR!

Nausea rolled through my stomach at the thought of Bryn ever finding out. He hadn't even been gone a week yet, and I had kissed someone else, or rather someone else had kissed me. I didn't think Bryn would see the distinction, especially because I had kissed him back, if only for a moment.

My phone beeped again, and I turned my focus back to the illuminated screen.

SPILL IT!

IDK y u think that...yeah, no.

Squirrels r chatty & nosey. Stop lying. :p

Damn Speakers! I always forgot about her sneaky little spies. The image of a little voyeur squirrel hanging around outside my window, running to Jenna to report any indiscretions on my part was absolutely horrifying.

And crazy, I typed back before turning my phone off. I could picture Jenna sitting in her room with steam practically coming out of her ears. I would probably have a full mailbox of angry texts when I turned my phone back on, but it was better than dealing with her now.

I slumped back into bed, blinking my eyes in the darkness. I glanced at my window, feeling oddly vulnerable. A whole army of squirrels could be hanging out in the tree across from my window, watching me. I stumbled across my floor and pulled down the shade, checking to make sure there weren't any gaps for nosey rodents to peek through. Once satisfied, I flopped back into bed and closed my eyes, yearning for nothing more than to dream about Bryn.

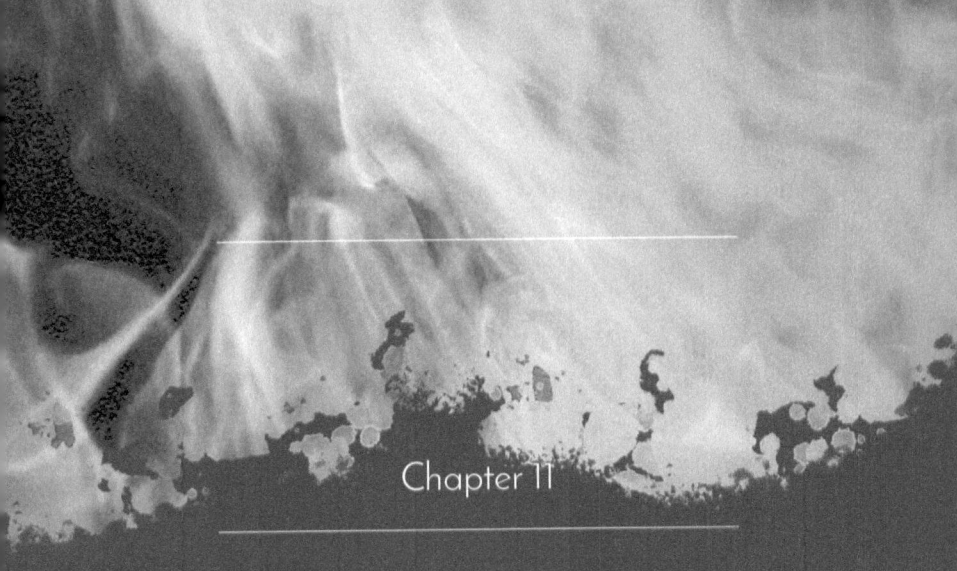

Chapter 11

"Rise and shine, my little Seer," Khol's raspy voice danced through my mind.

"No. Go away," I grumbled, pulling my pillow over my head. But pillows only buffer against noise on the outside of your head, so there was no escape for me.

"You agreed to get back to your life starting today if I left you alone last night. I did, and now you are."

"I lied just so you'd go away."

"I can come in person to wake you up, if you would like," amusement laced his tone.

I decided to ignore him. Soon enough, I dozed off again, the threat of Khol appearing in the flesh temporarily forgotten—until my pillow was snatched from my grasp.

"Hey!" I sputtered, my eyes widening to take in Khol's massive frame standing right next to me with my pillow clutched in his hand. In the light of day, he seemed to take up more space somehow, his dark auburn hair burning like fire in the morning sun. My nerve endings lit up from his vicinity and I suppressed a bodily shiver. *Damn ... not good. My powers really like him.*

His lips turned up into a slight smile, his creepy eyes sliding over me. "Would you like me to help you shower as well?"

Sudden self-consciousness overwhelmed me, and I pulled my covers up under my arms as a shield. I didn't want him getting any ideas and trying to kiss me like he had last night. "Eww...how old are you anyways, in your late-twenties? Early thirties? I just turned nineteen. I'm not quite jailbait but close enough for you."

Khol's smile wilted around the edges. "Nineteen is old enough where I am from. Besides, I am not human. Your societal norms mean nothing to me."

"Yeah, about that. Are you ever gonna tell me what you are?" *Besides creepy, that is.*

"All in due time."

"Fine. Whatever. So I suppose that if I don't get up and go to school today, you're just gonna harass me all day instead?"

"Harass? No. But I am sure we could find some very... entertaining...things for us to do to help you find the road to recovery." His gaze slid over me again, letting me know exactly what he was thinking. "The way your power hums to me constantly, calling to me, is like a siren's song, one that I yearn to answer with everything that I am."

My heart quadrupled in time as I stared at Khol. There was no point in denying that his words excited me, or more aptly, they revved my hormones, but that was beside the point. Because I was still a teenager, that really wasn't a huge accomplishment. "I love Bryn," I snapped. "There will be no answering of my siren's song by anyone but him."

Khol was a blur, my eyes unable to track his movements. When he stilled, he was kneeling beside me, hand outstretched. "You have no reason to fear me, my little Seer." His fingertips danced over the side of my face briefly, leaving heat in their wake. "I will not force you to do anything you do not truly desire to do. I am well aware that your heart belongs to another, for now. I am simply letting you know your options for when you realize he is not the one for you."

"What about the kiss last night?" I whispered, hating how my body responded to his. My skin ached with the need to rub against his, to follow the heat it offered.

"I regret having taken what should only be given freely, and for that, I am ashamed and I offer my apology. I simply needed to make a point, to show you that your life will go on without him." His warm fingers ghosted my face again before he stood, drawing away from me. "I want you to be able to trust me." His expression was solemn and oh so sincere. It made me want to give my trust to him—this strange man that wasn't even human.

My gut clenched. As a Seer I'd been taught to trust my instincts. I nibbled my bottom lip, studying Khol. I would trust him, even if he did scare me a little. It felt like the right thing somehow. "I don't know why...but I do...trust you, that is." I gave him a tentative smile.

His answering smile was instant and bright, making him look more handsome and a lot less creepy. "Now go ready yourself for school, my little Seer. I will be watching."

And just like that, he disappeared again. I huffed in annoyance. It looked like Khol would pester me until I got back to some semblance of normalcy. It wasn't like it would change much in the end. Bryn wasn't here whether I got out of bed and left my room or not and eventually we'd find each other again. Wallowing in self-pity wasn't going to bring him back to me any sooner. I'd just have to bide my time.

A slight breeze ruffled my hair, and I glanced over at my open window. *Khol must have opened it.* My gaze met beady little eyes that peered at me with curiosity. I sucked in a sharp breath. Perched on a branch in the big oak tree right across from my window was one of Jenna's little spies. *And to think I used to like squirrels.*

"Get out of here!" I yelled. "Go tell Jenna to mind her own business and to get the hell out of mine!" I yanked the curtains closed, muting the light from the bright morning. I shook my head in disbelief. *What has my life come to that I'm hiding from squirrels now?*

I HOVERED OUTSIDE MY KITCHEN, moving from foot to foot. My mom was preparing breakfast. Pots and pans banged, and the sizzle of things cooking filled the air. The occasional rustle of the paper let me know my dad was also in there. I currently held so much resentment towards them, and I didn't know if it would ever go away. I knew on some level they were exactly the same people they'd always been, the same people who had raised me so lovingly ... but now they were also the people who were responsible for ripping Bryn from my life. There are so many different kinds of love in this world, and I guess when push comes to shove, the romantic soul mate kind of love trumps everything else. *I wish things didn't have to be like this.*

I steeled my nerves, sweeping into the kitchen with a solemn face. All movement stopped, both of my parents turning to stare at me. My mom's relief at me being out of bed was palpable, but I wasn't going to make it that easy for them. I marched over to the pantry, grabbed a couple breakfast cookies and a bottle of water, stuffed them into my shoulder bag, and careful not to acknowledge their presence, marched out the back door without so much as a word. Things would never be the same between us, I knew that, and in some weird way, I suppose I was mourning the loss of my parents as well as Bryn. Because when all was said and done, I had made my choice, the only choice I could make, and when Bryn came for me in a year, I would leave with him no matter what.

As I rounded the corner, I saw Jenna, with rainbow-colored hair now, waiting expectantly for me. No doubt her squirrel spy had filled her in. She scowled at me, her eyes narrowing when they met mine. "Are you gonna tell me what's going on or not?"

"What? Your little spies didn't garner enough information to satisfy you?" I kept walking, not bothering to wait for her. She scurried to catch up, her shorter legs pumping hard. "Which by the way," I said without looking at her, "it's beyond creepy to have sent a squirrel to spy on me. No wonder everybody thinks Speakers are so weird."

It was a low blow, and I knew it. Not many of our kind gave Jenna the time of day, unless they were a guy interested in getting into her pants, and even then, that was short lived. Speakers had a reputation on the whole as being weird, and most of our kind steered clear. I, on the other hand, had instantly liked Jenna, mostly because of her quirkiness. I had always admired her for being true to herself and not giving a damn what other people thought —unless those other people happened to be me, as was the case now.

"That was just mean," she hissed. "I'm just gonna pretend you didn't say that, for the sake of our friendship."

"Just butt out of my business," I hissed back. "And you better keep your little spies away from me before I invest in a BB gun or something."

"You wouldn't," she gasped, completely appalled. "You aren't that heartless to shoot a poor, defenseless little animal."

I stopped abruptly, glaring down at her horrified face.

"Try me." I would never shoot a cute little squirrel no matter how annoying it was, but I was hoping Jenna couldn't see past my bluff.

She crossed her arms over her chest and glared back at me. I took that as a sign she wasn't buying my bluff. *Damn Speakers.* "If you want me to butt out of your business, then I guess I can stop defending you to everyone at school. The next time I hear another ugly rumor, I won't try to set it straight."

The blood completely drained from my face. "What are you talking about? What kind of rumors?" And seriously, community college was like high school 2.0.

Jenna's face softened to something resembling pity. "About you and Bryn, and how he got you pregnant...stuff like that."

"Oh God. How does anybody even know anything about me and Bryn?" Maybe school wouldn't be on my agenda for the day after all. I didn't know if I could face anyone if that was the kind of thing being spread around.

"Well," Jenna said, "I'm not the only Speaker who has little spies. Let's just say that a certain Miss Tina Sims is enjoying some newfound popularity over the info she's been feeding to the masses, even if most of it is bullshit."

Great. Now when I had a squirrel chilling outside my window, I had to wonder *who* it was spying for. At least Jenna was just doing recon for herself. Other Speakers obviously had agendas beyond curiosity. "Why? Why are people believing her?" I squeaked.

"Oh, P.J., you know why. People love to hear about

scandal, especially when it's about someone like you, who everyone thought was a goody-goody virgin. And you can't even deny that something happened, since Bryn has been shipped off, and you went M.I.A. at the same time."

"Oh." Jenna was right. The Bryn and P.J. rumors were probably the biggest scandal that had hit in a long time. I'd probably never live it down. *Not that I care all that much since Bryn is gone.*

We walked the rest of the way to the bus stop in silence. The ride to campus much the same. Only when the front doors to my new personal hell loomed in front of us did Jenna speak, "So are you gonna tell me who that guy was last night?" I knew she wouldn't be able to keep a lid on it for very long.

"Fine." I let out an exasperated breath. "His name is—" Khol's name seemed to just stick in the back of my throat. I opened and closed my mouth like a fish out of water, but nothing came out. I pursed my lips and tried to start over again. "His name is—" And again I couldn't utter a single syllable of his name.

Realization dawned. Khol had told to me the first time I'd seen him in the woods that he'd bound me from being able to speak to anyone about him. *Is that what this is? Am I physically not able to talk about him? What the hell? Who ever heard of such a thing outside of books and movies?*

I decided to try another approach to test out my theory. "He first came to me in the woods. He's—" *Aaaah!* I couldn't even describe what he looked like out loud. "Look, Jenna, I wish I could, if only to get you off my back, but I literally can't. I'm bound so that I'm not able to. In fact, I'm surprised I can even say that much. I physically can't say his name or describe him to you—the words just stick in my throat like friggin' super glue or something."

She eyed me with curiosity, tilting her head back and forth. "I can tell that you're not lying, but I've never heard of such a thing. Who bound you?"

"He did."

"Are you doing it with him now? Did Bryn completely spring you, and now that he's gone, you've already found yourself another *looover?*"

"No, of course not," I snapped. "I love Bryn. End of story."

"Then why were you kissing this other guy?" Jenna raised her eyebrows at me.

"I can't explain without running into what I can't say but let me just tell you that I didn't *want* to be kissing him. The only guy I wanna kiss is Bryn."

"Hmm," Jenna grunted.

It was then, as we walked up the front stairs to school, that people began to take notice of me, whispers following in my wake. *How many people from our high school go here now too? Seriously?* I kept my eyes straight ahead and pretended I didn't notice. *I so wish Bryn was here to hold my hand and make everything better.*

We pushed through the huge front doors, beelining for the hallway where our shared class was. I almost made it to the door unscathed. It was in my sights, when someone grabbed me by my wrist, pulling me to a halt. I suddenly found myself staring up into the dark eyes of Eddie Covington, a large Guardian-to-be who also attended our school. He was tall, like almost all Guardians, with a rather plain face and dark brown hair. He could be considered cute, but next to Bryn, he would be lucky if anyone noticed him at all.

"Hey there, P.J.," he said, smirking. "I heard you have a thing for us lowly Guardians. Now that Bryn's gone, I was hoping you might be looking to fill his spot."

"Get your hands off me." I shook free of his grip and rubbed my wrist while frowning at him. I didn't know what else to say, so I simply turned to leave.

Eddie crowded the space in front of me. "Oh, come on, P. J., there's no use in pretending anymore. I have to admit you had us all fooled with your little virginal act." His dark eyes roamed over me from head to toe, a lecherous grin spreading across his face. "Most Seers wouldn't touch one of us with a ten-foot pole, and here you've been, right under our noses, screwing Bryn the whole time. Us Guardians never get to *really* experience a Seer's powers. No wonder he was so protective of you. Guess he didn't want anyone getting their hands on his little prize. Although everyone should have known, with you being friends with a slut like her." He pointedly looked in Jenna's direction. "And who was the guy in your room this morning? Tina's already let all of us know about him. Another Guardian maybe? Older? Teaching you some things, things that maybe I'd be interested in learning?" His hand snaked out, grabbing my wrist again with force. "Come on, P.J., how about showing me what you're really all about?" His grip tightened almost painfully.

"Get your hands off me, asshole." I took a step back, but he followed. I knew we were in school, and I knew he couldn't do anything to me here, at least not out in the open, but my mind flashed back to the night at Ryan's party and the still un-named guy trying to force himself on me. Panic bubbled up in me and I froze. *Do something! You have to do something!* But because of my status as a Seer, I was never trained on how to protect myself. That was supposed to be Bryn's job. I had no clue how to physically defend myself.

"You heard her—get your hands off her, asshole." Eddie was abruptly shoved away from me, and I stumbled back into the wall behind me. Jenna rushed to my side. Eddie retreated fairly quickly, and my savior approached me. *What the hell is he doing here?* "Jeremy?"

His brow furrowed. "You okay?"

My face heated with sudden embarrassment. Who else had seen and heard what had just gone down between Eddie and me? And the bigger question was: *would it happen again?* "What are you doing here? At my school?"

He flashed me a smile. "It's my school now, too. My family and I moved here a week before our date. I enrolled here shortly after. I heard most of our kind go here after high school. Didn't I mention that?"

I frowned. "No, you didn't." That I would have most definitely remembered.

"Well, here I am. And just in time, I see." *Yeah, just in time to witness my complete and utter humiliation.*

"Ahem." Jenna cleared her throat, reminding me she was still there. "You never answered if you're okay. Eddie is such an asshole. Just ignore him. I always do."

I turned to meet Jenna's dark eyes, which despite her outward calm, were narrowed with tension. "Yeah, just fine." *Mostly, anyways.*

"What was that all about? A Guardian shouldn't be treating you like that." Jeremy rotated his neck and ground his teeth together, the muscles in his jaw twitching.

"Oh—you haven't heard. There're some rumors going around about P.J. and—" Jenna started, but I certainly wasn't going to let her finish.

"Shut up, Jenna," I hissed, turning to look at Jeremy, who now wore a slightly bemused expression. "It's nothing, don't worry about it."

"I've already heard the rumors, P.J. As the new guy around town, everyone was more than happy to fill me in on all the latest gossip." He took my bag from my shoulder and started walking, and since he was holding my stuff hostage, I had no choice but to follow. I assumed Jenna wasn't far behind us. "So what's the real deal? Because I'm not the type to buy into that kind of stuff."

I met his eyes briefly before deciding my shoes were really, really interesting. "I don't know. What've you heard? Although, I'm almost afraid to ask."

"Just that you're an easy lay, you prefer to do

Guardians, you were sleeping with your no longer future Guardian amongst a host of other guys, that he was shipped away after he got you pregnant, and your parents forced you to have an abortion." He paused briefly to inhale. "Also it's not just our kind that's talking. You seem to be the talk of both worlds. The Regs apparently have labeled you a slut as well, not that there are that many Regs at this school."

Our world was a bit behind the times when it came to things like slut-shaming but I expected a bit more from the sexual forward Regs. Maybe I was more naïve than I thought ... about everything.

I turned, glaring at Jenna who was a few steps behind us. "You never said anything about me sleeping with a host of other guys, or the abortion, or the Regs."

Jenna at least had the decency to look a tiny bit sheepish for once. "I didn't wanna upset you anymore," she mumbled.

"Because finding out this way is so much better," I snapped.

Jeremy touched my arm, and I met his deep brown eyes that burned with curiosity. "So what started these rumors?"

I chewed the inside of my cheek, mulling over what was safe to tell him. He seemed like a nice enough guy on our date, and he had come to my rescue with Eddie, but how would he react once he knew the truth? Our school was very clique-ish. None of the Regs realized most of the cliques were primarily divided between my kind and their kind, because we didn't look any different or dress any differently. We just had a tendency to gravitate towards people we could be more ourselves around without worry of exposure. I usually just hung with Bryn and Jenna, preferring to stay out of the clique game, that way I could be friends with whoever I wanted.

Unfortunately, my little group had been majorly downsized without Bryn as a member, and it was sounding more and more like I was the hot topic of conversation within all the major cliques in my school and around town. I could use as many allies as I could get. "Bryn was shipped away, and you know people talk. All of a sudden I'm the biggest slut this town has ever seen, apparently." I scuffed my shoe along the ground angrily. "I mean, hell, I've only been with one guy, and I've only had sex once. I was a virgin until recently." I inhaled and exhaled deeply, trying to calm myself. "It's so not fair."

"But it was Bryn, wasn't it? Who took your virginity?" Jeremy asked softly.

I whipped my head up, meeting his gaze sharply. I'm not sure what I saw there, but suddenly I wanted to tell him the truth. "Yeah, it was." My shoes became extremely interesting again.

Jeremy tipped my chin back up gently with the back of hand, holding his power in check, preventing it from connecting with mine. "It's okay. I won't judge. I already knew you had feelings for someone else when we had our date. I was just hoping I could compete. And you were a virgin then, I could tell."

"What? How?" *Just when I decide he's a decent guy he's probably about to spout some ridiculous nonsense he heard from his cousin one time about how a woman is a virgin if she wears a certain color nail polish or something. Ugh.*

He smiled. "I'm a strong Gatekeeper. Very strong. Not only can I sense and manipulate energy around the gates, but I can sense and manipulate *other* energies."

What? Ooooh—well, isn't that just friggin' fabulous? "Why didn't you tell me?"

"Yeah, because that wouldn't have freaked you out. By the way—P.J., I can —"

Despite myself, a laugh erupted from me, already knowing where he was going with his line of thought. "Yeah, you may have a point there." I snorted and shook my head. "I've never heard of a Gatekeeper being able to do that before." And thank my lucky stars I didn't until know because I would have been even more self-conscious than I already was, thinking that every Gatekeeper was all up in my sexual business.

He shrugged his shoulders. "Most can't. I can. No biggie."

Mmm ... definitely a biggie, but at least it isn't a common ability. What a relief.

Obviously no longer feeling very sheepish, Jenna took the opportunity to push in between Jeremy and me. She batted her eyelashes at him demonstratively. "Hi, I'm Jenna." Her voice was low and husky, leaving no doubt about what she ultimately wanted.

Jeremy's lips twitched up into a wry smile. "You have all the subtlety of a bull in a china shop, don't you?"

Jenna blushed, and I guffawed, causing Jenna to shoot me a glare. "That's our Jenna, blunt as can be."

"Well, I can be pretty blunt myself when I need to be. Sorry, Jenna, don't waste your time on me, I've already got my eye on someone else." He nodded his head at me, grinning.

The tips of my ears heated. "Jeremy, I—well, I—"

He slid my bag onto my shoulder, winking at me. "Don't sweat it. I know you have feelings for Bryn, otherwise you wouldn't have slept with him. I can tell you're the kind of person who doesn't do casual. But he's gone, and I'm here. And I have every intention of wooing you to the best of my abilities." He crowded my space, and for a second I thought he was going to try to kiss me.

Instead, he leaned over and whispered in my ear, his minty breath fanning along my cheek, "I've been on a lot of dates with a lot of Seers lately because of my Sudding, but none have piqued my interest like you have. Not only are you smart, funny, and stunning, but also, your power calls out to mine. You're who I want P.J., and I don't mind waiting around until you can be mine."

My heart thrummed in my chest, and it wasn't just because he was a hot guy and my hormones seemed to be set on overdrive lately. No, it was something else. Was it his power that was calling to mine like he claimed that mine called to his? Would the yearning to discover more grow with my developing powers? "Jeremy—" I tried again, but with a smile, he turned and trotted off down the hall.

"Wow," Jenna said, fanning herself. "Some girls have all the luck."

I grimaced. "Yeah, but it's not necessarily *good* luck."

"Only you would complain about having multiple hot guys vying for your attention." Jenna stuck her lower lip out at me. "Your powers obviously aren't stuck on zero like you've been thinking."

"Too bad the one I really want has been shipped off to who-knows-where, and I'm the one left here to deal with the fallout of everything. Or do you consider it lucky, too, that everyone in school thinks I'm easy prey now? Plus, I'd like to add, having guys chase after me simply for my power level isn't something. Sure, the power connection is nice, but it doesn't compare to having a real connection of the soul."

"Oh, stop being so dramatic. You and Bryn can eventually do whatever you want, you just need time to figure things out, to come up with a realistic plan. And things could be worse. At least you have Jeremy to keep you occupied so you don't waste away pining for Bryn." She smiled wistfully, causing me to roll my eyes.

"Seriously, what don't you understand? I'm not interested in Jeremy like that."

Jenna sighed. "Speaker here, something that you keep forgetting. I'm totally awesome at reading body language, and yours was saying something completely different just now. You might love Bryn, but Jeremy could definitely get you going if you let him. Why not use him until Bryn gets back?"

"Are you—are you actually suggesting that I use Jeremy —have sex with him until Bryn gets back?"

Jenna nodded eagerly. "Yep, that's exactly what I'm suggesting. It could be the solution to all your problems. You could marry Jeremy and take Bryn on as your lover slash Guardian." She clapped her hands together excitedly. "Then you could satisfy your duty and your heart." She opened her hand miming dropping a microphone. "Boom. Best plan ever."

I yanked at my hair in agitation, fighting back the urge to yell at Jenna since I knew she actually meant well. But her plan was a horrible idea, even if it were something that I was interested in. I could just imagine trying to explain it to the unwilling participants. *Oh, hey, Jeremy, even though you're my husband, I'm gonna keep on having sex with Bryn. Hope you don't mind sharing. And Bryn, you know I love you, but I need to have sex with my husband in order to try and get pregnant with his baby. You know, duty calls and all. You okay with that?* "You're absolutely insane, you know that, right?"

"Insanely smart." Jenna giggled, absentmindedly working some of her rainbow hair into a curl with her fingertips.

"Yeah, you keep telling yourself that." I grappled with moving some stuff around my bag without setting it down.

Dread must have peeked through my calm mask

because Jenna's face softened with sympathy. "The first day is always the worst. People will move on to the next big thing really soon."

I inhaled and exhaled deeply, trying to center myself. *Who does that ever really work for in real life? Seriously?* "All right, here I go." It wasn't just the rumors and whispers that were bothering me. It was also my first day back at classes without Bryn at my side. His absence left a big gaping hole in my chest.

Every head swiveled in my direction as we entered our class, whispers following us to our seats in the back row. I slid into my chair and slumped down, hiding behind a curtain of hair.

It's going to be a very long day.

IT WAS OFFICIAL: I was dropping out of school. I didn't need any kind of business degree anymore anyways, since being a future outcast from our society didn't translate to helping run the family business. *Hmm ... maybe I can now pursue a creative career, something like photography or graphic design?*

Not one single person had asked me how I was doing all day, and when anyone, male or female, deigned to actually utter a few words to me, it was always some kind of lewd remark or insult. The guys all wanted to sleep with me, and the girls all wanted to scratch my eyes out because the guys all wanted to sleep with me. I was beginning to think that Bryn was the lucky one, getting shipped off to somewhere where nobody knew who he was. But then again, he'd probably be getting all kinds of pats on the back if he were the one who was left behind instead of me. *Stupid ass double standards.*

"Hey there, my little Seer." I met Khol's vivid green eyes from my hiding spot under a tree in my backyard. I'd come there after school to mope. I wanted to be left alone, but my parents obviously wanted to be able to keep an eye on me. I guess they were worried I'd throw myself at the next available Guardian now that Bryn was gone.

"I'm not your little Seer," I snapped, focusing on a clump of grass in front of me. My nostrils flared as I tried to keep my breathing even. Khol's appearance had thickened the air, the pressure almost suffocating. A buzz of excitement burned through my system, which I was choosing to ignore.

Khol sat down, thankfully not close enough to touch. "Oh? But you are. We're linked, you and I."

I lifted my head to glare at him. "Look, I'm in no mood to deal with you right now. Why did you come this time? What do you want? Wait—" I glanced at my kitchen window to see if either of my parents had spotted Khol yet. "You better get out of here before my parents see you. After what happened with Bryn, they'll blow a gasket if they see me out here with some guy they don't know. Apparently, I can't be trusted around anyone with a penis anymore."

Khol chuckled, his laugh low and rumbling. "Well, I

don't think that is true. I think they just do not trust you in general now."

"That's all besides the point. I don't want them to see you here—with me." I glanced at my kitchen window again. Not to mention I didn't want any little rodent spies to see him either, although it wasn't like my reputation could get any worse than it currently was.

"They are busy at the moment. I can hear them talking." He tilted his head, smiling. "And I will be able to hear them if they approach."

Huh. Good to know. So he has superhuman hearing of some kind. I tilted my head to study him, almost mirroring his body language. "What are you?" I murmured. The more I was around him, the more comfortable I became, negating some of his creep factor. The less creepy he seemed, the more I noticed...other things.

For instance, how handsome he was, even with his ginormous proportions. And he had dimples. I'd always liked dimples. Bryn had dimples—*Bryn.* I couldn't let myself get distracted by Khol's handsome face and forget my Bryn. It was as if Khol was enchanting me somehow. "Are you using some kind of...I don't know—power—to distract me? Some kind of whatever-you-are mojo to make me forget about Bryn when I'm with you?"

Khol met my eyes, his gaze assessing. "I possess no such powers. Whatever you feel when I am near is completely you." He leaned closer to me, letting his leg brush against mine. The heat radiating from him washed over me, causing my breath to catch in my throat. Maybe what Jenna had said was true, maybe being with Bryn had sprung me, and my hormones were just going utterly crazy. If I knew that was the case, I could control it. *I have to control it.*

"Your friend Jenna knows nothing about these things," Khol rumbled.

"Stop doing that." I scowled at him. "It's creepy."

He didn't respond. Instead, he tucked a piece of hair behind my right ear, letting his fingers blaze a trail down my neck before they dropped away. My temperature skyrocketed, lava replacing the blood in my veins. I was practically panting, ready to combust, from a mere touch.

No. I won't let this happen. Just because my body was reacting to him didn't mean I would betray Bryn. I watched Khol, frozen in place, as he leaned closer, his face skimming along my neck. His breath was hot as it caressed my skin, but he was careful not to actually make contact. He followed a winding path up my jaw and towards my mouth, continuing not to make contact. He stopped when his face was level with mine, our breaths intermingling.

His lips ghosted mine as he spoke, "I told you, I will not take again what isn't freely given." I shuddered down to my core, my heart thrashing against my rib cage. I willed myself to move away, but I couldn't. It was if I was under some kind of spell. His fingers wound into my hair at the base of my neck, where he grasped tightly. *God, I want him to kiss me.* I was a traitor for wanting Khol's lips on mine, but I couldn't help the desire. I didn't have to act on it though. *I won't let myself.*

"No," I whispered. "Stop."

Khol tensed, his fingers tightening in my hair, and then ever so slowly he released me, exhaling heavily. A part deep inside me mourned the loss of his touch. *But I can't. I can't let myself feel that way.*

He squeezed his eyes shut, his voice a low rumble, "I want you, my little Seer. I will not pretend that part isn't true. Your power, your body, your very essence is what awakened me from my sleep. I am yours, your willing servant, linked to you first by choice and now by need."

I swallowed, trying to combat the sudden dryness of my throat. "Why do I seem to be the main attraction for all you guys around here lately? Why now? Why all of a sudden, when no one seemed to notice me before?" *Besides Bryn that is... Bryn always noticed me.*

With his eyes still screwed shut, Khol tipped his head back against the tree. "Because you were a pretty girl who is now becoming a beautiful woman—a beautiful and powerful woman who deserves to be worshipped, one that can no longer be ignored, one that I'm trying my best to keep my word to."

Moving lightning fast, his hands were cupping my face before I could blink, his gaze boring into mine. "I know a part of you wants me to kiss you, a part of you wants what I'm offering, even if you are not ready." I shuddered, unable to deny his words, knowing even if I tried, he would know. "But I will not take it from you, although I yearn to do just that. I will wait." His hands trembled against my cheeks. "We have more important things to worry about than our petty desires. I will come to you later when I have myself … under control." He stood abruptly and disappeared. *How the hell does he keep doing that?*

"P.J.!" My mother bustled out the back door towards me, barely containing her excitement. "You have a visitor."

I looked at her balefully. "I thought I was still being punished. Must be an important visitor."

"The fact that he wants to see you at all after what happened with Bryn—well, it means you still have hope, and I'm not going to let anything stand in the way of that."

"Oh, so it's a *he?* I guess it's safe to assume that he isn't a Guardian or anyone of that ilk, you know the unacceptable kind of guys for me to associate with, ones that won't be on your Sudding list." I crossed my arms over my chest and raised my chin defiantly. If my mother wanted me to see this guy, then I had no desire to do so.

"Now, don't you ruin this. I only want what's best for you, peanut," my mother whispered excitedly as I heard my father's voice growing closer. "He'll be out in a second."

"Fabulous," I grumbled. Well, I wasn't going to get up for whoever it was.

Much to my surprise, my father escorted none other than Jeremy into my backyard. Jeremy grinned as my mother hurried over to join my father, and the two of them went back inside without another word. *Well, I guess*

I can be trusted alone with a Gatekeeper, just not any Guardians. "What are you doing here?" I asked, trying not to sound too accusatory, and failing horribly.

"Just came to see how you were doing after your first day back in classes. I know it must have been pretty rough, all things considered." He sat down where Khol had been, and just like him, he was careful not to touch me.

I picked at some blades of grass, averting my gaze. "Yeah, don't really wanna talk about it. But thanks anyways." I lifted my head and met his deep brown gaze, unable to keep myself from being annoyed with him. "You know, I do appreciate you helping me today, and being so nice—I do—"

"But? I sense a 'but' coming." Jeremy's soulful eyes watched me intently.

I sighed. "Yeah, there is, if you come over like this, my mom is gonna start printing up our wedding invitations and naming our first child. She seems to think you're my only prospect at the moment, and well, I'm sure you know how it is."

"Yeah, I do. My mom is the same way. It's just, well, I wouldn't mind all of that—with you."

My mouth dropped open. "Wha-What? You can't be serious? You barely know me. You can't—"

"There's just something about you," he interrupted. "I can't quite put my finger on it. I wanna be with you, P.J. I thought girls all believed in the whole love at first sight kind of thing. I mean, I don't love you." Jeremy flushed. "Not yet anyways—but I could. I know that I could."

"Whoa, whoa, whoa." I waved my hands in the air. "You know I love someone else. You *know* that. It's been like a week since he was ripped out of my life. And I don't plan on giving him up so easily." Seriously, what did I just ask Khol about guys noticing me so much more all of a sudden? I'd gone from a drought to a flash flood. But the one I really wanted was nowhere to be found.

Jeremy frowned, picking at some blades of grass himself. "You *love* him? No, I didn't know that part. I just knew you had feelings for him."

"Even if I had feelings short of love for him, it's still only been a week." I sighed. "Look, Jeremy, you're wasting your time with me."

"So what do you plan on doing? He's a Guardian, P.J., and even though I would never judge you for your indiscretion, are you willing to give up your friends and family for him? Are you willing to become an outcast to be with him? To be completely shunned from our world?"

I didn't even have to think about it. I would do anything to be with Bryn. Absolutely anything. "Yes," I whispered. "I would do anything to be with him."

"Oh," Jeremy said. "Even still—I can't just give up on you. No girl has ever gotten into my head like you have. I can't stop thinking about you. And your power—the way it feels when it connects with mine is beyond unbelievable."

I let out a frustrated groan. "I don't wanna hurt you,

Jeremy. Despite not wanting to be with you romantically, I still like you. I still wanna be friends."

"Friends," Jeremy grunted, his lips twisting with displeasure.

He grabbed me, crushing his mouth to mine. I barely had time to mentally process what was going on before his tongue plunged in to massage and play with mine. And just like with Khol, I found myself kissing him back. A small moan escaped from me. *He's such a good kisser.*

And then it happened—I wasn't quite sure what it was at first, but I somehow knew it had something to do with his powers and my powers intermingling. I was yanked out of my body like when I had visions before, and yet at the same time, I was still very aware of Jeremy's body touching mine. I gasped into Jeremy's mouth as a vision slammed into me—white-hot light, images coming at me almost too fast to interpret. It was more of an impression than a vision, but it was bad, extremely bad—those things, those 'aliens' in so many people. They were everywhere, hiding and yet in plain sight. They had a plan, a plan they'd already set in motion. I could almost *see* it, and yet it was just out of my grasp.

I jolted back into my body when I felt myself begin to peak, all my muscles coiling tight. I was engulfed by Jeremy's powers. They swirled in and around me, pummeling all of my senses. My nerve endings were alight and spasming with ecstasy from little more than a kiss. I moaned into his mouth, my hands digging into his shoulders.

Little aftershocks were still racking my body when he pulled away. My eyes fluttered open, and I averted my gaze. I bit my lip, not knowing what to say. *Did that really just happen? Did he just make me have an orgasm from only a kiss by way of manipulating me with his powers? And I had another vision at the same time?*

Jeremy didn't have the same tongue-tied problem. "That was amazing," he murmured.

"What—what was that?" I sputtered. Guilt crashed over me like a tidal wave, threatening to drown me. First Khol and now Jeremy...what would Bryn think? Although what happened with Jeremy was a bit of a bigger deal considering how it ended.

"I'm not one hundred percent sure. I can manipulate all kinds of energies, but I've never been able to do *that* before. It was like I could feel our powers intertwining when we touched, and then..." His voice trailed off as he flushed, a small smile tugging at his lips. "You did, didn't you? You know? You did?"

My skin heated from the top of my head to the tips of my toes. I supposed there was no point in denying it. I got the sense that he already knew what he had done to me and was just pretending that he couldn't. After all, how could he not know when he'd known I was a virgin just by reading my energies? "Yeah," I breathed, still not making eye contact with him. "You?" I couldn't help but to be curious. I wanted to know if he had been affected the same way I had been.

"Yeah...no. I have a little bit more control than that over myself."

I narrowed my eyes, embarrassment morphing into anger. "What are you trying to say? That I have no control over myself? And that I'm easy to manipulate because of it?"

I knew my anger was misplaced. Jeremy seemed like a genuinely nice guy, and I didn't actually think he'd meant anything by his comment, and yet I needed to be angry with someone. I needed to yell at someone because I hated myself for betraying Bryn. "You did that on purpose, didn't you?" I hissed.

"No, and you know I didn't. Don't be mad at me because you feel like you betrayed Bryn or something. Maybe it's better you figure these things out now before it's too late."

Was I that obvious that he knew right away why I was actually angry? "Too late for what?"

He stepped towards me, and I backed up, causing him to throw up his hands in a sign of defeat. "Before you two do something really stupid, and then you figure out down the line that he isn't right for you."

"And I suppose you think you're right for me?"

His brown eyes flashed as his lips pressed into a thin line. "Yeah, I do."

"And why is that? Because you just made me...well... you know?" I couldn't bring myself to say it out loud.

Jeremy grunted, his lips turning up slightly at the edges

again. "Partly. You can't deny that we have good chemistry, P.J."

"I have *better* chemistry with Bryn. I love him. I don't love you." It was just like a guy to think everything was all about sex. There is more to chemistry than sex. Okay, fine, sex plays a huge part in it, but other things go into the mix, like emotions—emotions like love.

"So, you're not even willing to give me a chance after that? Won't you at least go out on a second date with me? Didn't that kiss at least warrant that much?" Jeremy's expression was pleading and not the least bit arrogant or cocky. I would have expected a touch of egotism after that little performance. Hell, I would be a little smug if the shoe were on the other foot, and yet his deep brown eyes only held a kind of desperation. "Please, P.J., give me a chance, a real chance. That's all I'm asking for."

I turned my head, not wanting to look into his sad eyes anymore. I wasn't cruel after all. "I can't. I'm sorry. I love Bryn."

"If you love him so much, then you shouldn't be worried about going out with me again. You could go out with me, give us a real shot, and if you really love him as much as you say you do, well then, I won't be able to steal you away. You owe it to yourself to find out, don't you think?" I didn't say anything, not really liking where the conversation was going. "The only reason to not go out with me is because you know you don't really love him, at least not the way you say you do. Don't you think you owe it to him to find out if you truly love him?"

"Stop," I said, my shoulders slumping. What if he was right? What if I was afraid to give anyone else a real chance because I didn't think I could be faithful? Would Bryn want to be with me if he doubted how much I really loved him? I knew Jeremy was trying to twist things to his advantage, trying to manipulate me into going out with him again, but even I couldn't deny he made some very valid points.

"All right," I said flatly. "I'll go out with you again." A huge grin spread across his face, his eyes shining. "But none of that again—don't do that to me again." I bit my lower lip and eyed him warily. *This could all be a huge mistake.*

Jeremy's grin turned sly. "I can't make that promise. I'm gonna use every God given gift to try and make you mine."

"Jeremy—" I groaned.

"Nope. You already agreed to go. I'll mention it to your mom on the way out—you know, so you can't back out of it later." He turned and loped back towards my house.

"That's playing dirty," I called after him.

He glanced over his shoulder at me. "Yep, but at least I'm in the game."

I slumped against the tree, running my fingertips idly over the bark. I froze when the texture of the wood dipped down into small jagged indentations under my skin. When Bryn and me had been little kids, we'd both carved our names into the trunk of the tree that I was currently touching. We hadn't put our initials together inside a heart or anything like that. We hadn't known about such things as romantic love yet, but both our names were there, just the same.

I had unerringly found the grooves that spelled out Bryn's name. My head lolled to the side, big fat tears slowly sliding down my cheeks. I'd just betrayed him—twice—and both times while his name hovered above me. My heart hadn't been in the kiss with Jeremy, nor the almost kiss with Khol, but my body had been, and it had called for more, not to mention its reaction to the actual kiss I'd shared with Khol in my bedroom last night. Bryn had been gone just over a week, and I'd already been unfaithful to him three times all in all. What kind of girlfriend did that make me? Not a very good one, that much I knew.

I loved Bryn, with all of my heart. I loved him more deeply and completely than I ever could anyone else. Plus he made my blood boil every time he was near me. So why did my body respond so willingly to both Khol and Jeremy? And how could I put a stop to things when they obviously were both dead set on having me for themselves?

Maybe when Bryn eventually comes for me, he won't want me anymore. Maybe he'll realize I'm the one that's not good enough for him.

Chapter 12

My brain was filled with cotton candy, and only one thing permeated the fluff in my head. I'd betrayed Bryn with both Khol and Jeremy. *I'm a shit person.*

In my pitch-black room, shades drawn to protect against the prying eyes of nosey squirrels, I fought the guilt that was eating at my insides. *I don't deserve Bryn and his love.* How could he ever forgive me? I had to tell him what happened, of course, but what if I didn't get the chance for months? Years? What if he came for me like planned, and I had to tell him what had transpired between me and two other guys? Would he hate me? Would he walk away from me forever?

"I feel your tormented emotions, my little Seer. Why are you torturing yourself?" Khol's low voice cut through the thick silence of my room.

I raised my head, blinking slowly. Khol's large frame

was crouched down beside my bed, his electric green eyes glowing in the dark as they roamed my face. He was one of the reasons I was so distraught, and yet I had to talk to someone. "I betrayed Bryn." A sob erupted from my chest. Saying the words out loud made it seem all that much real. "He won't want me now, after what I've done. And I can't really blame him. I'm not good enough for someone like him."

Khol snorted. "You know nothing of men if you think what you've done will turn him from you. He will want you until his dying breath."

What? "Shouldn't you tell me that he's not gonna want me anymore, and that he'll hate me, so you can swoop in and make your move?" Isn't that what a typical guy would do anyways?

Khol snorted again. "I won't resort to cheap tricks of manipulation to win your affections. You would only resent me in the end. When you finally come to me, it will be because you are truly mine, and there will be no doubts to hold you back." His white teeth flashed in the dark, illuminated by his eyes. "And when you are mine, you'll come to me alone for satisfaction, all other touches will leave you cold in comparison after I've branded you."

I shivered, goose bumps erupting in quick succession across my skin. There was something ancient and knowing in his words. His mention of branding me wasn't just an innuendo. It meant something more. It was like that with Khol sometimes. He would say something that seemingly meant one thing, but I would pick up on an undercurrent of secrets hidden beneath his seemingly benign words. I wasn't sure if he meant for me to feel those things, or if it was just a side effect of our link. Not that it mattered, because they were there. And it all scared the crap out of me. "I'll always crave Bryn," I said.

"When all others turn to dust, there will only be you and me."

Fear crept up my spine, his words ominous. "What's that supposed to mean?"

He stared at me for another moment, his face a mask that revealed nothing. "We must discuss the vision you had earlier...when you were kissing the Gatekeeper."

I eyed him warily. I knew he was changing the subject to something I couldn't ignore. "Yeah, fine. What about it? I couldn't quite make everything out. It was more of an impression than a vision."

"To you maybe, although that could be because you were otherwise occupied." His face twisted with displeasure for a moment before his mask of calm returned. "But I was able to look closer at your vision and discern what seemed to be just beyond your grasp." I waved my hand at him to continue. *Spit it out already.* "We've figured out what they want—these creatures."

"And?" I squirmed impatiently.

"They want this world for themselves. They wish to rule it, and to enslave humans. They've done it before, to other worlds. They implant themselves amongst the residents of that world, slowly take over, and once they have complete control, they use up all the resources. Eventually there is nothing left, and they move on."

"Holy shit!" I exclaimed. "It's like this movie I saw where these aliens attacked, trying to kill everybody so they could use our world up. Actually, it's kind of like a lot of movies I've seen." I frowned, wondering if someone, somewhere, was trying to tell us something.

"But unlike in your fantasy movies, the mass public doesn't know these aliens are among us. They look like regular humans to them. If you came forward, you'd probably be locked away and labeled insane," Khol stated matter-of-factly.

And he was right. I couldn't just point to people like Senator Bill Wexington and yell, "Alien!" People would lock me up and throw away the key. "So what do we do then?"

"We're coming up with a plan. In the meantime, you must just stay aware."

"Great. More of doing nothing. And who is this *we* you keep referring to? I'm hoping you're not using the royal we or something, because it's gonna take more than just you and me to take care of this problem." I noticed on several occasions Khol had said, "*We* are working on it" and "*We* are coming up with a plan." Just who was this *we*?

"More of my kind. Most of us still slumber, as I have said, but you and your powers have awakened more than just me."

My eyes widened. "Umm...so should I expect more pushy visitors like you to just drop by and harass me?" *Oh, please, no.* There was no way I could handle any more beings like Khol.

"No." Khol's jaw muscles popped as he clenched his teeth. "They are not to make direct contact with you. If any of them approach you, and trust me, you will know, call for me immediately, do you hear me?" He grabbed my shoulders, his fingers digging into my skin almost painfully. "Others of my kind are not as in control as I am. They won't be able to hold themselves back from you." Rage flared in his iridescent eyes, and I couldn't help but shrink back from him. "They will try to take from you what doesn't belong to them. They are too young and do not understand. I would kill them for it, but some of them would see it as a risk worth pursuing."

"And what makes you different from others of your kind?" I croaked.

"I have lived many lifetimes longer than most of them, and I understand things they do not. There is no need to fear them. They listen to me. I am their leader. But there is always a chance that one of them won't be strong enough to resist your call, and he will try to come for you." I shuddered at the thought. Khol reached one hand up, pushing my hair out of my face. "I will protect you. Please, I did not mean to frighten you." When I remained immobile with fear, Khol leaned in closer to me. "Do you trust me?" he rasped.

I did. For some reason I did trust him—truly. I finally managed to find my voice. "Yes. I told you before that I did, and I still do, despite everything."

"Good." He let go of me, his face growing pensive. "And don't worry, we won't sit by and observe for much longer. The time for action is growing near. Your very existence speaks of things to come. These creatures may think this world is ripe for the picking, and in many ways it is, but there are those of this world who will fight hard enough and champion the weak. The creatures will not win."

Purpose swelled within me. How many times had I thought recently that life had no meaning without love? That was true, but what good was love if we weren't free to express it? Things needed to change. Old ways needed to die in order to make room for the new, and these aliens needed to leave my world the hell alone so we could live in peace. *I can do it. I can help change things for the better.*

Getting rid of the aliens was the first step. As soon as that was taken care of then it would be time to change the thinking of my people. Bryn and me should be able to be together without being shunned by our own kind. My mind was spinning off to a thousand different places at once. *Wait...* "The aliens are behind all the chaos, aren't they? All the chaos and tension that's been worsening in our world?"

"Yes. Not only do they want to use this world and suck it dry, but also they enjoy the chaos. It makes them stronger and us weaker, in a manner of speaking."

"Oh. You mean like united we stand, divided we fall?" I asked, bouncing excitedly. Who knew history class would actually serve a purpose in my real life?

One side of Khol's mouth quirked up. "Yes. Precisely."

"And I wasn't gonna say anything, but what's up with how you talk? It's so *do not* this and *will not* that and all old fashioned in some ways."

Khol chuckled. "It's because I *am* old fashioned. As I've said, I was asleep for an extremely long time. I've been trying to update my manner of speaking. Haven't I been improving, my little Seer?"

I scowled. He needed to stop calling me *his* little Seer, but I supposed there was no point in arguing with him at that moment about it. "Yeah, I guess. I mean, before you probably would have said something like, 'Have I not been improving?' ...or something like that."

"Yes, indeed."

"And you just backslid." I laughed as his face twisted into a perplexed expression. "Nevermind, forget it." I smiled up at Khol for a second, before sobering. "I wanna do something. I need to help stop these asshole aliens."

"Even when it's time to move, you will not actively participate." Khol inched closer, running his knuckles along the side of my face. Much to my dismay, I sank into the warmth of his touch. *He's so friggin' hot.* And I wasn't talking about how he looked, nope. I was talking about his body temperature. I wanted to luxuriate in the heat his caresses brought my body. *I have to feel like ice to him.* "You're too precious to endanger in that way. And not just to me, I mean your visions. We would all still be in the dark about this if it weren't for you. Without you, we wouldn't stand a chance."

"But I can't just sit by and do nothing. I need to help, too." I watched as Khol's gaze dipped to fixate on my lips. He was thinking about kissing me, he practically vibrated with the desire. It stirred my own longings, causing me to tremble. I inwardly cursed myself for being so weak. I'd been tearing my guts out over what I'd done with both Khol and Jeremy, and now faced with it again… *I haven't learned my goddamned lesson.*

My eyes widened as I peered up at Khol. Fire seemed to dance behind the black irises of Khol's eyes. I felt compelled to touch him, drawn in like a moth to his flames. I pressed my thumbs on the outside corners of his eyes. "What are you?" I murmured.

His eyelids fluttered shut, a small tremor running through him. "Someone who can't seem to get control of himself when I'm around you." It sounded like he'd gargled with broken glass. "Your power sings to mine, like calls to like, and I desire nothing more than to forget my honor and claim you for my own when I am with you."

"But you won't." I shifted nervously, still holding his face. His eyes snapped open to resume staring at my lips. "Because I trust you."

Khol stumbled away from me, his legs visibly shaky. He regarded me with a small smile tipping the corners of his lips up. "Ah, and that's the truth of the matter. I will not betray your trust. It means too much to me. So remember, my little Seer, if you lose your trust in me, you lose all that stops me from taking what I truly desire."

I licked my lips. Khol's predatory eyes tracked the

movement. "And we're not just talking about sex, are we?" I had to know. I was already tired of the hidden meanings and games.

Khol's laugh was a dark rumble, low and seductive, and absolutely terrifying. It made me want to pull the covers over my head and hide like a little girl. "No, my little Seer, we are not talking about just sex. I want more—ever so much more from you than just that."

"What? What is it you want from me?" *Why do I trust him, again?* How was I even supposed to consider it when he scared the crap out of me on so many levels? And yet... I did. *I am seriously whacked in the head.*

"When you are ready to know what I am, then you'll be ready to know what I want from you. Until then, you can know nothing more than one day you will belong to me."

I raised my chin defiantly, despite the ice coursing through my veins. "I'm already Bryn's. He belongs to me, and I belong to him."

Khol grunted. "It's time for me to go...for now." And just like usual, he simply disappeared.

The depth of the darkness in my room suddenly seemed that much deeper with the absence of Khol and his luminescent green eyes. I had so much to think about and if I was being honest with myself...none of the emotional experience to deal with any of it.

A part of me longed for the innocent times before things had gotten so complicated with Bryn. Sure, I'd been in heavy denial, but at least things had been easy. To me, that night at Ryan's party was a clear demarcation of before and after, simple and complicated. Bryn hadn't been more than a friend, but I'd at least had him in my life. Plus there'd been no Khol and Jeremy hanging around trying to muck everything up, not to mention guys like the still un-named punk from Ryan's party and Eddie from school.

I used to crave attention from guys. I'd wish all the time that they would suddenly take notice of me, at least the good ones. What is it they say? *Be careful what you wish for.* And following that train of thought... I'd once been consumed with coming into my abilities as a Seer. That night at Ryan's didn't just mark a change for my romantic life but my life in general. That night had changed *everything* for me. I wasn't even sure I was the same person anymore.

I'm done with not doing anything. Done. I hadn't done anything when Bryn was ripped out of my life. I hadn't done anything about the visions that only I'd seen. I'd done basically nothing but lie around and feel sorry for myself. *I'm pathetic.* But what could I do, really? I was just one nineteen-year-old girl with no remarkable powers beyond having visions. My gift seemed to mirror the state of my life. I was a perpetual spectator, and I didn't know how to join the game.

I'D SPENT the entirety of my night ruminating about the issues I was facing. I'd remained an outward mask of calm as I stared at my ceiling, blinking into the darkness in search of a plan—any kind of plan. Ultimately, I'd come up with nothing. *Nada. Zilch. Zero.*

So of course, it was inevitable when my thoughts shifted to Bryn. He was ever present in my mind, sadly enough, even when I was liplocked with someone else. One would think that being consumed with Bryn would serve as a ward against other men. But, apparently, not so much in my case. At times it seemed as if my powers were a separate entity with a mind of their own.

And yet, my heart yearned for only Bryn and if I focused hard enough, I could almost believe he was still with me and I could physically touch him. My fingers twitched at the memory of his supple skin and how they felt exploring the warm expanse of his body. My nose tingled with his spicy scent as if I was really in his arms, pressed up against him. The gentle rumble of his laugh danced on the air as I trailed kisses down his throat, and his breath caught, his pulse thumping in his chest as I dropping lower … *Fuck. I miss him. He is my home. And I will always choose him over anyone else—always.*

It was like he'd taken a piece of me with him when he'd left. Without him to share things with, everything had taken on a surreal quality. My visions, my life, it all felt like a horrible nightmare without Bryn. I pushed my face deeper into my pillow and sobbed. *I need you, Bryn. I'm losing myself without you.*

"Oh, peanut." My mother's voice met my ears, the bed shifting under her weight.

Just go away. I didn't want comfort from one of the people who had ripped Bryn from my life. It was partly her fault I was suffering to begin with.

Her small hands softly stroked my hair. "I know you're upset now, but it's for the best, you'll see." I fought the urge to lift the pillow from my head so I could scream at her. Instead, I burrowed deeper into the comforting fluff.

"It could be worse. At least you didn't end up pregnant, and then you'd have to marry the first Seer descendant or Gatekeeper that would have you. At least this way you won't have to live a lie the rest of your life. You can move on from your mistake."

I wasn't sure what exactly tipped me off. Maybe it was the catch in my mother's voice, or the knowing way she seemed to speak, but in that moment I suddenly just knew.

I slowly lifted my face from my pillow, shock coursing through my system. "Oh my God," I rasped. "Oh. My. God. Is that what happened to you? Am—am I even Dad's real daughter?"

"Of course you're your father's, don't be ridiculous!" She snapped, her gaze darting away. "I just knew...a friend...a friend had that happen, is all."

But there was no missing panic right beneath the surface of her faux indignance. *Holy shit...* I'm not the biological daughter of the man I'd grown up thinking was my father.

I grabbed my mom's hand, my grip smashing her fingers together. She winced. "Tell me," I demanded. "I have a right to know. Wait—does Dad know? Does he know I'm not really his?" My mother slumped forward, her shoulders sagging. Tears welled in her eyes as she met my gaze.

It was then, for the first time, it occurred to me how young my mom was in comparison to all my friends' moms. "How old were you?"

"I love your father. I don't want you to ever doubt that," she stated, her voice shaking. "It's just I was young— so young—and he was—well, he was—he was like nothing I'd ever seen before."

"He couldn't have been a Guardian, that much I know, because I would've been a boy," I interjected, speaking my thoughts out loud.

"No, you're right. Your father," –her voice warbled as she swiped at a rogue tear making a break for it down her cheek— "your biological father, I mean—he wasn't human. Or not like any human I'd ever met before. He had these eyes—these iridescent blue eyes—and powers I've never seen before or since. He, well, I couldn't seem to resist him."

My mom swallowed, turning her head, unable to meet my gaze any longer. "I gave myself to him completely. I thought I was in love. I would have done anything to be with him. But when I found out I was pregnant, he disappeared. I never heard from him again." The dam broke and tears spilled from her eyes, running freely down her face. "He left me all alone. I didn't know what I was going to do, and then..." She paused, swiping at her tears again. "Your dad…well, he was in love with me, and when he found out I was in trouble, he wanted to take care of me, of *us*."

"What was his name, my father?" His eyes…although they weren't iridescent green like Khol's, I knew—I just knew that whatever Khol was, my biological father had been as well. The shock of what that meant coursed through my system, intermingling with everything else I just learned. "I'm not even fully human?" I didn't know why I was bothering to ask, since the answer was already clear.

"You're human—you're my daughter—"

"And something else. I'm human, and something else," I squeaked. *Okay, don't freak out. Don't freak out. You're still the same person, nothing has actually changed.*

Except that you're not fully human. My heart threatened to break free from my rib cage. *Shit. I'm totally freaking out.*

"Yes, peanut, but—"

"What was my father's name?" I demanded.

"Dragos. His name was Dragos." My mother sagged even more, defeat in her expression. "But he doesn't matter. The only father you need to know about is the one who raised you."

"I need to know *what* I am. Can't you understand that? It changes so many things. What if—what if I can't even have Seer children? Isn't that the only reason why I supposedly can't be with Bryn? Because of my duty? But what if that doesn't even matter?"

"No, no, that's not how it works. That's—"

"You're in denial. That's what all of this is. You don't wanna face the fact that none of the rules may apply to me. Get out. Leave me alone," I growled.

A part of me hated seeing my mother cry, the guilt of it twisting my insides into knots. But a larger part was nothing but a ball of anger. *How could she have kept this from me?*

She stood slowly, her silence hanging heavily in the air. Her face had drained of all color, and her lips were pressed together in a thin line. She trudged towards my door as if the weight of what she'd done was pulling her down. "I love you, my little peanut. None of this changes that. And your dad—none of that matters to him. You're his daughter, and he loves you, too."

She paused a few moments but when I didn't respond she left, shutting my door behind her.

Maybe my mom didn't have the answers I needed but I had a feeling I knew someone who did.

"Khol," I growled. "I know you can hear me, or sense me, or whatever. Get your ass here now."

He appeared in front of me. One second he wasn't there and the next he was. His glowing eyes lit up the dark. "You know," he stated without any preamble.

"Yeah, I do. At least the bit that I'm obviously part whatever you are. Care to share with me whatever that is now?" Every muscle in my body tensed as I waited for his words to drop like potential bombs to my psyche.

"You are half *arach*. Your father and I are both full-blooded. We are what you might call dragon."

Dragon? He didn't seriously just say dragon, right? I misheard him because dragons don't exist.

"And most people wouldn't believe you exist, either, or the creatures you've been having visions of exist." A tight smile turned up Khol's lips. His eyes darted back and forth over my face, studying, assessing ... waiting.

"Is that why my powers called to yours? Because of what I am?" It was if I was floating, my entire body numb. *I have to be in shock or something.* Despite that, there were so many questions that seemed imperative to ask.

"Yes, and why you awakened not just me."

"So you can, like, turn into a dragon?"

Khol nodded once. "Yes, a dragon is my other form."

Other form? My head was spinning. "Can I? Or will I be able to...?" My voice trailed off, not able to truly fathom the possibility.

"No. You were born with only one form. It's very rare for a mixed blood to have a second form."

I laughed, clearly on the verge of hysteria. "Good to know. I—" The room began to spin, but I pushed on with my questions. "What do you want with me? Really?"

Khol dropped to his knees in front of me, his large hands tenderly cupping my face as he locked his gaze with mine. "With my kind—*our* kind—when the female is ready to find a...mate, she sends out a call with her magic, letting the male dragons know she is willing. The strongest and most powerful have rights to her first, the right to try to claim her. I want to be your mate, P.J."

"Mate? What does that even mean?" I squeaked.

"I'm attempting to explain in a way that you might understand. The bond I'm referring to—we call it *Anam Cara*—loosely translated it means soul friend or soul mate. Humans have been using our term for centuries, but it means so much more for a dragon—more than mere words. It refers to the soul-deep bond we form with our desired partner. Our kind, once we find our desired partner, bond for the rest of our days."

"And how long is that? How old are you exactly? How old am I gonna live to be?" If I were a computer, I'd have been reading *Error, error, does not compute.*

"A very, very long time."

"Oh." *Bryn—what about Bryn?* I'd thought my new found heritage might mean I could be with Bryn, but it didn't mean that at all. What if it meant Bryn would die centuries before I did?

"*When all others turn to dust, there will only be you and me,*" I mumbled Khol's words. "That's what you meant, isn't it?" I looked at him sharply. "You don't care that I'm in love with Bryn now, because you think once he dies, it'll be just us, that I won't have a choice." *No, no, no, no, no!* Even the thought of me burying Bryn tore at my insides.

"Yes, you'll come to me eventually, and I'll claim what rightfully belongs to me." Khol's eyes blazed brighter. "I would prefer to have you now, to make you my *Anam Cara*, but I can be patient when I need to be."

So many of Khol's hidden meanings were coming to light. "And why do you think that I'm gonna be yours? Even if I go along with the logic that my magic calls to yours, and that I'm eventually gonna crave more—I'm assuming that has to do with our shared blood—then why you? Why not some other dragon?"

A low animal-like growl rumbled from Khol's chest, his countenance darkening. His voice echoed inside and outside of my head simultaneously. "I am Lord Kholkikos, ruler of the *rua arach*, and you will be *mo Anam Cara*."

"Lord, huh? Well, aren't you special? Isn't there a king or something? Why are you the ruler of, well, of whatever you just said?"

I raised my chin defiantly as I met Khol's gaze. Amusement flitted across his face, curling half of his mouth up. "I do like the fact that you are so...feisty. I find it an extremely attractive, and yet completely annoying, character trait."

I scrunched my face up at him, fighting the urge to stick my tongue out. He chuckled as if he knew what I really wanted to do. *Glad I can amuse.* "*Rua arach* means red dragon, and no, there are no kings, only lords of each faction—the red, the black, the silver, and the gold."

My curiosity piqued again, I temporarily dismissed Khol's display of testosterone-generated possessiveness. "Red dragon—is that what I am, too?"

Khol's took some of my hair in his hand. He wrapped it around his knuckles, pulling me closer. "You may deepen its shade, but you can always tell what faction a dragon is by the color of their hair. The older a dragon is, the deeper the shade of their hair becomes. One day you won't need to darken your hair any longer. It will be this way naturally."

"Really?" I couldn't help the smile that spread across my face, and I immediately chastised myself. With everything else that was going on, I was worried about my hair? *Ugh. Vanity be thy name.* "So, still, that brings me back to my earlier question: Why do you think I'm gonna be yours? Who's to say I wouldn't choose another dragon lord, like maybe a black, or silver, or—is that why you're so hot all the time?" My face heated. "Temperature-wise I mean? And I swear I saw flames in your eyes before. Is that—"

"No," Khol growled. "You belong with me. You will be my *Anam Cara—mo Anam Cara.*" He ignored my other questions, tugging me by my hair closer still. "I am the strongest of the red dragons, and you belong with your own kind."

His lips met mine with a brutality I'd never experienced before. His teeth scraped against mine, his tongue plunging into my mouth to claim and possess, not merely explore. I cried out as he pressed himself into me. His heat engulfed me, making me crave more. *Yes, more. Touch me more. More. I need more of you.*

It felt so right, so perfect as I writhed beneath him. And yet—*Bryn*—I could never betray Bryn so completely. I shoved at Khol, and he reluctantly relinquished possession of me. "You said not without my permission," I hissed at him. "And you don't have it. Only Bryn does."

Khol's eyes erupted in flames and they crackled as they

studied me with inhuman need. "Have you lost your trust in me then?"

I hadn't forgotten what he'd told me: if I lost trust in him, then he'd claim what he felt was his—*me*. But if I trusted him, because he ultimately wanted my trust, he wouldn't cross that line. "No. I trust you to back off now that I've warned you."

Disappointment washed over him, quickly replaced by approval. "You learn the game quickly, my little Seer." With that, he decided to just up and *poof* away again.

"Hey," I called. "I have more questions for you."

The marked silence was my only answer, and I heaved a huge sigh. Lately, every time I thought my life couldn't get any more complicated, the universe seemed to laugh in my face before hurling something new at my feet to deal with.

Chapter 13

C ollege is a joke, just like high school was. What's the point of any of it? What have I learned beyond how exceptionally cruel people can be? I hate college. And I hate all the people enrolled here. I morosely studied the bright red scroll on the wall outside one of my classes proclaiming *P.J. Stone is a slut.* It was obviously placed there for my benefit, the culprit probably somebody like Eddie, who wished the writing on the wall was just that.

Maybe a couple broken fingers will keep my tormentor from a repeat offense. Whoever said violence isn't the answer obviously didn't attend community college. A half dragon, half Seer with a pesky alien invasion problem to worry about shouldn't have to deal with such bullshit.

"Hey." Jeremy's greeting pulled me from my inner musings of vigilante justice.

I swiveled around, trying to use my body to block the script from his view. "Hey," I muttered back. My face heating when I spotted the anger burning in his eyes. Obviously, I hadn't moved fast enough to hide anything.

He pushed around me, scowling down at the wall. "Who the hell did this?" he asked through clenched teeth.

I shrugged, dropping my head. "Could be any one of many. Who can keep track of everyone who thinks I'm a slut at this school?"

Jeremy's scowl deepened. "Yeah, they just wish you were, from what I hear."

"My thoughts exactly." I started walking, hoping he would follow. I was tired of staring at the stupid wall.

"Well, at least it's the end of the day, and with any luck, the janitor will have it cleaned off by morning," Jeremy added.

"Yeah, okay, there are night classes though," I mumbled, my mood too dark to be cheered up. My day had sucked once again. It was beginning to follow a pretty routine schedule of me being ostracized intermingled with being harassed. I might as well don a huge letter A on my chest to complete my transformation to the most hated girl in town.

What really got me was that there were plenty of girls who actually did sleep around, and none of them were being persecuted the way I was. Not that I wanted them to be either. I was all about sexual empowerment after all, even if the people in my world where a bit behind the times when it came to feminism. It was just that the entire situation didn't make sense to me. I figured if I actually were what everyone was accusing me of, then no one would say anything, but because it was a lie, everyone was torturing me for something I didn't do. *Ugh. Fucking idiots.*

"So when do I get my second date?" Jeremy asked as he slid my bag off my shoulder. He lifted it like it weighed next to nothing, meanwhile I'd been like the damn Leaning Tower of Pisa.

As I studied Jeremy, a revelation hit me. Bryn was probably the hottest guy I'd ever laid eyes on, and he was mine. Now that Bryn was gone, Jeremy, the new hot guy, was falling all over himself to date me. Having seen myself in the mirror one or two times in the past nineteen years, I finally understood why I'd been labeled a slut. Of course no one could explain Bryn and Jeremy's interest in any other way—I had to be some kind of super slut. I groaned. *No wonder.*

"What?" Jeremy said. "Too soon? Don't forget though, you did agree. You can't take it back now."

I rolled my eyes. Obviously, my reputation was of little concern to him. All Jeremy was worried about was locking me down for his, same as Khol. Too bad neither one of them would acknowledge the fact that I was already taken by Bryn. "No, it's not that. It's just that something just occurred to me, and well, I think you wanting to date me isn't exactly helping my cause around town and in school lately."

Why do I have to care what anyone thinks about me? I shouldn't. I know that. It's just the name calling is accompanied by such hate and I kind of enjoy people liking me, call me shallow. Plus, I have this weird obsession with the truth, call me crazy, too.

Jeremy frowned. "You're not trying to find a way to wiggle out of our date, are you?"

"If I said no, would you believe me?" I batted my eyelashes, donning my best innocent face.

"Yeah, no, not even for a second." Jeremy laughed.

"Well, even if I am trying to wiggle out of said date, the other part is still true. You're not helping my reputation by wanting to date me."

"Mmm hmm. And I guess you're now gonna try and enlighten me as to how."

"Of course. The explanation is simple, all you have to do is to look at me, and then look at both you and Bryn." I waved my hand in the classic etcetera motion to let him know he should be able to continue with my line of thought on his own.

"I've never seen Bryn, and I couldn't pick him out of a lineup, but I still get what you're implying." He narrowed his eyes at me. "It's absolutely ridiculous."

"No, it's not. I know what I look like. Of course, everyone thinks I have to be using some kind of sexual mojo in order to get the two of you interested. There's no other logical explanation in their minds."

Jeremy stopped, pivoting on his heel to face me, his expression intense, angry almost. "You obviously need glasses."

He crowded me until I was pressed up against the nearest wall, his arms caging me in. I noticed that the few people lingering in the hallway, stopped to stare. *Great, this is all I need.* But none of that mattered when Jeremy's lips met mine. The moment the connection was made between the two of us, my mind blanked completely. His tongue tangled with mine, dancing within my mouth, making it hard not to curve myself around him. A small moan hummed in my throat, escaping when his power rose up sharply. It was if it was trying to coax mine out to play. Somehow, I found the strength to resist.

As he slowly pulled away, his face still too close for comfort, I stared into his deep brown eyes. *Huh. I never noticed they have gold flecks in them.* "You're stunning," he murmured, pressing another soft kiss to my lips. "Everyone's just jealous." Biting my lip, I ducked under his arm to make my escape. I made a mad dash for the main doors.

As I hurriedly made my way down the front steps of my school, a male voice called out to me, "Hey, P.J., after you're done with your latest play-thing, you should gimme a call."

I whipped my head around to spot Evan Thompson leaning against the railing. *Well, what do you know? He finally noticed me.* I waved my middle finger at him. He laughed. "Yep, you guessed right. That's exactly what I had in mind."

I didn't have the energy to deal with Evan and his sophomoric attempts to be clever. I turned my attention away from him, picking up my pace. *I just wanna go home.*

The world in front of me wavered, my head spinning

as an impending vision loomed. Gripping my bag tighter, I pinched my arm over and over in an attempt to stave it off, because if I went down, I was going down hard. *I hope I don't crack my head open.* Clutching at things blindly, I fumbled for something—anything to hold me up as my knees buckled. Abruptly I was yanked up and out of my body, my awareness going elsewhere.

It felt similar to what it might be like to stand in the middle of a 3D movie, as if I could reach out and touch everything, and yet I knew it wasn't real. I found myself in the middle of a high school, similar to my old one, but not mine. Students trudged by, making their way to their classrooms. If I had to guess, I'd say it was early morning because of the way everyone was making their way inside through the front doors.

My attention snagged on a boy standing a few feet away from me. He pretty much had the market cornered on the whole Emo look, topping it off with a long black trench coat. My gaze roamed over him, not sure why I found him so interesting. Until I focused in on his face. I gasped. One of those alien creatures was riding along inside of him. I could see the alien shining through from the inside, and yet the features of the boy weren't any different on the outside. As it had before, the dual imagery freaked me out, completely transfixing me.

Emo Boy reached into his trench coat, like it was the most natural thing in the world and pulled out a twelve-gauge shotgun. Screams of shock, pain, and utter surprise played in tandem with each shot that rang out in the small hallway. But I didn't look at the carnage that was all around us, no. Instead, I stared at the small ghost of a smile turning up the corners of Emo Boy's lips, even though the creature within him beamed.

I attempted to spring forward to tackle them when he stopped to reload, but I found myself unable to move. I was stuck in one spot. Panic welled up within me until I remembered I wasn't really there, that it was all a vision. With that realization, I was yanked away from the scene, but not before I zeroed in on the lifeless body of a girl lying on the floor in front of me. She was in a uniform, a cheerleader's warm-up uniform to be exact, a red and gold Indian decal emblazed on the front of her jacket. I committed the images to memory, knowing it would be important. I wouldn't have been sent the vision otherwise. Before I could see more, everything suddenly went black.

VOICES FILTERED into my subconscious as I began to wake up. "Don't move her. She could be injured from the fall," a guy's voice, older, probably a faculty member, commanded.

"Why'd she pass out? She was just walking and then boom," a girl's voice chimed in.

"She'll be fine. I'll take care of her," Jeremy's voice stated calmly. "I've seen this happen before, low blood sugar. I'll take her home and make sure she sees her doctor." Strong arms picked me up, followed by the steady rhythm of walking jostled me. My head lolled against someone I assumed was Jeremy. Surprisingly, no one put up any protest, not even the faculty member.

"Hey, wait up," another male voice called, but Jeremy didn't break his stride. "I said to wait up."

"Yeah, I don't think so," Jeremy snapped, although I felt us suddenly come to a halt.

"She had a vision, didn't she? I usually don't sense that kind of thing, but I could almost feel the energy around her. It's the only thing it could have been, but I thought she hadn't come into her powers yet."

"Get out of my way," Jeremy's voice vibrated with anger. We started moving again, and I thought whoever it was had gone away, but I was wrong.

"Do you think it was important? The vision she had? She must be pretty strong for me to sense it."

Jeremy sighed, obviously realizing the same thing I had: this guy wasn't going away until he got some answers. "Yeah, she's stronger than even I thought, and I can sense a ton more stuff than most Gatekeepers."

"Yeah? Huh."

"Yeah."

"Well, all right, I guess I should get going then."

"It's about time," I grumbled, letting Jeremy know I was awake. My eyelids fluttered open to meet his concerned gaze. The gold flecks in his eyes danced in the light.

"You feeling better?"

"I feel fine. Just drained, like I need a nap or

something." Jeremy nodded, his expression pensive. "You can put me down now, you know. I'm perfectly capable of walking on my own."

Jeremy smiled down at me, his eyes sparkling. "I was kind of enjoying having you in my arms."

I slapped at his shoulder. "Well, the fun is over. Put me down." He reluctantly set me on my feet. I swayed ever so slightly, reaching for his arm for support. Quicker than I had time to orient myself, Jeremy swooped me right back up into his arms. "Hey!" I protested.

"I'm not gonna have you fall over and actually hurt yourself. You were really lucky you didn't crack your head open on the pavement before. You need to learn how to control your visions better."

I shot him a death glare. "They're kind of new, and for whatever reason, whenever you kiss me, your power seems to feed them or something." Growling under my breath, I snapped, "So stop kissing me, and I shouldn't have any more problems."

"Or I could only kiss you when you're lying down." Jeremy chuckled, obviously finding himself very amusing. *That makes one of us.*

"Not gonna happen."

"Okay, how about leaning against a wall?" His eyes twinkled mischievously. I ignored the part of me that thought he was being kind of cute. That part of me was stupid.

"You know, I really don't have time for this. I have a vision to figure out and..." And what? What could I do except talk everything over with Khol as I'd been doing with my other visions? Unless... "And—and stop it," I whispered. Because that's what I really wanted to do. Stop it. I was tired of being a bystander in life, wasn't I? *The time for action is now.* Somehow, I just knew my vision was of the future. And if it hadn't happened yet, there was still time to stop it.

He glanced at me in confusion as he continued to walk. "That's not really your job yet. Leave it to the other Seers, the ones that have had years of training and experience."

"Yeah, that's kind of the problem. I think I'm the only one getting these visions."

"How is that possible?" Jeremy's eyebrows practically touched his hairline.

I mulled over how much I should reveal to Jeremy. I'd been in a similar situation with him before, and I had decided to go with the truth. The question was, should I again? After a quick internal argument and then deliberation, I decided that I ultimately had nothing to lose. If he didn't believe me, then at least maybe he'd think I was crazy and leave me alone. He'd either go away or help me. It was pretty much win-win, as far as I was concerned.

So I told him about my visions, leaving Khol's involvement out of the equation. Khol was my deep, dark secret, along with my recently discovered half dragon status. Of course, I wouldn't have been able to tell Jeremy those parts anyways, being that Khol had made it physically impossible to even utter his name out loud.

"Holy shit," Jeremy breathed when I'd finally finished. "You're telling the truth. I can tell these kinds of things, plus I could tell you had a real vision back there...holy shit."

He seemed to be handling it better than I'd hoped but with a generous helping of shock heaped on top. I stayed quiet while he processed. I could practically see the millions of thoughts running through his mind, and when he came to a decision.

A mask of determination settled onto his face. "What do you need me to do?"

And just like that, I have another ally.

"You—you wanna help me?" I stammered, surprised, despite me having hoped for just this outcome.

"Umm... Yeah, of course I'm gonna help you. I'm not just gonna let you run off trying to deal with this stuff by yourself."

"Yeah—uh—well—" I clicked my tongue and then grimaced. "I don't actually have a plan. More like a plan to have a plan."

We arrived at my front door, and he gingerly set me back on my feet, handing me my bag. "Can I come in? To talk about this?"

I chewed the inside of my cheek. "No, we better go around back so my parents can't hear. Whatever we plan, we can't let them know."

Jeremy nodded. "Good idea." He bent down to scoop me up again, and I hastily sidestepped him.

"I'm feeling much better now, and if my parents see you carrying me, they're gonna freak out, even if my mom does like you being here with me." *Liked him being here with me was the understatement of the year. If she could marry me off to Jeremy this instant, she would.*

He frowned. "Yeah, okay. I guess I can see your point."

I nonchalantly made my way around the back of the house. *La, la, la, no plotting or anything suspicious about to happen here.* Jeremy kept in step beside me, walking just a touch too close for my comfort. He was probably afraid I was going to topple over again. It was nice to feel cared for, but sometimes the men in my life took things a bit too far.

Um ... what? The men in my life? When did I start thinking of Khol, Jeremy, and Bryn as *the men in my life?* Bryn should be the only man in my life, at least if I was only counting from a romantic perspective. Nausea roiled my system and my gut twisted, but I managed to swallow it down because I had more important things to worry about at the moment, like saving innocent lives. An image of the dead cheerleader flashed briefly in my mind.

Jeremy settled beside me against the same tree that we had been under the other day when he'd had our little... kiss. It'd been a bit more than that though. My face heated at the memory. *Don't think about it, dumbass.*

"That was some kiss, huh?" I glanced up at him and blanched. It didn't matter why. I shouldn't be spending more time with him after that kiss. Every moment I spent with Jeremy or Khol was a small betrayal of Bryn, and yet I kept doing it. *What's wrong with me?*

"Yeah, I don't really wanna talk about that. We're here to figure out what to do about my vision." I closed off my emotions, meeting Jeremy's inquisitive gaze with cold indifference.

"And when exactly were you planning on filling me in?" Jenna's angry voice came from behind me. "I wouldn't know anything if not for the local friendly woodland creatures."

Closing my eyes, I sucked in a sharp breath through my nose and counted to three. When I snapped my eyes back open, I wasn't any less annoyed. "Nosy rodents are more like it. Are you having me followed all the time by them now? Because that's so not okay, Jenna."

"It's the only way I can find anything out from you lately." She lifted up a finger. "I would never have known about Bryn." She lifted up a second finger. "I would never have known about that other guy who you can't talk about." She added a third finger. "I would never have known about your visions, and"—she waved her hands at Jeremy— "when were you gonna tell me about him? Are you still my best friend or what?"

I crossed my arms over my chest, sighing again. "Of course I am. But that doesn't mean I have to tell you absolutely everything."

"That's exactly what it means!" Jenna cried out, clearly frustrated.

"Umm…" Jeremy chimed in. "What other guy that you can't talk about? Do I have more competition than I know about?"

"No," I snapped.

"Yes," Jenna said at the exact same time.

Jeremy frowned, looking back and forth between the two of us. "Well, which is it?"

I threw my hands in the air. "Bryn doesn't have any competition. He's the one I love, so all you guys can stop sticking your tongues down my throat because it isn't gonna do any good. When all is said and done, Bryn is who I'm gonna be with."

Jeremy's frown deepened. "So you're kissing this other guy, too?"

"No!" I exclaimed. "He's kissing me, just like you are. I'm not kissing anybody!"

"Does he go to school with us?" He snorted. "And you were trying to blame me for not helping your reputation." Jeremy stood and stalked closer to me. "All I want is a little honesty here."

"Yeah, what he said," Jenna threw her two cents in.

I gritted my teeth, trying to swallow back my anger. We had to get through this so we could come up with a plan to stop my latest vision from coming true. "No, he doesn't go to our school, he's—well, he's—" I still couldn't physically utter a word out loud about Khol. I growled under my breath, mentally cursing the stupid dragon. He was making my complicated life that much more difficult. "I'm bound magically not to be able to talk about him. The only reason Jenna knows anything about him at all is because of her little spies."

Jeremy glanced at Jenna for confirmation. "That's true." She nodded. "And that's another reason why I have to sic my spies on you: because who knows what else is going on with you lately that you can't tell me about? Your life has gotten extremely weird lately."

"Says the girl who has rodents spying for her," I grumbled under my breath.

"All right. I get it, okay," Jeremy said, his expression closing off. "Your life is very complicated right now, and apparently I have more competition than I originally thought. I guess I can deal with that."

"I really don't care if you can or cannot deal with it, Jeremy. I said I'd go on a second date with you, that's it. You know how I feel about Bryn. And this other—guy—he knows, too. It's not my fault you both seem to have thick skulls and aggressive tongues." I took a couple calming breaths, wondering for the millionth time who that ever worked for, and why I kept doing it. "None of that is relevant right now. What's important is figuring out what to do about my vision so we can save some innocent lives."

"I agree," Khol's deep voice boomed across the clearing, startling me.

All three of our heads whipped around, tracking Khol as he strode towards us in all of his otherworldly beauty. Although I wasn't really sure if I could really describe it as *otherworldly* since he was, in fact, from our world. *Dragonly* beauty? But I didn't know what other dragons looked like. It could just be Khol who was so magnificent. It was kind of hard to judge an entire species after only meeting one of its kind.

"Focus, my little Seer, you will have time to contemplate my good looks later," Khol said, mirth dancing in his heated gaze.

"I'm not doing anything of the sort. You're not a mind reader, so stop pretending to be," I snapped, my cheeks heating. I was beginning to wonder if he actually was able to read my mind and just wasn't telling me. It would certainly explain a lot.

"No, you just broadcast your emotions loudly, my little Seer." That was twice in a row he'd called me *his little Seer.* I couldn't help but think it was partly for Jeremy's benefit, who currently appeared to be readying himself to do battle with Khol.

"Oh. Oh my God. You didn't tell me—" Jenna scooted closer to me, digging her nails into my arm. "You didn't tell me he was so hot," she whispered.

"I couldn't describe him to you, remember?" Jenna's entire body trembled. I wouldn't have been the slightest bit surprised if she suddenly ripped off all of her clothes so she could offer herself to Khol right then and there. It would have been funny, if I suddenly didn't want to smack her. I didn't want Khol for myself, but—*Jenna does not get to touch him.*

I stepped out of her grasp, approaching Khol. "What

are you doing here? I thought you didn't want anyone to know about you?"

"It had become unpreventable now. I can't let you risk yourself like you're planning. I'll simply bind them like I did you." Khol glared at Jeremy, his body mirroring Jeremy's fight stance. *Friggin' ridiculous, the both of them.*

"He can bind me anytime he wants," Jenna purred.

"Shut up, Jenna," I hissed. "Stay away from him."

"Oh. Oh, I see. You think he belongs to you, too. Not fair."

"No, I don't think that, it's just…" *It's just what?* Why was the thought of Jenna going after Khol pissing me off so much?

"I do belong to her, little Speaker, as she belongs to me," Khol rumbled, his eyes still locked on Jeremy.

"Like hell she does," Jeremy said. "I don't even know *what* you are. Your energy is like nothing I've ever seen. P.J., Jenna, get behind me."

Khol laughed. "I would never hurt her, but if I did seek to, you could not stop me…*boy.*"

Jeremy glanced over at me. "I said to get behind me." His jaw muscles jumped and he ground his teeth together.

"Paige," Khol rumbled, his voice going low and smooth. "Come to me. If you want to stop your vision from becoming reality, I'm the one you should seek for help, not a *boy* like him. I won't stand by and watch you be injured."

"Paige," Khol said again, his voice echoing in my head.

"Yes?" I whispered.

Khol's power rolled out of him, wrapping itself around me, pummeling all of my senses. Every cell in my body vibrated in yearning for something I didn't quite understand. I was on fire, and yet I was freezing. My chest heaved as I rapidly panted.

Before, when Jeremy kissed me, his power had tried to coax mine to come out and play, and I was able to eventually push it aside. But Khol's power demanded where Jeremy's coaxed, and I was unable to deny its command. *More...more...I need more of this. Whatever it is. I need more.*

Khol's power called to the dragon half of me, a different side than Jeremy had been able to touch. In that moment, I was connected to Khol in a way that made me want to lose myself in his sweet embrace. *He'll make everything better. He knows exactly what I need.* I could almost hear his thoughts, but not quite. He wanted me, just like I wanted him. He would take away all my pain. *Yes.*

"It's natural for you to want me to claim you. If you were a full-blooded *rua arach*, you'd already bear my *Anam Cara* mark." His voice was a gentle caress inside my mind that only I could hear.

My vision tunneled, narrowing so I could see nothing but Khol and his beautiful visage. I began moving forward, consumed by the urge to give myself over to him —to accept what he was offering me. *Yes. I need to sink into his welcoming embrace, to taste the fire of his touch, to be consumed by Khol completely.*

"Tell me who you yearn to be with. Tell me who you want to lay claim to you," Khol continued to speak in my mind, but something else was there too. It was like a chant, an undercurrent of a song, rolling around in the back of my brain...over and over.

Suddenly my vision filled with an image of Bryn. It was so realistic I thought for a second that he was standing right in front of me. "Bryn." His name spilled from my lips with reverence, like a small prayer to the only man I would ever truly love. His sea storm eyes churned for me, threatening to pull me down in their undercurrent. His patented lopsided grin, complete with dimples, weakened my knees. All doubts caused by my want for Khol and Jeremy died instantly. No one would ever possess me the way that Bryn had. He owned my heart, body, and soul. I was his until my dying breath.

"No. That's not possible," Khol growled. My mind went silent, and the image of Bryn disappeared. I cried out in dismay. Even if it wasn't real, I didn't want to lose it. I dropped to my knees, hugging myself. "You will be mine," Khol grated.

I looked up sharply, sensing something about to snap in Khol, something that I couldn't let happen. I met his wild eyes with mine. "I trust you Khol. I trust you to help me with all of this, and I trust you to wait like you said. I trust you."

His iridescent green eyes sparked brighter, his nostrils flaring in distress. "I will not break your trust, but I cannot be in your presence any longer—for the moment."

His breathes were ragged, his voice nothing but a low rasp. "Call for me when you need me…for your plan. I will always be there for you when you need me. No matter what." He met my eyes with a longing so intense I shivered. Then he simply disappeared.

I choked back a sob. Ridding myself of Khol wouldn't be as easy a task as I'd once thought. He wanted me and thought of me as his already. Plus, he wasn't human. What if he eventually lost his patience and hurt Bryn? What if he tried to kill Bryn? I had no idea if a Guardian would be any match for a dragon, and I didn't want to find out. But I couldn't afford to think about any of that at the moment. I needed to focus on figuring out a plan to stop my latest vision from happening.

Wiping at my tears with the back of my arm, I turned towards Jeremy and Jenna. The two of them rushed towards me, but I lifted up my hands to stave them off. "No, I'm fine. And even if I wasn't, we don't have time to worry about it now. We need to figure out what to do about my vision. We have to save all those people."

Jeremy's features were lined with tension, and his gaze seethed with anger. "Fine. But we are gonna have a conversation about what just happened. I need to know how to protect you from—whatever he is."

I wasn't going to argue with Jeremy that it wasn't his place to protect me, or that I didn't think he actually could anyways, so I decided to placate him for the time being. "Okay. But not now."

"And me," Jenna chimed in, studying my face with that

look she got when I felt like she was seeing too much. "I need to know *everything.*" She caught my gaze and narrowed hers at me. Yep, she picked up on a lot more than I'd probably wanted her to. *Damn Speakers.*

I rubbed my temples, a headache blooming. "Yeah, okay, but not now. Now is the time to plan out what we're gonna do to stop my vision."

Jeremy and Jenna nodded in perfect unison. It almost made me want to laugh—almost.

Chapter 14

We were able to figure out the school from my vision by way of the cheerleader's uniform, and by browsing school websites. As luck would have it, the school was only a thirty-minute drive from where we were, which would have given us plenty of time—if it hadn't taken us the entire night to figure out where we were going. Even though Khol had been helpful in figuring out the few visions I had before, for some reason he couldn't get a lock on my latest, which was horribly inconvenient, to say the least.

With all of us packed into Jenna's bright yellow VW Bug, we sped towards our destination. And by all, I meant me, Jenna, Jeremy, and yes, even Khol. Why Khol felt the need to go with us in the car was beyond me. I had a sneaking suspicion it mostly had to do with Jeremy, and maybe a little bit to do with wanting to spend more time with me. Ever since the lifelike vision of Bryn, Khol had been…almost clingy. As if his confidence had been shaken somehow.

"When we get there, you point out the guy to us, and me and Khol will take him out. You and Jenna aren't going anywhere near this mess, in case something goes wrong," Jeremy stated firmly. As if he was the boss or something. *Delusional much?*

"Yeah, sure, whatever," I grumbled.

I was pissed. I wanted to help, too, but after the umpteenth time of me arguing my case, and both Jeremy and Khol threatening to tie me up and not let me go at all, I finally gave in. I should've been happy that they could at least agree about something—but I wasn't. My plan to get off the sidelines wasn't exactly panning out for me.

"Sure, no problem," Jenna added, obviously not feeling as put out by everything as I was. I shot her a glare. Maybe if we'd both argued my point with Jeremy and Khol, we would have won. "Stop glaring at me, P.J. I'm not gonna take your side just for the hell of it. They're kind of right about this one, as much as I hate to admit it."

I glowered out the window. Maybe she was right, but I didn't have to let her know that.

"There is no point for you to be there after you identify this boy from your vision. I would only be worried about you if you were there with us. That could cause me to make a mistake," Khol spoke softly, bringing his warm palm up to touch my cheek from the backseat. I hated the fact that my body wanted to lean into the heat he offered, hated that my body wanted more—so much more—from him.

"Hey. Get your hands off her," Jeremy growled. "She isn't yours."

"Oh, but she is mine, and I will touch her whenever and however I wish." Khol shifted, pushing his massive frame into the space between the front two seats. He cupped the back of my neck, crushing his lips to mine. I barely had time to process what was going on before Khol's tongue successfully laid siege to my mouth. Sparks of heat erupted across my skin, like kindling catching fire, and all coherent thoughts fled my mind. I may have moaned, much to my shame.

The car swerved severely, and Khol broke away from me with a curse.

"Stop! Just stop!" Jenna yelled. "No kissing and no fighting in my car! We're on a mission here, people, and it doesn't include a sword fight over who gets to mouth rape P.J. first!"

I slumped back into my seat, my face warming. "That wasn't my fault, and no one gets to mouth rape me because I already belong to Bryn." And rape? After what nearly happened to me at Ryan's party, the word alone made my flesh crawl. What Khol and Jeremy had done couldn't compare because I craved their touch on some level, even if I hated myself for it.

I peered around the edge of the seat, trying not to roll my eyes when I spotted Khol and Jeremy glaring at each other. *What am I gonna do with the two of them?* They just couldn't seem to get it through their thick skulls that I belonged to Bryn already. They were fighting over a perceived prize that was already claimed. In the end, it didn't matter if my body craved them, my heart only wanted Bryn.

"We're here," Jenna said, throwing the car into park. My head snapped up. The high school in front of us looked pretty much like any other high school. *Except this one apparently had murderous aliens enrolled.*

I gulped, the reality of the situation finally hitting me. *We're gonna do this. We're actually gonna do this.* My gaze locked onto the school, and everything seemed to fall away as I stumbled out of the car. Jeremy and Khol were speaking to me, but I couldn't decipher their words. All of my attention was centered on that school, especially when I saw the girl from my vision—the cheerleader—alive and well, and talking animatedly to a group of girls.

"This is it. This is really the place," I whispered. A large warm hand wrapped around mine, and I looked up to meet Khol's electric green eyes. "Won't your eyes, and well, how you look, stand out too much?" A thought that —as bizarre as it sounded—I hadn't even considered until that moment.

"No," Khol said as he squeezed my hand. "I can appear human when I want to." And just like that, his eyes went matte. I blinked in surprise. They actually looked like regular, everyday, green eyes. Without them, the rest of him appeared relatively normal, too. Well, if you could overlook how drop dead gorgeous he was... So okay, maybe normal wasn't the best word to describe Khol, but he could at least pass for human, like he claimed.

"Why didn't you ever do that before? I mean, at least when you first met me, so I didn't freak out as much?"

"I wanted you to see me as I truly am. I want no secrets between us."

"Oh," I said, flicking my gaze away. *He is good.* And yep, if Bryn weren't in the picture, I'd probably already have given him what he wanted: me.

Clearing my throat, I surveyed the school's surroundings us as we moved closer to the front doors. I glanced back to see Jenna waiting in her car, a scowl darkening her face. I hated to admit it, but I kind of, sort of, wished I were back there with her.

"Ready?" Jeremy asked as I reached for the front door of the school. I lifted my gaze to take in his tense expression, and Khol's almost identical one. I nodded once in confirmation before stepping into the main entrance of the school.

All background noise stopped. A whooshing sound filled my head, as if the ocean was rushing inside my ears, and a weird sense of déjà vu settled over me. I scanned the faces around me, but I didn't see the one I was looking for yet. What I really wanted to do was yell at everyone to run, to warn them that a crazy alien masquerading as one of their peers was about to use them for target practice. And yet I knew it would be useless.

"I don't see him," I whispered.

Khol squeezed my hand, and Jeremy stayed silent. I

knew they were both scrutinizing the crowd for danger, not liking that I had to identify the alien from my vision for them. If this guy didn't show up soon, they would probably carry me back to the car, kicking and screaming, being that they'd both morphed into Neanderthals. *Me Khol. Me Jeremy. Me protect. Me don't care what you want. Grrrr!*

Of course, when I'd almost given up hope, that's when I spotted him. His dark hair hung in his face, and as he walked in the front door, he flipped it out of his eyes, staring straight at me. All of the blood drained from my face, and my throat closed up as panic surge through my veins, the bloody images of my vision replaying in my mind.

The Emo kid's eyes narrowed as he studied me, and then Khol and Jeremy flanking me. My arm rose on its own volition, pointing straight at Emo Alien Boy. "That's him," I squeaked, tugging on Khol's arm. "That's him," I squeaked again.

Khol moved first, shoving me behind him, just as Jeremy reached for his power to do—well, I'm not exactly sure what because Emo Boy wasn't going to hang around to let me find out. He pivoted on his heels and made a mad dash for the front door. "Go!" Khol commanded, "I'll protect her."

Jeremy barely glanced at Khol before he took off running after Emo Boy. I started to move forward in an attempt to engage in the chase, but Khol had other ideas. He swung around, scooped me up in his arms and suddenly we were back in my bedroom. He deposited me on my bed, narrowing his eyes at me, which were glowing again. "Stay," he growled before disappearing.

I stared at the empty spot where Khol had just been, anger slowly bubbling up to the surface of my consciousness. *What the fuck?* Plus, why the hell didn't he just *pop* the lot of us over to the school instead of making us drive if he could transport other people? *Ohhh...That dragon and me are gonna have a looong chat very soon.*

"You get your ass back here right now, Khol!" I hissed into my empty room.

I got no response.

"I know you can hear me or feel me or whatever! Get back here right now!" A few moments went by, and then a few more, and still nothing. Rage vibrated through me. *That's it. I'm not going to just* stay *like Khol demanded. I'm not a goddamn puppy.*

I thundered down the stairs to the kitchen, not bothering to hide the noise since my parents were both at work and under the impression that I was at school. Without hesitation, I scooped up the keys to my father's new car, the one that was too precious for him to drive to work. I wasn't even allowed to breathe on the damn thing, but what he wouldn't know wouldn't hurt him. At least I hoped he wouldn't know when all was said and done.

Slipping into the shiny red Audi, I jammed the keys into the ignition and inhaled deeply. *Ah, new car smell.* I really hoped I didn't wrap it around a telephone pole or run it into a ditch. I certainly wasn't receiving any good driver awards anytime soon. I was lucky I'd passed my driver's test at all—it only took me three tries.

Desperate times and all of that. Well, here goes.

Shrugging internally, I tentatively eased my way out of the garage, which I didn't hit, so that was a step in the right direction. I stopped at the end of the driveway, adjusting the mirrors one more time before peeling out onto the street. My lips turned up in an involuntarily smile as I sped off to my destination. *Thirty minutes? More like fifteen at the rate I'm driving.*

I WAS ABOUT five minutes away from the school when something, or rather someone, caught my attention: Emo Boy. All I could see was the back of his head, and that stupid trench coat as he dashed down the sidewalk, but I was positive it was him. I stomped on the brake, screeching to a halt, causing him to swivel around to look at me. Our eyes met, and both of us froze.

Why haven't Jeremy or Khol caught him? Where the hell are they? And why is Emo boy still out running around? Shouldn't he be hiding at this point or something?

Remaining frozen with uncertainty, I gripped the steering wheel and continued to stare at Emo Boy. A hysterical laugh bubbled up within my chest. *Are we having a staring contest now? Because if so...I might be able to take him.*

The trance broke when Emo Boy reached into his

trench coat. I swore under my breath as he produced the shotgun from its hiding place, raising it to point in my direction.

This is not good. Should I simply duck and cover, or run him down? After all, he was pointing a gun at me. No one would blame me for turning Emo Boy into an emo pancake. The alien inside Emo Boy smiled, and it didn't take a rocket scientist to figure out what was about to happen. I ducked just as the front windshield of my father's car exploded all over me. *Shit. He's definitely gonna notice that.*

Without looking, I slammed my foot down onto the gas pedal, hurtling down the street for a short distance before I smashed into something hard and immovable. My forehead bounced off the steering wheel—hard. More shots rang out, shattering the remaining glass in my father's car. But the fact that I didn't resemble Swiss cheese yet, pointed at Emo Boy's lack of aim and hopefully my chances of survival.

I scrambled to get my seatbelt off while staying slumped down in the seat. Then I slowly pushed the door open, readying myself to make a run for it. My heart threatened to break through my rib cage as adrenaline coursed through my system. *You can do this. You have to.*

Clambering out of the car, I managed to stay low as I scurried across the pavement towards a row of houses. I only made it a few feet before something smacked into the back of my head. Black dots danced in front of my eyes as I hit the ground, my face scraping against the asphalt.

Panic riding me, I desperately clawed the pavement for purchase, managing to pull myself up to all fours.

Abruptly I found myself being shoved back down and rolled onto my back, a hostile Emo Boy looming over me.

"Guess you're out of ammo?" I quibbled, unable to keep my mouth shut apparently, even in a life and death situation.

"How did you know?" Emo Boy snarled as he reached down to grab me by my jacket. "How did you know what I had planned?"

The alien inside Emo Boy seemed to shine forth more brightly from him, and I found myself reaching up to touch his face, driven by some kind of eerie fascination. "Can you see it when you look in the mirror?" I mumbled, now feeling pretty confident I had a concussion. "Or do you even know he's in there? Who has control? Or do you share?"

"You *see*? That's not possible."

I smiled, blinking as something warm and sticky ran into my eye. "Obviously it's not...impossible." Sirens rang out in the distance, signaling that help was on the way. Emo Boy dropped me abruptly, causing me to hit my head on the concrete. "Ow. That's not very nice," I mumbled as my eyes slid shut. "And you didn't even answer my questions."

All went dark.

~

"YOU WERE SUPPOSED to keep her safe," Jeremy's voice vibrated with anger. "Not let her put herself in the goddamned hospital."

"I left her in her bedroom. I thought it was beyond even her to find trouble that quickly," Khol responded flatly. "And do not think for a second it doesn't cause me just as much pain to see her like this." Strong emotion flared in his voice as it went low and gruff.

"She's gonna be fine, guys. No need to fight," Jenna said, obviously trying to play the mediator.

"Yeah, but she could have died. We don't even know how close she came," Jeremy grated. "He was *shooting* at her."

"But she's not dead. She's fine. That's the important part," Jenna interjected. "And I don't want the two of you fighting and scolding her when she wakes up either." Khol grunted, the sound distinct and almost animal-like. Jeremy opted for silence as his response.

I inwardly sighed as I worked on opening my eyes. "Does my dad know about his car yet?" I muttered. At least my mouth was working. It seemed nothing ever put it out of commission.

"Your parents are on the way," Jenna answered just as I finally managed to peel my eyelids open. She was sitting in a chair next to my hospital bed, while both Khol and Jeremy were standing towards the foot. Both of their faces held a mixture of worry and anger.

"I told you to stay," Khol growled.

I narrowed my eyes at him. "Excuse you? I'm not yours

to order around, contrary to what you might think." I tried to cross my arms over my chest, but the IV got in the way. I turned my anger on Jeremy next. "And don't you say a word either. I do *what* I want *when* I want."

"I wasn't aware you wanted to get yourself killed," Jeremy snapped, crossing his arms over his chest, his brown eyes flashing with fresh anger.

I tried to sit up, but the black dots were back, accompanied by a sudden wave of nausea. "That wasn't what I was going for," I mumbled as I slouched back down into my pillow. My stomach settled after a few moments.

Khol stalked around the side of the bed, coming to stand beside me, and blocking out my view of Jenna. "Let me help you."

"How?" I asked, my eyes roaming over his set jaw line and tense muscles warily.

"I can heal you, if you let me."

"Then why the hell haven't you healed her already?" Jeremy demanded.

Khol ground his teeth together as he struggled to ignore Jeremy. He focused in on me completely. "I have to kiss you...touch you..."

Understanding dawned. "Oh," I whispered.

"Absolutely not," Jeremy said as understanding dawned on him as well. "I'm not gonna stand by and watch you maul her in the name of healing. It's the most—"

"Then don't watch," Jenna snapped. "He needs to do what he needs to do to heal her, Jeremy. Would you rather her stay how she is? Would—"

"Fine," Jeremy groused. "I'll be outside waiting for her parents. Tell me when he's done *healing* her." I watched Jeremy stalk out of the room so I didn't have to meet Khol's gaze. My heart had quadrupled in time the moment I realized what was needed to heal me. A part of me was excited by just the idea and eager to get started, while the rest of me felt like a traitor to Bryn for feeling that way.

Jenna cleared her throat. "I'll be outside, too." She turned, winking at me. "Try not to do anything I wouldn't do."

Staring after her, I gulped audibly. "So..." I said, the tips of my ears warming as I met Khol's heated gaze. "Umm..."

He leaned down, pressing his lips to mine gently. The familiar spike of heat slammed into me ... and then intensified. It was if his body was on fire, the flames from him surrounding every part of me. His large hands cupped my face, moving to run through my hair. A tingling sensation, coupled with the heat, skittered through me, healing and exciting in equal parts. It felt good. *Better than good. Amazing. Better than amazing...*

A small moan escaped from me as his hands slid down my torso, skimming over my hardened nipples on the way. *Wait. No. Too much. Stop! He needs to stop.* Bryn was the only one who had ever done anything beyond kissing me, and it should stay that way. It needed to stay that way. But my mouth was too busy kissing Khol to protest out loud. While his healing magic continued to make me whole, Khol's hands slowly explored my body.

I panted heavily, gasping when Khol slipped his hand underneath my gown to touch me between my legs. "No..." I moaned. I had become the cliché of the woman who knew she shouldn't be doing something and only gave a meager protest to ease her own guilt. I didn't really want Khol to stop. Or did I? Did I really want Khol touching me the way he was, helping me betray Bryn in the worst possible way? The answer of course was no, and yet I couldn't seem to help myself. *Stop. Stop. Please stop.* Another moan escaped my lips.

"Let me make you my *Anam Cara*. Let me lay claim to you," Khol rumbled, his voice roughened with promises of pleasure.

Alarm bells went off in my head. He didn't just mean sex—no, he wanted to claim me for his dragon mate—his *Anam Cara*. He would take me away from Bryn forever if he could, and I couldn't let that happen. I would surely die without Bryn.

My head cleared and I managed to push through my haze of lust. "No. Stop." I shoved at Khol's hand and scooted away from him, my face heating with embarrassment. I couldn't believe I'd let him touch me that way. Bryn should be the only one. Tears leaked out of the corners of my eyes. "That's not what I want..." At least not with him. *Bryn—only Bryn.* I'd been confused by the healing and my stupid hormones, but my head was on straight again. I didn't want Khol. I wanted Bryn.

"With me," Khol stated flatly, picking up on my

emotions. "It's not what you want with me, at least not yet."

"Never," I whispered, pulling the sheet up to cover me as if it were some kind of shield.

Khol's lips turned up into a small smile, his eyes blazing brighter. "Never say never, my little Seer. I'm sure you've heard that expression before." And as usual, he just disappeared.

Jenna and Jeremy picked that exact moment to come flying back into the room. *Thank God they didn't come back a few seconds earlier.* My face heated again. I was ashamed for letting things go so far with Khol. Why did I have such a hard time resisting him when I didn't really want him, at least not like I did Bryn? The guilt caused my shame to creep up to new previously unrealized levels.

Khol and Jeremy kept taking me to new lows emotionally. Had it only been such a short time ago that I'd been a virgin and had barely been kissed? I'd given myself to Bryn because I loved him, not just because my body craved his. I'd always wanted any relationship I had to go beyond the physical, I'd always wanted *more*. More... That word mocked me now, thanks to Khol. He'd said I'd come to crave it, and now I had.

"Oh my God!" Jenna exclaimed. "We just saw the news in the waiting room and—"

"I see you're all *healed*," Jeremy said, his voice dripping disdain. "That was pretty fast. And where is he? Did he leave with what he wanted?"

My face went slack as his tone fully registered. *Why the hell is he—oh. Right. I see it now.* Buried beneath his anger was accusation. He now thought what everyone else at school did—that I was a slut. Fresh tears rolled down my cheeks. "He's gone. And no, he didn't get what he wanted," my voice cracked. I liked Jeremy. And I liked that he respected me— or *had* respected me. I averted my gaze, no longer wanting to witness the look of incrimination that was directed at me.

"Hey," snapped Jenna. "Don't you talk to her that way. She's been through enough today, don't you think?"

Jeremy sighed, his anger melting away. "Yeah, I'm sorry, P.J. I didn't mean it. It's just that—I don't know—I guess I'm just jealous is all. And who the hell is Khol anyways?" His voice rose with fresh anger, "We all know he isn't human. How do we know we can trust him?"

I lifted my gaze to meet his. "We can," I said simply.

"He wants you for himself. He uses every opportunity to try and push his advantage. He—"

"You mean like you do?"

Jeremy opened and closed his mouth, bringing his hands up to push through his hair. "Okay, fine, you might have a point." At least he had the decency to look sheepish, something that Khol most certainly never did.

"Back to what we saw on the news," Jenna prodded impatiently.

Jeremy stood up straighter, his manners suddenly all business. "There was a shooting at another school today. Add that in with what happened to you, which made the news, by the way, and all of a sudden Senator Bill

Wexington has a lot firmer platform to lean on for gun control."

I considered the information that Jeremy had just shared as well as what I knew so far about the aliens. They wanted control of our world–they wanted to rule us, and there was no better way to start than to render us powerless, defenseless. They could situate themselves in positions of power, as in Senator Bill Wexington's case, and then push for bigger government control. Once they eliminated our will to fight back, they could make us do anything they wanted. It had all the beginnings of a conspiracy theory, except for one part: it was real.

I swore under my breath. The more things like the shooting that happened, the more people would be afraid, and there was no better way to scare people than to attack children. "Shit," I swore again. "And I'm guessing this is just the beginning."

"My thoughts exactly," Jeremy said.

"Yeah," Jenna added morosely. "I think we're in a bit over our heads."

I raised my eyebrows at her. "You think?" I almost wanted to laugh at the ridiculousness of the situation. There we were, a bunch kids in community college, and we were going to try and save our world—literally. *World Saving For Dummies, anyone know where I can get a copy?*

"We need to find a way to get them out of people's bodies. We can't exactly go around killing them. Plus, I would feel kind of guilty killing the people they were in," I mumbled, thinking out loud.

"What are they though? I mean really?" Jenna asked.

"I don't know, but they aren't from our world. That's not much to go on." I frowned, considering how little we did know about everything, even though it was a ton more than anyone else did.

"How are we supposed to fight them if we don't even know what they are?" Jeremy asked.

It was then I realized that Jenna and Jeremy were both looking to me for answers I just didn't have. They were expecting me to tell them what to do. How did I end up in that position? I wasn't any kind of leader. I was a chocoholic, boy crazy, technically still teenager, who was maybe a tad narcissistic.

I slumped back into the hospital bed. "I don't know."

Jeremy's face softened. He walked over and sat on the edge of the bed, taking my hand in his. "Let me be there for you. I'll help any way I can." A jolt of energy emanating from his fingertips shot up through my arm and raced through my body. I was suddenly extremely revved up, as if I'd just downed a couple energy drinks. I met Jeremy's eyes with question. He chuckled. "Better than coffee, huh? I'm very good at what I do." His eyes darkened as the double entendre left his mouth.

"What are we gonna tell your parents?" Jenna asked. "We need to hurry up and sync our stories before they get here."

I tugged my hand back from Jeremy, who frowned at the move. "Crap. How did I almost forget about that? How the hell am I supposed to explain any of it?"

"A vision," Jeremy stated calmly as he tried to recapture my hand in his. "Tell them you had a vision about something bad that was gonna happen, but it was so jumbled you didn't know what to think, so you just headed over that way to figure it out and voila."

"Yeah, that sounds like it just might work," I said, trying to keep my hand out of Jeremy's clutches without being too obvious about it. Although the wry look he was giving me told me he knew exactly what I was doing, and yet he persisted. *Thickheaded Gatekeeper.*

"Is that what we're going with? Because your parents are almost here." Jenna fidgeted nervously while looking down at the palm of her hand.

"How do you know they're almost here?" I asked, eyeing her palm with curiosity.

She lifted her head, and a small bug of some sort rose into the air. "I had some of the local insects keeping a lookout for me."

She smiled when I grimaced. "Fabulous. Now I have to worry about flies on the wall spying on me—literally? You Speakers are a lot more dangerous than anyone gives you credit for."

"Most people don't appreciate the advantages that having one of us on their team can bring them." Jenna smiled with pride.

Jeremy looked at her, running his hand through his tousled hair. "Yeah, I never really thought about what it really means to be a Speaker."

"Most don't." Jenna lifted her chin, meeting Jeremy's

gaze head on. "We're a lot more than just some weirdos that talk to animals. We're just as important as—"

"P.J.!" my mom exclaimed as she burst into the room with my dad hot on her heels. Jeremy backed away from the bed as my mom rushed to my side. "Are you okay, peanut? They said you were shot at and—" My mom's face crumpled up as she began to cry. "I was so worried."

I sat up straighter, letting my mom take me in her arms. "I'm fine, Mom. I shouldn't even be here anymore." *Thanks to Khol.* How was I going to explain my miraculous recovery to the doctors so I could go home?

She leaned back, running her eyes over every inch of me in that classic mom stare, as if she would know just by looking at me if I was okay. "How are you feeling?"

I pushed her hands away with annoyance. "Fine. Like I said. Maybe you guys can talk to the doctor so I can get out of here."

"What happened?" my dad demanded. I wanted to roll my eyes. What was it with men getting angry when you get injured? It was like they all get insulted that you let something happen to yourself they couldn't protect you from.

"Can't we talk about this later? I really just wanna go home." I implored my mom with my eyes.

"Well, I guess I'm gonna get going," Jenna said. I'd almost forgotten she was still there.

Jeremy cleared his throat to remind me of his presence as well. "Yeah, me, too. Call me if you need anything, P.J."

He met my eyes with meaning. "I'll get a ride home with Jenna."

"Bye." I waved my hand meekly. *Great, now I don't have the friend buffer.* "How about us going home?" I added hopefully, looking at my mom again.

"Of course, peanut, I'll just go find the doctor." My mom buzzed out of the room, already excited to get me home. She probably was more interested in what was going on between Jeremy and me, if her eyes lighting up with what he said was any indication. Luckily for me, she'd most likely gloss right over what had happened with my dad's car and Emo Boy, jumping right in to grill me about Jeremy. The lesser of two evils, I supposed.

"Why weren't you in school, and who told you that you could take my car?" I didn't look up from my sheet and fidgeted nervously with it and my IV. "Answer me, young lady." The tone in my dad's voice told me the big throbbing vein in his forehead was making an appearance, and even though I hated to admit it, when that thing made an appearance, it was time to run for cover.

"I had a vision," I mumbled.

"What?"

"I said I had a vision," I stated a little bit louder, although not much.

A loud crash echoed through the room, and I snapped my head up. My dad had knocked over a small table that had held ice water and some cups. *Yep, he's pretty pissed.* "You had a vision that had something to do with a kid and a shotgun, and you drove *towards* the danger?"

"It was all jumbled up—the vision," I squeaked.

"That's not an excuse. You should have told us about it before you went running off to put yourself in danger," my dad snarled vehemently.

"And then what? What would you guys have done? If you believed me at all?" Anger shot through my veins, giving me courage to face off with my dad.

"You dragged Jenna and Jeremy into this with you, didn't you? And where were they while you were getting shot at?"

"We saved innocent lives!" I yelled.

"I don't care about those lives—just yours," my dad yelled back at me.

"I'm sure their families don't feel the same way!" I gulped in air, trying to remain relatively calm, although it wasn't working. "I made a difference!"

My dad gritted his teeth and stared at me. "We'll discuss your punishment when we get home. It's going to be a doozy, let me tell you. You've proven time and time again recently that you can't be trusted."

I narrowed my eyes and laughed darkly at him. "Oh, really? What are you gonna do, forbid me to see the love of my life? Oh wait—you already did that. You've already ruined my life. Do your worst!" I screamed the last part at him, completely losing any control.

My mom chose that moment to come back into the room. "The doctor is going to be in to check you out soon, and then we'll see about getting you home." When neither my father nor I responded, she looked back and forth between the two of us. "Now what's this about?"

"I was just reminding Dad here that there wasn't any punishment that you guys could give me that would be worse than what you've already done by ripping Bryn out of my life," I growled, still glaring at my dad.

"But I thought you and Jeremy were—"

"Were what, Mom?" I snapped my head around, spearing her with a look of utter disgust. "Did you really think I'd get over Bryn so fast?" I raised my hand to keep her from responding. "No, wait. Don't answer that. Of course you did. But let me just tell you this. Even if Bryn were out of the picture—which he isn't—Jeremy would be my *third* choice. Not that any of that really matters because I still want Bryn."

"Third? But who?" my mom demanded.

I was going for shock value at the moment, and I knew the perfect way to twist the knife. "One of my kind. You know, what my *real* father is."

My mom staggered back as if I'd slapped her. "No—you can't."

"Why? Tell me why I can't be with someone of my kind if I wanna be. None of the rules of duty apply anymore now that I know. So you see, you might as well let Bryn come back because he's the lesser of the two evils now, isn't he?"

"How did you even meet one of them?" my mom asked, her face stricken.

"He sought me out. My power called to him,

apparently waking him up." I paused to let the news sink in fully. "You don't even know what I am."

My dad spoke up, my mom seemingly made speechless from my revelation. "You're our daughter. That's all we need to know."

"But I'm not *your daughter*, not really," I said as I met my dad's sad eyes. The look of anguish on his face almost made me crack, almost made me back down, but not quite. I knew that some people would kill to have a family that accepted them unconditionally whether they be blood or not, but I didn't quite feel like that was the case. I felt like my family loved who they thought I was, or wanted me to be, not who I was in reality. They couldn't accept who I was in love with because they deemed him not good enough for me. And yet, if they really loved me unconditionally, wouldn't they just want me to be happy? Bryn made me happy. Case closed.

"I have this whole other side to me that I didn't even know existed. Why didn't you tell me? Why did you keep me in the dark?" I blinked back tears and went back to studying my hands.

"We wanted you to feel accepted and loved, not different. Not—"

"Would you have ever told me? Or was this something you guys would have taken to your graves?" I brought my head up to study first my dad's face and then my mom's. The answer was clear in both of them. "That's what I thought."

I wanted out. I *needed* out. And despite what happened

between Khol and me less than twenty minutes ago, he was the first person I thought of to turn to for help. I called out to him mentally, hoping my desperation was crystal clear. *Please come. I need you.* I wasn't going to do anything completely stupid like run away with him, but I was planning on hitching a ride home with him. I needed space from my parents, even if it was just for a few extra minutes.

Khol appeared beside my bed in all his dragonly beauty, looking every bit as fierce as I knew he would. My mother gasped, and my father startled back a few steps. "You called, my little Seer?"

"I wanna go home." Khol inclined his head in question. I knew he was wondering why I'd called him for that, and why I didn't want to go home with my parents. But he didn't question me out loud. Although he was probably picking it right out of my head, for all I knew. "Please," I whispered.

Khol stepped forward to scoop me up in his arms, and my mom cried out, "No! P.J., no! You don't know what you're doing. You—"

"I'll see you at home, Mom," I said with steel in my voice.

"Paige Joplin Stone—" my father started.

"Stop. I need space from you two, and I'm gonna get it. There's nothing you can do. I'll see you both at home." Khol pulled me to his chest, and I wrapped my arms around his neck. "Let's go," I whispered. As we blinked out of the hospital room, my mom screamed out in anguish.

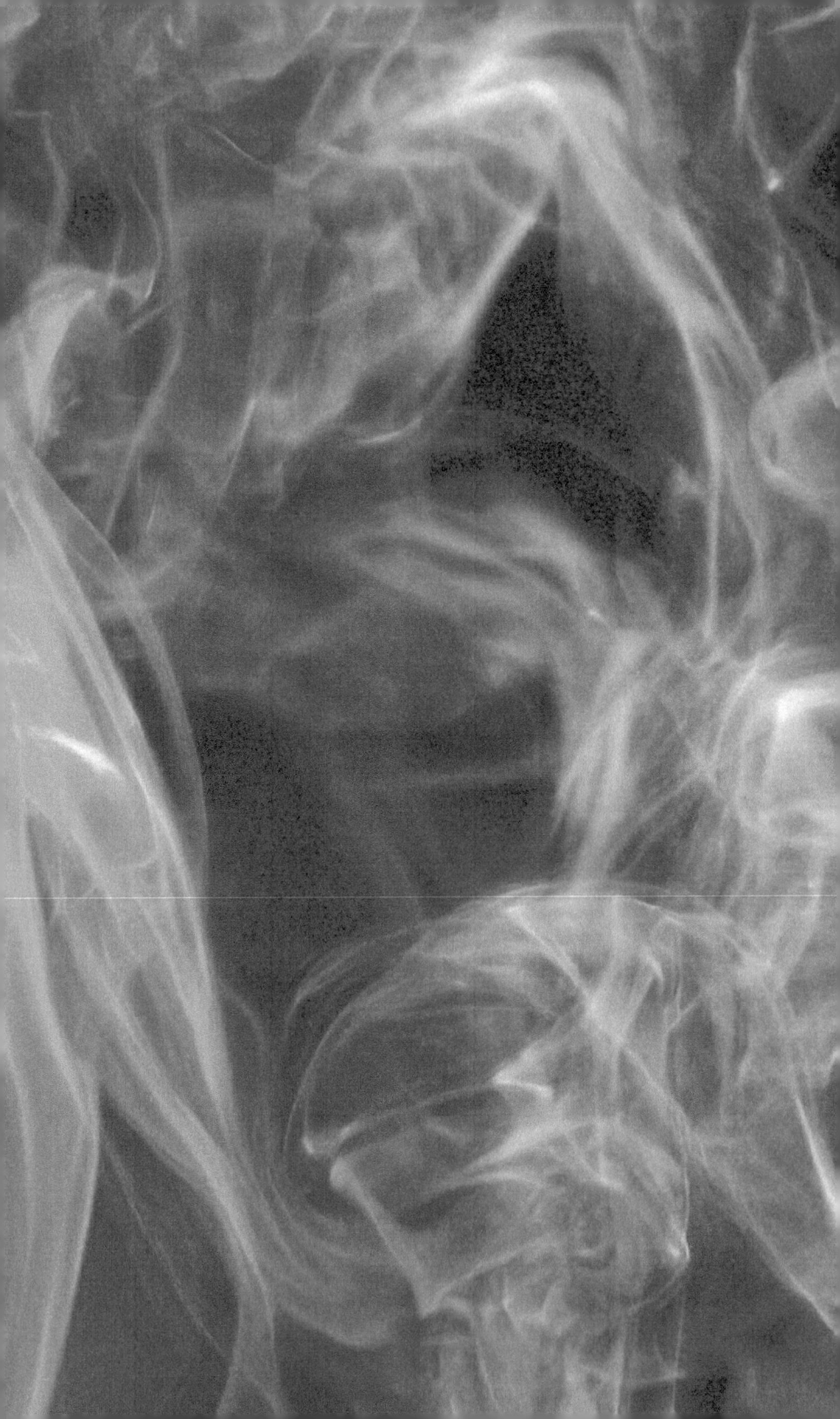

Chapter 15

Okay, so maybe I'd behaved like a spoiled brat throwing a bit of a temper-tantrum when I'd left the hospital with Khol. In my defense, I was exhausted both physically and mentally, and I simply snapped. And yeah, I was a bit spoiled because of my status as a Seer. Because of that, losing Bryn was my first big hardship, and I hadn't exactly developed the coping mechanisms to deal with it. Being angry and wanting space from my parents didn't mean I should treat them like complete shit though. For one, it clearly wouldn't bring Bryn back to me. Also, I knew my parents loved me and were doing the best they could, even if their views on my life were fucked up.

Although the damage seemed to be done. My parents seemed to be avoiding me since our fallout at the hospital. When I did actually see them, my mom looked at me with tears in her eyes, and my dad simply stared at me with sadness. They were probably afraid if they didn't give me the space I'd demanded, I'd disappear with Khol or something. Run off to never be seen again. If only they would bring Bryn back ...

Bryn. I sighed loudly as I conjured up an image of him in my mind. Of course, lately with my overcharged hormones, I always pictured him as he was when we'd been in bed together that first night—the night I'd given him my virginity.

I ran my hands through his silky, tousled hair, then down over his sweaty back. He shuddered at my touch, leaning forward to kiss me with a slow languidness that spoke of shared intimacies, and unspoken promises. "I love you, Peej. More than I can even begin to explain." His voice was so low and husky it seemed to brush things on my insides, making me shudder in turn.

That night had been perfect. Every little detail from our first time together was forever etched into my memory. The way his lips had felt on mine. His tentative caresses that turned to—

"Miss Stone, care to add anything to the discussion?"

I blinked, snapping back to the present—Mr. Edgington's psychology class. My face flamed as if it were written all over me what I'd just been thinking about. "No," I mumbled, wanting to disappear completely.

"I know that most of you take Intro to Psychology as an easy credit but how about you at least humor me and pretend to pay attention in my class, hmm?" Mr. Edgington raised his gray bushy eyebrows at me. I simply nodded in response. "Right. Now where was I? Nature versus nurture—"

I zoned out again, unable to help myself, only being yanked back to the present once again when everyone around me started packing up their stuff to leave.

"Remember to read the next two chapters for tomorrow," Mr. Edgington called to us, but I doubted anyone was paying attention.

One more class...one more class and I'm done until next week. Just one more class.

"Hey," Jenna said as she fell into step beside me. "Wanna stay over at my place tonight?"

"Yes," I answered without having to think about it. The tension in my house was unbearable. I would welcome the chance of being somewhere—anywhere—else.

"Your parents still acting all weird?"

"Pretty much. I think I broke something with them, but the thing is I don't know how to fix it, and I'm not sure I would if I could. They lied to me about some major stuff."

Jenna sighed. "Yeah, not telling you about who your real father is—well, that's pretty major."

I gasped, staggering against the wall. I hadn't told Jenna any of that. I was planning to—eventually, but I simply hadn't gotten around to it yet. "How the hell did you find out?" I closed my eyes and shook my head. "Please *do not* tell me you had a fly on the wall or something...literally."

I opened my eyes to a very pleased Jenna, a smug smile etched across her face. "You just told me."

"What?" *Shit.* She'd just pulled one of the oldest tricks in the book. I groaned and rubbed at my face. "But how did you even suspect?"

"Aside from the fact you don't look anything like your dad?" I scrunched my nose up at her. Lots of people don't look like their dads. Besides, I looked enough like my mom that it was obvious whose side of the family I took after. "But what really gave it away was when your eyes started to glow that day in your backyard. It wasn't much, but enough to make me wonder if you weren't part whatever Khol is, and you look a ton like your mom, so I don't think they found you in a cabbage patch."

My jaw dropped open. My eyes had glowed? *Holy. Shit.* "Why didn't you say something before? Did Jeremy see too?" I gulped. What other freaky dragony things were starting to develop in me that I had no clue about?

"There really wasn't a good time to bring it up before now. And yeah, unless Jeremy is blind, I'm pretty sure he saw, too."

I clutched my books to my chest tightly, concentrating on remaining calm. The thought of having to stay in school for one more minute suddenly seemed stifling. "I'm skipping my last class. I need to get out of here." I swiveled on my heel, marching for the front door.

Jenna scurried after me. "You just gonna walk out the front door right past your class?"

"That's the plan."

After a pregnant pause, Jenna responded, "I'll come with you. We can go scoop up your stuff from your house, and leave your parents a note that you'll be at my place. We can start our girls' night of fun early." She smiled up at me, but I couldn't manage to reciprocate.

"Hey. Where you guys going?" Jeremy appeared out of nowhere and fell into step with us. I didn't say anything and kept focused on my main goal: to get the hell out of school and off campus.

"We're calling it an early day and going over to my house. Girls' night tonight," Jenna said.

"Girls only, huh? I don't suppose I can tag along?"

"I don't know if P.J. is feeling up to it. She's kind of on the verge of freaking out right now," Jenna stated matter of factly.

"About what?" Concern seeped into Jeremy's voice.

"The whole eyes glowing thing from the other day, you know?"

"Oh. It's not that big a deal. Nothing to freak out about. Neither one of us look at you any different because of it, P.J.," Jeremy said softly.

"I'm not freaking out," I said between clenched teeth. "I'm a little bit upset is all."

"About what?" Jeremy asked.

"Seriously?" I glanced at him incredulously. "Finding out that I'm not even entirely human, and that my eyes are now doing some kind of weird glowy thing like Khol's? Not to mention my friends knew and didn't even tell me about it. Yep. Nothing to be upset about at all."

"Whoa, whoa, whoa," Jenna exclaimed. "What do you mean you're not entirely human?"

Really? What did she think after both meeting Khol and seeing my eyes glow? "Nothing," I muttered, quickening my pace to practically fly down the front stairs of my school. I was almost free and clear. As soon as my feet hit the front walkway, I broke into a full out run, unable to resist any longer.

"Hey. P.J., wait," Jeremy called, his feet pounding on the pavement behind me.

"P.J., come on. I didn't mean anything," Jenna called from farther back. She couldn't keep up with Jeremy and me with our much longer legs.

I ignored them both, jumping into my car and speeding off. Hurrying towards my front door, Jeremy snagged my arm, forcing me to face him. *How the hell did he get here so fast? I had at least a few minutes head start.* "I don't care if you're not entirely human. It doesn't change anything for me."

I met his deep brown eyes briefly before glancing away. "You don't even know what I am."

"So tell me." He tipped my face up with his fingertips, forcing me to meet his gaze again.

"*Rua arach,*" I muttered while trying not to count the golden flecks in Jeremy's eyes. He raised his eyebrows in question. "Red dragon. I'm half red dragon."

His brows furrowed together. "So Khol is a—"

"Full-blooded red dragon," I finished for him. "And he wants me for his *Anam Cara*—his mate."

Jeremy's hands balled into fists, and his jaw muscles jumped. "No," he ground out between clenched teeth.

"I don't know if I'll be able to stop it." I sagged with relief at finally being able to say my fears out loud. "Something about him calls to that part in me."

Jeremy's gaze danced back and forth between my eyes. "Do you want that? To be his *Anam*—whatever—mate?"

"No," I whispered. "At least I don't think so." He leaned forward to kiss me, and I turned, giving him the side of my face. "But that doesn't mean I wanna be with you either. I love Bryn. I still want him and only him."

He pulled away, exhaling loudly. "I know. So you keep telling me. It's just when I'm with you I feel this, I don't know, connection. And I don't understand how something so strong can be one-sided."

"I feel a connection, too. But it's to your power, and to you as a friend. I know it's not what you wanna hear, but it's the truth."

"Ahem. Why do I feel like I'm invisible lately?" Jenna grumbled from a couple feet away.

"Isn't that a good thing for spies?" I snarked.

She narrowed her eyes at me and flipped her rainbow hair. "I don't do the spying, my friends do."

"I know you feel something when I kiss you, more than a friend kind of thing," Jeremy interjected, as if Jenna was indeed invisible or not present at all.

I rolled my eyes at Jeremy. *Guys and their egos are completely insufferable.* "What do you want me to say,

Jeremy? You're hot, and you're good kisser. But I'm in love with Bryn. End of story."

A smile spread across his face, the gold flecks in his eyes dancing. "So I'm still in the game."

I threw my hands up in the air in utter exasperation. "This isn't a game—it's my life!" With that I unlocked the door and stalked into my house with Jenna and Jeremy close on my heels. *Funny, I don't remember inviting either one of them to come in. Guess what I want doesn't matter anymore.*

I internally bitched out my friends all the way to my room where I stopped short. My room was a complete disaster area. It was like a mini-tornado had swept through it, pulling out and destroying everything in its wake. *What the hell?*

"What's wrong?" Jenna asked before her eyes landed on the disaster I'd already seen. "What—what happened?" she stammered.

"I don't know," I whispered.

Khol appeared in front of me, his eyes glowing intensely. "Get whatever you need together quickly. It's not safe for you here anymore."

Jeremy pushed his way in front of Jenna and me to square off with Khol. "And how do we know you're not the one who did all of this"—he motioned to the disaster that used to be my room— "so you had an excuse to take her out of here?"

Khol barely spared Jeremy a glance, and instead, kept his attention riveted to me. "We don't have time to deal with any mistrust your friends may have for me. I need to get you out of here."

Did I trust Khol with my safety? Yes. Did I think that he'd use any excuse to get me alone so he could try to coax me into being his *Anam Cara*? Definitely. So the question was: which one was his motivator for the current situation? I couldn't afford to make any more mistakes. They could cost me Bryn, or my life, or both. "What happened? Why isn't it safe here anymore?"

"The aliens somehow know who you are. They came for you." His jaw muscles rippled and his hands flexed as if it was taking everything in him not to just grab me and disappear. And it probably was. I imagined his thoughts were something like: *Me Khol. Seer mine. Me protect what's mine.*

I shifted nervously, still not quite sure what to think. "How do you even know that?"

"I saw the one that shot at you leaving your house—"

"Why didn't you stop him from doing this to my room then? Why didn't you, I don't know, *get him* or something?" I asked incredulously as I waved my hands frantically at my trashed room. "And what were you doing lurking around my house?"

"I was in the area. Let's leave it at that." Khol sniffed indignantly. "And instead of *getting him*, as you so aptly put it, I decided to follow him to see if I could discover any useful information."

"And did you?" Jenna piped up.

"Yes, I did," Khol rumbled. "They somehow know who P.J. is, and they want to remove her as a threat."

"Remove me?" I staggered back into Jenna, who stepped out of the way for Jeremy to steady me. "You mean—" I couldn't bring myself to say it.

"How do we know we can trust anything he's saying?" Jeremy demanded while glaring at Khol.

"I trust him," I said without hesitation. Jeremy made a sound almost like a growl in the back of his throat, and his grip on my arm tightened. "So where are you gonna take me?"

"To my lair," Khol said. "I wish I could keep you away, at least until—" He shook his head violently as if dislodging some thought from his mind. "But your life will be protected there, even if it isn't the safest place for you right now."

"I don't understand. How isn't it safe for me there, but my life is protected?" Khol crossed his arms over his chest, his expression somehow conveying to me what he wasn't saying out loud. *Dragons*—other dragons—would be at his lair, and he was afraid they'd try to claim to me. "How will you keep that from happening?" I croaked.

"What?" Jenna asked with her head swiveling back and forth between the two of us. "Did I miss something?"

"Nothing that you need to worry about," Khol stated with finality. Lucky for me, Jenna liked to ignore such things.

"It kind of is, since I'm going with her."

My eyes widened. "You are?"

Jenna nodded once curtly. "Yep."

"Yeah, me, too," Jeremy rasped. "She's obviously gonna need protection from whatever danger you're dragging her into."

My face and neck from my friends' reactions. I hadn't expected them to want to go with me, and it kind of made me feel all warm and fuzzy inside, even if I could never let them go in good conscious. "Guys, I can't let you do that."

Jenna raised her chin, meeting me with a steel gaze that I would have recognized if I looked in the mirror. "You're not *letting* me do anything. It's happening whether you like it or not. You're my best friend, and we have to stick together."

"No," Khol growled. "I won't permit it."

Jenna narrowed her eyes and stalked towards Khol. "You're not the boss of me."

"Or me," Jeremy chimed in. "Regardless of how you feel about us, you know we'll come in handy in helping to keep her safe. And you want her safe, don't you?"

Khol's nostrils flared. "Of course." He brought his gaze back to study me. "If I bring you with us, you must listen to what I have to say. There will be many things you won't understand, and I don't have time to stop and explain everything all the time." I saw acceptance, although reluctant, wash over his face. "Fine," he grated. "I will bring all three of you to my lair."

"No!" I exclaimed. "You can't mean that."

"Jeremy's right. I must do whatever necessary, however unpleasant for me, to keep you safe."

"Who's gonna tell our parents? Who's—"

Jenna cut off what was about to be a stream of reasons why they shouldn't go. None of them would have stopped me if the shoe was on the other foot, but I had to try. "I'll have one of my friends tell my parents, and in the message, I'll tell my parents that they need to fill in both of your parents."

"Well, Khol said we have to leave now. You guys won't have time to go and get your stuff," I said, grasping at straws.

"That's okay," Jenna chirped, revved up from the excitement of what she probably perceived as an adventure. "I can borrow some of your stuff."

"But we're not the same size!"

"We've made it work before, we can make it work now." Jenna beamed at me, very pleased with herself.

"And as a guy, I'm sure I can figure out something there, right?" Jeremy looked at Khol, who nodded in affirmation.

Jenna began bouncing up and down. "Yay! It's settled! Now hurry up and pack so we can get going, P.J. I'm gonna find a friend to deliver the message to our parents for us."

"I just—I don't—what's happening?" I mumbled more to myself than anyone else. Just when I thought things couldn't possibly spin more out of control, they had. I rubbed at my temples, a burgeoning headache pressing along my skull.

But, wait. I was missing something. "Ummm... What

happened when you followed Emo Boy? I mean, besides you getting that…information about me?" I still couldn't quite bring myself to say the rest, that they wanted me dead. *Pretty harsh, even for would-be world-stealing aliens. After all, I wasn't even old enough to legally drink yet.*

"I was hoping he would lead me to others…like him, but I was only able to pick up the information because of a phone call he made." Khol's jaw rippled briefly with tension before smoothing out. "He would have harmed you if he found you here."

"And?" I prodded.

"And I took care of him after he ended the call." A dark smile spread across his face, sending a chill up my spine.

"What exactly does that mean?" I wasn't sure I actually wanted the answer.

"Just gather your things and rest assured that Emo Boy, as you referred to him, will no longer be an issue for you."

Referred, past tense. Did Khol kill him? The boy that the alien had been in was just a host, wasn't he? So what happened to the parasite inside him once the host was killed? Would he die along with the host, or would he simply try to move on? Maybe once the alien climbed into a host, they were joined, becoming one. Perhaps I should stop thinking of them as two separate entities and think of them as one.

As usual, it was like Khol just picked the questions right out of my brain. "Think of them as one. The creature takes control of the body, absorbing the person inside, at least as far as I can tell, and he won't be bothering you anymore."

Again I found myself wondering if he actually could read my mind and just wasn't telling me. *Because I'd be surprised?*

Annoyance flared within me. I didn't want Khol, or anyone else for that matter, poking around in my brain. "Stop doing that," I snapped.

He shrugged as if to say he couldn't help it, and I fought the urge to smack him. Instead, I focused my energy on scanning my room for clothes and other necessities to take with me. But because I was so annoyed with the entire situation, I just started shoving stuff into my bag with the hope that I was bringing with me what I would want later.

Oh well, it isn't as if I couldn't send Khol back to get something if I forgot it. I snickered to myself at the thought of turning him into an errand dragon. I wondered if he would actually do it if I asked. After a second's deliberation, I decided he would, in fact, fetch things for me because he was trying to get into my pants. I felt certain that males, of any species, were the same, and predictable when it came to that issue.

"Ready," I proclaimed after I swept my face wash and other necessary beauty products into my already overstuffed bag. "So how are we gonna do this?"

Khol raised his eyebrows at my comment. "I'll simply shift the three of you over to my lair."

I scrunched my face up at him, again, wondering why

he hadn't done that with us when we needed to hurry to the school to prevent my premonition. "Why didn't you just do that before when we needed to get to that school?"

"Because my powers are not back up to their full strength yet, having been in hibernation for many years. I will be exhausted after I do this, and that wasn't an option before."

I guess that made sense. "Oh."

"So it'll be mostly up to me to protect her until you fully recover?" Jeremy asked, his tone growing hostile. "How were you planning to do that before, when you were just gonna take her to your lair?"

"I would have only been taking her, which is not as taxing," Khol grated. "Do not doubt again that I can keep her safe, *boy*."

"You didn't do a very good job before." I could practically see the tension in the air radiating from both Khol and Jeremy. *Is it possible to asphyxiate from too much testosterone?*

"That was different, that was—"

"Boys, boys, boys." Jenna stepped into the space between the two of them. "There will be plenty of time to fight over P.J. after we get her somewhere safe." Tense silence permeated the air as Khol and Jeremy kept glaring at each other over Jenna's head.

I sighed. "Can we just go already?"

"You must all be touching me," Khol said without breaking his stare from Jeremy.

For Christ's sake...men.

I stepped into Khol and grabbed his hand, heat zinging up my arm. Jenna then moved to stand on the other side of Khol but decided to grip Khol's bicep with both her hands, sighing with appreciation. I bit the inside of my cheek to contain my nasty remark, tightening my grip on his hand to also keep from slapping her. Khol finally broke his stare off with Jeremy, his green eyes alight with mirth, obviously enjoying my little twinge of jealousy.

Jeremy approached us slowly, reaching up to touch Khol's arm with just his fingertips on the same side that I was holding his hand. Jeremy's eyes locked with mine, and then we were gone.

FOR SOME REASON, when Khol had said *lair*, my mind had conjured up images of something set inside a cave, or in the side of a mountain. I openly gaped at what actually turned out to be Khol's lair.

It's a friggin' castle.

It was a monstrous stone building that seriously could only be described as a castle, set on lush green lands that went on as far as the eye could see. *And I have 20/20 vision.* I felt like I was visiting a movie or TV set.

"Wow," Jenna said under her breath.

"My sentiments exactly," I muttered.

Khol lips twitched. "What did you expect, a cave?"

"No," I grumbled.

The twinkle in his eyes said that he knew I'd expected just that.

"My lord." A male with flame red hair, pale skin, and illuminated green eyes was suddenly kneeling in front of us, or more in front of Khol, really.

Even if I hadn't been prepared to expect more dragons, I would have immediately known what he was. The knowledge of it vibrated deep within me, causing my curiosity to ratchet up. As my eyes roamed over him, his gaze flicked up to meet mine. He was on his feet and stepping hesitantly towards me before I could blink again. I clutched Khol's hand tightly, having not even realized that I was still holding it.

A fine tremor rolled over the new dragon's body and his nostrils flared. "She's—"

"Not for you to consider," Khol rumbled, his eyes flaring brighter.

Still staring at me with an intensity that made me want to disappear, the other dragon took another step towards me. "Her power—it's—it's—unique, not cold like other female dragons. It calls to me with a heat I didn't think possible."

An inhuman growl rattled Khol's chest. "Back off, Macon," Khol commanded, his voice booming. A few heartbeats passed before he visibly relaxed. "I know the ability to resist is harder for one as young as yourself, but she's not for you."

Macon's face was filled with pain and confusion as he

met Khol's gaze. "Then why haven't you claimed her? She'll drive us all mad until you do."

"She's part human," Khol said, as if that explained everything.

And for Macon it seemed to. "Yes, my lord, I understand. I will try to avoid her until she bears your *Anam Cara* mark." With that, he pulled what I had come to think of as a Khol—a disappearing act. *Apparently, all dragons like such dramatics.*

I exhaled a long breath, my shoulders relaxing. "So that's what you were talking about?"

"Yes." Khol nodded. He tugged me forward, propelling us towards the castle.

"Why didn't you just *pop* us into the castle instead of out here?" I asked as my head swiveled around, trying to take in all the unfamiliar sights and sounds of this new place.

"Because I wanted you to see my land." There was a note of pride in Khol's voice that I couldn't miss. It made me wonder if stories of dragons and their acquisitiveness were based in reality. Because you know, sometimes fiction is loosely based on fact.

As we made our way inside through a side door, probably what would be called a servants' door, my senses prickled, letting me know that there were more than a handful of other dragons on the premises. My skin tingled, like little bits of electricity were running over the expanse of my body, and I trembled with the pleasantness of it.

"Why does it feel like we're sneaking in the back door?" Jenna asked. "I wanna tour of this place."

"P.J. needs to be isolated from the others here. You can have a tour after she's settled, if you wish," Khol said with a touch of annoyance.

The pleasant tingling slowly morphed to something much more...invasive. Suddenly my skin was burning, and my senses danced like I'd just downed a couple shots of Southern Comfort. Things spun and twisted. My entire field of vision narrowed down to Khol. I panted heavily, needing...wanting. I curled myself up against his side, even as we still walked. "Kiss me," I purred, not caring who saw. I craved the taste of him, needed the heat of his naked skin against mine.

"Not now. I must get you—"

I didn't hear the rest of what he said. *He's rejecting me?* If he wouldn't give me what I needed, then surely someone else would. "Macon," I called in a singsong voice.

Macon appeared directly in front of us, and I tugged free of Khol. "Macon," I purred. "You'll kiss me, won't you?" His eyes brightened in intensity as he came to me like a bullet out of a gun. His mouth slammed into mine, his lips searing, and I wrapped myself around him, greedy to get closer. I moaned loudly. *Yes! This is exactly what I need.* But before I could sink deeper into the kiss, Macon was ripped away from me and thrown into the wall. Khol scooped me up in his arms, and suddenly we were in a different room. A room with a rather large bed. *Mmmm. Yes, this could work too.*

My head swam as I reached out, pulling Khol towards me, capturing his lips with mine. "You know what I want," I growled. "Give it to me." I felt possessed, like someone else had taken over my body, and I kind of liked it. I'd never felt so completely free before. *Except with Bryn.*

I screamed, clutching at the back of my neck. It was if someone was pressing a hot iron to my skin, branding me. "Bryn!" I cried out. *Why aren't you here with me?* Bryn was who I needed, not Khol, and definitely not Macon.

Khol grabbed me, spinning me around to pry my hand off the back of my neck. "No. That's not possible. It can't be." His fingers dug into my skin.

The pain subsided as abruptly as it had begun, and left without it, I was suddenly too weak to remain vertical. I fell over onto the bed and curled into a ball, darkness already pushing at the edge of my consciousness.

"Bryn," I heard myself gasp. "Please. I need Bryn." And then I lost the battle—all went dark.

Chapter 16

"**M**y lord, how will we track them without her aid? None of us can see them for what they truly are, even you, without using her power. We can't let them get an even stronger foothold than they already have," a low male voice spoke urgently.

"I'm already aware of the problems we face, but we need to take care of her first," Khol said in response.

There was a pregnant pause during which I pondered why people were always talking around me when I lost consciousness. You would think people would want to let me rest and feel better instead of jabbering their jaws around me.

"How did you not notice until now, my lord?"

"It must have something to do with the black dragon's powers. He must be young, very young. Young enough to even pass for human. He might even be partially so, like her, which could explain it. He will come for her as soon as he can. He probably already feels the pull. He will know his partial claim is in threat. It will drive him mad."

"What will you do?"

"Claim her before he fully does so. Her *Anam Cara* will not be a *dubh arach*. She will be mine." Khol's words came out barely sounding human, which in fact, he wasn't. *I must be dreaming. What are they talking about?* I'd never met any kind of dragon before Khol had showed up to complicate my life, let alone one from a different faction.

"What will you do if he comes here?"

"I'll do what I need to do to ensure she fully belongs to me. I wanted to give her human half the time to get used to the idea, but I no longer have that option, this forces my hand."

"Wha? No," I slurred, unable to fully pull myself out of my stupor. "I trus ou." What I was trying to tell him, unsuccessfully, was that he couldn't claim me without my permission. I trusted him with that fact, and he said as long as I trusted him, he would wait. It didn't matter that I never planned on giving him permission. He believed one day I would. As for the rest, I still didn't know what he was talking about. Why did they think someone was coming for me?

"Shhh, my little Seer, you need to rest," Khol said as a large warm hand smoothed hair away from my face.

"I-I need Bryn," I somehow managed to say, *and actually make it sound like English.*

"No," Khol spat. "The only one you need is *me*."

I squirmed, trying to get away from his touch, but I didn't have the energy to fight him. Exhaustion began to pull me under again, my body too heavy to move. I was holding on to awareness by an extremely thin thread.

"She'll sleep for awhile longer, and then I will return for her," Khol spoke to the other dragon. *I don't like the sound of that.* "If the black dragon shows up, you know what to do." *I like the sound of that even less.*

"What about her companions?"

"Confine the boy to his room, but the girl is permitted entrance."

"Yes, my lord."

JOLTING AWAKE, I found myself in a strange bed, in a strange room. The last thing I remembered was the unsettling conversation between Khol and another unknown dragon.

"About damn time," Jenna's familiar voice said from beside me.

I let my head loll to the side, and there she was, lounging right next to me, reading a magazine. "I've been dying to talk to you." She folded the magazine, and met my eyes with her deep brown ones, which were currently sparkling with delight. "*Sooo...*" she drew out. "Me and Macon—"

I raised my hand, cutting her off. "Give me a second to orient myself before you hit me with what is sure to be another tale about how you got the latest notch in your belt."

Jenna thrummed her fingers against the folded magazine. *Tippity, tippity, tippity, tap. Tippity, tippity, tippity, tap.* Ignoring Jenna's impatience, I inhaled deeply a couple of times while I allowed my gaze to sweep my new surroundings. *Fancy, if not a little gaudy.* The room looked like it had been transported right out of Marie Antoinette's time; everything was marble and encrusted with gold. "Let them eat cake," I mumbled. Yep, if the outside of the castle hadn't answered my question about a dragon's acquisitory nature, then this room definitely did. *I wonder if there's a big pile of treasure in a vault downstairs somewhere.*

"Can I please tell you what happened between me and Macon now?" Jenna's whine cut into my inner musings.

"Fine." I knew she was about to tell me anyways, but I figured I might as well feign control of the situation.

"Well, you've probably already guessed that we did it." I nodded, unable to keep from rolling my eyes. "But what you can't guess, since you've only been with Bryn, is just how absolutely amazing and different it is to be with a dragon. They're just so…well, they're just so…" She started fanning herself as she searched for the right word. "Amazing," she finally settled on. *Maybe it's time I bought the girl a thesaurus.*

I couldn't keep the snide tone out of my voice, "Because you've been with so many dragons before. How do you know Macon wasn't an anomaly?"

"Hmm." Jenna turned pensive. "You're right. I think I should conduct a study while I'm here."

"For God's sake, girl, there are more important things on our plates than your sex life." *Like mine*, I silently added sheepishly.

"I think you should do it with Khol."

"Jenna!" I exclaimed.

"No, I mean it. At least for comparison purposes. You've only been with Bryn, and—"

Holy shit! Bryn. Was it possible? Everything that Khol and the other dragon had said while I was barely conscious came flooding back. No, it couldn't be, but then again, I was half dragon myself after all. "I think Bryn may be part black dragon." The words seemed even more ludicrous when I said them out loud.

Jenna laughed. "You'll do anything to change the subject, won't you?"

"No, Jenna! I'm being serious. I heard Khol and some other dragon talking, when I wasn't fully awake, about how some young black dragon, or at least partial black dragon, has the beginnings of a mate claim on me. I know from talking to Khol that the only way to claim a dragon mate is to do it during sex."

Jenna's eyes widened slightly as I continued on with my crazy theory. "Well, I've only been with Bryn, and Khol said all red dragons have red hair in human form, even ones like me who can't change forms, and well, wouldn't it make sense for black dragons to have black hair in human form? And who do we know that I've slept with that has black hair?"

When I put all the clues together that way, maybe it didn't seem that implausible that Bryn was part black dragon. I didn't think he was full-blooded because he looked too much like his dad, and he did have all the usual Guardian abilities. Which meant—"Holy shit! That means Bryn's dad had an affair with a female dragon. That's the only way it would make sense." Was that why Bryn and me had always felt so drawn to each other starting at a very young age? Had we started some kind of bonding process between dragon mates without even realizing it?

Jenna stared at me, her mouth hanging open. "Well, say something," I chuckled nervously. "I don't think, in all the years we've been friends, you've ever gone speechless."

"I—well, I—damnit, when you explain it the way you just did, it almost seems possible." She shook her head in amazement. "First you, and now maybe Bryn. Maybe it's true that Speakers can't be friends with our kind because if you're right, this means neither of you are one hundred percent Seer or Guardian."

I reached up and scratched at the back of my neck. It was beginning to burn. Nothing like before, but it was definitely uncomfortable. "Hey, will you see what's going on with the back of my neck? It was burning like crazy before, and now it's more burning slash itching, but it's annoying as all hell." I lifted my hair off of my neck, and Jenna scooted behind me to take a look.

"Umm... when did you get a tattoo and decide not to

tell me?" Jenna said with annoyance. "Didn't they tell you A & D ointment is the best thing for it while it's healing? It kind of looks raw."

"What?" I pulled away with alarm. "I didn't get a tattoo. What the hell are you talking about?" Jumping out of bed, I clambered over to a large mirror that was hanging on the wall. Contorting the best that I could, I tried to see the back of my neck, with no results.

"Hang on." Jenna reached down to the floor and into her purse to produce a small compact. She then joined me in front of the larger mirror while tilting it just right so I could see—

What the hell is that?

I gasped at the image reflected back at me in the tiny mirror. Sure enough, there was what looked like a black circular tattoo right below my hairline at the nape of my neck. "That's impossible." I pressed my fingers into the mark, wincing.

"Can't be impossible since there it is." Jenna studied me. "You really didn't know? How can you not know you got a tattoo?"

"I wish I knew," I said as I trudged back to the bed, my head reeling. Time and time again, I kept thinking my life couldn't get any weirder. *I really have to stop jinxing myself.*

A loud knock on the door preceded Khol entering the room. He gave me a tight smile as he met my eyes. "It's the black dragon's *Anam Cara* mark."

"Huh?" Jenna and me said in perfect unison.

Khol motioned to the back of his neck. "What you

think is a tattoo is the black dragon's *Anam Cara* mark—mate mark, or at least the beginning of one."

"What do you mean?" Jenna asked.

Khol answered while still holding my gaze. "Because it's black, I know it was made by a black dragon. All *Anam Caras*—dragon pairs—mark each other."

"So…" I started, finally finding my voice.

He picked up on my question before I could get it out. "Yes. He will bare a red mark on the back of his neck from you." Khol paused, turmoil rolling off him in waves. "This Bryn. *Your Bryn*," he practically growled the words. "I can no longer wait for you to be done with him before I claim you. This changes *everything*."

Fear shot up my spine, causing goose bumps to erupt along my skin. "I trust you," I whispered. But I knew it was too late for those words. Everything had changed. I could see it clearly in Khol's eyes.

For the first time since I'd met Khol, genuine sadness filled his eyes. "And I had hoped to keep that trust with you." He bared his teeth, snarling, "But I won't lose you, especially to a *dubh arach*."

"Whoa, whoa, whoa. What I think you're trying to say there, jagoff, is completely unacceptable. You better back off of P.J.," Jenna snarled back. "Nobody forces my best friend to do anything she doesn't wanna do."

A small part of me, the part that was slightly hysterical, wanted to laugh because Jenna had called Khol a *jagoff*. A larger part of me had already taken a mental vacation. I just couldn't seem to wrap my mind around what was going on. Or I was just in uber denial, which was most likely.

"Khol, please," I attempted. *Please, what?* Please don't force yourself on me and claim me for your mate when I want someone else? Laughter bubbled up in my chest.

"The mark isn't complete, that's why it's irritating you the way it is. I can guarantee you that his is doing the same. But once it's complete, there will be no going back. You would be his for the rest of your lives. And that I can't allow," Khol snarled again. "Especially not a damn black dragon."

He stalked towards me, and I shrank back until I hit the wall. I wanted away from him. I wanted to go home. I was in way over my head with him—with everything. "Drake," Khol called, his eyes not leaving mine for even a second.

A moment later, I saw someone male appear in my peripheral vision, but I didn't dare even glance away from Khol. "Take Jenna to her room and make sure she stays there."

"Yes, my lord," the same voice I'd heard when I wasn't fully conscious answered.

"No!" Jenna screamed. "You can't! She trusted you! *We* trusted you!" But Jenna's screams were silenced as the other dragon disappeared with her in his arms, kicking and screaming.

And then we were alone. Just Khol and me...me and a dragon intent on claiming me.

"Please," I whispered, my body trembling. "Don't do this to me."

"I'm sorry. You have no idea how much. But I don't have a choice anymore."

"It'll be rape. Are you telling me you have no choice but to rape me? I don't believe that," I warbled. I clenched my teeth to keep them from chattering and blinked rapidly to stave off the impending onslaught of tears.

He glided forward, stopping inches from me. His voice was barely a whisper, "You'll enjoy it, I promise. I know your body craves mine. That isn't rape, coercion maybe, but not rape."

He leaned forward to kiss me, and I turned away just in time so he got my cheek instead of my lips. "But my heart and soul will still crave Bryn. You'll deny me that for the rest of my life? Because once you claim me for your *Anam Cara*, I won't want him anymore, will I? At least not physically?"

"No, you won't. And it's better that way." He grabbed my wrists, pushing them over my head, causing my heart to thrash against my ribcage.

"I'll never forgive you for this," I hissed.

A small smile turned Khol's lips up ever so slightly at the corners. "But you will. You will because as your *Anam Cara*, only I will possess the ability to give you what you crave. And dragons are quite insatiable, especially the females. You haven't even begun to experience the full scope of your dragon side."

Bryn's image flooded my mind. *"Bryn!"* I mentally screamed. *"Please, somehow don't let this happen to me—to us!"*

I struggled in Khol's grasp, but he too strong for me. He managed to keep me pinned with just one hand, holding both my wrists as he tore at my clothes. I screamed with fury. I couldn't—*wouldn't*—let him do this. When he dipped his head to kiss me, I bit his lip. His eyes flared, the green growing brighter as a low rumble trickled from his chest. I tasted the tangy copper flavor of his blood as he persisted, delving aggressively into my mouth with his tongue.

"Get your hands off her. She's mine," a heartbreakingly familiar voice growled from behind Khol.

It was if time stood still for just a moment. Intermingled joy and relief played through me—until I registered the sly grin spreading across Khol's face, and the triumph glinting in his eyes.

Alarm bells sounded frantically within me. *It's a trap!*

"Bryn!" I screamed. "Get out of here! He wanted you to come for me! He'll kill you!"

Braking away from Khol, whose grip had loosened, I ducked under his arm, swiveling to his left to dash for Bryn. But before I could even get two steps, his arms snaked out, restraining me around my waist.

"Bryn!" I gasped, drinking him in with my eyes. He seemed bigger—more muscular than I remembered, even though it hadn't been that long since I'd seen him. He also seemed years older, his face set with grim determination as he stared at me. And his eyes—his eyes glowed an eerie blue that confirmed the fact that he was indeed dragon.

The one thing that hadn't changed was that he belonged to me. Every molecule in body buzzed with yearning to be in his arms. It felt quite possible that I would die right there if I couldn't reach him soon.

Bryn reached out for me as he stepped forward.

He still feels the same! He still wants me! "Let me go!" I screeched, clawing at Khol's arms. "Bryn!"

"Bind him," Khol commanded.

Three massive dragons appeared behind Bryn with chains. With blinding speed, Bryn's arms were bound by two of the dragons even as the third struggled to put a neck shackle on him.

"Peej!" Bryn roared, thrashing against his restraints.

Renewing my fight, I reached back and raked my nails down Khol's cheek. His blood burned my fingertips, but I didn't care. *I have to get to Bryn.*

Khol's grip slid from my waist to my wrists, yanking my arms behind my back. "Stop fighting me or he dies."

I instantly stilled. Khol was not bluffing.

"Bryn," I whimpered as I locked gazes with him. He was forced to his knees by the three dragons that held his chains. *No, no, no, no, no.* Hot, angry tears tracked down my cheeks. "You never intended on raping me. You just wanted me to believe it so I'd call out to him. It was all a trap. And I played right along."

"Yes. I couldn't leave to chance when he would come for you. He's young, his powers are just developing, and without such a motivator, he might not have been able to do what he just did." Confusion washed over Bryn's face with Khol's words. "He shifted right to you when you called out to him. He felt your bond was in danger, and the dragon in him knew he had to get to you."

"Dragon?" Bryn's full lips shaped the word with surprise.

"He doesn't know what he is. He probably hasn't processed what just happened. He reacted instinctually, which was what I was hoping for."

"What do you want with him?" I waited for Khol's answer, and when it didn't come, I knew what his silence was saying.

I choked back a strangled cry. "Don't hurt him. I'll do whatever you want. Anything. Just please don't hurt him." My eyes caressed every inch of Bryn that I could see. He was my everything, my reason for living. He owned my heart, body, and soul. How could I either choose giving myself to Khol or letting Bryn die? Either way, I wouldn't get to be with Bryn, and yet, at least if I gave myself to Khol, Bryn would get to live. There was some small comfort in knowing that my sacrifice would keep him alive.

Agony rolled over Bryn's features, pinching them. "No. Peej. Whatever it is, don't do it."

"I can't let you die!" I choked out. "He'll kill you if I don't do what he wants."

"It'll be like I'm dead anyways without you. Since I left, that's what it's felt like—like some part of me died because

I couldn't be with you, couldn't see you—couldn't touch you. I'd rather die knowing it was for your freedom."

I dropped my head, no longer able to witness the pain on his beautiful face. "I could never let you die for me." I started to turn towards Khol, and he shifted his grip to allow me. I met his gaze, hatred burning in mine for him. "I said I'd do anything you want as long as you don't hurt him. But you have to give me your word that you won't harm him in *any* way."

Khol's jaw tensed as he stared at me, blood from my scratches already dried on his cheek. After what seemed like an eternity, he grunted out a response, "We will keep him prisoner until I claim you, and then he may go free. Not a minute before. It will be your choice for how long he remains here. In chains."

I raised my chin defiantly. "He goes free now."

"No. You agree to my deal or he dies now. There will be no other compromises. It goes against all my dragon instincts to let him live at all." Khol ground his teeth together, and I sensed he was barely holding on to control. I knew in that moment if I wanted to keep Bryn alive, I couldn't push him any further.

"Okay. But not even one single strand of hair on his head will be harmed. Your word." I held my breath, waiting to see how he'd respond.

"My word to you that I will hold him as my prisoner until you agree to let me claim you. At that time, he will be released with no permanent injuries to his body or powers." Khol continued to grind his teeth together.

"That's as much as I can offer. Even that feels like too much."

I nodded once tightly, sensing it was the best I was going to get for Bryn.

"No, Peej. You can't. We'll find a way, I promise."

I wanted to believe Bryn, and a small part of me did. The part of me that still believed he could do anything— the part of me that still trusted him so completely that if he promised me something, that in itself would make it reality.

But I was no longer believed that we would get a happy ending.

My heart cracked and shattered into a billion pieces. I couldn't bear to look at Bryn, if I saw his face, even for another second, I might do something stupid, and I couldn't risk his life. I would give myself to Khol as soon as possible, so they wouldn't have time to hurt him in any way. I hadn't missed what Khol had implied with his words: no permanent damage. That still left a lot on the table as far as torture went.

"Don't make promises you can't keep," Khol growled at Bryn. "Take him away."

Bryn howled my name, chains rattling from the strength of his fight, and still, I refused to look at him. Finally, when all was silent and I knew he was gone, I lifted my gaze to Khol's, filling it with all the contempt I now felt for him. "I hate you," I said just as my vision swam and I collapsed to the floor.

Chapter 17

I slowly blinked my eyes open, my vison filling with Khol's pained visage. "I wish it didn't have to be this way." I sensed his words were sincere, and somehow that made them worse.

"Bryn and me are meant to be together. We always have been." Raw agony ripped at my insides. *I can't lose Bryn.* Because that's what it would be this time. Not a separation that would end after a year or two, but a permanent loss of him. I didn't know if I could go on without him. I'd never felt so utterly...hopeless before. I was trapped with no options and no way out. *No, that's not completely true. There is still one way out. I could take my own life—end this torturous game permanently. Take back my freedom from Khol.*

But what about Bryn? If I was dead before he was freed, I had no doubt that Khol would kill him. I would have to gain Bryn's freedom first. And that meant having to let Khol claim me. It was hard to believe that such a short time ago, a part of me had responded so feverishly to Khol's kisses, to his touch, when now the mere thought of his hands on me left me ice cold. Maybe it had something to do with the beginning of the *Anam Cara* mark from Bryn, or maybe the reality of possibly losing Bryn forever had finally hit it all home. I knew positively, without any doubts, I would never love anyone else the way that I loved him—he was my home—always had been and always would be.

"If you were meant to be with him, then you would end up with him, and I can assure you that won't be happening. You will be my *Anam Cara*, not his."

A strangled cry of frustration escaped from me. "Why?" I stared at Khol, studying his features for some kind of clue. "Why do you want me so desperately? It's not like you're in love with me, you can't be. Why not find some other nice lady dragon and claim her so that I can be with Bryn?" I didn't want to die. Not really. I was simply desperate for a way out.

Khol reached his hand out to me, and I shrank away. Hurt flickered within is gaze before a mask of indifference settled over his features. "Do not pretend to know the depth of my feelings for you."

Reasoning with him obviously wasn't going to work. I'd already come to that conclusion, and yet—yet I still had to try one last time. "I'll let you claim me, but I hope you know it'll still be rape because I'll only be doing it for Bryn, and I'll be thinking of him the entire time."

Anger sparked to life in Khol's gaze, and he grabbed me, his fingers pressing into the sides of my face. "Watch what you say to me, my little Seer," he snarled before roughly pressing his lips to mine. His tongue thrust forcefully into my mouth, dominating, before he yanked me away from him. The move made me feel truly violated for the first time since I met him, and it rendered me speechless. "You do not wish for me to show you the true meaning of the word rape. You would be wise to remember that I'm not human, and I'm attempting to observe human rules for your sake."

Gathering all of my meager strength, I smacked Khol across the jaw. A red handprint bloomed along his skin, and the sound of my palm meeting his flesh seemed to echo inside the large room. "I'm not entirely human either," I hissed, tensing for retaliation. But he surprised me yet again by disappearing into thin air.

I exhaled a shaky breath, my heart thudding in my ears. I had to trust in Khol's word that Bryn wouldn't be harmed, so he wouldn't suffer for what I'd just done. Although it still wasn't the smartest thing in the world to antagonize him either. After all, he wasn't human, as he kept reminding me.

Strung out and frazzled, I paced the room, every muscle in my body knotted with tension. I wanted— needed to see Bryn, talk to him, and make sure they were treating him decently. Given the chance though, I didn't think I'd be able to look him in the eyes knowing what I was going to do with Khol. I knew I needed to be worrying more about the alien infestation problem our world was suffering from, but how could I when my entire future hung in the balance?

Unbidden, images from me and Bryn's shared past kept skittering across my brain—all the birthday celebrations we'd shared, all the nights we'd platonically slept in each other's arms, and of course, when we'd first crossed that line, becoming more than friends. I wished I would have known at the time that those few moments I'd spent in Bryn's arms, letting him love me, would probably be the last I would ever have. Perhaps I would have been able to make them last longer, drawn them out somehow, etch every last detail into my mind. If only I could have figured out my true feelings for him sooner, we could have had so much more time together.

"Khol!" I screamed. "Just let me see him! Please! Don't cut me off from him completely!" If he cared for me at all, maybe he'd give in. He had to be sensing the torment his actions were causing within me. "I love him!" My voice cracked. "Please! You're going to get your way so just— please!"

Khol appeared, and he regarded me with the same mask of indifference as before, his illuminated gaze stony. "You know I can't let you do that. Not until after I've claimed you."

"Why are you doing this?" Lurching forward, I dropped on my knees before him, ready to beg—to grovel with everything I had in me just to see Bryn one more time before he was ripped away from me—again, but forever this time.

"You're pleading is pointless. I won't give you what you want." His voice was flat, devoid of all emotion.

"Why? Why are you doing this?" I asked again, my entire body trembling. No matter what he said, it just didn't make sense. *Why me?*

Khol's gaze flicked away, settling on a point above my head. "Dragons don't fall in love like humans. And there's a difference even between a male and female dragon." He paused, exhaling a ragged breath. "When a male dragon falls in love, it happens fast, and…it's forever. He will do *anything* to be with her, even fight to the death to possess her. For that reason, it doesn't work that way for female dragons, because some of her suitors could be killed off. Her bond doesn't become eternal until an actual *Anam Cara* mark is placed upon her."

"And what happens after the female bonds with one of her suitors? I mean, what happens to the male dragons who live but didn't bond with her?" I had to know what would happen to Bryn.

"They continue to love her, but they accept that she's out of their reach. Most of the time, they enter her service in some way in order to simply remain close to her."

"So they never bond with anyone else? They never fall in love with anyone else?"

"No."

"That can't be true—I mean Macon—I mean, he was with Jenna and—"

"It's true that Macon would have taken you up on your...oh so kind offer." Khol's jaw ticked with tension. "And he would have welcomed the chance to claim you for his *Anam Cara* because of your power—amongst other things, but—" He dropped to his knees so he could look directly into my eyes. "He doesn't love you. He doesn't love you—like I do."

Everything I was about to say dried up in my throat. *What? Love me? No. That can't be true.* But—but if it was true, then I could almost understand why he was being so ruthless about Bryn. Because if Khol loved me, it was either claim me for his, or live out the rest of his days loving me from afar, never being able to have me—or anyone else. So instead, he was dooming Bryn to that fate.

"How? How can you love me? You practically just met me," I finally managed to squeak out.

Khol gave me a tight-lipped smile full of pain and regret. "I wish that I didn't, for I despise what I'm doing to you. But you awakened me from my slumber, pulling me to you with your powers and then … it just … happened. I began to love you." He stood and walked away, talking with his back to me. "I was willing to wait. I was willing to honor your human side, for I knew your dragon side would come to crave more, and then I would make you mine. And it was happening. I felt your willpower to resist me weakening, despite everything else." His shoulders tensed as he balled his hands into fists. "But finding out that Bryn is part black dragon changed everything."

I inched forward on my knees as I stared at the back of

his head, willing him to listen to me—to really hear what I was saying. "It changed everything for you, but nothing has really changed. It's been this way from the beginning. I've belonged to Bryn since I was five years old. He's my home."

"*I* will be your home. *I* will be your everything. As you are already my world. Don't presume that I haven't picked up what you're feeling for him. I know your love for him is real, not the human puppy love your family all believes it to be." Khol's body trembled. "And I want that. I want you to feel that way about me." He whirled around to face me again, his expression half crazed, at least by human standards. "And you will. You will feel that way about me."

"No. It doesn't work that way. You can't make me love you."

His voice softened, and his gaze filled with unshielded longing. "You'll eventually come to love me because it's in your nature. You must be in love—you must feel that kind of passion. And it'll be easier for you to give in to those feelings once you're my *Anam Cara.*" He dropped down in front of me again. "I never thought it was possible for me to feel this way about anyone. I would give you anything —I would do *anything*—" His nostrils flared. "Except for one thing."

My lower lip quivered. "Except let me be with Bryn."

"Yes. Except for that." Khol rose from his crouch and began to pace. "He isn't strong enough to protect you. He doesn't have enough resources to give you the life you deserve. He is lacking in almost every single category as a dragon."

I dug my fingers into my thighs, trying to keep from launching myself at Khol. I wanted scratch him, hit him—hurt him. "I don't care about those things. He's who I want. He's who I've chosen. It's not fair for you to take my choice away from me."

"It may not be fair, but it is the way of the dragon, and you were both born into it."

"There's nothing I can say to change your mind then, nothing I can do?"

"No. There is nothing."

"Can I see Jenna? Jeremy?"

"Not for the time being. I think it's best if you're left alone with your thoughts so you can come to terms with the situation without your friends' influence. After all, they will never understand—they are not dragon." He stopped midstride and glanced my way, not meeting my eyes. "I will not come to you again until you're ready for me to claim you. Call for Drake if you need anything. You can trust him."

And with that, he vanished right before my eyes.

I WAS a bird in a gilded cage, or more accurately, a dragon in a gilded cage. Drake brought me any meal I wanted to eat, any book I wanted to read, and any random object I told him I required. It was kind of amusing to request odd things just to see if he'd get them for me, but that also got old fast. I had my own private bathroom that had a huge claw-footed bathtub that I'd taken to luxuriating in, but even a girl like me could only take so much pampering before I thought I'd go out of my mind. I had no contact with the outside world at all, and the only person I saw was Drake. He didn't seem to like me very much though, probably because he'd figured out what I was doing with my request game, so he spent as little time with me as possible.

I lost track of time, of how many days I'd been in my gilded prison, and it was tearing me up to know that Bryn was being held captive somewhere in the very same castle, and probably not with the same level of amenities. I knew what I needed to do to free him, but every time I thought I'd built up enough courage to give Khol what he was waiting for, the words lodged themselves in my throat.

The prospect of being with Khol, of having sex with him, made me feel sick, especially when I'd be doing it with Bryn under the very same roof. The thought of suicide still weighed heavily on my mind, but the biggest problem with that plan always returned to the point that I didn't want to die. I was just looking for a way out. And I'd still have to let Khol claim me first to ensure that Bryn would be released. I'd gone over and over things in my mind, and I couldn't come up with any other option to save Bryn. I was going to have to give myself to Khol to free him.

I just have one more question first.

"Drake," I called.

The massive dragon appeared seconds after I summoned him. "Yes." He eyed me with disdain. "What can I do for you?"

"I just have a question for you and then you can go." He tipped his head, waiting. "Khol told me that once a male dragon was in love, he would love her forever, even if she went on to bond with someone else. What happens if she dies?" His head tilted further, reminding me of a dog. "I mean, if something happened to me, would Khol continue to not desire anyone else, or would he be free to move on?" The real question was: would Bryn be free to move on?

"My lord would be free to move on if you died, whether you were bonded to him or not, in theory. Although some *Anam Cara* pairs, if they're bonded for long enough, die of grief when one of them is killed."

"Oh, okay. Thanks. You can go now." Drake eyed me speculatively for another few moments before disappearing.

Suddenly lightheaded, I dropped down to sit on the floor right where I was. Bryn would be free if I—if I—killed myself. He would be able to move on and love someone else someday, and even though the thought ripped at my chest, I knew I had to do that for him—I had to summon the courage somehow. I wouldn't doom him to becoming some kind of servant for me. He deserved better than that. I was out of options and time was running out despite my desire to hide in denial. I would let Khol claim me so that I could guarantee Bryn's freedom, and then I would end my own life.

Slumping over, I put my head in my hands as sobs shook my body. *I really, really don't wanna die.* My life had practically just started. And who would help track down the aliens to stop them from taking over our world once I was gone? *Someone else somewhere has to be able to see them, too. I can't be the only Seer in the entire world.* I stood abruptly and sniffled, wiping my tears away. None of that mattered as long as Bryn got a chance at true happiness. Bryn would always be the most important thing in my life, and I would always do whatever necessary to protect him.

"Khol," I croaked. "Khol—I'm ready." *Am I ready to die though? Can I really do this?*

Khol appeared in front of me only a few inches away, pushed me back onto the bed, and covered me with his body, his mouth aggressively slanting over mine. He was obviously ready to get down to business, and maybe it was better that way, so I wouldn't have a chance to lose my nerve.

My body responded to his scorching kisses, even as my heart froze like a block of ice inside my chest. As he tore at my clothes, I found myself arching up to meet him, wanting—at least physically—what he had to offer. Too soon, or not soon enough, we were both naked, and Khol was claiming parts of my body with his touch that I had sworn only Bryn would ever know.

Clawing and biting at Khol, I was overwhelmed by the urge to hurt him as he rocked into me, hating and loving what he was doing to me at the same time. Things with him were different than they'd been with Bryn. There was no soul-deep connection. There was no feeling of being exactly where I belonged. All I found within Khol's embrace was intense physical pleasure, which maybe would have been enough, if I didn't already know what I was missing.

Sweltering heat seeped out of Khol's pores, wrapping itself around me as the back of my neck began to burn. "You belong to me now," Khol growled as he stared down at me, capturing my gaze. "Say it."

"Yes," I gasped on the tail end of a moan, wishing I could deny the words, but I felt it—I felt his magic burning me, branding me, making me his.

"And I'm yours. Say it."

"Yes. You're mine."

And then I arched up one last time before blacking out.

I LET KHOL CLAIM ME, the words played over and over in an endless loop in my mind as I slowly fought my way back to consciousness. I was cold—empty. When I'd been with Bryn, I'd felt so good, so right, but being with Khol had been *wrong*—even if he had brought me pleasure. *Maybe it won't be difficult to take my own life after all.* Had Bryn felt our connection breaking? Surely he had to have. What must he think of me now, knowing what I'd done to make that happen?

Shame bubbled in my gut, shoving bile up my esophagus.

Blinking my eyes open slowly, I was surprised to find that I was alone. *No Khol. Well, isn't that nice? He finally got what he wanted, and he didn't bother to stick around afterwards.*

Lurching from bed, I stumbled towards the bathroom, not caring if I was naked or not. It didn't matter for what I was about to do. I shut and locked the door and started the water running for the bath. As the hot water filled the tub, I scanned the bathroom for options. My eyes stopped when they ran over a small hand mirror. I snatched it up and broke it on the counter, picking up the largest shard.

I have to do it—I have to do it now before I lose my courage.

I sank into the nearly full tub, hardly noticing when the hot water practically scalded me. I set the glass shard on the edge. When the water covered me up past my chest, I turned it off and picked up the shard, leaning back.

Passing the jagged glass back and forth between my hands, I watched the lights glint menacingly off its surface. *I have to do it—there is no other way.* I refused to doom Bryn to a miserable life. My death would bring him happiness—well, eventually anyways.

Besides that, the emptiness that was eating at my soul, knowing I could never have him again, was enough to make me want to end my life all in itself. *But I would never make this choice for myself alone.* I'd always thought suicide was the coward's way out, an easy escape from problems that would only make a person stronger if they stayed to face them. What would happen if the hero of a story died before they had a chance to become who they were really meant to be? I never thought myself capable of doing such a thing, but then again, maybe I wasn't the hero of this story, I was simply the main character in my own life.

But I wanted to live—even now as I readied myself for death—I craved life. There was still so much to do, so much to experience, the good and the bad. *I don't wanna die now.* I forced air into my lungs. *No—it isn't time for selfish thoughts.* This is for Bryn. *Everything is for Bryn.*

I held the shard tightly in my right hand, drawing blood, the pain not registering in my state of mind. Dipping my hands under the water again, I pressed the glass into my left wrist, slashing along the vein with all my might, quickly switching hands to do the right wrist. But the shard slipped from my numb fingers before I could repeat the process. Blood swirled around me, diluted by the water and I leaned back, hoping what I'd managed to do was enough. *It has to be enough.* My head lolled as the room spun and my eyes slid shut. *I love you, Bryn. I'll always love you and only you.*

"No!" someone roared, but it was far away—much too far away—for me to care.

Another voice joined the first. "Peej! No, no, no, no, no. Please, no. How could you do this? Save her! You have to fucking save her!"

But I was too sleepy to care about anything anymore.

Chapter 18

My eyes fluttered open, and I squinted into blinding light. *The sun*, it warmed and comforted me. I stretched as I yawned, sitting up in the middle of a pallet set up in the center of an immense garden. Strong, warm arms held me at my waist, and I looked down with a smile as I recognized the long masculine fingers. "Bryn," I murmured, twisting around to take in his sleeping face steeped in the brightness of the day. I stroked my fingers down his cheek and ran my hands through his silky mane of black hair. *I must be dead*, I mused, *for certainly waking up in Bryn's arms is heaven.*

Just then he stirred, his dark lashes cracking open to showcase his sea storm eyes. "Peej," he rasped, his voice raw with emotion.

I suddenly found myself on my back with him pinning

me down. His face became a mixture of anger and agony. "Don't you *ever* do something like that again. Do you hear me? Never again. What the fuck were you thinking?"

His fingers bit into my arms, and I wriggled against him. "I don't understand." My brow furrowed with uncertainty, was I dead or not? Because angry Bryn wasn't one I wanted in my own personal heaven. Maybe I should clarify? "I did it for you. Everything was for you."

"You tried to end your life for me? Why? Why would you think that's something I could live with?" Bryn growled.

Not dead then. I squeezed my eyes shut, wanting to escape his anger. "I had to free you. I wasn't gonna get you either way, so I at least wanted you to have a chance at happiness. Once I was dead, you would have been free to love someone else, bond with someone else."

Bryn shook me, causing my eyes to snap back open. "When did you get to be so stupid? Dead or alive, I'm never gonna love anyone else." He continued shaking me until I felt sure my teeth were going to rattle out of my mouth, then he lifted me up and wrapped his arms around me. "God, Peej, I'll never be able to erase that image from my mind—I thought you were dead."

"How am I not?" I whispered into his chest. "And where is Khol? Why is he letting us be together now?" My throat constricted with panic. If I wasn't dead, then that meant I was bonded with Khol. *No, no, no, no, no.*

"He healed you. He was releasing me when he felt

something was wrong with you, and he brought me with him since he was touching me and he was in a panic."

I stiffened and pulled far enough back from Bryn to meet his gaze. "So, I'm still bonded with him?" *I tried to kill myself for nothing.*

Tearing away from Bryn's grasp, I stared down at my completely unmarred wrists. Something in me snapped, or maybe it had snapped a long time ago, and I'd never been the same. I started clawing at my wrists as I cried out in frustration, "You should have let me die!"

"Stop," Bryn commanded as he grabbed my hands. "You're not bonded with him anymore. You were dead for a second, or near death—I don't really know which, and honestly I don't want to know. But your soul left your body, breaking the *Anam Cara* magic. You're not bonded with either of us."

My heart fluttered with fresh hope. "So we can be together? Me and you, like it's supposed to be?" If he still wanted me after what I'd done that is. And I wasn't talking about the attempted suicide, I meant about letting Khol claim me. I'd been with someone else besides him. Maybe he wouldn't want me anymore. "Unless...unless you don't want me anymore," I added, voicing my fear out loud.

Bryn looked at me like I'd sprouted two heads. "Maybe you have lost it if you think that. Why would you think that?"

"Because I was with him—I let him—oh God—" I crumpled to the ground, unable to stop the sobs from wracking my body.

Bryn took me in his arms, enveloping me in his warmth. "That doesn't matter. I'll always love you no matter what happens. You didn't betray me on purpose. I know you never would."

"But I enjoyed it. It felt good," I croaked into his chest.

"I don't get it. Are you trying to talk me out of wanting to be with you?"

"You have the right to know. You need to know that you deserve someone better than a slut like me."

"What?" He pulled back just enough to snag my gaze, his expression incredulous. "Are you seriously slut shaming yourself right now? For something that was essentially forced on you? I just—I mean—fuck Peej— don't you know that I could never want anyone but you? I love you unconditionally. Always. None of the rest matters. That's what unconditional means since you obviously forgot. "

Bryn's lips came crashing down on mine, his tongue sweeping into my mouth with a mixture of his unique taste and salt from my tears. It was a heady flavor, thick and rich with hope for a future together. My hands tangled in his hair as I struggled to get closer to him. *Home*, he was my home.

Bryn's hands ran over my body as if he were checking to make sure I was real before his movements changed into something with more intent. I wrapped myself around him, needing to feel his skin under my hands, needing to absorb the taste of him on my tongue. I hadn't really thought about what I was wearing, but when the cool air touched my heated flesh as Bryn parted the front of my robe, I shuddered as goose bumps erupted all over me.

"Is it too soon? Do you want this?" Bryn paused before going any farther, hesitation evident in his voice and body language.

"Yes," I rasped as I pushed my bare skin up against his hands. "I need this—with you." What I left unsaid hung in the air between us. I needed Bryn's touch to wipe away the shameful feelings Khol's had left behind.

My words set Bryn's lips and hands into motion again, and I moaned with satisfaction. "I'll never let anyone else touch you again, I promise. You're mine." Bryn's vow wrapped his power around me in a cool caress, claiming what was rightfully his. He slid into me easily, his rhythm soft and slow at first, and then faster as we were both swept away in our passions.

I scored my nails down his back, crying out his name as a feeling of ultimate possessiveness washed over me. I looked up at him, capturing his glowing electric blue eyes in my sights. It was time to make my claim. "You're my *Anam Cara*. No one will ever tear me away from you again." I knew it was the dragon part of me jockeying for control, but I didn't care because all of me wanted him, and all of me *would* have him.

"Yes," Bryn rumbled, his pupils dilating as he bowed his head to claim my lips again. Our powers rose up and twined together, becoming one. *It's perfect, all so perfect*, I thought as Bryn and me cried out our releases together and collapsed into each other's arms. We were one, as we were always meant to be, and nothing short of death could change that now.

Bryn cradled me to his chest as he wrapped one arm around my waist while the other smoothed my hair back from my sweaty face. I had so many questions floating around in my head now that we were done getting reacquainted. Like where was Khol now, and why had he let Bryn claim me for his *Anam Cara* after everything? Where were we for that matter? "Why did he let this happen now, after he fought so hard to have me himself?" I mused out loud.

"Maybe it would be better if I answered that for myself," Khol replied, his tone raw.

Stumbling to my feet, I refastened my robe, and Bryn wrapped his arms around my waist as I turned towards Khol. "What are you doing here?" I asked, my stomach twisting.

A bitter smile turned his lips up ever so slightly. "This is my land. I am free to go wherever I wish within my domain."

"Why? Tell me why you let him claim me? After you put us through—all the rest."

His gaze dropped to my wrists before snapping away. "I miscalculated how human your emotions are. I never thought you'd do—" He clenched his fists, nostrils flaring. "—what you did. I was forced to realize that I would never have you for my own." The rest passed from him to me silently. It didn't need to be said out loud. In his way, he'd done exactly what I'd done for Bryn. He'd sacrificed himself for the happiness of the one he loved—me. My heart broke just a little for him.

"Thank you," I murmured, not knowing what else to say.

"I will protect you. You will stay here as planned, out of reach of the aliens."

"And Bryn?"

"He is your *Anam Cara* now. I can't expect you to stay and for him to not. We must regroup and gather our strength so that we can make our move against those creatures soon. The time for action is nearing. We can no longer wait on the sidelines." He turned as if to go and then looked back at me with sorrow in his glowing eyes. "I never meant—I never thought—please forgive me," his voice cracked.

"I forgive you." And I did. I wasn't sorry for what I'd done. It led me back to Bryn after all, but I wasn't going to hold a grudge against Khol. Maybe he was too dragon to fully understand what he was doing before, but at least he had righted the wrong.

"Thank you," he whispered just before he disappeared.

"Well, I don't fucking forgive him," Bryn muttered under his breath.

"Bryn," I chastised, swatting him with my hand playfully. "He's not human."

"Yeah, and neither are we apparently." Bryn's face settled into hard lines, as he no doubt considered the betrayal from his parents that truth represented.

"At least we have each other, for real now." I wrapped my arms around his neck and stood on my tiptoes so I could reach his lips with mine.

Bryn scooped me up and settled on the ground with me in his lap. "This is all just a little surreal. I didn't even know dragons existed."

"Yeah, me neither," I rasped against the skin of his neck as I darted my tongue out to taste him. Would I ever get enough of him? My whole body seemed to buzz in anticipation of his touch. I nibbled on his ear next, causing Bryn to fist my hair to hold me close.

"Oh God, Peej. Is it just my imagination or does everything feel better than before? Because I didn't think that was possible."

I moved to straddle him, my ankles locked behind his back. "Khol said dragons are insatiable, especially the females. He said we haven't even begun to experience the full scope of what it means to be dragon yet, and now we're *Anam Caras*." I slid my hands over the hard expanse of his back, his muscles rippling under my fingertips. "And because we're *Anam Caras*." I nipped at his bottom lip, and his large hands dropped from my hair to cradle my bottom. "You're the only one who can give me what I need."

Bryn chuckled low in his chest. "I swear I've had dreams about you that began like this."

I stopped kissing him and raised my eyebrows. "Oh yeah, and how'd those dreams end up?"

He chuckled again, tugging at my robe. "I'm a guy, how do you think they ended up?"

I snorted. "That's what I thought." Sobering, I studied his beautiful face, a face I'd known practically all of my life, and now a face I would know intimately for the rest of it. "I love you more than I can ever explain to you." My words were similar to ones Bryn had said to me the first night we were together. The night I'd given him my virginity. "I would die for you."

I felt rather than heard a low growl erupt from his chest. "You almost did." He pulled my robe wide open to expose my naked skin to the warm afternoon, and yet I still shivered under his rapt gaze. "How the hell did I get to be so lucky?"

Heat gathered in my middle, and despite having been with him, it felt like it'd been an eternity since his intimate touch. I met his illuminated cerulean eyes, which were still a slight shock to see, and reached out to him. "I need you," I rasped low. He welcomed the invitation eagerly, staying in my embrace for the rest of the afternoon until the sun began to dip low behind the horizon.

"P.J.!" Jenna yelled excitedly, setting me in frenzied motion to cover Bryn and myself up. I so didn't want her to get a look at Bryn's goodies. They were for my eyes only.

"No. Not yet. I don't wanna deal with her yet." Bryn's grip

around my waist tightened as he sleepily protested Jenna's arrival. "Let's pretend she's not here, and maybe she'll just go away." I harrumphed, knowing that wasn't likely to happen.

I clambered to my feet just in time to see Jenna and Jeremy running towards me. Bryn remained where he was, but with his hands propped under his head. He seemed so relaxed and snuggly that I pouted at him, wishing I could in fact just ignore Jenna and remain with him just awhile longer.

Jenna leapt at me, throwing her arms around my middle in a crushing bear hug. For someone so small she was extremely strong. "Oh my God! I was so worried! Macon told us what happened!" Her eyes flicked down to Bryn, and she tackled him next. "Bryn! I missed you!" A low growl rang out around us, and Jenna paused to glance over her shoulder at me with horror. "Was that you, P.J.?"

"Just don't touch him right now, okay?" I didn't know why I was being so possessive and jealous. It really wasn't like me, and I knew Jenna didn't mean anything by what she'd just done. Maybe it was the *Anam Cara* thing, or maybe it was my dragon side, or a combination of the two; but regardless, Bryn and me were going to have to find out what else being dragon mates was going to mean for us.

Jenna stood, raising her hands into the air in mock surrender. "Touchy, touchy."

"So you're Bryn," Jeremy said with an undercurrent of hostility that made me grimace. Bryn didn't know yet that I'd been hanging out with him, or that he'd kissed me.

Maybe he wouldn't care now that we were mated. *Yeah, right.* He'd probably want to beat Jeremy into a bloody pulp. How could I forget how he'd reacted when Jeremy and me had our first date? He was crazy with jealousy when I'd gone to see him that night, and he had barely begun to come into his dragon powers. Or maybe his dragon side is what drove him to be so jealous in the first place? I hadn't thought about that before. *Huh.*

Bryn stood abruptly, gaze locked onto Jeremy, his nostrils flaring as his eyes lit up again. The blanket that I had thrown over his middle to cover him up fell to the ground as he pulled on his pants.

"Damn," Jenna breathed as her gaze zeroed in on Bryn's nether region. "No wonder you're in love with him. What, Khol didn't stack up? *And* he's part dragon? You are so lucky."

I elbowed her in the side, causing her to grunt. "Keep your eyes to yourself. He's mine," I hissed. Yeah, I really had to get my jealously under control or we'd never be able to go into public again. *And the problem with that is?* a small voice inside me whispered.

"Yeah. I *am* Bryn. Who are you?" Bryn's menacing tone brought me back to the bigger problem at hand. *Bryn had seen Jeremy pick me up for our date. What's the point in pretending that he didn't know him? It must be some stupid male thing. Ugh.*

"Jeremy."

Bryn's gaze snapped to meet mine. "What the hell is he doing here?"

Jeremy notched his chin up and smirked. "I came to help protect P.J. We've gotten pretty close since you've been gone. Or hasn't she told you?"

"She's mine," Bryn growled, and I stepped into his side, placing my hands on him. I could sense his dragon moving closer to the surface, and I wasn't going to let him do something he'd regret, like kill Jeremy. Although with his current murderous expression, I wasn't so sure he would ever come to regret it. *Geez*—Bryn and me both had gone our entire lives without knowing dragons existed, let alone that we were half-bloods, and now we were both acting more dragon than human. *What's going on?*

"Bryn," I whispered as I grabbed him by the side of his face, tugging him down so I could capture his mouth with mine. I pushed my tongue forcefully past his full lips, and it only took him a second to respond by pulling me into his body and fisting my hair. I couldn't help the moan that escaped from me as he tugged my neck back by my hair so his mouth could latch onto my throat. He nipped lightly as if to leave his mark, and then he lifted me up so I could wrap my legs around his waist. His lips reclaimed mine ferociously. I forgot where we were and who we were with as I let my fresh lust for Bryn consume me completely.

I suddenly found myself back on the pallet with Bryn's body weight pinning me down. I spread my legs so he could settle into the cradle of my body I offered. He ground himself against my hot core, jean against bare skin, and I moaned at the delicious friction.

"Ahem," Jenna said demonstratively. "Don't mind us or anything."

Bryn and me both froze, our heads snapping in the direction of Jenna's voice. "Shit. I forgot they were here. How could I forget they were here?" Bryn's face flushed with embarrassment as he sat up slowly, carefully making sure everything of ours that should be covered actually was.

"You guys look seriously freaky with those glowing eyes." Jenna laughed.

I wanted the ground to open up and swallow me whole. If Jenna hadn't said something, would Bryn and me have gotten down to business right in front of them? Well, not that they would have stuck around—hopefully—but if they would have, for the sake of argument, would we have? My face heated as I realized the answer. "I-I'm so s-sorry," I stammered, unable to meet Jenna or Jeremy's eyes. "I just meant to distract him, and then—well, I guess we got a little carried away."

"Well, you definitely distracted everyone," Jeremy muttered bitterly.

"No one asked you," Bryn growled.

I placed my hand on his arm. "Bryn. Stop. I'm yours."

He shook his head as if trying to dislodge some random thought. "Yeah, I know, it's just I feel so possessive. I don't know what's going on with me."

"You're newly bonded *Anam Caras*," Macon, who

appeared from nowhere causing Jenna's face to light up, stated dryly. *As if that explains everything.*

I raised my eyebrows questioningly at him. "And that's supposed to mean something to us?"

Macon shrugged. "Newly bonded *Anam Caras* act as if crazed for each other. But don't worry, it doesn't last forever, just a couple of decades."

"A couple of decades?" I squeaked. "So what you're saying is we shouldn't be allowed in public for a couple of decades, and then what? Do the feelings just go away?" The jealousy, the possessiveness could go away yesterday as far as I was concerned, but a little pang of sadness swept through me at the thought of losing some of the intensity between Bryn and me.

"No, from what I understand, the feelings never go away. You'll just get better at controlling them," Macon said with an amused smile. Could he read what I was thinking from my face?

"Oh." I slipped my hand into Bryn's large warm one. I sighed in contentment as my body hummed in pleasure at the mere touch of him. It was as if we were completing a circuit.

"Great," I heard Jeremy mutter under his breath.

I glared at him, wondering if he was spoiling for a fight. If he kept up with the little jibes, there would be no doubt that a battle between him and Bryn would erupt eventually.

I directed my attention back to Macon, choosing to ignore Jeremy and his annoying comments. "Is there anything else we should know about being new dragon mates—I mean, *Anam Caras?*"

Macon's face turned pensive. "I'll have to think about it."

"Why can't there be some kind of introductory manual or something? You know, like for expecting mothers—*So you're going to be a newly bonded Anam Cara, what to expect the first few decades.*"

"I'll see what I can find," Macon said as his attention turned to Jenna. "I was looking for you."

She reached out to touch his arm while biting her bottom lip. "*Reeeally?*" she purred. "And why is that?"

He drew her to him, and she molded her body to his, wrapping her arms around his waist. "I think you know," he said with a lascivious smile.

She giggled. "Oh, you dragons are so naughty."

"You know it," he growled low in his throat as they disappeared.

"Hey, get your asses back here!" I called with annoyance. "I wanted to talk to Jenna!" But I got no response except for another snarky remark from Jeremy.

"Could have fooled me. There seemed to be only one thing on your mind that you wanted to do, and it wasn't talking, and it definitely wasn't with Jenna."

"All right. That's about enough out of you," I snapped as I dropped Bryn's hand and stalked towards Jeremy. "I told you from the beginning that we were never gonna be anything more than friends." I narrowed my eyes at him. "I told you I loved Bryn."

Jeremy narrowed his deep brown eyes back at me. "But the chemistry we both felt when we kissed—you can't deny that was there."

"He kissed you?" Bryn growled from behind me. *Damn.* I was hoping to get the chance to tell him myself before Jeremy blew me out of the water.

I turned around to meet Bryn's angry gaze. His eyes were lit up like two flashlights. "I wanted to tell you—I was gonna tell you. I didn't want you to find out like this."

Bryn's chest heaved with barely controlled rage. "Get out of here. Now. Get out of my sight."

"Me?" I asked, trembling. I knew it. Bonded or not, he was pissed.

"No. Him."

"I'm not leaving you here with him like this." Jeremy crossed his arms over his chest stubbornly.

"Now!" Bryn bellowed, causing me to grimace.

"I said I wasn't—"

"Please, Jeremy. Just leave us to sort this out ourselves. He won't hurt me if that's what you're implying. He would die before he ever hurt me." Jeremy met my eyes with uncertainty. I could see he was ready to throw down with Bryn over this, and that was the last thing I wanted. "Please," I begged.

"Yeah, okay." Jeremy stalked off with tension wafting off of him in palpable waves.

Bryn stood utterly still, not uttering a word, until he was completely out of sight, and then yanked me into him. "Tell me."

"There's not much to tell. He wouldn't take no for an answer, and he kissed me. End of story." I bit my lip as I studied him, hoping he wouldn't push the issue any further.

"And?" *Crap.* Bryn knew me too well. He sensed there was more to the story.

"And what?"

"*And* did you like it? *And* how many times did he kiss you? *And* did you kiss anybody else while I was gone?" Bryn's voice broke an octave lower than normal.

I flicked my gaze away, unable to meet his angry glare anymore. How would I feel if he'd kissed other girls while he was away? My gut clenched. *What if he did?* "I couldn't help but like it. He used his Gatekeeper power on me. He can manipulate energies…" I let my voice trail off, hoping I wouldn't have to explain.

Bryn's fingers bit into my lower back. "What does that mean *exactly*?"

"I…umm…you know…when he kissed me the first time. Okay? Is that what you wanna hear?"

Bryn's body trembled, and his voice came out as a low rumble. If I hadn't been so close to him, I wasn't sure I would have heard it. "Did you do anything else with him?"

"No," I squeaked.

He tipped my chin up with his fingers so I could meet his gaze. He did it so slowly and so carefully that a wave of fear shot up my spine. "Who else?"

My eyes widened as I stared into Bryn's lipid pools. He was different—changed, his dragon side riding him hard

AVA WIXX

at the moment, pushing to have complete control. Despite that, I forced myself to remember that he was still my Bryn, still the same Bryn that I'd known practically all of my life, and now he was my *Anam Cara*. I had no reason to actually fear him.

"Khol," I finally muttered.

"That's it? Anyone else?"

Anger simmered in my gut. "No. I didn't go around kissing everybody while you were gone, Bryn. I love you. I'm bonded with you. I tried to kill myself for you." I knew the last thing was a low blow and still fresh, but it was the truth.

He released me, lurching back a few steps. "Goddamnit, Peej. These feelings, I know they're not right, I'm trying to fight them, but—I just wanna throw you down on the ground right here and right now, and I wanna just—just—" His gaze flicked away from me, as if ashamed of what he was about to say.

"Just what?" I asked softly.

"I wanna take you so long and hard that you won't remember anybody else ever touching you other than me. Because there won't be anybody else ever again," he growled.

A thrill ran up my spine at his words. *I have issues. Or maybe I should say my dragon side has issues.* "Then do it," I whispered.

Heat flared to life in Bryn's eyes. "It won't be like it's been between us before."

I swallowed in anticipation. "I know. I want you to."

And I did, I wanted him to do whatever he needed to do to me to make things right between us.

"You can't mean that," Bryn said the words with an undercurrent of hope. He wanted me to mean them but didn't quite believe that I did.

I tugged my robe from my body and let it drop to the ground by my feet. "I do." I trembled slightly in the cool air as I waited for him to react. "Take me any way you want. I'm yours."

Bryn's powers had gotten a major boost because he came to me almost as fast as Khol could move. He shoved me to the ground and flipped me over so I was flat on my stomach. I lay utterly still, my breathing erratic, as I listened to him pull off his pants. Then he reached down and yanked my lower half up into the air, sliding into me as he held my neck down with one hand. He took me fast and hard, setting a blistering pace, and honestly, if it had been anyone else, I would have rebelled against such treatment. But it was Bryn—*everything with him is different.* Always had been and always would be. Maybe that was the one good thing that had come out of being with Khol; I now had a way to compare exactly how different.

"Mine," Bryn grunted from behind me.

"Yes," I managed to rasp.

I wanted to belong to him completely and in every single way possible. Bryn branded me brutally, and I know most people would never label what we were doing as making love, but somehow, to me, it still was. My heart swelled, knowing that he loved me so completely, and wanted me so desperately that he felt the need to take me in such a manner.

When we were finally both spent and I was hoarse from expressing my enthusiastic approval of this particular manner of lovemaking, Bryn settled me onto his chest and held me there tightly. I didn't protest, and merely fell asleep, content with the knowledge that I was exactly where I was always meant to be.

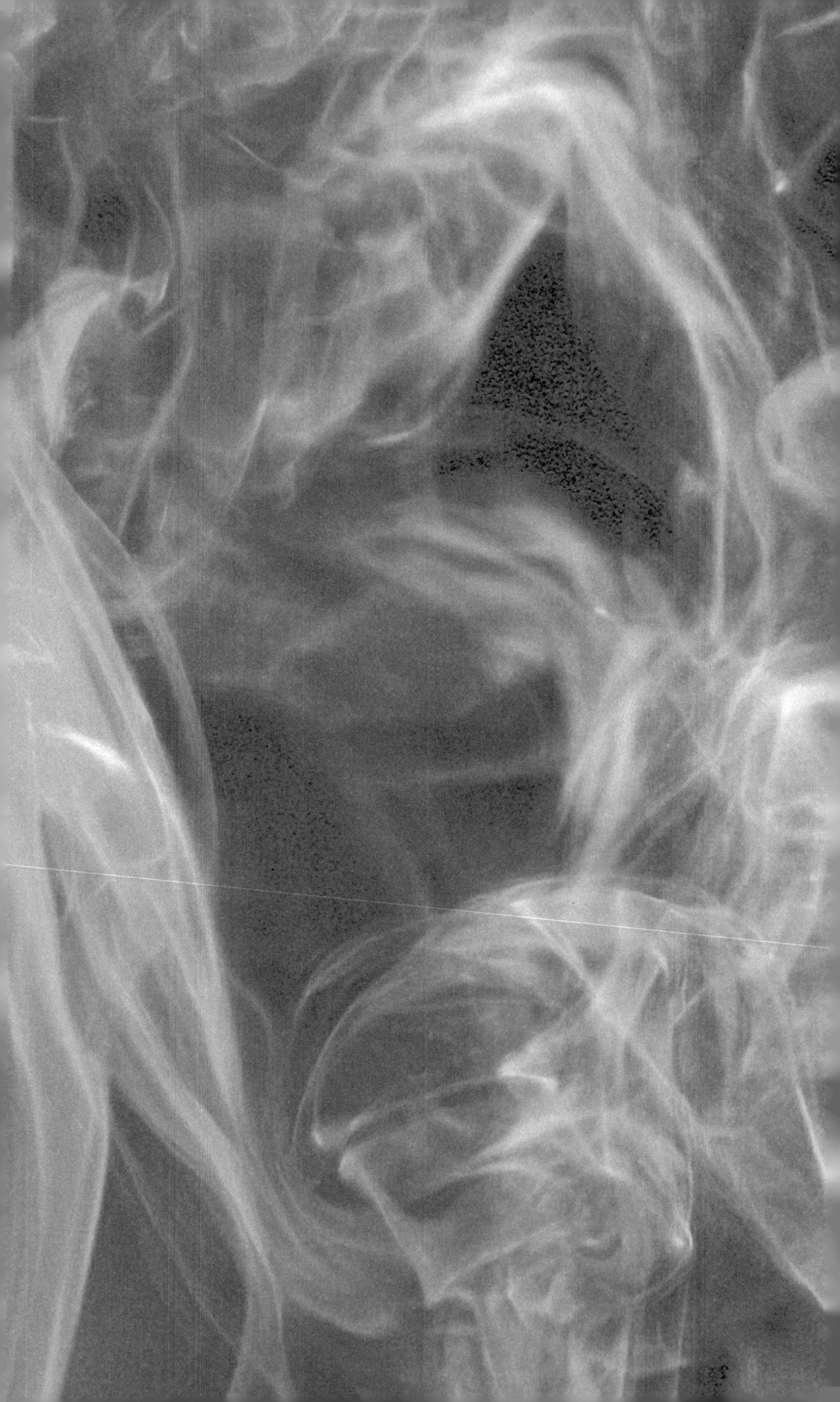

Chapter 19

Sometime the next morning, Bryn and I walked hand-in-hand back to Khol's castle floating on a cloud of euphoria. Bryn seemed satisfied in the solidity of our relationship after marking his claim on me again and again late into the night. I wished we could have stayed in that garden for days, if not months, just enjoying each other's company, a step removed from all the problems that existed in our normal lives. But I knew that was unrealistic, plus I really needed a shower, and I sternly informed Bryn that there would be no more naked time until I got one. He begrudgingly agreed and was mollified when I invited him to join me.

I glanced over at Bryn, my heart speeding up at just the sight of him. He was the most beautiful guy I'd ever laid eyes on. Plus, the more he touched me, the more I craved him, and not just when we were being intimate, since that was still a relatively new addition to our relationship. It had always been that way between us. There was a comfort in feeling his skin against mine, almost like a security blanket, and until it had been ripped away for a while, I'd never realized just how important it was to me.

I hung back a few steps while our hands remained intertwined, trying to catch a glimpse of my *Anam Cara* mark on the nape of his neck. Every time I saw it, a thrill shot through my veins. *He's mine—well and truly mine.*

"Are you trying to look at it again?" Bryn studied me, amusement in his dark blue eyes.

I smiled sheepishly at him. "I can't help it. Show it to me, please?" I batted my eyelashes at him and bit my lip.

He groaned. "All right, but this is the last time." He hunched over and bent his head forward as I released his hand and came to stand behind him.

I reached my right index finger up to trace it. My *Anam Cara* mark on him appeared nothing like his on me. It was a deep crimson red, shaped like a lopsided star. "This means you're mine," I whispered in awe.

Bryn spun me up in his arms, and I laughed. "We never needed those marks to know we belong to each other."

"And to think you once tried to resist me. Remember back when I first figured out my feelings for you, and you tried to shut me down?"

Bryn grunted. "I was young and stupid. I thought you were too good for me."

I scrunched my nose up at him. "Bryn, it's only been a few weeks. What do you think now?"

"It seems like a lifetime ago though, doesn't it?" He

kissed the tip of my nose, and grabbed my hand as he started walking again. "I still think you're too good for me, but I'm smart enough now to not look a gift horse in the mouth. If you wanna be with me, I'm not gonna fight you."

"Yeah, whatever." Bryn was so out of my league in so many ways it wasn't even funny. I still couldn't figure out what he saw in me.

"You just don't see yourself very clearly."

"I see myself fine," I muttered, not wanting to talk about it anymore.

"Come on, seriously, Peej. We were born to be together. Can't you see that? What were the chances of us both being half-blooded dragons and meeting the way we did? It was meant to be, and that's all there is to it. Plus, we're bonded now. It puts a whole new meaning to the words *till death do us part.*"

I didn't respond because I couldn't exactly disagree with him. The oddities surrounding us were too much to not believe that fate had brought us together.

I sighed, my mind wandering to the problems we were going to have to face in the real world—and soon. "What are we gonna do about our families? School? Those alien things? Everything is such a mess, Bryn."

"It could be worse. You could be bonded to Khol, or you could be …" A grimace swallowed the rest of his words and he quickly changed the subject. "Have you had any more visions? About those things?"

"No. Don't you think I would've said something? That's not exactly info I would keep to myself."

"Huh," Bryn grunted.

"What? It's not like I get visions on a regular basis..." I trailed off as I studied Bryn's suddenly pensive expression. "Tell me what you're thinking."

"It's probably nothing, but ever since I got here, I've been feeling more...dragon and less Guardian. And now you tell me you haven't had any more visions with all that's going on, factor in your much more dragon tendencies and..." He lifted his eyebrows as he stared at me as if I should know where he was going with his current train of thought.

I didn't. "And?" I prodded.

He pursed his lips. "All right, it might sound stupid, but I feel like this place is stifling our Seer and Guardian sides for some reason."

"That just doesn't make any sense though, I mean, it's not like..." My gut twisted the more I considered his theory. I mean, it wasn't completely ridiculous. "Maybe we should talk to Khol."

Bryn growled under his breath. "I don't trust him."

"You have no reason not to. He's never lied, and he's been totally upfront about himself and his motivations since I first met him. Besides, if he wanted to keep me from bonding with you, he could have." Bryn scowled in response and I glared at him. "Well, I'm gonna talk to him whether you like it or not."

"I'm not gonna let you talk to him alone."

"Fine. Whatever. I didn't say I wanted to."

I wasn't about to have a stupid argument with Bryn.

He had nothing to worry about with Khol. Bryn and me were bonded, and Khol had saved my life. *What's the big deal?* Okay, so maybe the fact that I'd slept with Khol was kind of a big deal, especially because it sort of wasn't my choice, not rape exactly, but not one hundred percent my call either. But with everything that happened after... Well, I was willing to try and forget about it at least—*I want to forget about it. All of it. Have it permanently wiped from my mind.*

"Khol," I called. "Hey, Khol, we need to talk to you, please."

Instead of Khol, Drake appeared. "Yes, what can I do for you?" he snapped. *Boy, he really doesn't like me.*

"Where's Khol? I need to talk to him. No offense," I added, trying to be nice, not that I cared all that much. I knew there was little hope of changing Drake's opinion of me now.

"He is...indisposed at the moment. Unless it's an emergency—"

I waved him off. "No, no emergency. I was just hoping to talk to him about some stuff. When's he gonna be *un*-indisposed?"

Drake smirked. "It could be some time. He is currently occupied with a guest—of the female persuasion."

"Oh." My cheeks heated. "But I thought—well, I thought..." I knew our bond was broken, but I thought it might take Khol more than five minutes to get over being in love with me. *But wait ... didn't he say that male dragons couldn't move on? I guess I misunderstood. What a relief.*

"Oh, yes, that." Drake met my gaze knowingly. "He will love you and desire you until the end of time, but he knows you are out of his reach now. So he will try to forget you the best way he can. Pointless, really, but he has little choice."

I blinked several times, confusion nettling. "I don't understand." *Or maybe I don't want to.*

"Oh, come on, Peej, he's trying to forget you by burying himself in some other female dragon," Bryn said with disgust.

I shook my head in dismay. "Yeah, okay, but won't he bond with her then? And if he bonds with her— nevermind, I don't wanna know anymore." I obviously didn't understand the dragon mating process as much as I thought. Or maybe I'd been freaking out so much when it was explained to me I didn't hear it right. I obviously didn't know the rules.

Drake's eyes lit up as he glared at me with unmasked hostility. "But maybe you should know. Maybe you should know what he sacrificed for your…happiness." He raked his disapproving gaze over Bryn before returning it to me.

"He'll never be able to bond, never be able to love another, and he'll never father a child. He'll be able to desire other women, have intimate relations with them, but it won't be the same. It'll be sex, and sex only, for the rest of his very long life. Yes, the *Anam Cara* bond is broken, but a male dragon loves forever. If only he hadn't fallen in love with you, and merely wished to claim you for your power, then he would have lost nothing. Or if you would have stayed dead."

My heart fisted as it sunk in what it would really mean for Khol, but what could I do? Both Khol and Bryn would have been completely free if my suicide attempt had been successful. I thought that since my attempt had broken the *Anam Cara* bond, it had broken everything else. Apparently, I was wrong.

Bryn growled. "It's not her fault Khol fell in love with someone that didn't belong to him. She's been mine since way before he came into the picture."

Drake growled back, his body tensing as he stared down Bryn. "You don't deserve her. You are no match for my lord. It shouldn't matter that she is part human. He won her fair and square by the way of the dragon, and he should not have let you have her."

Anger spiked through my system. "Hey! Stop talking about me like I'm some property to be claimed or inherited and fought over. I chose Bryn. Besides, you don't even like me. I would think you'd be ecstatic that Khol didn't get stuck with me."

"It makes no difference if I care for you or not, only that my lord does. I would have served you regardless. What you did—we would have all been better off if he hadn't saved you."

"Don't talk to her that way," Bryn snarled through clenched teeth.

Drake smirked at Bryn. "Or what? What are you going

to do about it, little dragon? You're too young and too weak to play this game with me."

Bryn growled low in his throat, eyes blazing bright, as he stalked towards Drake, who didn't seem alarmed in the least. "I'll show you who's too young and too weak. I'm going to make you regret how you just talked to her."

I clutched at Bryn's arm, but he shirked me off as if I were nothing. "Bryn, please. Let it go."

"You should listen to your little *Anam Cara*. Maybe she's not as stupid as she seems."

"Hey," I exclaimed, "I'm not stupid."

"Then you would have stayed bonded with my lord," Drake spat, "and not have chosen this *baby* dragon."

A red haze dropped over my vision, and a growl erupted from my chest. *How dare he insult Bryn again and again. He has no right.* I charged at Drake, my hands stretched out towards him instinctively. Before I had a chance to process what was happening, Drake was engulfed in flames—flames that were coming from my palms. I froze, staring dumbfoundedly as Drake dropped to his knees screaming in agony, and yet I had no control over what was happening with my body, the flames just kept shooting from my palms.

"No." Khol stepped in front of the flames, drawing the fire into his own palms. "Control your *Anam Cara*," Khol snarled at Bryn.

"I don't know what to do," Bryn snapped. "Tell me what to do."

"There's no time for that." Khol absorbed my flames

into him as he moved closer and closer, one tiny step at a time. When he was scant inches away, he reached out and interlocked his hands with mine. It was as if all of my power was completely sucked away in an instant. With its sudden loss, I dropped to my knees, my vision filling with brightly colored spots. My eyes fluttered shut, and someone caught me before I hit the ground.

"What did you do to her?" Bryn demanded. "Give her to me."

"I did what needed to be done to save Drake. She could have killed him," Khol snarled. "Follow me inside. I'll restore what I took, but not here."

"Wait," I heard Bryn say before I sensed we were inside. Khol must have just shifted us there.

"I don't feel good," I mumbled into Khol's chest. "What did you do?"

"I'm sorry, my little Seer, so sorry I had to do that to you, but you'll feel better soon, I promise," Khol's voice had lost all its harshness as he whispered tenderly to me.

"That's her, isn't it? I can tell by the way you're looking at her. What is she doing here?" a female voice demanded with scorn.

"Leave. I don't want you here anymore," Khol responded, cold as ice.

"But—but—I at least thought—"

"You thought what? You are dragon, you should know better. Now leave before I throw you out."

Even though I was physically weak, my mind was still

reeling. Was the woman that Khol was currently speaking to the one that he'd been *occupied* with? I was almost one hundred percent sure from how they were talking that she was, and he was just going to kick her out like that? *Wow, what an asshole.*

"I'll remember this, *my lord,*" the woman hissed.

"See that you do, so next time you'll remember your place."

"She's not even full-blooded, and she's a child. How could you want her over me? In fact, how could you want her at all?" The women's voice had taken on the tone of a petulant child. *And she was calling me one. Psst.*

"The heart wants what the heart wants," Khol muttered. "Now get out. I don't owe you any explanations, Shannon."

"You're an asshole," I managed to say in a normal tone, my eyelids still too heavy to lift. "You can't just use someone and throw them away like that." I was outraged for Shannon. Women needed to stick together instead of fighting over assholes.

She laughed darkly. "Maybe I do like her after all, even if she is a naïve child."

"I'm not either of those things," I grunted as another wave of dizziness slammed into me. "I just don't feel good."

"Well, I'm leaving," Shannon said just before the door slammed. Couldn't she shift, or was she just being dramatic? I'd probably never know.

Khol settled me on what felt like the bed, which despite my current physical condition got an instant reaction out of me. My eyes snapped open, even though I couldn't quite focus, as I clutched at him. "Ew! No! Don't put me down on used sex sheets! Someone else's used sex sheets!" I'd have to burn my skin off. *Good thing I can now probably do that.*

Khol pushed me back down easily because I was about as strong as a newborn baby at the moment. "We didn't have sex in the bed, so don't concern yourself."

"Oh. Okay."

"Now, let me give you back what I took before Bryn comes storming in here."

"Why didn't you just—" My words were cut off as Khol exhaled into my mouth, his lips pressed firmly against mine. He tasted warm and sweet, and a tang of power swam onto my tongue and down my throat, wrapping itself around my core. My eyes snapped open with the sudden jolt of energy, and I sat straight up in bed as Khol broke contact with me.

I met his gaze with wonder. "Wow. What did you just do?"

"I gave you back the energy I took. You would have eventually regenerated it yourself, but it could have taken days." He stood and backed away from me, flicking his gaze to the side. "I'm not an asshole."

"What?" Was he actually going to try and defend himself after what I'd just heard?

"Shannon is dragon, and she knows what my situation means. She chose to be with me under no false pretenses."

"That still doesn't mean you had to be so callus towards her. You were just plain mean." I grimaced as Khol slumped into himself at my words. For some reason I felt sorry for him.

The bedroom door flew open and a wild-eyed Bryn hurried through its frame. "Peej!" he exclaimed. I rose as quickly as I could, running into his open arms. "You're fine now?" he murmured into my hair, his grip tightening around my waist.

"Yes," Khol answered for me. "I returned to her the energy I stole." He began pacing. "This is why young dragons such as yourself don't usually find themselves with *Anam Caras*. It's your job to keep her under control. If I hadn't shown up when I did, Drake would be dead."

I gasped, horrified that I'd almost forgotten what I'd done to Drake. "But he's gonna be okay now, right?"

"Yes. But no thanks to him," Khol spat in Bryn's direction.

"This isn't his fault," I hissed. "It's mine. I don't even know how I did that."

"You're just coming into your powers, strong emotions are normal triggers. What happened was normal, but what happened after was not." Khol continued pacing.

"Tell me what I need to do, so it doesn't happen again," Bryn said softly. I looked up at him with surprise, not expecting him to accept the blame that Khol was trying to place on him.

"You'll need to train to do it and even then…" Khol met my eyes with some unknown emotion. "I'm not sure how long it'll take a black dragon to be able to do what I did."

Well, I don't like the sound of that. "Wh-What do you mean?"

"You're a fire dragon, all red dragons are, it's our element to control. All dragons have some fire, but not like us, and you're stronger than even I guessed."

I glanced back at Bryn before I met Khol's gaze again. "What does that mean exactly?" I swallowed to try and combat the sudden dryness of my throat.

"It could take decades before he can do what I did today, if at all."

"But why? If all dragons have fire?"

"Black dragons are water dragons. They have fire but not the same level or control as a red dragon. Plus, I'm what you would call ancient, which means I have more power than most."

"Can't I just use water to douse her flame then?" Bryn asked.

"No!" Khol exclaimed. "Promise me you'll never try. With the both of you being so new to your powers and so out of control, you could kill her."

"No. I'll never try then," Bryn said as his arms slid around my waist again, pulling me up against him.

"Where are all these dragon powers coming from? I don't understand why they're just appearing all of a sudden. And I haven't had any visions since I've been here. Something's wrong. In fact, that's why I called Drake to us, because we wanted to talk to you about that."

"Yes. That is a problem," Khol said, his voice growing pensive. "I will admit, I've been a little...distracted. There are some things I hadn't taken into consideration when I brought you here."

Bryn squeezed me once as if to say *I told you so*. I glared at him briefly before focusing back on what Khol was saying, having missed part of it. "—the gates for your power. It would explain why your dragon natures are emerging so fully here." We stared at him blankly. Khol narrowed his eyes at us before continuing. "You might need to go back in order for your Seer gifts to work."

I shifted within Bryn's grasp, still confused. "But why would being here make that much of a difference? There are gates all over the world. I'm sure there's bound to be one close enough."

"We exist in your world and yet...not. Dragon magic helps to keep us concealed here. You simply may not be strong enough to receive visions through the barrier yet." Khol shrugged.

"So being cut off from our other sides has allowed the dragon magic to be pushed to the forefront," Bryn said as the pieces began to click into place.

Khol nodded. "Exactly."

"What are we gonna do?" Going back to all the problems I left behind seemed like a horrible idea, and yet

I knew it was my responsibility to fight the alien creatures simply because I was the only one getting visions about them. "We're gonna have to go back, aren't we?" But I already knew the answer.

"I'm afraid so," Khol responded through gritted teeth.

Fabulous.

Chapter 20

After a lot of discussion—okay, argument—it was decided that our little band of misfits; made up of myself, Bryn, Khol, Jeremy, Jenna, and Macon, who seemed unwilling to leave Jenna's side, were going to venture back to Pittsburgh. The primary goals were to see if I could get any helpful premonitions/visions and to see what had happened there since Khol had taken me on an involuntary vacation to Dragon Land. I couldn't shake the overwhelming ominous feeling that the fallout of my leaving was going to be more than I was going to be able to handle.

Khol and Macon shifted us into the quiet dark of my parents' backyard. *Funny how I've already stopped thinking of it as my backyard.* It was early evening, and yet my parents' house, along with all the neighboring houses, was silent and dark—uncharacteristically so. I swallowed the sudden rise of bile in my throat, sliding my hand into Bryn's large

349

warm one. "Something's not right," I whispered into the night.

"I don't sense anyone nearby," Khol muttered in response.

"I don't feel any weird energies though. That's something," Jeremy said, his voice strung tight.

Dizziness swept through my head, my vision blurring, just as pain abruptly tore through my skull. What I *saw* was like watching several different channels on T.V. but all at once. Most of it was too convoluted for me to make sense of—except for one scene—one that threatened to rip my heart out of my chest.

Cops wearing black S.W.A.T. gear battered in the front door of my parents' house, taking Bryn's family and mine by surprise. Bryn's father was the first to react with his superior Guardian reflexes and abilities—and then everything happened so fast, or maybe I just couldn't focus on it properly. Screams erupted, shots were fired, and my family's living room left in shambles. In the end, both of our families were led out of the house in handcuffs. Bryn's father was bleeding from a bullet wound in his arm, but at least he was still alive.

My vision continued, and I watched as every family in the neighborhood that had any Seers, Gatekeepers, Guardians, or Speakers in it, was taken away in much the same fashion. There was no doubt why they were targeted, why they were taken to who knows where: because of me. It was obvious the alien…riders felt threatened by the fact that I could see them and have visions about them, so they were trying to remove all of us. Until I'd tried to interfere with the school shooting, my kind hadn't even registered on the Riders' radar, but now things had changed.

I slammed back into my body, finding myself in Bryn's arms. He peered down at me, his face pinched with concern, and his eyes churning with dark emotion. "What did you see?"

"Nothing good," Khol answered for me. "Her visions were jumbled and more confusing than normal, but I was able to understand the gist of what she saw."

I fought the impulse to demand how Khol was still able to share my visions with me since I was bonded with Bryn, especially because a small part of me was glad for his deciphering help. We'd all be screwed if I had to figure it all out myself.

But Bryn wasn't above demanding answers from Khol. "How did you share her vision? If anyone should be sharing her visions, shouldn't it be her *Anam Cara*? Which is *me*."

Khol gave Bryn a feral smile. "Yes, well, it seems your *Anam Cara* bond doesn't translate out here where your Guardian and Seer sides are dominant."

"Hey, yeah," Jenna piped up. "Those tattoos are gone from your necks. Weird."

"What?" I exclaimed, twisting to try and see the back of Bryn's neck. I reached my right index finger up to trace the spot where it should have been. A soul-deep sadness seeped into me despite everything else that was going on. *It's gone.*

Bryn caught my hand and tipped my face back so he could look into my eyes. His voice went low and gruff as he spoke, "I told you before, the marks don't matter, and we don't need them to know we belong to each other." It was just with the marks, it somehow seemed to guarantee that we would be together. Without them, it felt like we were right back where we started.

I blinked heavily to stave off my impending tears. Bryn was right, and besides, how shallow was I that I was worried about the lack of some stupid marks on the back of our necks when our families had essentially been abducted?

Biting my lip, I turned towards Khol. "Why were they taken? I mean, what reason was given for S.W.A.T. to take them? Obviously, it's the aliens that wanted them, but they came in using the police and government under the guise of something else—what was it?"

"Suspicion of plotting terrorist acts. They have fake intel, of course, that I'm sure also implies all the families here were part of a cult."

Bryn tensed, and for the second time since I'd known Jenna, she was temporarily rendered speechless. Jeremy spoke first. "Explain," he said flatly.

"They took our families—those things, those alien riders—by using the government and law enforcement as their tools. And who would stop and question them? Once all of our kind are out of the way, there won't be anyone to stop them. They'll take over—they'll rule this world just like they did all the others before this one. Oh God—what do we do now?" I slumped against Bryn.

What could we do? Who was going to believe us? It was probably all over the news about the cult that was planning major terrorist activities. In fact, the whole situation could serve as a double whammy—they'd probably 'find' all kinds of weapons and whatever else they needed to push any kind of agenda they wanted. Fear was always the best motivator, after all.

"What do we do?" I mumbled into my hands.

"First things first," Khol took on an authoritative tone. "We need to get all of you out of here. Just because no one is here now, or spotted us yet, doesn't mean it's safe to be out in the open like this."

Macon strode forward, as if by silent command. "Where should we take them? P.J. needs to be able to get her visions but also be somewhere safe."

"Don't state the obvious," Khol snapped.

Macon bowed apologetically, averting his eyes. "I'm merely thinking out loud, my lord."

Khol spoke as if Macon hadn't said anything. "We'll set up temporary quarters in the caves just outside the boundary line of the spells covering my land. My—" Khol stopped short, eyeing me warily. "*P.J.* will be able to get her visions, and you'll be safe there until we can figure out something better."

"We have to save them!" I exclaimed. "I'm not going

back into hiding and leave them to fend for themselves. I'm the reason they were taken to begin with."

Bryn tightened his grip around me. "They're obviously being kept alive because of you—us. They'll probably offer them in some kind of exchange for you."

My eyes pricked with tears again. "Because of my visions." Yep, and to think just a short time ago, when I hadn't yet come into my Seer abilities, I had prayed and wished for visions to come to me. Now look at the trouble they'd caused. *Be careful what you wish for* was really hitting home for me. "I wish I'd never started getting visions. I wish we could go back to the way it was before." I turned my head, burying my face in Bryn's chest, not wanting to deal with any of it.

"But then who would protect our world? Who would know the truth?" Bryn said gently before kissing the top of my head. "Ignorance isn't always bliss, Peej."

He was right. Of course, he was right. I knew in my heart if I actually had the chance to go back to the way things were before, I wouldn't take it. I simply wished things were as simple as I thought they were before, even though they never actually were anything but complicated.

"Let me just talk to some of my friends before we go," Jenna said over her shoulder before skulking off into the woods. By friends, I knew she meant of the local furry persuasion.

"At least we have an entire team with us," Bryn muttered.

"Yeah, that's at least lucky," Jeremy agreed. "Maybe we should try contacting some of the other teams that are centered around the other gates. Surely they haven't been affected by all of this. Maybe the Riders don't even know about them yet."

"I'll send out some scouts," Khol said. "We'll know shortly who our allies are."

Jenna came scurrying back to our little group with a grim look of determination on her face. "The good news is that my friends are able to see the Riders inside of people, too. That could come in handy in the future."

"Yes. We can use any help we can get." Khol bared his teeth in a mock smile. "Now let's get out of here before we're spotted."

"I LIKED OUR OTHER ACCOMMODATIONS BETTER," Jenna grumbled. She slumped down onto her makeshift bed that was nothing more than an air mattress with a bunch of blankets.

Macon smiled at her indulgently. "This is only for tonight, and then we'll figure out something better. I'll stay here with you."

"Yeah, yeah," Jenna muttered as Macon disappeared to probably get more unnecessary things for her. When he was gone, she scooted over to sit by me, rolling her eyes in exasperation. "I wish he would give me a little space, you know?"

"You seemed really into him before. What happened?"

"He just wants sex all the time. I'll be lucky if he doesn't break me," Jenna said, sighing.

Laughter exploded from me. "Could it actually be true? Could you have actually met your match?" *Wow. Who would have thunk it?*

Jenna scrunched her face up at me with annoyance, flipping her rapidly fading rainbow hair over her shoulder. "I guess I never had a guy stay interested in me for so long." She glanced around to make sure Bryn, Jeremy, and Khol were still setting other things up around the cave and not paying attention to us, before leaning in to whisper, "What do you do with Bryn?"

"What do you mean?"

"You know—when he wants to get it on and you're not in the mood, or he wants to do something you're really not into?" She stared at me.

"Well, Bryn and I haven't been having sex all that long, but—" Had I ever not been in the mood when Bryn wanted me? Had I ever not been into something he wanted to do to me? My cheeks bloomed with warmth as I realized the truth. I didn't know if I could actually deny Bryn anything he wanted from me. He owned me in a way I wasn't sure I wanted to let anyone else know about.

Of course, I knew in my heart that Bryn would never be able to deny me anything either—he was mine as much as I was his—but things like that are still hard to explain to an outside party. "B-but—" I stammered again. I didn't want to tell Jenna, but at the same time, with her Speaker abilities, she'd probably figure it out eventually and just be mad at me for not telling her to begin with. I really didn't need the headache. "But whenever and wherever Bryn wants it, I don't deny him. I just don't want to. I love him too much."

Shock played across her features. "So you're telling me that no matter what, you'd give him what he wanted?"

"I mean ... Yeah, I guess that's exactly what I'm saying." When Jenna didn't say anything right away, I had the urge to explain more, just to clarify. "I love him. I mean, I love him with everything that I am. I would lay down my life for his. Hell, I almost did," I said, thinking about my botched suicide attempt.

Jenna started twirling a piece of her rainbow hair around her fingers, her eyes glazing over. "I wish I could find that."

I was incredibly lucky to have Bryn, and I, too, wished that someday Jenna would find with someone what I had with him. "Me, too. So Macon's not him? Even with his superior dragony lover skills?"

Jenna flopped onto her back, exhaling loudly. "No, he's not him. Even with his superior dragony lover skills." She sighed again, making me smile at her dramatics. "I wonder what's going on with our parents right now?"

I frowned, not wanting to consider the possibilities. In fact, I'd been trying very hard not to think about that subject at all, hence why I had let Jenna distract me with her sex talk without any of my usual complaints. "I think it's best not to contemplate the possibilities so we don't drive ourselves insane."

Leaving Jenna on the bed, I walked over to where the guys were talking quietly to each other in harsh voices. My brows drew together as I strained to hear what they were saying, but as I got closer, they all shut up completely. "Hey, what were you guys talking about?" I didn't have to be a Speaker to know they were trying to hide something from me.

Furtive glances passed between the three of them before Bryn rose and gave me a tight-lipped smile. "Nothing you need to worry about." He reached out one of his large hands to snag mine, but I batted it away with annoyance.

"Don't think you can keep secrets from us and tell me it's nothing." I turned my suspicious glare on each of them in turn. "Now, who's gonna tell me what you guys were whispering about just now?"

By this time Jenna had come up to stand beside me, donning an angry expression to match mine. "Yeah. No secrets. You guys better spill it before it gets ugly up in here."

Khol met my gaze steadily. "It might be best if you didn't know for now."

"No," I said, bunching my fists into tight little balls. "No secrets."

Bryn glanced back at Khol and Jeremy, letting another guarded look pass between them before he nodded once tightly at me. "All right, it's just we didn't wanna upset you anymore."

"Stop stalling and tell us," Jenna exclaimed as she threw her hands in the air. I looked to Bryn, waiting for him to explain.

He cleared his throat and shifted nervously from foot to foot. "We're the last ones left," he blurted out. "The last complete team of Seer, Guardian, Gatekeeper, and Speaker not in custody of some sort."

All the blood drained from my face and a wave of dizziness assaulted me. There was no way I was hearing what I thought I was hearing—absolutely no way.

"Holy shit," Jenna whispered.

"It's true," Khol said. "My scouts just reported back to me. Those creatures—"

"You mean the Riders?" Jenna asked for clarification.

Khol tilted his head as he looked at her. "Yes, the Riders, if that's what we're calling them now. They appear to have planted themselves in every major government in the world. They—"

"So it's all up to us?" I interrupted. My world tilted, and I clutched at Bryn for support. The full implications of what Khol was saying were finally sinking in. "We're the world's first and last hope—literally?" Bryn's warmth engulfed me as he wrapped his arms fully around me. "We can't even legally drink yet, and it's up to us to save our entire world?"

The cave grew silent as tension permeated the air.

How the hell are we gonna pull this one off?

Chapter 21

"It's not fair," Jenna whined for the umpteenth time as she studied herself in the mirror before meeting my gaze in the reflection. She batted her eyelashes furiously against the unshed tears in her eyes. "I'm so plain now—just plain ugly." With that the dam broke, and wetness flowed down her cheeks.

I struggled not to roll my eyes at her obvious pain, returning my attention to my own drastically altered image in the mirror. My long auburn locks had been shorn off into a short angled bob, the front longer than the back. I still had chunky pieces of auburn in my hair, but the majority of it was now a midnight black. "I'll trade you," I said, sighing. Jenna's only response was a guttural sob.

"You look beautiful," Macon cooed to Jenna as he appeared and dropped down on his haunches in front of her. He lifted his arm to show her the offering of flowers that he had brought to cheer her up. "You'll never be plain. You just look more…natural now."

I grimaced at his choice of words. Clearly, just because Macon had been having sex with Jenna, didn't mean he knew her at all. "Natural?" Jenna stood, snatching the flowers from Macon's hands. "Who the hell wants to look natural?"

Unable to resist, I waved my hand in the air and scrunched up my nose. "Umm. Hello? Me. I would love to have a shade of hair that looks like I could have been born with it. Not this" —I tugged at my black and red do for emphasis— "punk rock wet dream."

"My hair is brown," Jenna hissed at me. "It's the color of shit."

"You know what, Jenna? It's actually the best I've seen your hair look since I've known you, but besides that— well—" I tried to clamp down on my anger. "It's not about just us anymore. Do you think I want my hair to look like this? Do you think my self-esteem is soaring when I look at myself in the mirror?" I breathed in and out a few times before continuing on. "Do you think I wanna live in these caverns, even if they look like one of those home makeover shows got a hold of them? It's up to us to save our world, and if going through some unwanted makeovers—both in our appearance and living conditions —helps, then you're gonna just have to suck it up."

"Easy for you to say, your hair doesn't look like shit— literally."

I threw my hands up in the air in utter exasperation. "I

can't deal with you anymore right now," I said as I swiveled on my heel and stalked out of the room. Jenna was my best female friend, and there was a time when I probably would have been as distraught over my hair as she was with hers, but…things had changed. *I had changed.*

I let my feet carry me blindly as my thoughts turned pensive. What if our efforts all turned out to be useless? What if my little band of misfits just didn't have what it took to defeat the alien riders that were trying to take over our world?

"I feel your worry, my little Seer." Khol's deep voice startled me from my internal list of worries—the *what ifs* of self-doubt.

I looked up to see his large 6'7" frame leaning against a tree to the right of me, his dark auburn hair illuminated by the late afternoon sun, making it blaze like fire. I decided to overlook his term of endearment for me because, after all, with me being bonded to Bryn, it had little meaning anymore—except to him maybe. "I really don't like that you can still feel my emotions. That shouldn't be happening with me being bonded to Bryn."

Khol pushed himself off the tree and strolled towards me. I didn't miss the bitterness that showed from behind his glowing green eyes. "As if you have any idea what's normal or not with an *Anam Cara* dragon pair." He let out a long sigh. "Besides, the two of you are hardly typical, neither of you being fully dragon." He began to walk, and I followed behind him, a part of me wanting to comfort him. Khol was in love with me, and being fully dragon meant he always would be—not my fault—but I wished it didn't have to be that way. I wished that he, too, could find true happiness like I had found with Bryn.

"I don't want your pity," Khol rasped harshly, angling himself towards me. "Never give me your pity." I stopped abruptly to stare up into Khol's angry visage. I knew the anger was simply covering his pain, so I wasn't frightened. He would never hurt me. He had already sacrificed his own happiness for mine when he let me take Bryn as a mate despite his prior claim. Even though it took my attempted suicide to make him understand that I would do anything for Bryn, and that he stood no real chance.

"No pity," I said as I touched his arm. "I just wish I could comfort you, make you feel better. I...regret the way things turned out for you."

Khol shifted into my touch, and he relaxed just a little. A sad smile curled the corners of his lips up. "What I would need to be comforted, you would be unwilling to give."

I let my hand fall away from him. "No, you're right. I'm not willing to give you what would really make you feel better."

Khol's hand snaked out to grasp some of my hair between his fingers. "I'm glad you listened to me and left some red in your hair." He frowned as he watched my baby fine strands slip out of his grasp. "It's necessary to alter your appearance, but you still must hold on to the core of who you really are: a *rua arach*."

I had the feeling he was talking about more than just

my hair color. Had he been sensing some of the intrinsic changes that had been slowly taking place over the last couple of weeks? It was as if my hair was simply another symptom—a visible one—of my internal makeover. The old P.J. was too soft, too concerned with unimportant things. I had to become someone who could handle whatever my new life would throw my way.

Bryn appeared suddenly beside me, his dark blue eyes narrowing briefly at Khol before he swept me up in his arms with a laugh. "I think I finally got this teleporting thing down, Peej." His full, supple lips met mine, and I allowed his tongue to sweep in briefly to explore my mouth before I pulled away.

I met Khol's sad eyes, giving him a weak smile. "Don't worry, I wouldn't feel like me if I didn't have some red in my hair. I guess that's the dragon side of me."

"Yes. Most likely," Khol responded flatly before popping out. I was no longer surprised when he did that, but it didn't make it any less rude. *At least say goodbye or something to let a girl know you're about to disappear. Geeze.*

"I don't like you being alone with him," Bryn grumbled.

Choosing to ignore Bryn's ever present jealously of Khol, I gave Bryn a genuine smile. "I'm so happy for you that you have the whole teleportation thing down." I stuck my lower lip out in an exaggerated pout. "But it's not fair that I don't seem to be able to do that, not to mention your other abilities from your Guardian side."

"Nice aversion tactics, Peej. The Queen of Subtlety, as always."

"It's not like I care if you know what I'm doing. You're being ridiculous, and you should know it. It's just I'm not really in the mood to tell you that—again." I crossed my arms over my chest, glaring at him.

He let out a loud, long, and pained sigh. "I can't help feeling territorial around you with him. Blame it on my dragon side. I don't know, even with knowing how things are, I still... Well, I still..." Bryn's voice trailed off as he let his eyes fill me in on what he couldn't say out loud. He still couldn't get the mental image of Khol and me in bed together out of his mind. He hadn't actually seen it with his own eyes, but we all know that sometimes what we imagine is so much worse than the truth.

"I—well, I—" What could I say that he didn't already know? I let Khol claim me to save Bryn's life. Yes, it brought me physical pleasure, but it had ripped my heart out in the process.

Seeing the pain in my face, Bryn grimaced briefly before taking me in his arms. "That wasn't fair. I'm sorry. I'll get over it. I love you too much not to."

I leaned back in the confines of Bryn's arms to study him. His was the face of a fallen angel, or what I imagined one might look like. Pale, flawless skin was drawn taut over high cheekbones, a perfectly sculpted nose hung over full supple lips, and thick black hair—it all made him a study in contrasts. I'd known his face practically all of my life, and when I looked into it, I felt at home in every sense of the word.

"I hate it, too, Bryn. I wish that I didn't have to let him claim me to save your life—but I didn't have a choice. You know that." Tears that I hadn't realized were brewing spilled from my eyes and rolled down my cheeks. "I wish my number was still one." I choked back a sob, hating the fact that I could never again claim Bryn as my only lover. But I couldn't change the past, no matter how much I wanted to.

Bryn buried his face in my hair and inhaled. "It doesn't matter. None of it does, not really. We're together now— *Anam Caras*—and we love each other. I hate that I let it get to me sometimes."

"No, Bryn, it's not your fault. I don't know how you do it. I would curl into a ball and die if the situation were reversed." I fisted his T-shirt and closed my eyes. "I kissed Khol and Jeremy while you were gone, I betrayed you in more ways than one..." Another sob stole the rest of my words. If I found out he had done the same thing to me, I probably really would have curled into a ball and died.

Bryn squeezed me tighter to him. "Let's not think about any of that anymore. We're together now. Forget about the rest." He dipped his head to nip at my earlobe before nibbling on the side of my jaw. I exhaled all my tension, melting into his embrace.

"I love you, Peej, more than anything."

"I love you, too," I murmured as Bryn's hands slid down my body to mold my languid form to his firm, hard one. I let myself luxuriate in the feeling of being surrounded by him for a few moments before pulling away. I met his eyes briefly before focusing over his shoulder, not wanting to get sucked in by the heat for me I saw in them. "We really don't have time for that now. We need to get back—" My words were swallowed by Bryn's fierce kiss, temporarily blanking my mind, which I'm sure was his goal. I moaned into his mouth as his callused hands slipped under my sweater to skim my suddenly overheated skin.

"We have time," Bryn whispered hoarsely as he nibbled his way down my neck, causing white-hot heat to pool in my middle. Sometimes I hated how easy it was for him to manage me, even though I knew the reverse was also true.

"I'm so sick of seeing you guys groping each other everywhere I go. Can't you two be a little more considerate of the rest of us?" Jeremy's angry voice was like ice water being poured over me, and I wrenched away from Bryn's grasp. I looked up to see Jeremy's eyes glittering with jealousy and something else I couldn't read.

I flushed under his scrutinizing gaze. "I'm sorry," I croaked.

"Well, I'm not." Bryn pulled himself up to stand at his full height, which although wasn't as tall as Khol's, was a good deal greater than Jeremy's 6'1", not to mention Bryn's larger frame and muscles were more daunting as well. Jeremy was by no means a tiny or scrawny guy, but he certainly seemed it standing near Bryn.

"Of course you're not," Jeremy said. "You're more than happy to rub it in all our faces that she's yours anytime you want."

"Hey!" I exclaimed indignantly. "That's not what this is all about."

"Like you'd be any different with her," Bryn growled, taking a step towards Jeremy who squared off with him, not intimidated at all.

"Why don't you give me a chance to be with her and we'll see."

"I don't share."

Did Jeremy realize how close to pummeling him Bryn really was? Did he realize how close *I* was to pummeling him for that matter? I strode forward and smacked him across the face with as much force as I could muster. His head snapped to the side before his startled brown eyes met mine. "Don't you ever talk about me like that again." I inhaled and exhaled deep shuddering breaths, trying to rein in my temper. Thank God we weren't in Khol's realm at the moment because Jeremy would have probably been toast—literally—from my dragon fire gift. Even as it was, my palms heated, ignited by my fury.

Fresh anger replaced Jeremy's surprise, and his lip curled into a sneer. "If he would have stayed gone a little longer—"

"Don't say it," my voice vibrated with fury. "Don't you dare say it."

"—I would have gotten my chance to seduce you, too, and then maybe you would have made a different choice."

"It's not all about sex!" I screeched, my voice going up a few octaves. "You knew I loved Bryn from the beginning!"

"And yet you still kissed me—"

"*You* kissed *me*!"

"You enjoyed it. Or was your orgasm all for show? Imagine what I could have done if I actually touched you." Jeremy laughed darkly. "Khol got his shot, what about me?"

Images of Khol and me in bed together skittered across my brain, followed by what I had attempted to do right after—take my own life. The soul-deep agony that was still there but that I suppressed washed over me, pulling me under in one brutal wave. I dropped to my knees, screaming as flames erupted from my palms. They weren't anywhere close to the strength they had been when I burned Drake, but I could feel the power to do more damage lurking just below the surface. And I didn't think I could control it any more than I had the first time.

Bryn rushed forward, panicked. "Peej!" he exclaimed.

"No! Stop!" I croaked. "I don't wanna hurt you!" I met Bryn's eyes as he dropped his arms and let them fall helplessly at his sides.

"Khol," I whispered. Before his name had completely rolled off my tongue, Khol appeared in front of me, and grasped my palms within his. The sudden lack of heat and power caused my world to go dark around the edges, and I fell forward. Warm, strong arms caught me and scooped me up before everything went completely black.

Chapter 22

"Why the hell do I have to be the one who keeps passing out?" I grumbled, my eyes fluttering open to a dimly lit room. I met Bryn's worry filled gaze and wondered why I was still so tired. The last time Khol had siphoned off my power, he re-energized me shortly thereafter—*so what gives?* "Why am I still so tired?" I asked out loud.

"Khol was trying to teach me how to give you some of my power. He thought it would be a good way to learn the pull and push that I need to know to do what he does." Bryn turned away, his face falling into shadow. "But I'm not very good at it." He stood abruptly, his back facing me. "I'm not very good at any of it."

"Hey," I said, pushing myself up onto my elbows with a grimace. Good thing Bryn couldn't see or he would have felt worse about how much I was struggling. "We're both new at this. And we wouldn't have to deal with all of this so soon if I could keep my temper under control."

"Maybe Khol was right. Maybe being with him was the best thing for you," Bryn whispered, causing my heart to flutter.

"You don't mean that." *He's just upset.* I sucked in a deep breath, trying to combat the feeling that my chest was about to cave in. "Don't ever say something like that." When he didn't move or respond, a fine tremor ran over my body. "Bryn?"

In a blur of motion, Bryn took me into his arms, dropping his face into my hair. His muffled voice rumbled low near my ear, "I'm sorry." He didn't say anything else, just continued to hold me tightly in his arms. Afraid to speak, I let him.

What was he thinking? Was he having regrets about being with me? Was I, with my newly emerging powers, too much for him to handle? "It's too late for buyer's remorse," I joked, trying to make my voice sound lighthearted. "You're kind of stuck with me because of the whole dragon *Anam Cara* thing..." My voice trailed off as more self-doubts swirled around in my head. Ever since Bryn and me had left Khol's realm and our dragon sides hadn't been dominating us, our *Anam Cara* marks had disappeared. We hadn't returned for fear of me missing out on an important vision, but the worry that out here—in the real world, so to speak—Bryn and me weren't really bonded was ever present in my mind. Maybe Bryn saw it as a way out, a loophole for him to back out of being with me. "Bryn?" His name seemed to hold all the questions I was unable to speak out loud.

"I would never let anyone else have you." Bryn's voice cracked. "I love you. You know that. Always."

"But then—"

"It just makes me sick that you have to rely on him for anything. I wanna be the one who you turn to for everything. The fact that I can't take care of you kills me a little more every time something like today happens." I kneaded his shoulders where I could reach in an attempt to comfort him, but he pulled away and stood with his back to me again. "Some days I feel every bit the baby dragon he thinks I am. And I hate it." I watched as Bryn's fists clenched and unclenched in frustration. "I need some time alone," Bryn muttered before popping out ala Khol style.

"Damn it!" I growled as I feebly punched the bed. "Not you too now." It was annoying enough that Khol popped in and out all the time, but now Bryn seemed to be following suit with that unacceptable behavior. *Stupid dragons!*

"They're killing the wolves!" Jenna exclaimed in a panic as she burst into the room brandishing her laptop. "We can't let them kill the wolves!"

"Okay, calm down. What are you talking about?"

"The government is letting people kill off the wolves in Idaho and Montana!" Jenna said in a rush. "I found info about it online!" She paused to inhale and exhale a few times, her face flushed with anxiety. "You know who it really is: the Riders! We can't let them do it! Oh my God, I can't breathe!" She gasped, clutching at her throat. "Can't breathe!" She clawed at her throat, her breathing becoming short little gasps as her face flushed even more.

Holy shit! Was she having a panic attack or could she really not breathe? "Khol!" I cried out. "Khol!" Maybe with his healing abilities, he could help her. It was worth a shot anyways.

Both Khol and Macon appeared. Macon rushed to Jenna's side, worry creasing his brow. Khol turned his eyes to me. "What's the problem?" he asked calmly.

I waved my hands frantically in Jenna's general direction. "I think it's pretty self explanatory!"

"She's having a panic attack. They're not unheard of," Khol stated blandly.

I narrowed my eyes at him. "Well, can't you fix it or something, you know, with your healing powers?"

Khol frowned at me. "Since there isn't anything actually wrong with her physically, and since the panic is caused by her mind, there is nothing I can do. It will pass, and she'll be fine."

My gaze shifted to Jenna. Macon had scooped her up in his arms in an effort to comfort her. She was still gasping for air and babbling about us needing to save the wolves. "She says they're killing off the wolves—the Riders. What can we do?"

"We must pick our battles. Right now, the most pertinent problem on our hands is rescuing your families, or would you disagree?"

I swallowed at the sudden lump in my throat. As much as I wanted to help the wolves, I, of course wouldn't rate their lives above those of my family, and I didn't think Jenna would either. "No, I don't disagree," I whispered, almost ashamed to say the words out loud. Unfortunately, in a war there would always be casualties, and if I wasn't mistaken, we were technically at war with the Riders.

Khol nodded once tightly at me and then disappeared. "Yep, thanks for your help," I grumbled to myself.

"Don't worry, I'll take care of her," Macon said to me just before he disappeared with Jenna still in his arms.

I sucked in a startled breath when I noticed Bryn standing perfectly still in the shadows cast by the slightly ajar door. I wondered how long he'd been standing there when he spoke. "And again you called to *him* for help," he said, his eyes dark with unfounded jealousy.

"I—well, I—" I started to stammer, emotionally steeling myself. I loved Bryn and had no reason to feel guilty for calling out to Khol for help. After all, Bryn didn't possess the healing capabilities that Khol did. "He has healing powers that you don't. I won't feel bad for asking for his help. He's a part of our team now, Bryn—get used to it."

Bryn ground his teeth together as he glared at me, his sea storm eyes raging with dark emotion. "Yeah, well, maybe you can ask for his help tonight to keep you warm." He swiveled on his heel and stalked away from me.

I remained paralyzed in shock for a few moments before I gave him chase. "Bryn! Wait!" I scurried to catch up to him, and when I did, I grabbed at his arm. "Bryn!

What the hell is the matter with you today? Stop being so ridiculous!" I yelled, exasperated. "You have no reason to be jealous, so why are you?"

Bryn halted, exhaling loudly and slumping his shoulders. He stared at the ground in front of him for what seemed like an eternity before lifting his head to meet my gaze. "After everything... I still don't feel good enough to be with you sometimes."

My stomach twisted. "You can't be serious. I thought we were past that. If anything, you're too good to be with me." I still had trouble wrapping my mind around the fact that Bryn loved me. He was so perfect in every way, and well—I'm just me, enough said. How could we both think the other one was too good to be with us? Or was that just a part of being in love, putting the object of your affection up on a pedestal?

"Bryn," I tried again, reaching up to run my fingers through his shorter, spikier hair. A part of me mourned the loss of his longer locks, but just like the rest of us, I knew he had to change his appearance the best he could in case we were out in public and spotted by Regs on the lookout for the wanted and missing cult members' children. Thinking about how I missed his hair, I wondered if he thought I was as pretty with my new hair. "Do you still think I'm pretty?" I couldn't keep the words from spilling out of my mouth. Maybe I was just as vain as Jenna in my own way.

Bryn turned to regard me with a twinkle in his eyes that reminded me of the old carefree Bryn, the one from my childhood. "Just because you've gone all punk rock slash emo on me doesn't mean I'd kick you out of my bed," he teased.

I punched him in the arm, which didn't even cause him to flinch. "Hey, don't be mean. It's not like I had much of a choice."

His expression grew serious, and he reached up to touch my hair before cupping my face. "You'll always be beautiful to me, Peej, no matter what." I closed my eyes and sank into his hand. To have someone like Bryn love me, despite the utter mess I knew I was—how did I get to be so lucky?

"I love you," I murmured, opening my eyes to stare up into his beautiful face.

Bryn's hands moved down my back, and he pulled me closer to him. "I need you," he said gruffly, his voice breaking an octave lower than normal. "Now."

His words ignited a wave of heat inside me that quickly spread throughout my body. I suddenly needed him now, too. But he didn't make a move. He just stood there staring down at me with enough heat in his eyes that I was afraid he would actually burn me. I bit my lip and pressed my body against the length of his, wrapping my arms around his neck.

"So..." I prodded. When Bryn was in this kind of mood, I knew he liked to take charge, and I didn't mind at all, but if he didn't get a move on it soon, I was going to be the one tearing his clothes off.

"I want it—"

"Rough, I know. I told you before, I'm yours—any way you want me."

Bryn's eyes glittered with pure male satisfaction, and without any more preamble, he whirled me around and pushed me against the wall face first. I braced myself with my hands as he pulled down my pants and underwear all in one motion. A shiver shot down my spine as I stood there waiting, fully exposed to him. When he finally slid into me, I called out his name and rocked back into him.

The things he made me feel—not just physical pleasure, but emotional intimacy—I knew only he could give me. I'd only fully come to understand that after I'd been with Khol, and I wished I could make Bryn fully understand that as well, because if he did, he would never be jealous. It always was as if Bryn was making love to me even when he was being his most brutal.

"You're mine," he growled. "Never forget that."

"Never," I gasped, every molecule in my body buzzing with ecstasy. He leaned over, gently biting the side of my neck right above my shoulder. Then his teeth sank in as he snarled his possession of me again against my skin. *Ow! What the fuck!*

When he finally pulled away from me and released my neck, I whirled around to glare at him. "That hurt," I snarled. I brought my hand up to the tender spot on my neck and pulled it back again. It was covered in blood. I stared wide-eyed at the red liquid and then brought my gaze up to Bryn who looked almost...surprised. "You drew blood. What the hell, Bryn?"

"Yeah, I don't know what happened." He glanced away sheepishly. "I'm sorry, Peej."

I yanked up my pants and stalked over to the small mirror that was hanging on the wall. I ground my teeth together when I got a look at the damage he'd done. He'd bitten me hard enough that I could clearly see where all his teeth had been, marked by bright red oozing out of the little indentations. "This better not scar," I said, meeting his eyes in the reflection of the mirror. He stood behind me, his gaze dropping down to his handiwork, a small smile tugging at his full lips. "Hey. That better not be a smile on your face, Mr. O'Bannon."

He lifted his gaze, and a full, patented smile, complete with dimples, spread across his face. "I don't know why, but" —he reached his forefinger down to lightly touch my wound— "this makes me happy."

"You can't be serious," I ground out, trying to keep my temper under control. Luckily for Bryn, my energy was low so I wouldn't accidently set him on fire, because I was that pissed at him in that moment.

He bit his lip in a failed attempt at containing his smile. "I can't help it. Something inside of me feels…happy that I bit you, and the thought of you scarring, well" —he cleared his throat— "that makes me almost ecstatic."

I gaped at him. "You're kidding, right?"

"I wish I was," he muttered, running his hand through his hair.

"Yeah. I'm gonna go check on Jenna," I said as I stalked

past Bryn towards the door. He didn't make any move to stop me and didn't say anything else. *Smart man.*

I swung out of our room, stomping down the hall towards Jenna and Macon's room. At least I hoped I was, I hadn't exactly memorized the lay of the land yet. *I'm probably going the wrong way.* I was so caught up in thoughts about why the hell Bryn had bitten me, that I almost ran face first into Khol's chest. "Oh," I muttered. "Didn't see you there." Why the hell was he standing smack dab in the middle of the hallway anyways? *Stupid dragon.*

"His behavior is beginning to concern me," Khol said softly, his brows furrowed with concern.

"What are you talking about?" I absentmindedly brought my hand up to touch the wound on my neck.

"I think you know exactly what I'm referring to," Khol murmured as he brought his hand up to move mine off of my wound. "You should let me disinfect and bandage that. It could scar."

I frowned. "I think that's what he wants—for it to scar." I looked up to study Khol's face as his eyebrows arched up to practically skim his hairline.

"Did he say that? That he wants it to scar?"

"Yeah, actually he did. He said something inside of him felt *happy* that he had marked me, and that the thought of me scarring from it made him feel almost *ecstatic.*"

Understanding swept over Khol's features before he schooled his face into a neutral mask. "Mmm hmm," was all he responded with.

"Oh, don't give me that. I know you know what's going on now. It was written all over your face before you tried to hide it. You're not the only one good at reading people, Khol." I crossed my arms over my chest and glared up at him as his lips quirked up slightly at the corners.

"Very well. It seems that his dragon side is struggling with the disappearance of your *Anam Cara* marks. He feels the need to mark you in some way—any way—to satisfy his dragon half. We need to figure out a solution before his dragon side loses control and he does something reckless."

A knot of worry twisted in my stomach. "Like what? What could he do?"

"Come." Khol motioned for me to follow him. "We will talk more as I dress your wound."

My hand instinctually shot up to cover Bryn's mark on me. "No!" I exclaimed. "Just leave it alone." I couldn't fight back the unexplained panic at the thought of losing Bryn's mark.

Khol stopped short to study me, and I backed up a few steps while trying to get my breathing under control. "It appears your dragon side is having some issues as well."

"No, it's not," I snapped. I was angry that Bryn had bitten and marked me, wasn't I? I mean, wasn't that why I'd stormed out of our room to go check on Jenna to begin with?

Khol quirked one auburn eyebrow at me. "You could have fooled me."

I exhaled loudly, slumping in on myself. I supposed

there was no point in trying to deny it. "Fine. Bryn and me are both having some...issues. So what do we do about it?"

"I don't know," Khol stated flatly.

"What do you mean you don't know? You're like this ancient dragon, so you have to have run across something like this before, right?"

"I have never, in fact, run across a situation even remotely resembling your and Bryn's."

"What?" I asked incredulously. "How is that even possible?"

"Most half-blooded dragons end up with full-blooded dragons, and that solves the problem. With the two of you, only time will reveal the solution—if there is one." Khol turned away from me when he said the last part, causing my pulse to speed up.

"Explain," I squeaked.

"If you had remained bonded with...me, for instance —" His eyes blazed bright with longing. "—then my magic would have been strong enough to sustain the *Anam Cara* marks for the both of us, until and if yours matured enough to be up for the task. As it is now with the two of you, neither one of you has fully matured into your powers and it appears that outside of my realm, your human magic is more dominant than your dragon. It could take some time for them to balance out. In the meantime, the dragons inside of you are struggling to clarify the *Anam Cara* bond. Out here, it's as if you haven't been fully bonded yet. It's why the marks didn't appear the first time you were together sexually, but only appeared when in my realm."

My heart was pounding in my ears. "So theoretically, out here, our *Anam Cara* bond is still in danger."

"Yes."

"Oh." I gulped. "That means that some other dragon could still force me to be his dragon mate."

"I won't let that happen," Khol stated firmly as he stepped forward, tipping my chin back so he could look me fully in the eyes. "You have chosen, and I won't let someone take that away from you."

"Take your hands off her," Bryn growled from behind me. "I've heard about enough. I know what you're trying to do, and it won't work. She's chosen—and she belongs to me." Bryn seemed to take up more space than he normally did, and as I turned to face him, I swore that his eyes flashed a bright dragon blue. It happened so quickly, I wasn't sure if I had imagined it.

"Bryn—Khol was just trying to help. He was—"

Bryn bore down on me, and when he was close enough, he swept me up in his arms. "He was trying to help himself to you is what he was trying to do," he snarled. "He was trying to take away my mark."

I looked up into Bryn's face as he moved swiftly towards our room with me in his arms. "Bryn, please." And that time when his eyes flashed bright dragon blue, I was sure I wasn't imagining things. I swiveled my head around to peer at Khol over Bryn's shoulder, and when I turned my pleading eyes towards him, he took a step back, raising his hands as if to say he wasn't getting involved. I scowled at him, letting him know it was a little too late for that. He simply shrugged and disappeared. *Typical.*

"Bryn, you acting like this is completely unacceptable. I feel like you're dragging me back to your cave by my hair." I ground my teeth in anger when he didn't even dignify me with a response. I smacked at his chest. "Put me down. Now."

When we made it back to our room, Bryn deposited me gently on our bed and backed away from me slowly. His face was a mixture of anger and torment, making him appear much older than his nineteen years. "I'm sorry. Again."

He spun around and punched the wall, causing bits of rock to rain down on him. "You just have to stay away from him—at least for now—until we get this figured out." His shoulders rose and fell heavily as he tried to get his breathing under control. "It's just every time I see you with him, I can't stop myself from losing it, Peej. I wanna kill him. No joke—actually rip him limb from limb."

A lump formed in my throat, and my eyes burned. I sucked in several ragged breaths in an effort to calm myself, and then, my face scrunched up against my will as racking sobs tore from my chest. *I'm trying to be strong. Why can't I be strong?* I curled into a ball in the middle of the bed, hugging my knees to my chest.

Everything is such a mess! Our families had been kidnapped by crazy aliens hell-bent on taking over our world, we'd been forced to go into hiding and drop out of school, Bryn was acting like some sort of overly possessive caveman—I didn't know who I was any more. I was not currently acting like the new tough me that I so desperately wanted to be—and, and I hated my new hair! Things couldn't get much worse.

Bryn came and scooped up the little ball that was me, and held me in his arms as he stroked my hair. "Things will get better, I promise, Peej." He chuckled dryly. "Because they can't really get all that much worse."

"Bryn, we just don't have time to figure out all of our dragon bullshit right now, not with everything else that's going on." I sobbed into his shirt.

"Yeah, I know," Bryn said, reassuringly. "It'll work out. I swear it will."

And yet the old feeling that I used to get that just because Bryn promised me something, it would come true wasn't there anymore. I knew he would do everything in his power to keep his promise to me, just like he always did, but somewhere along the line I had begun to doubt him. None of it was his fault—after all, he was human... mostly—I just wished I still believed anything was possible just because he said it was. I guess that meant I was growing up. *Growing up sucks.*

"Please do not tell me this weak sniveling *child* is the P.J. you chose over me," a female voice I didn't recognize asked sharply from the open door of our room.

"Nala?" Bryn said with surprise. "What the hell are you doing here?"

Why the hell do females around here keep referring to me as a child? I lifted my tearstained face from Bryn's shoulder and blinked away the blur from my eyes. I inhaled sharply and wiped at my cheeks self-consciously because in our doorway stood a friggin' supermodel, or at least someone who looked like one. She was at least my height, if not taller, with the long, lean muscles of an athlete. She wore black leather pants that were molded to her body, and a matching black leather bustier. Her hair hung long, black, and silky halfway down her back, and her eyes were almost the same bright blue as Bryn's—except they glowed. *Dragon,* I realized belatedly. She was absolutely gorgeous, her pale skin flawless, and if I wasn't mistaken, Bryn knew her.

I turned my face questioningly towards his and saw that surprise was still the dominant emotion displayed on his, so I decided to take the lead, despite my current emotional breakdown.

"And you are?" I sat up and arched my brows at the would-be supermodel.

She crossed her arms over her—yes, of course—more ample than my own bosom, and gave me a haughty sneer. "I don't have to answer to you. Bryn knows me."

I fought back the urge to say something snarky and turned back to address Bryn instead. Annoyance flared regardless. "Well? Care to fill me in on the random dragon female who seems to know *you* and that *I* don't know."

He had to have met her when he was away. There was no other explanation. My stomach knotted at the thought. And then her words from when she first appeared slammed into me... "Bryn?" His name held all of my unspoken questions, and when I saw the look on his face I knew. *I just knew.* "Oh my God." I stood, my hand fluttering to my mouth. "I told you—but you didn't tell me. *How could you not tell me?*"

"Peej." Bryn reached for me, anguish in his eyes—and guilt. There was definitely guilt there, too.

"You let me babble on and on about how awful I felt about what happened with Khol and Jeremy while you were away and—"

Sucking in a ragged breath, it fully dawned on me. With everything that had been going on, I had absolutely no idea what Bryn had been up to when he was away— hell, I didn't even know *where* he'd been. "And you just kept saying not to worry about it, that none of it mattered because we're together now." Anger coursed through my system. "Oh God—how could I be so stupid? You just didn't *want* to tell me what happened—or *who* happened while you were gone."

"Her hair isn't even really black, is it? She's not even a black dragon. What is she, Bryn?" The bitch dragon's scornful voice sliced into my head like a red-hot poker. I whirled around, facing down the bitch that thought she was going to steal Bryn from me. Sure, I was currently angrier than I ever had been with him, but who was I to call the kettle black? In the end, I didn't want anyone but him, and no stupid bimbo black dragon was going to lay one finger on him.

"I didn't even know what I was before—or her, or you. I just—"

"Shut up, Bryn," I hissed. I was, for the first time, mentally reaching for my fire, and even though I was still weak, I could feel it bubbling up inside of me, fueled by my burgeoning rage. *I am going to fry this bitch until there is nothing left of her. I am going to make her pay with her life for what she tried to do.*

"Oh shit!" I heard the bitch exclaim just as I felt the flames burst to life in my palms.

"Peej, no!" Bryn exclaimed as he rushed towards me.

But before I could do any real damage, Khol appeared in front of me with a bewildered expression on his face. He grabbed my palms, essentially dousing all hopes of me killing the bitch dragon. "What's going on?" he asked, much too calmly for my taste.

"Did you sleep with her?" I demanded of Bryn with a white-hot fury I'd never felt before. "*Did* you?" I belatedly realized I hadn't passed out after Khol had taken my flames. *Go me.* But I had little time for patting myself on the back. I needed answers from Bryn, and I needed them *now.*

"I would never—" Bryn started but was cut off by bitch dragon's high-pitched voice.

"She's *red?!* She's a *crazy* red dragon?"

"Are you actually standing there openly insulting me and my faction, when we both could strike you down with barely any effort at all?" Khol's voice was calm, but I could feel the anger rolling off of him in waves. "What are you even doing here? I don't recall issuing an invitation to any *dubh arachs.*"

"I came for Bryn," bitch dragon said, fear in her eyes despite her false bravado.

"I don't want you here, Nala," Bryn said. "What happened between us didn't mean anything to me. I love P.J., and I always will."

"You can't love her. She's a red dragon—you're black." She tapped her leather-clad leg impatiently as if it explained everything.

"He's mine!" I screeched, struggling to get to her, but Khol was a lot stronger than I ever hoped to be.

"Give her to me," Bryn growled at Khol, his eyes flashing a bright dragon blue.

"Don't touch me!" I hissed at Bryn, and even though I was still within the confines of Khol's arms, my flames were pushing to erupt from me again. I was that pissed off.

"It would be best if you left her to me for the time being," Khol informed Bryn.

But he wasn't having any of it. "I said to take your hands off of *my Anam Cara* and give her to *me.*"

"*Anam Cara?*" bitch dragon said. "Impossible. I don't see any marks."

"It's complicated," Khol stated dryly.

"Maybe I should go—for now." Bitch dragon eyed Bryn with a longing that set my blood on fire, which caused actual flames to burst up from my palms again.

"If you come anywhere near him, I'll burn you alive," I

seethed. And in that moment, I absolutely meant it. I had attempted to take my own life for Bryn—I wouldn't hesitate to take another's if they stood in our way.

Bryn didn't seem to care about any of that anymore though. His only goal was to get me away from Khol. He crowded closer to me as Khol desperately attempted to get me under control.

"Give her to me," Bryn repeated, this time with utter coldness. I could sense he was on the verge of snapping. *Fabulous.* That would make two of us.

I threw my head back, screaming in frustration and fury. Raw power like I'd never experienced rushed through me, but only for a second, one painful second, before everything went completely black.

Chapter 23

A familiar lilting song wound into my ears as I struggled to wake up. "Mom?" I murmured, my eyes fluttering open.

"Hi, peanut." My mom smiled as she leaned over to caress my face while I lay in bed—my bed, or rather, my old bed in my old room. My heart clenched.

"I'm not really here, am I? This is a dream, isn't it?"

"No, I'm not really here, and neither are you. But I am communicating with you through your dreams. I'm asleep where I am now as well."

I sat up, eyeing my mom keenly. "Oh, okay, so we are kind of really here then." I smiled at her before tears erupted from my eyes, cascading down my cheeks in twin rivers of regret. Despite all that had happened between us recently she took me into her arms without hesitation. "Mom, I'm so sorry. All of this is my fault. Are you okay? Is Dad? You guys know I didn't really mean all that stuff I said, right? I was just angry. So angry because of Bryn. But I still love you both so much."

I sucked in a shuddering breath. "I should have warned you somehow—warned all of you. I was worried about so many stupid things—things that could have waited. If only I would have tried harder to make you believe my visions —if I only would have—"

"Honey, you can't dwell on all the *what ifs* of life because they'll eat you alive. You can't focus on any of that. You need to look to the future and remember how much we've always loved you."

Something's not right. Beyond what I already know. "Mom?" I sat back, studying her face, which had suddenly been drained off all gentleness.

"You need to listen to me, peanut. I don't know how much time I have here."

"Okay."

"They're going to kill us. Exterminate us all."

"No!" I gasped, the shock of her words were like a fist punching into my chest. "We're gonna save you! We're coming for you! We just don't have a plan yet! But—but we're figuring one out now!"

My mom's shoulders curved inward, and her lower lip trembled slightly. "Oh, honey, my little peanut. You mustn't try. The only reason I'm able to come to you now is because they're letting me. They expect you to come for us—they want you to because it's a trap—and that's why you can't."

"No. We're gonna save you. None of the rest matters."

My mom's eyes glistened as she shook her head. "Our world matters and protecting it still does. You and your friends will be the last hope this dimension has. If they kill you, then this world will die, too. You can't let that happen. This is our purpose for being here—this is what we've trained for—even though no one ever thought it'd really happen. I'm so sorry we've failed you, so sorry all of this falls on you now." A rogue tear crept down her left cheek.

"Mom, no—"

"Peanut, please, you need to let me finish. I need to say these things to you before it's too late."

She's saying goodbye. My mom is saying goodbye to me before she's taken away from me forever and murdered by the alien riders. Numbness rolled through my system.

"I'm proud of you, honey, so proud. And I know things aren't turning out for you the way you had hoped. But you have good people surrounding you—people who love you —don't forget that. And Bryn—I'm so sorry for everything your father and I did—you're going to need him now more than ever. Do you love him? Truly love him?"

"Yes. I love him more than I thought possible," I rasped, my throat tight.

She smiled wistfully. "Then don't let anything stand in your way. Our people have forgotten many things, forgotten that love is more important than anything sometimes, because life is short—too short."

She wrapped her arms around me again and squeezed. "We'll always be with you, peanut. We both love you more than I think you understand." She sat up, staring off into space as if she were seeing something somewhere else, and who knows, maybe she was. "I have to go now. I love you."

"Mom, no!" I reached for her, but she was fading away right before my eyes. "I need more time!" And then she was gone. "No!" I screamed. "No!"

Jolting straight up in bed, I squinted into the dim light of my and Bryn's room. Bryn opened his sleep-encrusted eyes and reached for me. "Peej," he murmured. "She's gone. Don't worry."

I stumbled out of bed in a panic. "We have to save them! Before it's too late!"

Bryn slid out of bed and caught me by the elbow before I could do a face-plant. "Who? What are you talking about? Did you have a vision?"

"Our families of course! Who the hell else?"

"Tell me what happened."

I froze, everything my mom had just shared fully sinking in. "We're—we're not gonna be able to save them, Bryn. It's gonna be too late. My mom—" My lower lip trembled uncontrollably. "My mom said they're gonna exterminate all of them—soon. It could be happening now."

Bryn went rigid, his expression blanking before he slumped down on the bed. He ran a hand down his face. "I just thought—maybe hoped—that they would try to ransom them or something, give us some time. My God— *all* of them?"

I nodded numbly.

Bryn abruptly stood, determination replacing the empty look of sorrow that had been in his eyes just moments ago. "I'm gonna go gather everyone together for a meeting. Get dressed and I'll see you in the common room in ten." He pulled on sweatpants and a T-shirt with jerky movements before stalking from our room without another word.

I didn't know what he hoped to accomplish with the meeting, but at least we'd have everyone in one place so I could tell them the unfathomable news I'd just received.

EVERYONE WAS ALREADY ASSEMBLED in the common area by the time I got there. Judging from the tension in the room, Bryn had already filled them in on what I told him.

"What are we gonna do?" Jenna blurted out before I could even settle down beside Bryn.

I bit my lower lip, trying not to let her expectant face tear my heart out. She really thought I had a plan or an answer of some sort. "There's nothing we can do." I cringed at my own words.

"What? You're just gonna let them die? You can't mean that!" Jenna stared at me in shock.

"This is about more than just us, Jenna. I wanna save them just as much as you do—Goddamnit!" I swore, letting my anguish and frustration take control of me for a moment before I reined it in, throwing it in the box with everything else I wasn't emotionally capable of dealing with at the moment, and sealed the lid . "My mom came to me in my dream. Told me what they were planning. I got the feeling—" I swallowed at the lump in my throat that seemed ever-present lately. "I just got the feeling that—she was saying goodbye. She told me goodbye. They're probably already dead."

Despite my calm delivery of the news, my entire body shook like I had the chills even though I was sweating. "They let my mom reach out to me when they haven't before so we'd be in a hurry to get to them. But we won't find them alive if we go. It's a trap."

Jenna shook her head frantically. "No. No, they can't just do that! They can't kill them all when they didn't do anything!"

"They've already done things they shouldn't be able to do but that didn't stop them," I said.

"No! We have to try!" Jenna cried out in anguish as she collapsed against Macon, who wrapped his arms around her.

"We have to save this world—our world—from the Riders. We really are this dimension's first and last hope. Before, when we found out everyone but us had been captured, we knew everything fell on our shoulders, but there was still a chance for reinforcements—still a chance that we might get help."

"Now we really are alone," Bryn chimed in, his voice flat.

"You're not alone. You have the support of the red dragons," Khol's voice echoed through the room loud and clear, plucking a note of hope deep inside of me. "We can't let their deaths be in vain. We can beat the Riders. And we will." Khol placed his hand on my shoulder, and I looked up into his eyes. "We will succeed."

I nodded once tightly, acknowledging his promise. "What about the other dragon factions? Do you think they'd be willing to help?"

"I can guarantee you the black will," bitch dragon said. She strolled into the room as though we'd been expecting her.

I must have noticeably tensed, because Bryn slid his large warm hand over to cover mine, and I moved closer to him and out from under Khol's touch. This was war, and sometimes you had to work with allies that in normal times—well, I don't know—let's say who you might want to burn to a crisp. I loved Bryn and I knew he loved me, and that's what really mattered. We'd have our little talk about what happened while he was away later—and in private.

"I'll send a messenger out to the gold and silver factions immediately," Khol informed us before he disappeared.

I stood and walked over to where Macon was still holding a sobbing Jenna. I reached my hand out tentatively to touch her, letting it fall without contact. "Jenna," I whispered. "We'll make them pay. I know it won't bring them back, but we'll make them pay."

She hiccupped once and then abruptly stopped crying. Her head lifted up just enough from Macon's chest so she could meet my eyes. "Good," she croaked.

We stared at each other for a few moments, neither one of us saying anything out loud, as we reached a silent understanding. We were on the same page with this. The Riders would pay for what they did, and we would be the ones to deal them their hand of justice.

I turned to look at Jeremy next, who also met my gaze with the same grim determination as Jenna. It was good to know that despite his feelings of bitterness towards Bryn and me, Jeremy would have our backs where it counted.

"Tomorrow, after we've all had a chance to rest as much as we can, and after Khol has hopefully heard back from the other dragon factions, we're gonna come up with a concrete plan of action. No more waiting around. We can't afford to for one second longer." With that, I strode back over to Bryn, took him by the hand, and headed towards the door.

When I got close to bitch dragon, I flipped my new shorter hair, turning my nose up at her. She could covet *my* Bryn all she wanted, but he always had, and always would, belong to me.

AS I LAY in bed sprawled across Bryn's bare chest, I let my thoughts wander. I knew there was little hope for any real sleep for me, and I could tell Bryn wasn't really sleeping either, but I was too tired to talk, and I knew he was, too.

There would be a time for me to question him about bitch dragon, but it wasn't now. And maybe it wouldn't be for a long time. We were at war, and who knew how long we'd get to be together before something happened to one or both of us. Everything was unstable and uncertain about our future, all of our futures actually, so we had to take refuge in all the small comforts as they came our way.

I tried not to think about the fact that our families were dead, otherwise the guilt would eat me alive. Instead, I attempted to believe they were somewhere far away from us, somewhere that didn't get U.S. postal service or long-distance phone coverage. I knew I wasn't coping and was in some sort of denial—or maybe that was my way of coping. But our cause couldn't afford for me to have any more emotional breakdowns. Somehow, I had taken on somewhat of a leader position in our little group, and with that came greater responsibility. So instead of shattering into a million pieces like I really wanted to, I thought of my mom, and took inspiration from one of her favorite movies.

"After all, tomorrow is another day," I said into the dark, a small smile on my lips.

Oh yes—the Riders would rue the day they messed with me —with us.

About the Author

Ava Wixx escaped into books at a young age and decided to stay there. It was only a matter of time before she was driven to create her own fantasy worlds from fear of running out of places to explore.

Reader, writer, dreamer … Ava only toils in reality when absolutely necessary. She lives in North Carolina with her husband, and spoiled mini-poodle.

(If you want up-to-date info on book-y things then visit Avawixx.com and don't bother with the social media. Because let's face it, Ava is an online slacker and she signed up for some accounts but never actually posts.)